LEFT NO CHOICE

K.W. HARRIS

LEFT NO CHOICE

JON BLAKE BECOMES J.J. TRACKER

TATE PUBLISHING
AND ENTERPRISES, LLC

Left No Choice
Copyright © 2014 by K. W. Harris. All rights reserved.

No part of this publication may be reproduced, stored in a retrieval system or transmitted in any way by any means, electronic, mechanical, photocopy, recording or otherwise without the prior permission of the author except as provided by USA copyright law.

This is a work of fiction. Names, characters, and incidents are either the product of the author's imagination or are used fictitiously, and any resemblance to actual persons, living or dead, or events, is entirely coincidental. Additionally, this work of fiction is in no way intended to be seen as factual where the integrity of authority figures in named locales are concerned.

The opinions expressed by the author are not necessarily those of Tate Publishing, LLC.

Published by Tate Publishing & Enterprises, LLC
127 E. Trade Center Terrace | Mustang, Oklahoma 73064 USA
1.888.361.9473 | www.tatepublishing.com

Tate Publishing is committed to excellence in the publishing industry. The company reflects the philosophy established by the founders, based on Psalm 68:11,
"The Lord gave the word and great was the company of those who published it."

Book design copyright © 2014 by Tate Publishing, LLC. All rights reserved.
Cover design by Rtor Maghuyop
Interior design by Honeylette Pino

Published in the United States of America

ISBN: 978-1-63418-600-1
1. Fiction / General
2. Fiction / Thrillers / General
14.10.15

ACKNOWLEDGMENTS

My wife, Samantha. Sam's loving patience, understanding, and fortitude are a gift from God.

Ms. Lewan, my seventh-grade English teacher, for planting a seed of confidence in 1975 that took root and still thrives today.

Edwin James Charlon (Jim). Posthumously, for being a great mentor; Jim was the most honorable man I have ever known.

The four Js—Jessica K., Jeremiah B., Joshua N., Jonathan M., plus Alexandra P. Harris—my children and light of hope for our future.

E. A. Davenport, for her loving and tireless support for our entire family.

PROLOGUE

"Are you out of your mind, Blake? You're already well on your way to one of the brightest careers in the history of the United States Army. Your battlefield sense during and after the Gulf War saved *hundreds* of civilian lives and many US soldiers too! I've served with many great men in this man's army, yet I can count on one hand those I believe to be like you. Jon, you take this letter and toss it, or I will," General Granger said impatiently.

"Sir, I cannot express how honored and grateful I am by your belief in me. However, with all due respect to you and the army, I've seen, heard, and done things while wearing this uniform that I will forever regret. I can no longer be a part of it, sir," Sergeant Blake explained while standing rigidly at attention before the general. "I've given this country six years of my life, yet I will be haunted by those six for the rest of it. I'm done, sir; I can take no more."

General Granger clearly recognized the emotion in the man's words as they hit the air. He had heard enough to know that trying to change Blake's mind would be a waste of time and end in failure. Blake truly wanted out. After a long silence, he spoke.

"So, Jon," Granger asked as he clasped his hands before him on the desk, "what will you do?"

"I've decided to go back to school, sir, to learn the business of finance," Blake said with conviction as he kept his gaze fixed on the window above the general's head. "I've decided on a career in banking, sir."

"*Banking?*" Granger's tone could hide neither his surprise nor his disbelief. Blake sensed that Granger seemed insulted by this and prepared himself for the general's verbal attack. He was not about to be intimidated by this man or any other, regardless of their rank.

"*Yes, sir!*" he said crisply.

The general snorted, still unable to believe what he'd just heard. As a war-hardened Medal of Honor recipient, he was insulted. He sat looking at Blake with a facial expression that reflected his disdain. Blake could feel the general's eyes burning holes into the ribbons on his uniform. Silence filled the room as the general continued to stare angrily at Blake.

After what felt to Jon like an hour, the general slapped his palms down onto the desk and then rose slowly from his chair, leaning across the desk toward him. He stared now into Blake's eyes, but Blake did not return the gaze. As Granger had risen, Jon had averted his gaze slightly upward above the general's head. In his peripheral vision, Jon Blake could now see clearly the expression on Granger's face. It was bottled rage.

Granger was visibly battling his desire to let loose a barrage of disparaging comments in retaliation. He took it very personally when anyone cast so much as a shadow upon his belief in what the US Army stood for and did, let alone one of its most promising soldiers. His lips were pressed together so tightly they had lost their color and his hands were shaking. With a reddened face, he slowly shook his head as he stood upright and turned toward his

LEFT NO CHOICE

window. It took Granger a moment to compose himself; then he spoke over his shoulder to Sergeant Jonathan Blake.

"It is not my place to question or comment on a man's chosen path once he has left the army, Sergeant, no matter how tempted I am to do just that. You have served your country as only a handful of others have that also lived through it. The selflessness that you've shown in battle reflects honor and a commitment to excellence that far exceeds the ordinary soldier, and for that reason, I hate to lose you. However," Granger said as he turned to face Blake, "it is also for that reason that I will not stand in your way any longer. Your request for terminal leave is granted, and I shall see to it that the paperwork for your discharge is put through expeditiously. Dismissed."

"Thank you, sir," Blake said, then pivoted to exit.

"No, Jon, thank you," Granger whispered to himself as Blake made his way out. "Sergeant Blake!" Granger called out as Jon was passing through the door.

Blake stopped, turned, and snapped to attention. "Sir?"

Granger moved across the room and stopped directly in front of Jon, his hands clasped behind him.

"For all that you've done to help ensure the security of our allies and this great nation, I pray that God will grant you the understanding of why He chose to make you the warrior that you are. Take care of yourself, Jon Blake." Granger's words and tone reflected both his admiration and his understanding. He paused, took a deep breath, and changed tone. "Now get the hell out of my office and gather your things. You're out of here as of right now."

For the first time in his career, Jon Blake looked a superior officer directly in the eyes while at attention. He stretched out his hand slowly, and when Granger noticed it, he looked into Jon's eyes with appreciative surprise. For a moment, he and Jon shared many thoughts with their eyes only, and then the General took Jon's hand and shook it firmly.

"Thank you, sir. For everything."

With a smile and a nod, Granger patted Jon on the shoulder and said, "Dismissed, Sergeant," then watched as Blake closed the door. As Granger walked back to his desk, he said to himself, "From Green Beret to Banker. Unbelievable. Well, son, I wish you good luck," he said, raising his coffee cup to the door.

"Sergeant Blake! Sergeant Blake!" came a voice from behind him as he was exiting the Command HQ building. He turned and saw a young woman in uniform running toward him gripping a folder of some type. An officer was about to step into her path from the hall on her right. Her speed seemed too much to avoid an embarrassing and forceful collision. Then it happened. He watched in amazement as this young corporal nimbly and gracefully sidestepped the hall entrance just in time to avoid the officer, without breaking stride. "I'm sorry for yelling but the general asked me to make sure you signed these before you left, Sergeant. He said to tell you he couldn't process your request without them," she explained.

Jon couldn't help but notice her smiling stare as he gazed into her eyes and commented as he reached out to accept the documents. "Thank you, Corp…oral…" He looked at her questioningly, waiting for her name.

"Tomkins. Joan Tomkins," she said hesitatingly as she too finally looked directly into his eyes. She had heard clearly almost all that was said in the general's office due to how loud the two men were. She was so impressed with this sergeant's comments she even found herself drawn in and hoping for him to get all that he wanted without delay. She hadn't looked at him closely as he entered the general's office as she was used to dozens of visitors a day. However, the more she heard him speak to the general, the more she wished she had. And now that she was face-to-face with him, try as she might, she couldn't take her eyes from his, or hide her desire to learn more about this man away from the sterile formality of a US military post.

LEFT NO CHOICE

Jon read all of this fairly well as it happened often when he was stateside, but for the first time in his life, he found himself wanting the same thing. He just didn't know how to say it.

"Tomkins. Thank you, Corporal Tomkins. You're right," he said as he opened and breezed through the file, "these are my terminal leave request forms. I couldn't get out of here without signing these."

She mustered a little courage and took a chance. A *big* chance.

"You're welcome, Sergeant, and please, call me Joan."

Jon only locked up for a second before he raised his gaze to meet hers again, but she caught it just the same. He truly was a little out of his element here.

"Joan. Hello, Joan, my name's Jon. Jon Blake," he said, smiling and extending his hand. "I have to ask. How did you know there was someone coming into the hall?"

"By the look on your face, Jon" she said innocently, smiling and taking his hand as she spoke.

Strangely, his emotions stirred when he heard her say his name.

"And how did you know that I'd like to…that I really wanted to know your first name?"

Joan didn't miss a beat. "By another look on your face," she said cheerfully as she looked up into his eyes, one to the other and back again.

She released the handshake and Jon unwittingly glided his fingers gently across her palm as she withdrew. Joan felt a warm tingle travel from her palm to her heart. She had been moved a few times before, but it had never felt like this. She was absolutely taken with this man, and he with her.

"Joan, would you care to join me for lunch or dinner, tonight?" Jon asked nervously, realizing his heart was pounding as though he'd just finished a long run.

"Okay, Jon," she replied, still looking into his eyes.

"Which one?" Jon asked, chuckling, still nervous.

Joan composed herself even though her heart was also racing and said, "Lunch, I think. Yes. Can you meet me here at thirteen hundred?"

"Thirteen hundred it is, Joan," he said as he looked deep into her eyes again, smiled, and turned to leave.

They had dinner together too. Within a year, they were having breakfast as husband and wife.

Over the next nineteen years, the Blakes truly enjoyed their lives together. A wonderful marriage, a son who showed promise in all his chosen endeavors, and career successes for Jon that vaulted him to within two promotions of becoming a vice president for the regional headquarters of Security Pacific Bank in Albuquerque. He never spoke of his career in the army once he entered the private sector except to say that he had served as a soldier during the Reagan and Bush administrations. Not one friend or coworker knew he was once a Green Beret. Only Joan knew. Jon wanted to keep the door to his military past locked forever, so Joan never pushed. Life was now pleasant, rewarding, and filled with wonderful memories.

But fate was fickle, and very few things last forever. It was about to force Jon to make a choice. Either reopen the door to his past or turn his back on righteousness. It would have been an easier decision twenty years ago, but he was now a husband and a father. This time, he would not be walking through alone either. He would have to take his wife and son through with him.

1

"Okay, gentlemen, I want to know what's going on," Anthony Joseppe Tracerio Sr. said impatiently as he rose and lit his after-dinner cigar. All eyes had been fixed on him periodically throughout the meal, yet only when the men were sure he was not about to look back. Tonight was not the night you wanted to have prolonged eye contact with Tony Tracerio. As usual, dinner itself went by without one word about business, but when the table was clear and the servers had left, business was the only acceptable topic to Tony.

Not one man of the eight seated at the table wished to be the first to answer. Each looked at those across from them, silently, waiting. Finally, one cleared his throat and spoke.

"Mr. Tracerio, I know what I saw. Those packages were definitely from the farm. I can't say for sure how they got there, but there is no doubt they were yours."

"You're positive of that, Gus?" Tracerio asked.

"Yes, sir, I am."

"Then it is time we figure out who is responsible for stealing then selling my product to my competition! In fact, I want the name of every man who is or just could be stealing from me, and I want it tonight. It's time a message is sent to all those in my employ about my views on the subject."

Every man there knew what that meant as they locked gazes with each other. Tony Sr. had had enough, and now, people were going to die. Tony didn't really care who died either. He knew that once he had a few men killed the thieves would stop, at least for a while, and he may just get lucky enough to hit the right ones anyway.

As the meeting went into the fourth hour, it was decided that only three men had opportunity to stiff Tony Sr. out of his own money in that part of Albuquerque, but no one could accurately pinpoint which of the three were truly responsible. After another hour of debate and conjecture, Tony Tracerio Sr. was far past his limit of patience.

"It seems to me that no matter how much longer we sit here jacking our jaws, we will come no closer to figuring out who's really behind it, so all three will just have to pay. Is that clear?"

"But what if one or two of them aren't involved?" his son Tony Jr. asked.

"I said *all three will pay*, and that's the end of it!" Tony Sr. barked angrily, then said, "Victor, get my coat. We're leaving. You geniuses stay here and figure out how and when. But by noon on Monday, it had better be done."

Tony locked eyes with each man seated at the table for a second, and each nodded or spoke their acknowledgement. Then he said as he headed through the door, "Good. I'd hate to hear on Monday that I was going to have to replace any of you."

No one played Tony Tracerio Sr. for the fool regardless of how long they had been with him. His orders were clear. Hank Foster, Fred Johnson, and Howard Bell were each to become unwitting participants in Tony Tracerio's latest "staff memo." They each would receive notice of their separation from the organization on Sunday night, and now there was nothing anyone would do to stop it. Tony Sr. had spoken and, right or wrong, that was enough.

Everyone believed Hank Foster's trucking company had to be booming. They had no idea Hank's lavish lifestyle wasn't coming from the legitimate side of his trucking business. In fact, he wasn't keeping his company afloat at all. Tracerio was. Tony used Foster's trucks to haul his product from the farm to distributors all over the Southwestern US, so Tony made sure Hank always had enough money to make payroll. But Hank was responsible for his drivers, so if one of them was pinching a carton or two per shipment, it was Hank's fault whether he knew it or not. The second man, Fred Johnson, operated a massive egg farm that proved to be the perfect cover for their manufacturing and packaging plant. There were thousands of square feet of otherwise useless space beneath the main hen house for them to work out of, and the number of regular employees coming and going every day allowed the specialists working below to go in and out relatively unnoticed.

The other factor that made the egg farm perfect for their operations was the ventilation system. The hen house needed to stay very cool and, in the desert outside Albuquerque, that was no easy task. The poisons in the air from the chickens were filtered constantly, which meant the ventilation system was running 24/7. Who could know it had other uses? They had been manufacturing methamphetamine for years right below the hen house and had never drawn a single suspicion from the law. The Tracerio family had liked it that way, but now, they would have to put someone else in there to run it because Fred's people could be shelving a few cartons per shipment that were to go onto Foster's trucks.

Tony Sr. had learned that the group syphoning and distributing his product without his knowledge was currently under surveillance by the DEA, which infuriated him. He had already lost untold amounts of money because of these thieves, and now, they had been caught with his dope.

Gus Cantonelli, a lieutenant on the Albuquerque PD and one of Tony's inside men, was sure the DEA didn't know the source of the product as of yet but told Tony it was only a matter of time unless the skimming stopped. If the DEA caught some fool before he could repackage the stolen Meth, they'd have one of Tony's shipping cartons. Then Fred Johnson's egg farm and Tracerio's entire nonchalant distribution system via Foster's trucks would have to be shut down.

Tony could manufacture elsewhere and set up a new distribution system, but the current operation using the egg cartons could be conducted during daylight hours right in front of a cop. After all, egg deliveries to grocers were commonplace at every store in America. Tracerio's operation went so smoothly he was fast becoming the South's biggest supplier, so he chose to plug the leaks in his ship over building a new one.

The third man, Howard Bell, was just a small-time street vendor. He ran his little piece of their operation from the back of his produce market. He had worked for the organization for twenty-five years, so when he said that he'd had to cut his prices because of the competition, no immediate questions were asked.

Tracerio's take from Howard was much less than any other street vendor handling the same volume of product, which Tracerio had let slide until now. The police raid that Cantonelli led on his competitor's place was only two buildings down from Howard's store. Cantonelli noted that there was no lab, just product. If Howard had been skimming and selling to them, it would explain why Tracerio's profits were much lower there. The following Sunday had been chosen for many reasons as the day to hit all three. First, the farm only ran two shifts, so all employees would be gone by nine. That meant Fred Johnson would be in the main house alone except the security guards. However, they

LEFT NO CHOICE

worked for Tracerio, *not* Fred. Second, Gus knew from his days walking a beat that Howard Bell closed the produce store at five on Sundays, then walked down the street to a tavern to have a few drinks before going home. He never left the tavern before seven thirty and usually stayed until well after eight. Then he'd walk the three blocks back to his store, head down the alley, get in his truck, and drive home. He wasn't supposed to make it back to the truck that Sunday. Third, Hank Foster never threw parties on Sundays as most of his guests still had to work on Mondays. He had a habit of spending Sundays in the city with some of Tony's girls and driving home around ten. The plan was to catch him while he was winding his way back up the hill to his house.

David Sharpe and Marcus Greenhill were Tracerio's resident professionals. They were instructed to handle Hank Foster and Fred Johnson. They flipped a coin, and with the win, Sharpe chose to visit Fred, leaving Foster for Greenhill. The third team of George Ashland, Tim Covington, and Dennis Jeffries were bank executives by trade and were only used for this kind of work when the other two were unavailable. They had handled all previous tasks without problems but still were not as experienced as Sharpe or Greenhill. For that reason, they were given the easiest assignment—Howard Bell.

Hank Foster's accident was a tricky one to pull off, which is why Marcus was glad that Sharpe had chosen to take out Fred Johnson. Marcus loved a challenge, and making Hank's death look like an accident gave him one. Location and timing were everything. The road to his house wound its way up the hillside with numerous sharp turns. If any of those turns were taken too fast, or if the outside front tire blew at just the right moment, Foster's vintage Ford Bronco would crash into the light duty guardrail. Its momentum would cause it to flip over the rail and down the embankment with him in it. His uphill driving speed they could not control, but a blown tire was a different story.

Greenhill lay there on the embankment just off the road, waiting for Foster's Bronco to go by. His rifle was outfitted with a state of the art laser-targeting device and a silencer. His plan was to shoot the tire from behind and below, so the bullet would have an upward trajectory as it exited, never touching the roadway or another part of the vehicle.

The real trick to this was hitting the tire at just the right angle. His aim had to be low enough on the tire so the bullet would not hit the rim but pass through the rubber twice. Upon hitting the steel belts inside the tire, the bullet's face would be flattened, making for a much bigger hole as it exited the other side. Then the bullet would just fly off into no man's land, never to be found. After the Bronco blasted through the guardrail and sailed down the embankment, he would just climb down and fire it up. Should Foster be ejected prior to the vehicle coming to a stop and have lived, he'd just break his neck with a quick flick of the wrists, set the blaze, cover his tracks, and leave.

Regardless of how or where Foster died, Greenhill knew the Bronco had to burn. That was the only way to assure the tires would melt, destroying any evidence that one had been sabotaged. Greenhill's aim was on the money, and the Bronco swerved so quickly Hank had no time to react. The Bronco crashed into and through the guardrail with so much force that it could not be stopped. It flipped end-over end through the air parallel with the hillside for one full revolution, and the force of the heavy Bronco's grille hitting the ground some seventy feet below was enough to make metal tear like paper. The Bronco was vintage no more.

Greenhill could hear shattering glass, crunching metal, and Hank Foster's screams of terror as the Bronco flipped one last time. Marcus calmly walked toward the spot in the severely damaged guardrail where the Bronco had gone airborne to survey the scene. The vehicle had settled on its roof in the center of what looked like a dry riverbed that was as wide as a football field. The Bronco was almost unrecognizable. The whole vehicle was now a torn mass of metal. The fiberglass portion of the roof had been smashed, sending large chunks in every direction. Foster's screams were the only sounds filling the night now and Greenhill could clearly hear the agony carried by each of them. Greenhill was shocked that Foster was conscious, let alone still alive. Marcus was actually pleased that Foster had survived. Now he could tell Foster that this was no accident, that the worst was yet to come. He stood motionless for a moment taking in the sight, priding himself on his work. He then began to make his way down the hill, careful to erase each track as he descended.

The three bankers were to go to the office, log in on their terminals of the mainframe computer, then leave for Bell's store. Once there, they'd collect the few special egg cartons from Howard's office and catch him in the alley as he headed for his truck. The plan was to make it look like a mugging turned deadly. Afterward, they'd return to the bank and await calls from Greenhill and Sharpe confirming completion of their assignments. Once Ashland received both calls, the trio would log off their computers at random intervals and head for home. Ashland would notify the upper echelon the next morning as to the outcomes.

Howard Bell never made it to his truck. Within a few steps of the driver's door, two of the three bankers stepped out of the shadows. Tim Covington whipped the bat around with such force that it became slightly imbedded in Howard's skull. As George Ashland stood watch, he heard the sound of Covington's bat and turned to see the result. He saw Covington jerking it away as Howard fell face first onto the cement and then watched as Dennis Jeffries moved in with the knife. Dennis knelt beside

Howard and surveyed the damage. After seeing close-up the destruction one swing of the bat had done, he realized Howard was most likely dead already. Blood was pouring out of Howard's skull at a sickening rate, but Dennis was still not satisfied.

"Man, I was hoping to turn this guy into a Pez dispenser, but I guess I should try out for a major league baseball team instead," he whispered excitedly to Covington as they rifled through Howard's pockets, taking everything.

Ashland stood watch in the shadows as the other two searched Howard's truck yet found nothing worth stealing. He glanced down at Howard's lifeless body and saw a pool of what looked like oil in the dim light of the crescent moon encircling Howard's head and body. He thought it strangely curious how blood could look like oil as he turned his eyes back toward the street.

Since the security force worked for Tracerio, they let Sharpe walk right into the main house on the farm. Fred Johnson had just settled into his inground hot tub on the east patio when David Sharpe came through the back door. Johnson was sipping a drink and watching TV with his back to the house, unaware that he had a visitor. Sharpe stood there behind him for a moment, smiling broadly. He couldn't have planned this one any better. The TV Johnson was watching was on a stand about five feet from the hot tub. Not close enough to fall into the water yet but that was easily remedied. Sharpe also noticed there was a great deal of slack in the extension cord and coax and chuckled to himself. He walked around into Johnson's vision with the Beretta, now drawn, pointed at Johnson's head. When Fred saw him, he started to rise, but Sharpe barked at him to sit back down or eat a bullet. Johnson reluctantly obeyed. He watched as Sharpe walked over to the TV and squatted.

LEFT NO CHOICE

"All I want is information, Fred, so just relax. Somebody from here has become quite the entrepreneur with Mr. Tracerio's product. He just wants to know their names. If you tell the truth, he'll probably just make you reimburse him for his losses. If you don't, well…"

As he was talking, he had nonchalantly reached into his jacket pocket, pulled out what Fred knew to be a silencer, and screwed it onto the business end of the Beretta. Johnson figured his only chance for survival was to play it cool and deny any involvement in skimming from Tracerio.

"Man, nobody working for me is stupid enough to steal from Tony. Tell Tony that it must be Foster's drivers or his distributors. I keep a close count on every carton that leaves here, David, and Tony knows it," Fred said with conviction, albeit unconvincing.

David Sharpe gave him a 'that makes sense' facial expression and nod. He removed the silencer, rose, and holstered his pistol. Fred's fear began to subside when he saw this, but it returned when Sharpe rolled the TV stand to within two feet of the water. His mind raced as he watched Sharpe. He thought of trying to get out and run but knew he couldn't outrun a bullet. And Sharpe had come right past the security guards. That meant Tracerio was truly orchestrating Sharpe's play. No, he thought, there was no way to escape. His best course of action was to continue playing the innocent stooge.

"Listen, Fred. Mr. Tracerio sent me here to recoup his losses. Now, the way he sees it, even if you personally didn't steal from him, you were in charge so it was your responsibility. Right? Right! So how can you and I rectify the situation, huh? Let me think. Um…um…I've got it! I'll tell him you didn't realize someone was skimming because you've been working so hard your brain is fried!"

With that, his expression turned wildly sinister, and he tipped the stand. Fred stared in horror as the TV fell toward the water. He moved as fast as he could to climb out of the hot tub but not fast enough. The current invaded Johnson's body, locking Fred's muscles up so tight he looked like a seizure victim. Sharpe had never seen a man electrocuted before and enjoyed every second of it. The last sound Fred Johnson would ever hear was the crazed laughter of David Sharpe. The entire house was dark as Sharpe made his way out because the circuit breakers had flipped. He instructed the head of security to run out back, look at the scene for no more than fifteen seconds, then to call 911. By the time the ambulance arrived, Sharpe would be miles away.

It took almost two minutes for Marcus to traverse the steep hillside, all the while listening to Hank Foster's cries for help. He did not hurry, for two reasons. First, he wanted his footprints to be as shallow as possible so they'd be easier to erase. The second because he knew Foster lived in so secluded an area that the nearest home was close to a mile away on the other side of the mini-mountain. As there was no line of sight and echoes would be traveling away from the neighbors, no one could hear or see the crash. Since Hank's estate was the highest on the hill, no one would be driving by either.

"Is someone there? Dear God, *please* help me! I-I can't seem to move. I-I'm bleeding all over and I th-think my legs are broken. Ple-e-ease help me! *Hello! Who's there? Answer me, please!*"

Foster's eyes darted in all directions as he heard what he thought and hoped to be the sound of footsteps. Steam was rising from his wounds as his warm blood met the chill of the night air. His upper body was wedged between the steering wheel and the seat, and the back of his head was touching the partially collapsed roof. He could feel the weight of his body suspended in midair by his seatbelt, and the pain in his left shoulder was becoming more excruciating by the minute because of it. The smell of his own blood seeping out and saturating his clothes filled his nostrils.

He could feel it's warmth as it slowly flowed across his neck and dripped down onto the headliner. His arms were pinned against his chest by the steering wheel, and both his legs were definitely broken. His right leg had suffered only minor fractures while his left was much worse. It had been caught between the dash, the seat, the door, and the steering column during the initial impact. Both his tibia and fibula had snapped like twigs. They tore through his flesh more than once as the vehicle rolled over, and now, only small strips of jagged skin joined his lower leg to the rest of him. When Greenhill finally arrived, Foster's screams had subsided into moans and pleadings to God. Although the Bronco had not caught fire, the pungent aroma of gasoline was almost sickening. Fuel was coming out of the fuel pipe past the gas cap in a steady stream, creating a little river that ran down the hill past the driver's door.

"Hello, Hank! How's it hangin'?" Marcus said jovially as he knelt beside the driver's door and peered in.

"K-Kevin? Is that you? Kevin?"

"No, I'm not Kevin. Who's Kevin?" Greenhill asked with mock jealousy as he surveyed the damage to man and vehicle.

"M-My neighbor down the hill. But it doesn't matter. I'm glad you showed up, whoever you are, 'cause I r-really need your help. I'm hurt b-bad, and I c-can't get out," Foster said in a pained and dazed voice.

"I see that, Hank. I'm really surprised you're still alive. I guess seatbelts really do work, huh?"

"N-No offense, m-man, but could you dispense with the chitchat and h-help me get out of here? P-P-Please? I-I-I'm really hurtin' here," he said as he began to shake.

"Well, the way I see it, that's gonna be a problem, becau—"

Foster's dizziness cleared for an instant as he realized this man had called him by name. "H-Hey! H-How'd you know my name? W-Who are y-you?"

"Who I am doesn't really matter, but who I work for does. See, man, we both get paid by the same guy. Or should I say we both *did get paid* by the same guy."

"What? I own m-m-my company. I don't work f-for an—"

At that moment, the answer to his "why me" question hit Hank Foster like a fully loaded freight train. A fear like he'd never known before filled him; the fear of impending death.

"P-Please, man. I'll give you anything. Anything! Just please help me g-g-get out of this. Tracerio doesn't have to know. I-I'll disappear and never come back. I'll make it worth your while, man. I'm serious. I've got money. Lots of money! Just get me the hell out of here and it's all yours! You'll never see me again!"

"Save it, Hank! No amount of money could make me cross Tony. You crossed him for money and look where *you* are now."

"*Listen to me, man!* It's almost *three hundred grand*! That would set you up in style in any country you want! And it's yours just for letti—"

"*I said save it!* Don't you see? This is really going to happen. You are going to die right here, upside down, in the middle of nowhere. And you wanna know what really gets to me, Foster?" Greenhill asked through clenched teeth as he closed the gap between their faces. "That every one of you begs like a whimpering fool when it's your turn to pay the piper. Not one of you has faced it like a man. Well, hear this, Hank. This time, you stole from the wrong man."

"P-P-Please! Don't kill me! I'll make it right with Tracerio! I will! Please!" Hank Foster begged, sobbing uncontrollably.

"I was sent here to make it right with Tracerio, fool! You burned him, and now I'm gonna burn you!"

He looked into Hank Foster's terror-filled face for the last time. He took out his lighter, reached through the broken back window, and struck the flame. He held it there until the back seat caught, then he rose, grabbed the branch used to erase his presence, and stepped back. As he backed away, Foster begged and pleaded through a voice filled with panic and hopelessness. Words were coming out so fast they blended into one garbled utterance. Greenhill had applied just enough pressure to make him snap. Marcus watched him trying desperately to get free, to no avail. The fire reached the drizzling gasoline and sped through it. Simultaneously, the fire climbed up toward the gas tank and down the little river of fuel. As Foster saw the flames run past him on the ground, his utterances reached a new crescendo of fear and panic. He was now screaming. Greenhill rather enjoyed this part and swept the ground quietly while he backed away so as not to miss a word. By the time he'd made his way back to the road, the vehicle was engulfed in flames reaching twenty feet high, and the unmistakable smell of burning rubber was proof enough for him that the tires were melting in the flame's intense heat. He could no longer hear screams from Hank Foster. As he turned away to go back to his car, the vehicle exploded, silhouetting his form in the eerie glow of the red-gray smoke. Hank Foster had been dispatched—Greenhill style.

Ashland had already spoken with Sharpe when the call from Greenhill came in. After they hung up, he spent a few more minutes working on the file he'd had on screen. Then he logged off and went to the offices of Covington and Jeffries to tell them to do the same. The three men stopped at a bar before going their separate ways and as usual, ended up staying until closing time.

Ashland awoke at his usual time the next morning but not because he wanted to. His head was still spinning as was his stomach. He threw up twice before leaving the house, yet knew better than to call in sick. He had to inform his superior about the three assassinations, and to do that securely, he had to be at the bank. Stories about Johnson and Bell were already in the newscast he listened to on the drive to work. He figured someone would realize Hank Foster was missing in a day or two and go looking for him. As he shuffled by his assistant's desk and noticed her absence, he remembered she had left Friday on vacation. He silently cursed himself for getting drunk the night before. Without her there, he was facing one horrendous Monday. Once in his office and logged onto the system, he selected the outgoing e-mail icon on his screen. He addressed it to Jack Edwards, vice president.

> Jack, three for three. Confirmed. One not yet discovered.
> His Bronco is sitting near the bottom of a ravine with him
> in it, possibly still smoldering. Should be fou

Another wave was coming fast. He staggered quickly around his desk to his private bath and closed the door. As he knelt with his head hovering over the toilet bowl, he decided he'd finish the message, send it, delete it from his sent folder, then take the rest of the day off. His heaving drowned out all other sounds, so he didn't hear the knock on his door or his name being called.

Jon Blake had been completing some loan documents for one of Security Pacific Bank's commercial customers and needed to put them with the rest of the file. He knew George Ashland, his department's senior executive, had been trying to decide whether to award the client the loan. The documents weren't due for a few days yet, but Jon was always focused on staying ahead of his workload. He left his office and walked toward Ashland's. Jon someday hoped to move into that office. He'd heard rumors that George was being considered for a senior vice presidential position. Ashland had a fifth floor corner office with a private bath and balcony. It was quite large and impeccably decorated in an effort to impress potential clients and subtly calm existing ones.

LEFT NO CHOICE

Virginia, Ashland's administrative assistant, had a generous space too. Her desk was just outside Ashland's massive double doors. It was separated from the rest of the offices on the 5th floor by a long hallway that displayed a good number of original sculptures and other works of art. Jon's office was closest to George's and everyone on the fifth floor believed he would most likely replace George should Ashland get the rumored promotion. On the lower floors, the employees worked in cubicles or open spaces, but once you hit the fifth, it was a different world entirely. If you weren't standing in the halls, you couldn't see anyone unless they walked by your door. Jon had never really cared for that look, other than Ashland's office. He preferred a somewhat open floor plan normally, but on this day would be grateful the architects hadn't seen it that way.

Since Jon knew Virginia was on vacation, he just walked right through Ashland's open door while knocking and said, "Hey, George, I finis—" He stopped speaking as he realized George wasn't there. Standing silently for a few seconds, he heard familiar sounds emanating from Ashland's privy.

He knew George drank too much quite often, so Jon decided not to ask if he was all right. He definitely didn't wish to embarrass George. Instead, he'd just find the file, put the loan documents in it for Ashland's review, and then go back to his own office. He decided to email George to let him know the documents were back in the file. That would save George the trouble of having to be face-to-face with anyone while he felt as he did. Jon walked around George's desk and began flipping through the stack of files when one slid off and grazed his computer's mouse. Every terminal's monitor in the entire company had screen savers set on three minutes, yet you could bring back the working screen at any time by touching any key or moving the mouse. When that file brushed the mouse, the screen came to life. As the dark screen saver was replaced by George's bright email screen, Jon couldn't help but to glance at it.

> Jack, three for three. Confirmed. One not yet discovered. His Bronco is sitting near the bottom of a ravine with him in it, possibly still smoldering. Should be fou

Jon's face showed his confusion, even though there was no one to express it to. He read it again. It was addressed to Jack Edwards, and Ashland obviously had not finished it yet. Blake suddenly became aware of a possible meaning for this strange message as he too had listened to the radio on the way to work, and a shiver ran down his spine. He felt the hair on his hands and neck stand up of their own accord, and his pulse quickened. He restacked the files on George's desk, picked up the documents he had brought with him, and started to leave. He only hoped Ashland needed at least two and a half more minutes in the bathroom to regain his composure so the screen saver would come back on. Jon was just passing into the foyer when he heard the toilet's flush, and it startled him. He thought quickly as he heard the sound of water running in a sink. He took several quick steps out into the hall, turned around, and waited. As he took those steps, he looked down the hall and saw that it was empty. He hoped no one had seen him enter Ashland's office. While he stood there listening for the bathroom door to open, he started flipping through the loan documents he was carrying. If anyone saw him now, it would appear as though he had stopped right there in the hall on his way to Ashland's office so he could look over the documents again before presenting them to his boss.

The bathroom door opened, and to Jon's dismay, not much more than a minute had passed. He had no choice now. He had to go back in. He took a deep breath, waited one more second, and started walking back to Ashland's office. He was hoping to catch sight of George and call to him, drawing him out into the hall. If Ashland said to come in while he made his way around the desk instead, it could get ugly for Jon. Ashland may notice his screen. That would not be good. As Jon was taking his third step toward the door, Ashland came into view.

LEFT NO CHOICE

"Hey, George!" Jon called out cheerfully, slightly quickened his pace. Ashland turned in his tracks and walked toward Jon. Although they didn't live by the same rules and the conversations they did share were pretty much strictly professional, Ashland actually admired Jon.

"Yeah, Jon, what have you got?" Ashland said while trying to fake a refreshed smile.

Jon took two more steps before he was face to face with Ashland. They were now standing just outside Ashland's office in the foyer.

"Good morning, sir. I just finished the loan docs on the Pierreson merger and wanted to know if you'd go over them to make sure they are right. When you have the time, of course."

Jon was surprised at how well he was able to maintain his composure. It had been almost two decades since he'd been in a situation requiring deliberate deception. Ashland didn't seem to notice anything unusual either. Jon hoped Ashland would strike up an "attaboy" dialogue, at least for another minute and fifty seconds or so. He was right, but Ashland had reasons of his own for not wanting Jon to follow him into his office. George may have forgotten about the screen saver but not the unfinished email he was typing. He couldn't risk Jon seeing it. George did a good job trying to cover up his hangover and gave Jon sincere accolades about his performance and dedication. He even jokingly brought up the rumor of his impending promotion to senior vice president and said that if it ever came true, he would recommend that Jon replace him. He was lying. Jon could never replace him and he knew it. Jonathan Blake was not the kind of man to involve in Tracerio's business, and whoever held Ashland's chair must be willing to work on both legitimate and illegitimate files.

George finished the conversation by saying he would read the documents the next day, and that he was very confident he'd find nothing wrong. He said he wasn't feeling well though and wouldn't be staying for very long. He asked Jon to handle any emergencies that arose, then asked not to be bothered for the remainder of the day. With that, he went back into his office and closed the door.

It was going to be close, Jon thought. Maybe it had been three minutes, but he really didn't think so. As Ashland made his way around the desk, he stopped. Jon was almost back to his own office when George's door opened, and Jon heard his boss call his name. He turned around to see Ashland walking toward him with a pained look on his face and motioning for Jon to come to him.

"Uh, Jon, I don't know how to ask you this without sounding like a complete heel. I mean, you've been a big asset to me for such a long time." Ashland's facial expression was tightening as he spoke which disturbed Jon. Ashland saw the look on Jon's face and mistook it for bewilderment, then went on. "Oh, it's no big deal, Jon, relax. I just want to know if you'll have your assistant field all my calls today and tell everyone I'll be back in the office tomorrow. Can you do that for me?"

Jon shook off his tension, smiled, and said, "Sure, George, no problem. Whew! The way you started out, I thought I had done something wrong." His heart was beating so vigorously he thought he could hear it.

"Of course not, Jon. Don't be ridiculous. You're a big part of the reason we're doing so well here on the fifth floor. I just feel awkward because I'm throwing more on you for the day than you should have to deal with. Now, if you'll take care of that, I'll finish a few things that need to be done right away, and then I'll be off. Thank you, Jon, and I'll see you tomorrow." With that, he walked back to his office to finish the e-mail to Jack Edwards.

Jon stepped into his office, closed the door, and sat down. He called Frieda on the intercom and instructed her to take messages for George for the remainder of the day. Then he became angry. With the situation, yes, but moreover, with himself. It took him a full half-hour before he was calm enough to function normally

LEFT NO CHOICE

again, and even then, he wasn't able to keep his focus on the bank's business. He kept chastising himself for not using his intelligence training. He had been in much worse predicaments than this as a Green Beret. Yes, it had been almost twenty years ago, he told himself, but that was no excuse. He tried to assess the situation as best he could throughout the day. However, he wasn't able to piece everything together until the ten o'clock news came on and gave him his answers. One by one, the newscaster filled in details of the three deaths. Jon grew angrier and more disgusted as the reporters spoke. After hearing the police's ridiculous explanation for the death of Fred Johnson, he decided to begin an investigation of his own. There was no way the wind could be responsible for Johnson's electrocution and for the investigating officer to even suggest such a thing was absolutely ludicrous.

Jon realized that he had stumbled onto something and that even some of Albuquerque's finest may be players. Who, besides Ashland, Edwards, and possibly some cop or cops could be involved? What were they doing that warranted murder? How was the bank connected? How long had this been going on right down the hall from his office? Had they killed before? If so, who had they killed and why? He didn't sleep that night. He pondered the situation and possible solutions all night long and well into the following day in his office too. No tougher decision had he faced in his life than this one. To ignore what he knew would mean condoning bribery of police officers, extreme brutality, and murder. However, to become involved would definitely put the lives of his wife and son in danger. As he played out every conceivable scenario, they all led back to the same place. Eventually, his close proximity to Ashland would cause him to be a target, meaning his wife and son would be as well. And if he were to resign from the bank so soon after the three murders, suspicions could rise about how much Jon knew. That ended his indecision.

He went home and had a long, emotionally draining conversation with Joan. In the end, she understood his views on everything and his initial plan of action. They held each other in silence, exhausted. Each of them wondering why they were put in this situation, and if they'd survive it. Over the next seven weeks, Jon spent many nights at the office, piecing together quite a collection of document copies he believed to be valuable. His efforts had remained relatively unnoticed too, yet that was about to change.

2

It was closing time on Friday night at the Regional Headquarters of Security Pacific Bank, and as usual, George Ashland, Dennis Jeffries, and Tim Covington met at the elevator on their way out. Every Friday, the three of them went out together after work to drink and act like single men. They were waiting for the elevator to arrive and carry them to the parking garage when Jeffries picked up on it. The fifth floor receptionist was having a conversation with the night janitor, and they were discussing Jonathan Blake.

She was waiting for her husband to pick her up and the night janitor had arrived early, so he wasn't on the clock yet. Jeffries tapped the other two and beckoned them to be silent. He pointed in the direction of the receptionist and the janitor, then pointed to his ear. As the other two watched, he flipped his head to the side, motioning for them all to step away from the elevator and listen. They moved out of the sight line of the receptionist, yet well within hearing distance. The janitor was telling her that for several weeks, Mr. Blake had been coming back to the office almost every night after nine. They listened as he went on to say the man had been working until eleven or twelve each time before leaving again. He opined that Mr. Blake must be bucking for a promotion or something, and that he was constantly using the copier. The receptionist commented on how odd that was as Mr. Blake's administrative assistant could make whatever copies he may have needed the following business day. The two passed it off as just another executive trying to impress his boss, and the janitor left saying it was time to punch in.

The three men walked back down the long hall to George Ashland's office after the conversation broke. They agreed they should inform their superiors immediately. Jack Edwards's phone rang as he was putting the key in the ignition of his Land Cruiser. Ashland hurriedly told him that there was a problem, a very serious one. Edwards was usually a very unshakable sort of man, but Ashland could sense his nervousness as Jack Edwards responded. Edwards said he'd call Theodore Danbury, the bank president, right away and instructed all three to wait for him in the conference room adjacent to Danbury's office on the top floor. Edwards knew Ted Danbury would still be in his car, so he dialed Danbury's cell phone number. Once Danbury had heard enough, he barked a few things at Edwards and hung up. He whipped his Lexus LS460 around and sped back toward the office. He yelled out loud at nobody as he drove, getting angrier by the minute. Jack Edwards had only heard that tone used by Danbury on two other occasions and both were extremely dangerous situations. Jack wasted no time in getting back up to the conference room where all three men were waiting. He told two of the men standing before him, Ashland and Covington, to carefully search Blake's office while Danbury was making his way back to the office. He instructed the third, Dennis Jeffries, to keep watch for the janitor. He reminded them to be thorough yet most importantly, to leave no trace they had been in his office. They were told to get out of Blake's office by eight, whether they were finished or not. Edwards didn't want to risk an encounter should Blake come back that night.

They were to reconvene in the conference room immediately after leaving Blake's office. It took thirty-five minutes for Danbury to get back to the bank. In that time, the two men had thoroughly searched Blake's office once and were doing it again when Ashland received a call from Jack Edwards. The ensuing meeting lasted over two hours. They had found nothing suspicious in Jon's office and had noticed no changes in his behavior other that the fact that he was coming back at strange hours. They discussed the possibility that he was just getting ahead on his workload as he was a dedicated man. They were about to put everything on hold and start watching him closely when Danbury spoke again.

"So you found nothing in his office. So what?" he said impatiently, then continued. "There is absolutely no reason for Blake to be here after hours at all, no matter how dedicated he is. He is doing *something* he doesn't want anyone to know about and that cannot continue. Whether the result of his late-night antics brings the law down on him directly or to Tony's organization, we simply cannot risk it. Jon Blake must be dealt with, and I mean tonight!"

All had to agree with that. Danbury then sent Ashland, Covington, and Jeffries to pay an immediate surprise visit to the home of Jonathan Blake and family. Once there, they were to learn what Jon Blake had been making copies of, where all those copies were, and who he had already involved. Then they were to collect all incriminating documents and bring them back to the office. Lastly, they were to eliminate everyone in the house, period. If only they had known of Jon's past as a decorated warrior with the US Army's Green Berets.

Although he wasn't aware that they had discovered him, Jon had been preparing for just such an event. More importantly, he had prepared his wife, Joan. He had meticulously laid out a plan of action for her on what to do and where to go should they get to him before he had enough evidence to expose them. Danbury's fear, surprise, and inexperience at dealing with situations like this one should have been enough for him to call Tracerio. Instead, his immense ego won out, and he sent three bankers to Blake's home to do the work of professionals. The team of Ashland, Covington, and Jeffries had done jobs like this before, but even those had only been accomplished after careful planning and guidance. They departed the office at 8:45 p.m., stopped at Ashland's house to get weapons and other necessities, then headed for the Blake residence, completely unaware of who and what awaited them. They were not experienced enough to take on someone who was ready for them, let alone a man with Jon's lethal combat skills. They foolishly assumed that Blake wouldn't know what hit him and went so far as to joke about it in the car en route to his home. They even had the audacity to discuss the bonuses each would receive from Mr. Tracerio for their quick and decisive action.

The Blake family lived in a quiet neighborhood on the outskirts of Albuquerque that had attracted them because of the full acre lots, modest cost, and outstanding privacy. On this particular night, Jon and Joan were sitting on the back patio. Both had after dinner glasses of Courvoisier Cognac, trying to quell each others' fear and tensions over the situation that had been tearing their happy lives apart over the last seven weeks. They were speaking in nervous whispers to keep their son Lance, who was inside watching TV, from hearing them.

"But I still believe you can take what you already have to the police and let them handle it, Jon," Joan whispered.

"Honey, if I could, I would. But with the amount of money that's involved, they must have allies on the force. If I gave this information to the wrong cop, those in charge would find out, and they'd come after us too. We just cannot risk it until I can figure out who's sitting at the top of all this. Then I can send everything I've found anonymously to the FBI, and they can deal with it. I don't want anyone to even suspect our involvement."

"Why is it important for you to remain anonymous? Won't that impede the investigation?" Joan asked.

"Because the authorities will try to force me testify as to how I came by all the evidence. Then we'd need to go into the witness protection program and live the rest of our lives in hiding. I can't do that to you and Lance, Joan, I just can't. Which means I've got to get enough proof together that they won't even need testimony, or the name of the anonymous donor," Jon said sadly.

He knew that it could be any number of vice presidents, or even the president of the bank himself that was laundering all those millions through the bank, but for whom? And for what? Jon had already come to the conclusion that it had to be profits from sales of drugs or guns, or both. His biggest fear was being forced to be an active participant in the ensuing trials once he'd handed everything over to the authorities. There just had to be a way to avoid that, he told himself. There just had to be. Then it dawned on him. *There was a way!*

"Joan, if I can avoid being discovered, we won't even have to disappear. I think I can make it look like one of their own ratted them out by mailing everything to the FBI in one of their names"—Jon was thinking aloud—"and they'd eventually request a deal in exchange for testifying against the rest of them. I'll make sure there's enough proof against that one in the package that even if he wanted to deny involvement he couldn't. The only way that one could possibly stay out of prison would be to cut a deal and testify. Then all the focus will be on that one person. No one else who's involved would even think twice about it being a setup."

Joan didn't seem convinced, so Jon leaned forward, laid his hand lovingly and gently over hers, and explained further.

"Sweetheart, when the FBI contacts the man they think sent the package and letter, they'll do it discreetly and spend enough time with him to convince him that he has no choice but to testify, or face life in prison. They'll promise him a new identity, a new job, and a move to another part of the country. Even if he did refuse to cooperate with the FBI, which is a million to one odds, no one would know it was really me who had sent it. Not the FBI, not the ringleader, not anybody. As a last resort, a simple note saying 'I think they are on to me, get me out now' left where his cohorts could find it would ensure they go after him and never even consider anyone else. Do you see how much sense that makes? Or am I completely crazy?" Jon asked.

Joan looked out into the night with a solemn expression. Her eyes, though focused on nothing, moved from spot to spot in the sky as she considered what Jon had said. Jon watched her intently, then let his gaze join hers out into the night. He couldn't tell what she was thinking, but knew she would speak the truth when she did speak. He wished so much that there was a way to keep her and Lance out of this but knew that was impossible. Then Joan looked to the heavens, took a deep breath, and spoke.

"Yes, Jon, it does make sense," she said sadly.

She had been trying every day to convince him to go to the police, but the more she heard, the more she understood his reasons for not going. Moreover, after having ample time to look at all the possible scenarios and their likely outcomes, she believed this course of action to be the safest too.

"I just pray we can get through this without you being caught. I love you so much," she said as a single tear slipped from each of her now glistening eyes.

LEFT NO CHOICE

The embrace and whispers they shared at that moment were both gentle and empowering. Each found the courage in the other's love to do what was necessary to save the family. Each secretly believing that the other carried enough strength to get them all through this alive. Joan's forehead had just settled into his shoulder when he heard it. In all their years in this home, he had never heard sounds this loud from behind the house, ever. After all, their home backed up to a barren desert hillside. But now, he did. And they were the unmistakable sounds of footsteps over moisture-starved brush behind the back gate!

He squeezed Joan hard, then whispered, "Stay calm, it's time for the three Gs. I love you, Joan. Remember to follow our plan step-by-step. Go!" Then he looked at her seriously, flashed his eyes toward the house and told her he loved her again. Her mind raced as she realized what was happening. Something was wrong, and she needed to do the "three Gs" as Jon had called them—Get Lance, get to the car, and get away, now! Lance was playing a video game on his Nintendo System in the family room when Joan rushed in. She noticed that he was still wearing his shoes, and for the first time, she was glad that he had forgotten the "no shoes on in the house" rule.

"Son, I don't have time to explain, just come with me! Quickly!" she said with as much courage and urgency as she could muster.

Lance could tell by the look on her face that she meant it. He dropped the controller, took her outstretched hand, and followed her quickly through the kitchen. She grabbed the shoulder bag she and Jon had prepared and the car keys. She led Lance through the back door, down the steps, and past where his father was standing. Her eyes locked into her husband's for a quick moment, telling Jon all she felt for him with that glance.

Jon Blake looked at his son as they passed and said almost in a whisper, "Son, go with your mom, and I'll see you a little later. I love you!"

Lance, though confused, nodded and obeyed. He hadn't had much choice anyway as Joan was pulling him along even as Jon was speaking. Joan whispered to Lance to get in her car fast and quiet and to lock the door. She did the same and just in time. As she started the car, a man burst out of the house from the back door and lunged at Jon, striking immeasurable fear into both Joan and Lance. Jon dodged the lunge, delivered a sweeping elbow to the man's back, then ran past him into the house. As she put the car in drive, another figure came running up the driveway toward them from the front corner of the house. Joan stepped on the gas and intentionally steered toward the man in the driveway, but he jumped clear of her attack. Lance got on his knees in the seat and turned to see the man who jumped away from the car. That man started running after them as yet another man appeared and came running toward the house from the back gate.

Lance became so scared he began screaming, "What's going on, Mom?" over and over again. As they drove past the front of the house and down the long driveway, Lance could see two, then three human shadows cast against the closed curtains in the living room. He watched as the man who had tried to chase them entered the front door and slammed it shut behind him. By now, Lance was screaming his request for answers. Joan although scared out of her wits too tried to calm him down. She wished she could call in the law on her cell phone, but Jon had told her not to use it unless the thugs were chasing her and Lance, no matter what happened to him. She was looking carefully in her rearview mirror as she drove for vehicles that might be following her.

The Blake family was very lucky, if you could call it luck, that Jon was much stronger and more agile than his assailants had anticipated. This grave underestimation of Jon's abilities forced all three men to direct their attack at him alone, which gave

LEFT NO CHOICE

Joan enough time to escape with Lance. As they drove down the street, Lance could see silhouettes through the curtains. Lance was horrified. He slowly slid back down into his seat, crying in extreme anguish. Joan was also crying and calling out loud to God for his intervention. A few minutes, later Joan and Lance were within a mile of the I-40 freeway, her first goal in the escape plan. She sped up to get through the Unser Boulevard and 98th street traffic light before amber turned red. As she cleared the intersection, she glanced over to the oncoming traffic lanes and her heart leaped up into her throat. The first car facing her in the left-turn lane was a police cruiser, and the officer's eyes met hers as she flew by. She looked down at the speedometer and gasped. Fifty-eight miles an hour! She was way over the speed limit and could only hope he wouldn't follow.

Through her rearview mirror, she saw the cruiser do a U-turn and it's lights began to flash. Joan knew they were for her. She became suddenly aware of how frightened she was and remembered something Jon had said. He had told her not to talk to anyone about this, the police included. The fear was overtaking her almost as fast as the police cruiser, and her voice sounded shattered as she said over and over to Lance not to say anything to the policeman, that she would handle it and explain everything to him later. Her hands trembled as she pulled to the shoulder. She watched in her side mirror as the tall, deep-bronze skinned African-American officer rose from the cruiser and closed the door. As he drew nearer, she could see a look of controlled frustration on his face. It seemed an eternity before he arrived at her window.

"Ma'am, practicing for the Indianapolis 500 isn't against the law, but doing it on the streets of Albuquerque is, even on Unser Boulevard. Could I see your license and registration, please?"

Just then, Officer Rhodes noticed the look on her face. It was not the normal look of fear, anxiety or frustration those he caught speeding had. This woman was teary-eyed and very upset about something.

"Are you okay, ma'am? What's wrong?" he asked as he leaned down and looked across to the passenger seat. He saw that the young boy sitting there was as terrified as she was.

As Joan was about to tell him she'd had an argument with her husband, his hand radio came to life. "All units in Paradise Hills sector. We have reports of a house on fire at 4715 Great Hills Drive. All available northwest units are ordered to evacuate the immediate vicinity and clear fire lanes. Fire and rescue are en route."

As the dispatcher repeated her instructions Officer Rhodes looked at Joan and said, "Ma'am, are you all right? If you're not, I'll try to help you. If you are, I've got to go."

Joan knew that Jon needed help more than anything right now, so she looked up at him and told him she was okay. As she spoke, she saw the genuine concern in his eyes and said in the most stable voice she could muster, "We'll be all right, Officer. I'll slow down. Thank you."

With this, Officer Rhodes ran back to his car, flipped a U-turn, and sped away in the other direction with lights and siren on. Joan ran what she had just heard the dispatcher say through her head. A home on fire in Paradise Hills the dispatcher had said. 4715 Great Hills Drive she'd said. Their home.

On that fateful night, Officer Michael Rhodes had dropped his partner off and was heading home when he saw the speeding car. Even though he was off duty, he wheeled the car around after watching the woman drive so fast through the intersection. It surprised him to see a woman in the driver's seat so much he immediately went to talk with her after pulling her over. Michael knew running the license plate was standard procedure, yet in

LEFT NO CHOICE

this case, he chose not to. As he walked toward the car, he saw both her hands go clearly onto the wheel, so he went right to the window. He leaned down to make eye contact with her and used the Indianapolis 500 line, which was his favorite for speeders on the West Side streets bearing Al Unser's name. It was then that he saw her face fully for the first time.

This woman was frightened to the point of panic, and this must be the reason for her unsafe speeding. He decided to forego the lecture about her driving. He wanted to find out what had terrified her so badly. He noticed the boy beside her in the car and saw the striking resemblance. He assumed the boy had to be her son, who was also crying and scared. Michael's experience told him this was probably the aftermath of a heated argument with someone but asked to be sure. As he was about to start digging, the dispatcher came on the air. *If this lady needed help, she would say so*, he thought. If she refused it, she was probably just upset and capable of calming herself down. How she responded to his offer of assistance would help him decide whether to stay with her or to hightail it over to the address given. The dispatcher was repeating her instructions again while Michael offered help. The woman declined, so he took off toward the fire as he knew he would definitely be needed there. He said a little prayer for the woman and her son as he drove, truly hoping they could resolve their problems.

In his time on the Albuquerque force, he had been told numerous times how dangerous any fire could be due to the dry brush everywhere. The powerful winds, which could change direction without warning, added to the hazard. When he arrived at the scene, he saw the fire reaching up and out of the windows on both floors. He could feel its heat from a surprising distance. The sirens of the fire department vehicles were clear, and from their volume, close now. He had radioed in when he arrived and saw other officers on scene so he ran to the adjoining house to evacuate the neighbors. While he was running up the driveway, as if on cue, the family came out to see what was going on. He asked if everyone in the family was standing there, and the mother replied in the affirmative. He asked her to take the kids and the dog to the end of the block. He asked the husband if he knew how many people lived in the house that was on fire. The man told Officer Rhodes the names of the Blake family and their approximate ages.

Michael then instructed the man to knock on all the neighbors' doors and tell them to gather their families and take them to the end of the block as well. He watched these two adults turn and do as they were asked, then headed toward the back of the burning house. He circled it as close as he dared, looking for any signs of life either within the house or on the grounds close by and saw nothing. He ran back to the front. The fire department was now on the scene connecting hoses to hydrants, preparing to stop this ferocious and hungry beast from consuming the entire neighborhood. They knew there was nothing they could do for the Blake home, so they concentrated their efforts on keeping the adjacent homes from catching fire. Officer Rhodes ran swiftly across the front yard of the Blake residence toward the fire crews to assist them. Out of nowhere came a sound more deafening than the fire itself. He felt himself being picked up and thrown like a rag doll against a tree. The force of the blast was so great the sheer impact caused him to lose consciousness. This was the last thing he would remember about that fire.

After watching the officer do a U-turn and drive off in the other direction, Joan started the car and drove to the freeway on-ramp. She looked at Lance who was now trying very hard to keep his own tears in. His valiant effort was to no avail as the tears kept streaming down his reddened face. This made Joan realize that she had to regain her composure, think clearly, and not lose control as she needed to be there for Lance. Jon had told her not to go to the police if something happened to him as he didn't know who she could trust on the force and instead, to follow their pre-planned disappearing instructions. If he were able to escape his assailants, he would contact her through the personals in the newspaper of Portland, Oregon, her destination city, and eventually follow them there. Jon had truly tried to think of everything. Joan only hoped now that Lance would still have a chance to get to know his father.

His father. No greater man had there ever been in the eyes of his son. Jonathan Blake was kind, funny, generous, and wise. His body was that of an Olympian and his face had been chiseled handsomely by the hand of God. He had eyes of sky blue, blonde hair, and a strawberry blonde mustache that was trimmed to perfection. His only vice was a pipe and Captain Black cherry tobacco. The first stop she made was in Edgewood, a town approximately twenty miles east of Albuquerque. Jon had told her to go there, pull the maximum amount of money from the automated teller machine, fill up the car with the only credit card Jon hadn't taken, then double back, and head for the Arizona line.

As Jon donned the helmet, he knew in his heart that no matter what his emotions were telling him, he was doing the right thing. There was just no way to protect them all the time. He had to bring the whole bunch down before they would ever be truly safe again. Jon knew how fortunate he was to have a wife like Joan. She was strong-willed, capable, and very smart. He knew she would do everything within her power to follow the plan they had made, and knowing this made it easier for him to be away from her and Lance for awhile. Their lives would be disappointing ones at best if he put them all in the witness protection program. And should they ever be found, he couldn't bear to think of the consequences. He just had to eliminate all of the threats before he could rejoin his family. This was now the hardest decision he ever had to make, but make it he did.

Jon Blake had not told his wife this part of his plan. He knew she would argue its absurdity, and he was afraid she might be able to convince him she was right. If he were lucky enough to live through the initial attack, he would lead the criminals far away from his wife and son, then double back under his new alias of J. J. Tracker. He had already acquired IDs, placed a large amount of money in a different bank, and purchased the motorcycle and trailer. He also bought a 9mm under that name, prior to being discovered. He had come to the conclusion that if there were only one or two credit card transactions made to the east by the Blake family, any direction of travel was still a feasible possibility. However, a third, fourth, and fifth transaction, each further east than the last, would solidify the impression that they were probably headed for the Atlantic Coast. Those chasing them would believe Jon must have forgotten that those transactions could be traced.

Even though within just a few days, the FBI could also be looking for him; they didn't concern Jon. He knew they'd probably just be looking for Joan and Lance at first anyway, thinking him to be dead. That would give him more than enough time to pull everybody on both sides of the law into a wild goose chase toward the Eastern Seaboard looking for Joan's car. They would fall for it, he was sure. The cops would believe she didn't know not to use the cards, either, so they'd assume they were getting closer with each new transaction until they caught her. The depraved mind that started this would never even entertain the thought that an upstanding family man like Jon Blake would leave his family to fend for themselves. That meant everybody would follow the trail he was leaving. This suited J.J. just fine as he wanted them to follow him, not his wife and son.

J.J. knew not to sign anything anywhere as Jon Blake so he'd pay cash for gas and most of his food on the trip. He'd register under J.J. Tracker in motels if he stopped and again pay cash. He wanted Jon Blake to remain dead as long as possible. He wouldn't have to sign anything at teller machines, so while he was still assumed dead, the cops would believe Joan was using them. The only way they would discover it wasn't her was to look at the ATM security videos where the money was drawn. He figured the law wouldn't do that until they found out Jon Blake was still alive, which was still at least a few days away. He'd also be careful not to let the Harley be caught on the videos. Parking it a block from each of the banks he would visit should do the trick. He'd leave the helmet with the bike each time too. He didn't want anyone on either side of the law to start looking for a man on a motorcycle.

He'd been as ready as he could be for an attack although he really thought they'd come for him while he was alone somewhere, like they had those other three. That's the main reason he hadn't sent Joan and Lance away in the beginning. There were other compelling reasons for Joan and Lance to stay in Albuquerque too. Jon didn't have any idea how long it would take him to collect enough evidence to bring everyone down. If he sent Joan away with Lance and they were gone for longer than a few weeks, talk between Joan's friends would begin. That was a huge problem as Joan's friends were the wives of Jon's fellow executives. Once the husband's heard, they'd begin to ask Jon questions and suspicions could arise—"Where did she go?" "Why did she go?" "Were they having problems?" "What kind?" "Why hadn't she confided in any of her friends?" "Even if she were mad at Jon, surely, she'd want their support, wouldn't she?" "Were they coming back?" "How serious were these problems between them?" There were just too many questions Jon would have no good answer for. That in itself would make it immensely difficult if not impossible for Jon to continue digging under the radar as all eyes would be upon him and most conversations would be about him. He was upset with himself, however, as he thought about what might have happened to them that night because he hadn't sent them away.

Underestimating his adversaries was not a mistake he would willingly repeat. He was glad now that he'd thought to take Jeffries upstairs to his bedroom and put him on the bed before he jumped from the window. He'd hidden the Harley in the shed since the day he purchased it. He wasn't worried about anyone finding or stealing the bike out there, and since his car was still there, all this would make it seem to the cops like Jon was the one in the house when it went up. The crooks may believe differently due to what they'd hear from Ashland and Covington about Jeffries' absence, but they sure as hell weren't going to tell the cops that. He hadn't expected Ashland and Covington to run out of there while he was grappling with Jeffries, though. He fully expected all three to stay on him until they had finished him. The other two must have been intimidated when they saw that he had put Jeffries down for the count while they were setting the fire. Maybe they thought he could take them out too. Or maybe they were afraid of getting trapped by the fire. No matter. At least he and his family were still alive and on the move.

J.J. wondered what they would tell their superiors about how they were able to get out and Jeffries wasn't. Maybe they would use Jeffries as a scapegoat for fouling up the attack so they wouldn't be blamed. Maybe they'd say he took off out of fear. Nonetheless, these things didn't matter now either. J.J. was just glad that one of them was already out of the way. Now he had to go back after the others. He'd thought long and hard about how to move around without attracting too much attention. He decided to pose as a motorcycle jockey because they were known for traveling from town to town while living a nomadic lifestyle. This would make it easier for him to get in, get done what had to be done, and get out without being noticed too prevalently.

LEFT NO CHOICE

The first order of business once he had left the eastbound trail for them to follow was to double back and head for the cabin he had rented just outside of Chimayo, New Mexico. The cabin was located roughly eighty miles north of Albuquerque just outside the Santa Fe National Forest in a heavily wooded, lightly traveled area known for its wild game. He chose this place because he needed to have a wide array of weapons at his disposal but didn't want to attract undue attention in the process. All those who had cabins up there had their own little arsenals and most stayed to themselves, which suited J.J. perfectly. Being up there would also let him regain his sharp shooting skills with the weapons he would purchase as J.J. During and after Operation Desert Storm and the Gulf War, he had become a crack shot with both rifle and sidearm. He hoped relearning those would happen quickly. He was still pretty good in hand-to-hand combat as he had just found out. However, he was sure he needed a lot of work where his bows and knife were concerned as he hadn't loosed an arrow in twenty years. It would be necessary to get back into the shape he was in while he was stationed overseas too. All these things that had to be done would take a good bit of time, so he prepared himself to be in training up at the cabin for at least a month.

The arsenal would be funded by money he had earned through investments that his wife had known nothing about. For years, he had been secretly stockpiling it, in hopes to one day walk in the door at home and surprise her with the announcement, "Honey, I quit my job at the bank today. I've been putting a little away here and there over the years and it has finally grown to the point that we can now live very comfortably without working. So, where in the world would you like to live, sweetheart?" It was his goal to do this before his fiftieth birthday, which would be long before she would expect him to be able to retire. The amount he had accumulated was almost seven figures, and he still had six years of investing to go. He had never even considered the possibility that he would be using this money to protect them and quite probably save their lives. He had only thought of what the look on her face would be when he told her that he was retiring because they were multi-millionaires.

Well, J.J. concluded, *at least the money will be used to perpetuate justice and that was the second best thing it could be used for.* With that, he fired up the bike and drove as quickly as he dared out of the neighborhood toward the freeway. He was running four miles an hour over the limit on his way to Edgewood in hopes of catching up with Joan before she left there to tell her he'd made it. Their plan was for her to get the money from the account and get back to the freeway as quickly as possible. They had eliminated Edgewood as a rendezvous point during their discussions as Jon wasn't sure how long it would take him to get away if they did come after him at home. No, it was best that she not wait for him. He would contact her in Portland within ten days through the personals in the paper. He missed her at the bank by only moments but recognized the Intrepid as it merged back onto the westbound freeway while he was approaching the eastbound on-ramp. He felt overjoyed that they had made it, and she had indeed headed to Edgewood. He wanted to catch up to them to let them know he too had survived but knew better. He glided past the on-ramp, accelerated, set his cruise control for sixty-eight, and headed for the Texas State Line.

Joan drove through the night and well into the next morning before she stopped for the second time. She was already well inside Arizona and would reach California by nightfall. She needed to refuel and she had to get them something to eat. While Lance sadly picked at one of the sandwiches she'd purchased at the mini-mart, she explained to him what was happening.

"Lance, what I'm about to tell you will be hard for you to understand, but you must try," she said as her voice broke and the tears began flowing down her face onto her pink blouse. "Your father was working for some very bad men, but he didn't know that until just recently. I'm going to tell you what he's told me but you must promise never to repeat it. We are doing right now what your dad asked me to do, in case he was found out and didn't have time to leave with us. Your father said they'd kill us if anyone ever found us, so you must promise me you won't ever tell this to anyone, okay?"

She began sobbing as her words reached her own ears. Pictures of what might have happened to her husband mercilessly filled her mind. Lance had put down the sandwich and listened while keeping his gaze fixed on his feet. After a short time, Joan composed herself and proceeded to tell Lance everything. When Joan finished, she told him they would follow the plan and pray that soon they would hear from him so that they could be reunited and start their lives over. Lance asked Joan if she thought his dad was dead. Joan thought for a moment then decided it was best to be completely honest.

"Son, I won't lie to you. Yes, it's possible that those men killed your father last night. But, somehow, I know in my heart they didn't. I cannot explain why. I wish I could. It's funny, but as we were getting back on the freeway in Edgewood, I had a strange feeling that he was right there with us. I know that sounds crazy, Lance, but I really believe he made it out of there."

She went on to explain to Lance with a great deal of difficulty that if he had not made it, he was already with God and Jesus in heaven. That they shouldn't feel bad for him because he would feel no more pain. She told him how God only took really special people from the earth in this way and that his father must be very special for God to call him to heaven while he still had a family. This seemed to appease him outwardly, so they drove on in silence.

3

Michael Rhodes woke the following morning in the hospital around ten thirty, and standing beside him was his friend and partner, Ralph Davis. Ralph had been on the force his entire adult life, but came to trust Michael as the best partner he'd ever had. Ralph's big brown eyes began to brighten as he watched his friend's head clear.

"Man, even though you're standing two feet away, your nose is too close for comfort. Move that sorry excuse for a circus tent back, would ya?"

Ralph smiled, showing all of his "nothing to write home about" teeth, and threw back, "This nose has sniffed out more bad guys than you'll ever catch, so if I were you, I'd be trying to figure out how to reward it. Maybe a new snowblower for the peak, huh?"

Michael smiled as his friend grabbed and squeezed his hand reassuringly.

"I'll tell you, man, you are one lucky 'hunk of lard' to be alive," Ralph said and went on, "when that gas main went, it not only leveled the house and spread debris a quarter mile, it took out the whole side of the house next to it too."

Ever the cop, Michael asked, "Did everybody make it? What about the folks that lived there? Did anybody find out if they were home?"

"Hey, hey, *hey*, now. You just relax and try to heal yourself, would ya? God knows you need all the help you can get doing that," Ralph said, admiring his friends concern for a family he'd probably never met.

"Come on, Ralph. Give it up, man. You know I'm not gonna just let it go. So tell me, did they all get out okay?"

Ralph's tone changed to one of sadness as he informed his friend about the body that was found in the debris. It was most likely an adult male judging by the size, but the body was badly burnt. Ralph went on to say that this was the only body found, though, so if anyone else had been there, they had gotten out in time. He told Michael of the Fire Marshall's pending investigation. Once the fire marshal was able to ascertain the cause, he had promised to let Michael know all of his findings personally. Although as of this morning, there was no word on the wife or child of the deceased. The department was still trying to locate them. Ralph went on to tell Michael that the detectives assume she and the child were out of town as they had not shown up at the house yet. He just hoped he wasn't the one on duty there when they finally did pull up from their trip to see their house burnt to the ground. He didn't want to have to be the one to tell them that one of their family members hadn't survived.

Michael listened as Ralph told of the department's intent to question the man's coworkers at Security Pacific. The questions would range from living relatives to travel habits to favorite family retreats and so on. He cautioned that this might not produce any leads. They could only be sure the wife had driven to where she took the child as her car was gone. Michael hoped they hadn't seen it on the news. If they had, he hoped they were with loved ones. Ralph said he had to go but promised he would be back later with some of the guys and a deck of cards if Michael felt up to losing some money. After Ralph left, the nurse checked on Michael. The doctor came by later to explain that he had suffered a severe concussion and a badly bruised back. However, his tests showed no signs of permanent damage. He told Michael he was going to order more tests for the next morning and if all went well, Michael would be out of there in two days and back to work in a week.

By mid-afternoon, the majority of the staff at Security Pacific's Regional office had heard about the fire. All were shocked and saddened by the news of Jon Blake's apparent death, and most who knew him were visibly and vocally mourning him. However, early that morning, on the highest floor of the bank, a different discussion regarding his untimely "death" had been held. The president, a vice president, and two of the three executives sent to the Blake residence were in attendance. Four other well dressed, distinguished looking men sat in the president's personal conference room, and yet another three men were standing. Everyone was trying to put all the pieces together concerning the previous night's fiasco.

This room had been used for many such meetings as it had been designed for complete privacy. It was almost completely soundproof, with translucent glass walls that gave anyone looking through a heavily distorted, incomprehensible view. It had only one entrance, which required passing through two doors, with classical music playing and a ventilation system in the hall between the two doors that could only be controlled from inside the conference room. The ventilation system was designed to force air toward the inner door to keep sound from traveling out. The room had its own lavatory, bar, refrigerator, telephone voice scrambler, and paper shredder. Even these safeguards against traffic and information going in and out were not enough to make those in charge comfortable. Prior to all meetings, the room was checked for bugs, and there were doormen stationed for good measure; two guarded the outer entrance while two more were stationed inside the conference room. These features allowed those within the conference room to express themselves in any manner they saw fit, without regard to being heard. This was why the small framed man known as Tony Tracerio Sr. angrily thundered away at George Ashland and Tim Covington.

"I just cannot believe that three of you couldn't handle one measly pencil-pusher, a housewife, and a little kid! How could you screw up such an easy hit?"

The emotion in his voice was almost an uncontrollable rage. He was nearly seething he was so angry. All who were present knew that meant some of them might not see the sun rise in the morning. George Ashland shook in fear as he feebly tried to explain.

"Mr. Tracerio, we were very careful when we went over there. We split up and closed in from different directions to prevent escape. We had a contingency plan ready in case they saw us before we got to them. Each of us was responsible for one of them. Since Dennis was the youngest and strongest of us, he took Blake himself, but there was no way we could know he was so strong and quick. He took Dennis out like *he* was a little kid. I think somewhere in Blake's past, he had martial arts training. You should've seen this guy. In all honesty, I'm surprised all three of us aren't dead. I mean, had we known this guy was ready for us, we would not have gone in the way we did, sir. We would have requested your assistance in bringing professionals in to handle him. We just thought we—"

"You thought! I can't believe I'm hearing this! If you *had* been thinking, you would have called me before you ran over there trying to be heroes! And you"—he was now pointing and glaring in the direction of Danbury, the bank president—"I want to hear from you why you took such a high profile matter into your own hands!"

At fifty-three years old, Theodore Danbury, known as Ted to those few that he let close to him, was a man that most around him admired. He was meticulously groomed and always well dressed. He was also strikingly handsome with his six-foot-three-inch frame, salt-and-pepper hair, and steel gray eyes. It had been said he could probably convince Fidel Castro to turn Cuba into a democracy if he had enough time with him. Yet at this moment, he was a frightened mass of reddened flesh just hoping to live through the day. He mustered as much courage as was possible under the circumstances and began.

"Tony, I did exactly what you have instructed me to do in each of the previous situations like this one," he said with some conviction. As he went on, he changed his inflection to that of a regretful, subordinate man who had tried to please. "I only did so without consulting you this time because I really believed this to be the course of action you would have instructed me to take."

Danbury knew Tony Tracerio's thought process very well and knew that if he showed any cowardice or disrespect, he would be strangled where he sat. He also knew that cowardice and fear were two different things. Further, Tony Tracerio Sr. could easily tell the difference between the two, so Danbury tried very hard to make sure his face clearly reflected some of the fear he had running through him. Tony liked keeping otherwise powerful men around who feared him as it somehow gave him added confidence. Danbury's manipulative expertise showed as he went on to explain everything that had happened, hoping that the great Tony Tracerio Sr. would admit to himself that he would have made the same decision. He closed his explanation with the riskiest statement he had ever spoken, knowing if he didn't hit the mark with Tony now, he could very well be a dead man.

"Tony, all you would have known about Blake was what we knew before we went over there. You have always instructed me to use these same men to solve problems. I only did what I knew you would have ordered me to do anyway, sir. The only difference I can possibly see in the chain of events is the timing of your involvement. I am truly sorry for that and must take full responsibility for it because I chose not to let anyone bother you last night."

All those present during Danbury's dissertation would never forget his masterful use of the English language as his words and inflection visibly soothed Tracerio's rage. Tony had not been handed his position by an aging relative, or because he was a trusted "second" to the boss. He started his world from nothing. He had used his remarkable wit to outsmart his adversaries on both sides of the law, and with this he had acquired a devoted following. As he listened to Danbury, he did quietly admit to himself that he undoubtedly would have ordered the same three men to do exactly what Danbury had instructed them to do. As all present watched in silence, Tony moved to the window, hands clasped behind his back. He had already silently dismissed the events of the previous night, thanks to Danbury, and was working out the details of how to repair the damage before it got worse. The silence seemed like hours for Danbury, Edwards, Ashland, and Covington.

When he did turn and walk back to the head of the table, he said, "Okay, here's what we are going to do. First, all of you who work at the bank start looking into an embezzlement conspiracy that seems to point to Blake and Jeffries. Nothing too big, just leak it that there are some discrepancies in the books, and these two both had access to the funds. In one or two more days, the rest of the staff will notice Jeffries isn't around and will begin to ask questions, or worse yet, call the cops. If someone files a missing persons report and the chief doesn't follow up on it, he'll be under the microscope and that won't do. Leak it that Jeffries had been talking about just packing up one day and going off somewhere where there was no stress. This will buy us time where Jeffries's disappearance is concerned. Even if his disappearance is reported later and the feds show up, that story coupled to the conspiracy seed should lead them to the probability that Jeffries and Blake were partners in some scam. Jeffries must have gone to Blake's house that night for whatever reason and their disagreement turned deadly. Then the one who lived disappeared with the wife and kid.

"If Blake lived, he was just disappearing from the law. If Jeffries did, then he and Blake's wife must have been having a secret affair, and after killing Blake, they ran off together with the boy and the money. Either way, nothing points to us. This also helps solve our little problem of the real discrepancies in the books. I'll make sure the fire marshal rules the fire accidental, which keeps him and the chief from being forced to order an autopsy. That buys us more time. Next, close up all loose ends and any potential paper trails here that could lead anywhere but to those two. I want that done before one o'clock today. Then, shut this whole damn operation down. I don't want anything strange to happen here at the bank after these two have disappeared from the picture. That will make an even stronger suggestion that they were running the show. The janitor seeing Blake hanging around at night lately should work to our advantage if we do this right."

His voice was level and his thoughts focused, a complete reversal from just a few moments before. He went on.

"Now, since they only found one body in the debris, we must assume its Jeffries becau—"

"What if Blake's dead and Jeffries took off to escape your wrath?" Tony Jr. interrupted. "What if he skipped out 'cause the wife and kid got away and he figured you'd kill him, so he's gone into hiding, or even gone to the feds?"

Tony Sr. glared impatiently at his namesake and explained.

"Son, if Blake was dead, I think I'd already have been informed that his wife and kid were in protective custody somewhere. Without him to protect them, I'm sure they would have gone to the police by now. Even though the cops think otherwise for the moment, we know they weren't on any trip last night when all this happened. There are only two logical explanations for their complete disappearance. One, that they have gone to the cops and are being hidden away. But since I own the cops, and they don't have them, all that is left is option number two. Blake did not go to the cops and is taking his family as far and as fast as he can away from here."

As Tony spoke, his voice grew louder until he was screaming at the top of his lungs on the last few words. He took a few deep breaths, calmed himself, and continued. "After all, it seems he had already prepared his family for our hit. How else would they be able to get away so fast and so clean? He must have known it was only a matter of time before we'd be coming for him. Right?" As he looked around the room, all eyes were on the table, but all heads nodded in agreement. "Okay, then. This is the question we should be asking ourselves, gentlemen. Why would he go to the trouble of copying all our files and preparing for a hit, instead of spilling his guts the second he discovered something? Because he didn't know who to trust at the bank or on the force, that's why. He must not have enough evidence to involve the authorities yet, or I'm sure I'd have heard about it from the chief by now. I wouldn't have gone to the law if I were Blake, either. No, this guy took his family into hiding somewhere. I'm sure of it. Nonetheless, we know that eventually the cops may be forced to do an autopsy on what's left of the body. It's a matter of when. It will either be when the conspiracy theory spreads far enough because Jeffries is also missing or when they realize they just can't locate the wife and kid. Either way, we need to find all of them, and I mean fast."

Tony Sr. thought silently for a moment then spoke again. "We also need to put out a search for Jeffries in case you're right, son. I'll see if the chief can get me an ID on the corpse without involving the medical examiner. That'll let us know who's still alive and who to be looking for. Has anyone thought to check for transactions made last night through the banks automated teller system by either the Blake family or by Jeffries?"

Danbury had been waiting for this question to arise. He was well prepared to answer it.

"Yes, Tony. I checked this morning, and Mrs. Blake's card was used within an hour of the attack to draw $300.00 from our branch in Edgewood, and she used it to get gas there too. A little over four hours later, they used one in Amarillo at another bank, again to withdraw cash. Two hours ago, another transaction in Oklahoma City. All were Blake's or his wife's cards, and none whatsoever by Jeffries. However, we're monitoring all savings, checking, and visa accounts the Blake's and Jeffries have with us."

"Very good, Ted, very good. They're definitely headed east then. I want all of our friends in the east to have pictures and descriptions of these people and their car by tomorrow night. I want to know if they have any relatives or friends and where they live. Let our people know I'm putting a $100,000.00 bonus up to anyone that finds them for us. I also want Greenhill and Sharpe on their trail as soon as possible. Son, tell them to find out what Blake knows, collect all documents, and kill all of them, including the kid. I want there to be no loose ends left." Tony paused for a moment to let his orders sink in. He turned to face the table, then said, "Well, take a good look around the room, gentlemen, because we will never meet here again."

He looked at one of the goons by the inside door and said, "Have my car taken to O'Donohue's Pub. I'll meet it there shortly." Then, as he donned his suit coat, he said, "All of you who work here, pay attention, as I will not repeat this. All discussions regarding this situation are over where you are concerned. Do not speak between yourselves no matter where you are. Do not 'speculate' as to where they might have gone, don't even think about it. All you are to do now is drop hints about a potential embezzlement conspiracy, and only a few at that. If you get questioned, and you may, play stupid or you'll be playing dead, do you understand?"

All heads nodded in unison, including those not being spoken to.

"Are there any questions?"

No one dared ask any, even if they wanted to. They were just relieved that all of them were still alive.

With no responses from the group, Tony Sr. said, "Okay, that's it. Get Greenhill and Sharpe moving now. Son, let's get out of here."

Marcus Greenhill and David Sharpe had been raised in the same neighborhood, and the two of them were very close indeed. They had done everything since grade school together, from cheating in class, to dating much younger girls that were too lonely or too infatuated for their own good. These girls were so impressed with how cool Marcus and David seemed they would do anything, and that means anything, Sharpe and Greenhill told them to do. Then, once our "heroes" had persuaded them to do everything, they dumped them coldly and without compassion, leaving unsuspecting parents to try to pick up the pieces. Unfortunately, their list of accomplishments doesn't end there. They graduated to stealing cars, mugging defenseless seniors, running and selling drugs, and then to the worst of violent acts—rape and murder. They were as loyal to each other as they were inseparable, and this made the pair a very dangerous enemy if they really didn't like you or if you had something they wanted. By the time they reached adulthood, they had broken every law regarding human life there was. This earned them quite a reputation on both sides of the law, and many job offers on one. They accepted most.

It was hard to tell which was more dangerous. Sharpe and Greenhill's sadistic enjoyment of committing gruesome, evil acts or the people with the coldly calculating minds that paid them to carry them out. They ended up in the employ of some very powerful, self-serving men that actually liked having them around to handle any problems that arose. They were also hired out occasionally as contractors to others that were in need of their talents. Within fourteen hours of the family's disappearance, Sharpe and Greenhill were on the road. They knew that the family had left Albuquerque heading east, and so were they. They also knew they had to find them before the cops did. The cops believed the old man was dead, at least for the moment, but sooner or later may have a look at the credit card transactions themselves when the wife and kid didn't come back.

The cops would discover that the first one was just after the house went up and come to their own conclusion. They would most likely say she did the dastardly deed then ran. To make matters worse for the Tracerio organization, the cops would also see the withdrawals made in Amarillo and Oklahoma City, which would prove she had crossed state lines. That meant they would have to notify the FBI, and the feds would have to come in on the case. If the FBI got involved, Tracerio's world could be turned upside-down. The feds had the manpower to watch every major airport and boat dock as well as almost every major road that lead into Mexico and Canada. For obvious reasons, Sharpe and Greenhill had to find them before the feds did and hopefully even before they became involved, no question about it. They had met with Danbury and Ashland to get all available information on Blake prior to going after him. His entire personnel file, all of his account histories, and his office phone records had been copied and carefully returned to their respective cabinets. The copies were given to Sharpe and Greenhill for tracking purposes.

Both secretly felt that box full of intelligence was a serious waste of their time. After all, this guy had stupidly been leaving them quite a trail by using his credit cards along the way to get cash.

"Doesn't this idiot know if he uses his cards anybody can track him?" Sharpe asked Greenhill as Albuquerque faded in the rear view mirror of their Crown Victoria. Marcus Greenhill laughed.

"Man, what are you complaining about? As long as we find 'em before the feds do, it'll be some of the easiest money we ever make. Besides, Blake might be tryin' to save all his cash for a jump out of the country or somethin.' Let's just catch up to 'em and put some holes in them before they skip out or get snatched by the Fibbies. Oh, and you need to stop at the next town so I can get some rubbers."

"Rubbers? What do you need them for?" Sharpe asked, puzzled.

"'Cause if the wife looks as good in person as she does in this picture, me an' her's gonna get real friendly before we take her out. I jus' don't wanna leave no evidence it was me, okay?"

Sharpe looked quickly at Greenhill as if he were crazy, then turned his eyes back to the road and said, "Who said you get to go first, Marcus? If we gonna do this, I think we should flip for it. Besides, you went first last time, man. Now it's my turn."

Greenhill pushed Sharpe, saying, "All right, man, stop whining. You can go first." Then after a slight pause, he said, "But that means you gotta spring for the rubbers."

"Deal!" Sharpe said, and they looked at each other and laughed. Both were too arrogant to realize it, but for the first time in their careers, they should have been very worried.

She couldn't get it out of her mind, no matter how hard she tried. She was positive her husband had made it. She had felt that way even before she left Edgewood. Joan and Lance had traveled almost nonstop the entire day, using cash for everything since Edgewood. She really had no need to use her regular credit card at all, even in Edgewood, as Jon had given her new ones under a different name and over $9,000.00 in small bills to take with her for the journey. He had only wanted her to go there and use one to mislead their pursuers. Jon had told her that if he hadn't left with them, there was a chance he wouldn't leave at all. In that case, she must leave a trail to the east, then double back. The scumbags would put everybody they had on the road eastbound looking for her car, Jon had said. By the time they realized the car wasn't to be found and the electronic trail had dried up, she should be in California, or already have arrived in Portland. The important thing was to make sure she had dumped the car within two days, no matter where she was.

The plan was for her make it to North Hollywood in that time and abandon it there, keys in the ignition. Jon had seen many insurance loss reports from the banks branches there and had actually been able to pinpoint a three-block area in North Hollywood where theft was almost guaranteed under the right conditions. Auto theft was big business everywhere, and North Hollywood was no exception. The car had to disappear with no trace, period. North Hollywood not only carried a sizable theft rate, it also had a very low recovery percentage. Almost every car that got snatched was never seen again and that was precisely what the Blakes wanted. Joan knew it would be a very long journey to Oregon, especially having to stop in Southern California first. Once she and Lance arrived in Portland, she could try to relax a little while she waited for Jon to contact her. She just had to make it to Portland.

J.J. made it to Amarillo just before two in the morning, then waited until two thirty to go to the bank. He and Joan both usually drove the speed limit and his constituents knew it. He wanted his pursuers, should they think to calculate his average speed, to believe he was trying to avoid being noticed by the police. That should make Ashland's other boss relax just a little. After all, if he was still leaving a trail, he couldn't be in custody, protective or otherwise. J.J. believed that if the men who wanted him dead felt the family was in protective custody, they would order a nationwide manhunt. The reason for that was the leaders would know the feds could take the family anywhere to hide them. Not just to the east, but anywhere. That would mean they could eventually look in Portland and that was absolutely unacceptable to J.J. He wanted to grab a motel room in Amarillo after visiting the bank but knew he had to ride straight through to Oklahoma City. Anything he could do to make Ashland and Edwards's bosses believe the whole family was together was top priority. What better way than to make it look like two people must be sharing the driving? One drives while the other sleeps. For the Blake's to cover that much ground in that short a time span while obviously driving the speed limit, they had to be switching off. There could be no other logical explanation. J.J. knew it was possible that even if he did stop and rest, they might not realize the family wasn't together, but why risk it? No, he had to make it to Oklahoma City before taking a break, period. With that, he weaved the Electra Glide back onto the I-40 and rode on.

4

"I just can't believe how stupid this guy is, Marcus. He worked at a bank, for pete's sake!" David Sharpe was beginning to show his boredom. He often did when they were traveling as he had always been a fidgety sort. Marcus had learned over the years that when David felt that way, he was easy to mess with and Marcus almost never missed an opportunity.

"Man, just relax, okay? This fool will slip up again too. They all do. It's only a matter of time. We just need to be close enough when he does to finish the job and collect that $100,000.00 bonus!" With that seed planted, Greenhill looked over at Sharpe, tapped his chest with the back of his hand, and asked, "What are you going to do with your share of the money, David? I mean $30,000.00 is a lot of cash."

Sharpe chimed in without thinking, "Oh, man! I'll tell you what. I'm gettin' me a n—wait a minute, Marcus. How do you come up with my share bein' only thirty grand? There's only the two of us, and half's got my name written all over it! Man, don't even try pullin' that crap with me. You know me better than that!

LEFT NO CHOICE

Either you've gotten stupid over the years or I just never realized you don't know how to do long division."

"Just trying to see if you were still awake, man. So, what *are* you gonna do with your $40,000.00?" Marcus was grinning from ear to ear as he said this, knowing that his *compadre* had a short fuse where money was concerned.

"I'm gonna kill you too, Marcus, you jerk. Just keep it up. One stray bullet and you go to see your maker when these poor schmucks do!"

"Yeah, but if I die, you won't have anybody around who can think for you, or put up with your smell. Man, haven't I told you a thousand times your deodorant should be called 'reodorant'?"

"That's it, smart guy. If you don't lay off me right now I'm gonna pull this car over and whip your butt so bad you'll beg me to shoot you just to get it over with."

Marcus Greenhill was laughing so hard now that his eyes were watering, and he was doubled over in the seat. All this did was frustrate Sharpe even more. David Sharpe had never been known for his intellect or his charisma. He had a reputation for being a brute with no reasoning power and whenever Greenhill chided him, he always went off. Marcus didn't do it very often, but when he did, he knew Sharpe well enough to know just which buttons to push. In a matter of minutes, he could turn Sharpe into a red faced, crazy-eyed contract killer. Marcus always knew how to soothe the savage beast too. This is the main reason they worked together so well for so long.

Through his laughter, Marcus said, "David, David. I'm just messin' with ya man. You know that. Chill out. Jeez! Don't we always have each other's back?"

Sharpe was still visibly upset but had to agree that they had always protected each other. "Marcus, man, I don't know why you do that to me. You know it frosts me to no end. Just quit doing that crap to me, okay?"

Now down to a large smile and an occasional chuckle, Greenhill looked over at his friend and said, "All right, man. I was just messin' with you. I'll really try not to set you off anymore. So what *are* you gonna do with your $40,000.00?"

Sharpe went crazy at this, swinging the car over to the right shoulder and cussing Greenhill out while he did. He was really mad now, which made Marcus laugh so hard he could no longer breathe. Sharpe slammed on the brakes, put the Crown Victoria in park, and leaped across the seat onto Greenhill. Marcus pleaded through his laughter for Sharpe to stop, that he was just jivin' him, and the more Sharpe tried to get his outstretched hands around Greenhill's neck, the harder Marcus laughed. This went on for quite a few minutes as it did every time Marcus played with David's ego. Eventually, though, with Sharpe completely on top of Greenhill in the seat, Marcus stopped laughing long enough to promise not to do it again. As David moved back over under the wheel, Marcus looked at his beet red buddy while sporting a cheesy grin. Sharpe cussed Greenhill out under his breath as he pulled back onto the freeway. He occasionally backhanded Marcus on the left bicep, repeatedly telling him to shut up. Sharpe referred to him as an ugly hyena, then started smiling himself. As they drove and the humor of the moment subsided, David changed the subject back to business. Not just because he wanted to get back to business but because he didn't want to go through the ribbing anymore.

"Okay, Marcus, if you were a guy who worked in a bank and this stuff happened to you, what do you think you would do? Where would you go, especially if you had a wife and kid in tow? I mean, if it were me, I'd be trying to start over in Canada or someplace like that. Wouldn't you?"

Marcus had been thinking a great deal about that same question and, as of yet, had come up with no other solution than the one Sharpe had just touched on.

"That's what I think I'd do too, man. Both Blake and his wife were their parents' only kids, and all their parents are dead. There's no family to keep them here, so leaving the US makes the most sense. But Tony's payin' us to be out here, so let's just keep looking and having fun while we are. Sooner or later, if we can't find them and they don't turn up somewhere else, you know we'll be called in. I'm gettin' hungry, man. Messin' with your mind gave me an appetite. How much longer 'til we get to Amarillo?"

Sharpe looked at the mile marker beside the freeway, thought for a few seconds, and answered, "About forty-five minutes. But I'm hungry too. Lets stop in the next town and get somethin' to eat, then head into Amarillo, okay?"

"Yeah, okay," Greenhill agreed and went on. "Hey, man, isn't Amarillo the place with that restaurant that serves a really big steak? You know, it's somethin' like seventy-two or seventy-five ounces, and if you eat the whole thing, you get it free?"

"Yeah, it is. In fact"—Sharpe perked up at the thought of finally trying to take that steak on—"we passed a billboard a couple miles back with a picture of it. Tell you what, Marcus. Let's eat dinner there instead. Whaddaya say, huh?"

"Sounds goo-o-o-d to me, man, Sounds goo-o-o-d to me. Pull off up here in this next town, man, so we can get their number and call ahead. I am starvin'."

Joan pulled off the freeway in Barstow, California, just before six. She needed gas and Lance needed to use the bathroom. She had driven straight through, only stopping for food, fuel and the bathroom. Her goal was to make it to the Greyhound station in time for the late night bus to Portland. Joan thought this was the best time to board as there would be fewer travelers and less people to deal with. She still had to get to North Hollywood and dump the car before they could go to the Bus Depot, though, and she was cutting it close. The last bus left around midnight, so time was short. She had come to terms with her situation and was hoping Lance would break free from his dazed state soon. She had considered trying to distract him, yet felt that gamble could backfire. He might get angry and close her out completely if she made it seem like she was ignoring the previous night's events. Instead, just being prepared to answer any questions as best she could was the plan of action she chose. Throughout the drive, Lance had been thinking about a lot of things. From happy moments to sad, from exciting events to tragic ones and all led him back to the last twenty-two hours. He was actually quite a resilient youngster and had gained a firm grasp on the reality of their situation long before they had crossed into California.

As Joan made her way through the city streets back toward the freeway, she wondered if she would ever see Jon again. Their love was truly an unbreakable bond, no matter the circumstances. They had faced many small hardships together in their past and had always triumphed. But this was no small problem. It had taken all of her will power to stay quiet when the policeman stopped her, but she knew she needed to trust Jon. He had told her during one of their discussions that should they have to leave separately, he would contact her through the Personals section of the Oregonian, Portland's largest paper, within ten days of their departure and every ten days thereafter. He told her that if ever she had not heard from him within a ten-day span, she should take one of two final steps—either go to the FBI in Portland, or drive up into Canada and catch a flight to Sydney to start a new life. Jon had made her aware of all the possible dangers she and Lance could face if she did go to the FBI. He explained how they would be taken into hiding by the FBI until trial, but even that would not completely guarantee their safety. There was a very real possibility that even the FBI could not protect them no matter what measures were taken. The men who were behind this had killed before and with a lot less at stake. Jon was sure they would pull out all the stops over something of this magnitude. No amount of money or risk would be too great for them as she could surely bring them all down if she ever made it to the stand. After all, millions and millions of dollars were involved, and professional hit men worked for much less.

For her and Lance to go into protective custody and testify before the Grand Jury by choice should be a last resort, Jon had said. The problem wasn't with the men she could name as they would most likely be whisked away to jail immediately. The problem was the men she couldn't name. They would still be on the street, and to make matters worse, they were the ones really in power. Plus, they had already proved they would kill others to protect themselves and their interests. Even if those she could name turned state's evidence, it was doubtful they would divulge who the real boss was. The FBI would have to keep climbing the ladder of power one confession at a time until they got to him, but he would most likely disappear long before they knew his name. He could orchestrate the elimination of every single person who could testify against him, including her, and time would be of little consequence. Joan and Lance would be hunted for the rest of their lives if she testified.

However, if she could successfully escape detection from everyone long enough, the bad guys would eventually give up the search. They would come to one of two conclusions, and both were to Joan's advantage. The first was that she must not have known anything anyway, because no indictments had come down and no arrests had been made. The second was that she had chosen not to reappear to testify for obvious reasons. Either way, if the FBI didn't show up and start arresting people, Joan and Lance would be safer. If he didn't make it, he told her, she would be much better off just leaving the country with Lance. Jon had moved a great deal of their money into another bank, yet not under the name Joan Blake. It was Catherine Lake's account, the alias she had chosen for herself. Australia, Jon had said. They would fit in well there. Joan had actually laughed out loud when he'd said it and asked him where he had come up with that one. She smiled again as she thought of that moment. It was one of the few times they had laughed at all since Jon had told her what was happening. Yes, he'd said, Australia. The weather was good, the language the same, the economy was similar, and no one would ever think to look for them there. It would be as safe for them as it would be beautiful. Besides, he'd said, since American TV wasn't big there. Even if they were being sought publicly here, they would be able to live freely there, without worry of being recognized. She hoped she'd never have to book that flight and refocused her mind on getting to Oregon.

Once in Portland, she'd buy a cheap car and rent an apartment right away as Catherine Lake. She and Lance would set up residence and wait to hear from Jon. She prayed that he would come for them before school started in the fall as she didn't want to be that long without him. She also didn't want Lance to have to field any questions from the local kids about where they were from, what brought them to Portland, etc. The risk that their pictures may be circulating soon was too great for Catherine to work outside the home, so she and Lance would just stay pretty much to themselves. Since there was plenty of money to tide them over, she had less to worry about. She just had to get there.

The sun had already gone down in Arkansas where J.J. was by the time his wife and son had arrived in Barstow, California. J.J. used every card with the Jon or Joan's name on it to draw cash one last time just outside Little Rock, then destroyed and disposed of everything with the name Blake on it. He was done leaving a trail to the east; it was time to head back to New Mexico. But this time, as J.J. Tracker. He rode southwest on the I-30 now, toward Texarkana, where he would finally get some sleep. He had

LEFT NO CHOICE

driven straight through and had traveled quite a few more miles than Catherine because he did not have to stop as often. In the morning, he would get a good breakfast under his belt, then start the journey to the cabin above Chimayo, New Mexico. It would take a lot longer to get back than it took to get to Little Rock, though. J.J. had decided it best to take a different route home, through Abilene and El Paso, then up the I-25 through New Mexico to Chimayo. He would be adding almost five hundred miles to his trip by going this way, but he couldn't risk using the same roads he came in on. After all, if he stopped for fuel at the same time and place as someone sent to look for him, that would be "all she wrote." No, it was safest to go back the other way. Besides, it would give his beard an extra day to grow in. He wanted the beard to be full enough to dye it and his hair dark brown before he had to encounter people for longer than it takes to pay for fuel or food, anyway. He wasn't used to the growth on his chin and neck, though. He had never before worn a beard, and it itched—a lot. He'd get used to it and to being somewhat unclean, he thought. He needed both effects to be able to carry out his plans virtually unnoticed in and around Albuquerque.

Officer Rhodes said good-bye to his friends and thanked them for letting him win the card game as it was the first time he had. They'd talked a great deal about the house, the fire, and the body that was found. Some speculation as to where the wife and son might be came up, but it passed quickly as the game began. He was doing well, the doctor said, and would be able to go home in the morning. He couldn't return to work, though, until the following Monday, which was still nine days away. His back had to heal as did the cuts to his scalp. He argued with the doctor about that being too long, until the doctor asked him if he could really protect himself or his partner if things got physical. He knew he was in no shape to be in a fight and that quieted him quickly. He decided to make the best of it when he got home by catching up on his reading. But the more he thought, the more restless he became. He decided that he would take the trip to Jamaica he had always wanted to take and heal his back on the beach in the sun. He had researched the costs months ago, and they were surprisingly small. He would call the travel agent in the morning and make the arrangements. He smiled at the thought of finally going, and it consumed him until he drifted off to sleep.

5

She had arrived in LA late on a Saturday night, so the freeways were a breeze. They made good time to North Hollywood and stepped out of the Intrepid for the last time around nine thirty. She had thrown all the manuals in a dumpster during her stop in Barstow and now grabbed the registration, insurance cards, and all other ownership documents from the car. She put them in her purse to be destroyed and discarded at the bus station along with any ID that didn't belong to Catherine Lake. Jon had told her to make sure the car was left in an undesirable area, so she had to drive around the streets for a while to find the best spot. Under normal circumstances, she would have been frightened to be traveling in such a downtrodden section of town at that time of night. However, after what she and Lance had been through the last two days, the walk back to where streetlights were in abundance was an easy one.

As they walked toward the bus station, she worried that the police might find the car before thieves did. That worry was put to rest when she saw it cross the intersection in front of her only three blocks from where their walk had begun. It was still bearing their New Mexico plate too. Catherine chuckled nervously and nonchalantly as she pointed it out to Lance. She did it to let him know his dad had been right, but it didn't seem to faze Lance in the least. She sighed and kept walking. She surveyed the buildings as they continued on and tried a few times to involve Lance in conversation by asking him to look at things, then asking what he thought of them. She was getting through even though she didn't know it. Lance was listening, and when she wasn't looking at him, he was looking at the things she had pointed out. He just wasn't ready to speak yet. Why should he? He had no idea what to say to any of this. His dad may be alive, but he may not be. They might be a family again soon, but they might not be. He just kept thinking that this stuff only happens in the movies. This stuff only happens in the movies!

Tony Tracerio Sr. had to make a lot of routing changes in his laundering operation since being forced to shut down the operation at Security Pacific. It took him and his bookkeepers three days just to account for all the money. He was livid that he would have to leave almost one and a half million dollars sitting in various Security Pacific accounts. He knew it was too risky to pull it even though the accountant was fairly confident they could do it unnoticed. He consoled himself with the knowledge that once the heat was off he was going to kill Ashland and Covington personally. He knew he couldn't do it when he originally wanted to, which was right there in the conference room in front of all their cohorts. That would have been just too many disappearances from that one building. It was something he'd have to bide his time on, so he shelved it. He'd have Danbury transfer both of them in a few months or so to separate branches of the bank, using the logic that they all needed to split up because the heat was finally off. Tony would give each man a "good job keeping your mouth shut" bonus of fifty grand in cash. Of course, before they could spend a dime of it, he would have them yanked from their beds and brought to him. He wasn't sure how he'd do them yet, but he was positive their deaths would be slow and filled with pain. For now, though, he still had the loose ends known as the Blake family to clean up. Tony's contacts in law enforcement had heard nothing regarding these people, except that they still hadn't surfaced.

This made him breathe a little easier. The longer the Blakes stayed away from the law, the better Tony's chances that they never would contact them. But Tony knew he had to find them before the law did, because even though he controlled some people, he didn't own them all. This made the Blake family a very dangerous liability. If some "out for justice, self-righteous badge carrier" got to them first, he knew Blake would have no choice but to tell all, and Tony didn't need that kind of exposure. He secretly hoped that this guy was smart enough to leave the country but would never voice it as he didn't want anyone in his employ to get the idea they could do that and successfully escape. He just had too few contacts outside the states and even those were shoestring at best. He was hoping to resolve that problem by the time Tony Jr. was ready to assume control of his empire. He made a mental commitment to begin building a network that reached around the globe as soon as this current crisis was over.

Tony Jr. had been sent to a boarding school as a lad, which is where he met and befriended Victor Edward Hanes. Victor E. Hanes, nicknamed *Victory* by his classmates was now the head of Tony Sr.'s security force at his estate. Hanes had proven himself to be quite resourceful and ruthless in everything he chose to do. This impressed Tony Sr. enough to fund his collegiate education along with Tony Jr. on the condition that he watch Tony Jr.'s back at all times. They both did very well scholastically, so well in fact that Tony Sr. didn't have to pull any strings to get either of them into UCLA. He just had to fork up the tuition. Tony Jr. received his Law Degree there, with a minor in tax accounting. Hanes's degree was in behavioral psychology with elective classes mainly based on self-defense techniques. These fields were Tony Sr.'s idea. He wanted this six foot three inch mountain of foreboding muscle to be able to handle people with his brains as well as his brawn.

Tony was very proud of his son for choosing the fields of Law and Tax Accounting as those were the two he would undoubtedly need most upon inheriting the family business. Tony Jr. had grown to five feet eleven inches, which surprised his father as he and Tony Jr.'s mom, who'd passed away giving birth to Tony Jr. were both under five feet six. Tony Jr. was street-smart, too. He was quite adept at outthinking most people. He was even asked for his opinion on many situations, which is why Tony Sr. had requested his son's presence at the estate. Tony Jr. knew why he'd been called, and was working on several scenarios during the drive.

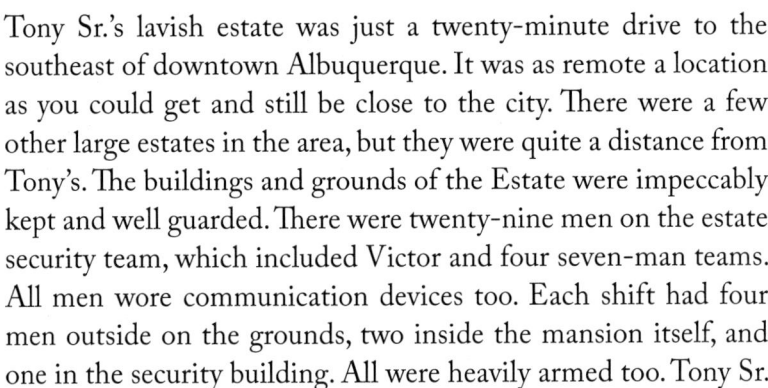

Tony Sr.'s lavish estate was just a twenty-minute drive to the southeast of downtown Albuquerque. It was as remote a location as you could get and still be close to the city. There were a few other large estates in the area, but they were quite a distance from Tony's. The buildings and grounds of the Estate were impeccably kept and well guarded. There were twenty-nine men on the estate security team, which included Victor and four seven-man teams. All men wore communication devices too. Each shift had four men outside on the grounds, two inside the mansion itself, and one in the security building. All were heavily armed too. Tony Sr.

had made quite a few enemies during his rise to power, so he and Victor decided to leave nothing to chance. The two men inside the mansion and the four on the grounds did staggered roving patrols, but the ones who manned the security building only left that post when relieved. Someone had to be on watch there at all times. This position was the highest next to Victor's, and he screened each man heavily before allowing him the responsibility of that job.

There were cameras everywhere on the grounds that were connected to live-feed video screens in the security building, so every square foot of ground was monitored 24/7. Tony had refused to allow cameras in the main house although Victor and Tony Jr. had put up quite a fight about it. Tony Sr. didn't want these soldiers watching his movements in his own home, and that was that. Victor compensated by having alarm circuits installed on every door and window of the main house, which were also monitored from the security building. Victor and Tony Jr. had left nothing to chance where Tony Sr.'s safety was concerned. All the men on the security teams were handpicked by Victor. All were well paid, well trained, highly motivated, and loyal. Twice, Tony had told Victor to take men from the house to handle "messes" that needed cleaned up in the city, but Victor vehemently refused both times. He explained to Tony that to weaken the security of the house even for a night was unacceptable.

Should Tony's enemies ever discover that and wish to attack the mansion, they'd simply need to create a diversion in the city one time. Victor also convinced Tony never to use any of the men hired to guard the house for any other "jobs" while they were off duty. Keeping them singularly focused was too important, and once word of that policy got out, it should deter anyone from trying to attack his home. Victor had done a fantastic job in setting up the protection systems for the estate, and Tony rewarded him handsomely for it. Tracerio's security measures worked so well that no one ever tried to breach them. Tony liked it that way as it kept his home's atmosphere a peaceful one. He didn't have to worry about the men getting complacent either. Victor made sure each team trained both physically and with their weapons twice a week. Victor was very confident that the staff was ready to take on a force of just about any size.

Tony Sr. had wanted to get his son's thoughts on the Blake situation, hoping Tony Jr. would come up with something he hadn't already thought of.

"Come in, son, come in. Thank you for driving out from the city. I really appreciate it. Would you like something to eat, son? Something to drink?"

"A glass of Frederick's wonderful iced tea sounds good, Dad, thank you."

Tony Sr. looked over to his long-time butler Frederick and raised an open right hand in the air, saying, "You see, Frederick, my son and I agree. You make the best iced tea in the world. Why don't you bring us both a glass."

Smiling ever so slightly, Frederick bowed and said, "Sir, would you like any snacks with your tea?"

Tony Sr. declined and off Frederick went.

"So, Dad, any news?" Tony Jr. asked.

"That's why I requested you to come visit me, son. Our people are searching every nook and cranny looking for Blake and have so far come up with nothing. I'm hoping that you and I might be able to put our heads together and figure out where a man with a family might go to escape people he knew were trying to kill him."

"Well, Dad, I have been pondering that very thing day and night. I think it depends on how much he knows about what's been going on and whom he thinks is behind it. If he thinks it's just a bunch of bankers, he's probably just going to another state trying to start his life over. However, if he knows who you are and that you are the one calling the shots, his smartest moves would be to leave the country or go to the feds for help. Let's say for a moment that he's afraid to go to the authorities because he believes protective custody would be an eventual death sentence for him and his family. This takes us back to the theory that he would be smartest to leave the country. Either way, I don't think he'd risk his family's safety on that roll of the dice, and neither would I. So, if I were him, I'd try to leave the country."

Tony Tracerio Sr. listened intently to his offspring's thoughts and nodded all the while Tony Jr. was speaking.

"Now, Dad, let's look at another possibility. What if he isn't afraid of going to the authorities but doesn't think he has enough hard evidence to use as a bargaining chip where his family's livelihood is concerned? We're already fairly sure he hasn't gone to the cops as of this morning, and it's been three days since they disappeared. It could be that he's still digging on his own, but that is truly a long shot."

"A long shot? Now that's the understatement of the year, Tony. To do that, he would have to stay close to Albuquerque, keep his whole family hidden, and have enough money and time to dig. Not to mention that he'd have to come out in the open to get information, which would put them all in jeopardy. No, son, I think anybody who was smart enough to escape us the first time couldn't be that stupid," Tony Sr. said with a tone of disbelief.

"So, if we're sure he's not here in Albuquerque trying to blow our operation wide open, he's almost assuredly planning on disappearing," Tony Jr. said.

"Perhaps," Tony Sr. said pensively, "but perhaps he did go to the feds and they assisted him in getting out. That would explain how this nobody escaped with his family and cannot be located."

Tony Jr. hesitated for a moment, then said, "I've thought about that possibility a great deal, Dad, and I really don't think he's made contact with the law."

"I don't either, son. If he had, we wouldn't be seeing a trail of credit card use day after day. If the feds had him, that wouldn't happen."

"Exactly," young Tony agreed and went on, "So I think our best option is to get more eyes in southern airports and on the docks, raise the bounty, and keep distancing ourselves from the bank as well as the two flunkies that fouled up the hit."

Tony Sr. agreed and would get word out all over the south that he'd raised the bounty to $250,000. He'd also keep Sharpe and Greenhill on the trail the Blake's had left. He asked his son to meet with all key people within the organization personally to let them know to watch what they said and did around Ashland and Covington and to keep their eyes and ears open when around these two. All operations had ceased at the bank; he'd already taken care of that. And these two were not involved in the new setup happening in Phoenix, so he only had to worry about what had already happened that these two knew about. Tony was now very glad he planned to kill these two when the time was right. He finished his tea in silence after his son left to arrange things, then decided not to let this situation overtake him. He called for Frederick and had him make reservations for two at his favorite restaurant. Then he made a call to his "flavor of the month" and told her to be ready around six. After all was arranged, he changed clothes and went out to the pool for an afternoon swim.

Victor was coming toward the house from the security building as Tony approached the pool and they talked for a while. Victor was well aware of the Blake situation too. Tony Sr. briefed him on the conversation he'd had with his son and asked for input.

"It sounds like you've got everything as under control as is possible, sir," Victor said, then continued his patrol. Tony watched him walk toward the house after that, feeling even more confident that he was doing the right things.

LEFT NO CHOICE

The police investigation into the whereabouts of Mrs. Blake and son had only brought more questions and no answers. The Blake case should have been moving up fast on the priority list of the detectives, yet it wasn't. One detective had suggested the body found in the house be autopsied but that request was denied. Chief Richter was having a tough time covering Tony's boys on this one, and he was especially angry with Theodore Danbury. If Danbury had called him in advance of the Blake family hit, Richter could have made arrangements for a different man to be on duty as the lead detective that night. That would have made things much easier on him and on Tracerio. So Richter's only choice was to control the rest of the investigation the best he could. He ordered the detective handling the case to come to his office. The detective didn't just want an autopsy. He wanted to put out an all-points bulletin (APB) for the wife and son. He'd also learned that another employee of the bank had not shown up for work in the few days since the fire and wanted to follow that up. Additionally, some executives at the bank seemed to be curious about some high-dollar entries in the accounting ledgers. They'd said the entries could easily be simple accounting errors, but then again, maybe not. He didn't know if those events were connected, but wanted to dig deeper into that too. Then he asked for more manpower and that is where Richter saw an opportunity arise.

"You were kind of doing fine up to the point where you asked for help, Detective Singer, but we'll get to that in a minute," Chief Richter said calmly, then continued. "First, an autopsy on that body is a waste of taxpayer's money and therefore out of the question. The fire marshal has determined the cause of the fire to be accidental and that Blake died while he slept. You know all that, yes?"

"Yes, sir, but th—"

"But nothing, Singer. Let's move on to my second problem. Since there's been no crime here, Mrs. Blake and her son are not suspects, or even persons of interest for that matter. So requesting an all-points bulletin on them is absurd. It's a lawsuit waiting to happen, Detective. Especially when she learns that we've hunted her down to interrogate-slash-notify her in the cruelest of ways about an accidental fire that tragically killed her husband, took the boy's father, and destroyed her home. What are you thinking, son?"

Detective Singer sat speechless. Chief Richter could now plainly see that the man was ready to throw in the towel, so he spoke again, this time as a mentor.

"Detective, I think you're going to have a great career in law enforcement and am pleasantly surprised by the amount of energy you've put into this, but you're out of line on this one. You're not the first detective I've had to say this to, and you won't be that last, so don't feel bad. I'm not demoting you, Singer, because I want you out there on our team. However, I am replacing you as the detective handling this man's death as of right now. I hope, though, this will be the last time you get so gung-ho before thinking about the consequences." Then Richter touched the intercom button on his phone and said, "Gladys, tell Lieutenant Cantonelli I want to see him, okay? Thanks."

"I'm sorry, Chief. You're right, sir. I should have thought it through," Singer said.

"I agree, but that's all water under the bridge now. Just give Cantonelli everything you've collected on the missing banker, the accounting irregularities, etc, and get onto another case. Dismissed, Detective Singer."

Lieutenant Guiseppe "Gus" Cantonelli was on Tracerio's payroll with Richter and the fire marshal, so all the attention this case was getting should fade away and quickly. Richter sat back in his chair quite pleased with himself, then called Tracerio.

LEFT NO CHOICE

Officer Ralph Davis had been watching the events and decisions regarding the case from afar and was becoming frustrated. The decisions made by the chief seemed to be strange ones, but he was still the chief. Maybe the wife and kid really would show up in a few days and all these goings-on were coincidental. He wished his partner Michael Rhodes was home instead of recuperating in Jamaica so he could talk to him about it but that was still five days away. He decided to keep his mouth shut and leave the detective work to the detectives for the moment but to keep watching.

Joan Blake, now going by Catherine Lake, had slept a lot on the bus ride to Portland. They took the back seat of the bus so they could avoid as much human contact as possible. Catherine made sure that she and Lance kept their faces conveniently hidden as often as possible. Either under a hat while they slept or buried in a pillow against the window. Whenever the bus stopped, only one of them would go off at a time while the other made sure no one else would sit in their seats. For the majority of the night run, there were very few people on the bus, so she and Lance were three rows back from any other passengers. This allowed them to talk as Lance was finally ready to. She filled the ten-year-old in on what she thought he could understand. She explained in detail his dad's entire plans and thoughts, including what might happen to them if anyone ever found out who they really were. He seemed to understand all of it, which relieved Catherine somewhat. After that had been discussed and between dozing times, their conversation turned to what to do once they arrived there while they waited for word from Jon.

Lance was also sure his dad was still alive and was now strangely excited to be a part of this cat and mouse game. He promised his mom he would not let her down, and he would tell everyone he was from Las Vegas, like he was supposed to. That would be easy for Lance to do as his maternal grandparents had lived there his entire life before they died. He had spent many summer months there with them and knew the city pretty well for a boy of ten. His paternal grandparents had passed on before he was born. They had died in a plane crash just a year after Jon finished serving in the US Army. He knew that his dad had been a member of the Green Berets. This was one reason he was sure his dad had lived through the attack. No way could just three guys take his dad. Jon didn't talk about his time in the military, even with Joan. She surmised it was because the things he saw were too painful and saddening to relive, so she avoided the subject. It was a good thing that they never talked about it, too. Since no one else knew of Jon's decorated past in combat, they didn't know that three average guys didn't stand a chance of taking him down in a surprise attack. And now that his dad had become J.J. Tracker, Lance was sure as Catherine was that the bad guys were in big trouble.

J.J. rented a car-sized storage facility in Chimayo on his way to the cabin so he could hide the motorcycle trailer where no one could discover it's contents. That little trailer held every copy of every document he'd taken from the bank. He then made it to the cabin without incident, but he was exhausted. He had been traveling in one direction or another for almost three days. When he finally arrived, he slept for eleven straight hours. He hadn't done that since he'd had Mono as a teenager. When he awoke, he was fully refreshed and very hungry. He was glad now that he had stopped for groceries on the way to the cabin even though he was almost sleepwalking while in the aisles at the store. He bought stuff he would never use too, such as beer, two bottles of whiskey, and potato chips. He figured it was best to get those to keep up the façade; both in the store and if he ever had unexpected visitors show up at the cabin. He didn't expect any, but he didn't know what liquored-up hunters do when they come across another guy out there. He figured he'd need some on hand to offer if the situation did arise.

The cabin needed a good cleaning, but Jon decided to leave it messy. He opened the first bottle of whiskey and poured more than half of it out to make it seem as though he had been drinking it. He did the same with three bottles of the beer, leaving the empties in the overflowing kitchen trash can. He figured it was best if he looked like a lazy, heavy-drinking slob should anyone happen by as this might deter them from coming by a second time. He would leave the door unlocked, and the only thing he would keep clean was the bike. That should solidify the look he was after. He would store the majority of the weapons and gear he'd purchase in a well-hidden hole not far from the cabin, all wrapped in water-tight plastic. He'd leave just a few guns and a bow in the cabin itself. The weapons stored in the cabin would be those used by hunters. A rifle with a scope, a shotgun, one revolver, and a bow would be enough. The bow would be a compound bow, with arrows designed to bring down a large animal in one shot. The hole that would serve as his storage room would be easy for J.J. to create and conceal. As a Green Beret, he had been taught how the North Vietnamese excelled at this particular talent. They had tunnels with exit holes that were within just a few yards of American soldier campsites, and many times, the soldiers didn't know it until it was too late. Their skill at jungle camouflage was unsurpassed by anyone in the world, and J.J. had learned how to do it just as they did. No one would find his storage room, even if they were standing within inches of it.

The first order of business after he finished eating was to scout the perimeter of his new home. He needed to find the right location for the storage room, so he had to familiarize himself with the trails made and used by both man and beast. More importantly, he had to learn how close the neighbors were and how often they passed within visiting distance of the cabin. After grabbing his hunting vest, license, and shotgun, he headed out into the woods.

6

Catherine and Lance only had to spend two nights in a motel as Jon had set up an outstanding credit profile for her under her new name. She found a nice little Dodge Shadow with reasonably low miles at a dealership for $3,700.00 and found an apartment a few hours later. The cozy, two bedroom apartment had a loft and was just off Sunnyside Road in Clackamas, a southeast suburb of Portland. By signing a one-year lease, she was able to get the first month's rent free, and although it was not furnished, it was worth it.

She had found that most of the furnished ones were very pricey for where they were and what they were, so she decided to find an empty one and furnish it herself. She would have to wait a day for credit approval before she could move in, they had told her. That was fine with Catherine, though, as she needed to go out and find the furniture for it anyway. She was very glad there was no sales tax in Oregon. This saved her money on her car and on the furniture. She was also quite pleased to find an apartment that had so much to offer for her and Lance. The complex had a pool, Jacuzzi, playground, game room, and fitness room. Within a mile was a huge mall with restaurants, movie theatres, a video arcade, and even an ice skating rink. She hoped all these things would keep her and Lance preoccupied until Jon came for them.

Jon. Where was he? Was he okay? Did he really make it? Or was she just wishing so hard that it felt like he had? It was less than a week until his message should appear in the personals, but with every day that passed, her anxiety grew. She hid it well from Lance, though, she had to admit to herself. He was seemingly unaware of her worst fear. She involved him in each purchase decision, from his own bedroom set to the living room sofa. They went out and bought dishes, pots and pans, and tableware, and stored it all in the hatchback until they could move in the next day. The furniture store would deliver everything she had purchased the following afternoon, and she had paid the surcharge to have them stay and set it all up for her. This would give her and Lance time to set up the kitchen, and then go buy some clothes, some linen, and some groceries. When they got back to the motel, the message light was glowing red on the phone. Her heart leapt with anticipation. Jon knew she was going to stay at one particular motel in Gladstone as they had a restaurant right there on the premises. Her hands shook noticeably as she dialed the voice mail number.

"Ms. Lake, this is Julie from Treeline Terrace Town Homes. I wanted to let you know that you're application has already been approved and you can move in anytime. I guess your credit was so good that even though you'd lived all these years with your mom in Las Vegas, they went ahead and approved you without a rental history. So, congratulations, and welcome aboard! I am sorry to hear that she passed away, though. Anyway, someone is in the office each night until seven, so if you decide to come down tonight, please do it before then. Thanks. Otherwise, we'll see you tomorrow!"

LEFT NO CHOICE

As soon as she heard the voice, her heart sank. She was praying it would be Jon. Well, at least they had the apartment, she thought. But for how long would they need it? She shook all of it off as best she could and told Lance the news, then called the furniture store to arrange delivery. Over the next few days, she and Lance got the place set up with all the basic comforts of home and had purchased a modest amount of clothes to get them by. They visited the Zoo, Multnomah Falls, and Seaside, a small coastal city about an hour west of Portland. It seemed to help time pass more quickly until the day they should see the message in the paper from Jon. Each night, Lance asked her what they would do if there were no message. Each time, she told him that they would have time to discuss that if, *and only if*, that happened. She knew he was scared, so she didn't let impatience get the best of her. She fielded all his queries calmly and always left him with the thought that she knew he was still alive. That the message would be there. It had to be there. It just had to be.

J.J. took two whole days to scout out the area surrounding the cabin before deciding on a place to put the weapons. He walked the area both day and night, sleeping as best he could during the day. He knew most of his work would be safest if done after dark, so he was trying to get his body to adjust its cycle. He sat quietly for hours each night out on the stoop of the cabin, just listening. He listened for all the right reasons too. Just like a combat zone, any change in the normal night sounds of the wilderness usually meant trouble was near. He wanted to know those sounds and know them well. After he sat on the stoop for two full hours each night, he would do the same thing from inside the cabin for another two. The sounds were dramatically muffled with the door closed, but he could still hear them and wanted to get used to them that way too.

He pondered many things while in silence, doing isometrics and stretching exercises to help tone his muscles while he listened. He thought a lot about Joan and Lance. In fact, he was constantly battling with his own mind to keep them out of it for the time being. He needed to focus on what would eventually bring them safely back together, not what had caused their separation or how they might be feeling during it. Yep. Focus. That was what he needed again. That and his survival instincts, honed to a quick and deadly edge. He would do whatever it took to protect his family, even if that meant never seeing them again. But the more he thought of that possibility, the more focused on his objective he became. One average man fighting to defend his home and family was worth a dozen hired guns, and he knew it. But he also knew that if he could revive what he had spent years trying to bury in his memory, twelve men wouldn't even be close to what they'd need. They'd need an army.

Michael was feeling much better. The daily massages and the nightly hot tubbing had done wonders for his back. He had three more days on the beach at the Montego Bay Resort and planned on enjoying every moment of it. He was feeling so good he had decided to climb the terracing water steps known as Dunn's River Falls, just outside the city of Ocho Rios. He hadn't thought much about work, but what little he did allow into his mind surrounded the fire, the man who burned to death in it, and his family. He hoped it would all be over by the time he got back as he wanted to forget it. Little did he know that he would never be able to forget it, or that the hand of fate was about to throw him right in the middle of it.

LEFT NO CHOICE

Sharpe and Greenhill had followed the trail to Little Rock where the last transaction had been reported. They did some poking around and came up empty. They updated Tony Jr. by phone, and he instructed them to head south to New Orleans. Both Tracerios had a feeling Blake had taken the family there so look for them there they would. It wasn't just an act of pin-the-tail-on-the-donkey map reading either. Both father and son knew it was very easy to disappear in that city and that it was almost as easy to leave the country from there. The boys were excited to hear that as they loved New Orleans. They'd spend a third of the time hunting, a third partying, and a third eating and sleeping. They just wished they had brought extra cash with them. In their profession, cash was the only way to do anything. Never leave a paper trail, no matter how insignificant, was rule #1.

They thought of calling Tony Jr., but knew he could easily figure out why they wanted the extra cash. After all, they had been given quite a sum to start the journey with and should not need more for weeks. They decided that if they ran out, they'd just rob some poor schmucks as needed to tide them over. And if the idiots fought back, well, bonus! They got to kill somebody for free. They were getting a little concerned that the trail had dried up though. The Blakes had been using their cards consistently until two days ago, and now, nothing. All interested parties assumed they must have finally realized they could be traced and quit using them. But that meant Blake would run out of money soon and forced to use one. The Tracerios just wanted Sharpe and Greenhill within striking distance when they did, and they believed it would be in New Orleans.

Ralph Davis was getting more disturbed about the way this case was being handled. He and Michael had been told they'd be kept in the loop due to Michael's obvious involvement at the scene of the fire. Now he couldn't even get a few words out of Lieutenant Cantonelli that he didn't already know. Ralph decided to give up, stay out of it and tell Michael that Cantonelli just didn't care. It wasn't that Ralph was a quitter or naïve that made him stop pressing the issue either. Ralph truly had not even considered the fact that there could be a concealment conspiracy going on right under his nose in a department he had worked in for fifteen years. He didn't know it, but giving up on the case saved his life and the lives of his wife and children. Ralph wasn't looking deep enough into what was going on or he would have become silent much quicker than he did. Since Ralph and Michael were beat cops, they didn't get much information on accidents or homicides that they were not the first on the scene for, which were rare. Ralph couldn't possibly know to question all the recent accidents that had produced fatalities.

Gus Cantonelli was almost to the end of his rope with Ralph's questions. He was only one confrontation away from making Ralph become a routine traffic stop statistic. His wife and kids would have been dispatched in accidental fashion, just in case he had told her of his suspicions regarding the investigation. Cantonelli wasn't happy about being put in the hot seat on this one either but did what he was told by Chief Richter and Tracerio. He'd handled all of the investigations that needed a quick burial over the past decade and had been compensated heavily for it. In three more years, he would have enough to go back to the Old Country and live well because of them. He just had to make it three more years.

Tony Sr. met his son and his four most trusted employees every Wednesday night at Tony's favorite restaurant, *Ciao Bella*, for dinner and talk. This tradition had been going on for years, and when Tony requested your presence, you didn't say no. So each of these men made it a part of their weekly lives and scheduled all other personal activities around it. This particular Wednesday, there were two additional guests seated in Tony's private dining room—Chief Thomas Richter and Lieutenant Gus Cantonelli. Neither had been invited to dinner by Tony in years, and both were understandably nervous. The first course of the dinner menu was served promptly at seven, but Tony's guests were to make their appearance no later than six thirty. All knew this meant six-fifteen, including Richter and Cantonelli. Since Tony was a partner in the restaurant, he had it closed every Wednesday at four. All regular staff members were given the night off, except the head chef and his assistant. The head chef, Joseppé Furia, was renowned for his ability to create dishes like they were served in the Old Country even though he was missing half of his left pinky finger.

They knew to schedule all their outings, including vacations, around this Wednesday tradition too. If they went anywhere out of the city, they had better be back by Wednesday noon to begin preparing dinner. This meant always plan to be back in town on Tuesday, to give them a day cushion for unforeseen delays in flights, etc. Tony's chef that worked at the mansion had been called once to fill in because the regular one was stuck in Atlanta. It was during the Air Traffic Controllers strike, but even this was an unacceptable excuse to Tony Sr. The man should not have gone on the trip at all if there was the possibility of a strike. It didn't matter that he had been planning the vacation for almost a year. He needed to be taught a lesson in commitment. After all, Joseppé could still prepare food for Tony and the boys without the tip of his pinky finger.

All had arrived by six ten. They would have drinks in the lounge until about six twenty-five, then move to the dining room and take their seats. The only members of the dinner party not in the lounge were Victor and Tony Sr. Victor was already standing guard in the dining room, and Tony was in the kitchen. He always taste tested the food and complimented Joseppé on his expertise. He usually stayed in the kitchen talking with Chef Furia about ingredients, temperatures, times, and spices until around six thirty. Then with a look at his watch, he would pat Joseppé on the back, tell the assistant to watch and learn, that someday he might be as good, and head for his private dining room.

All stood as he entered, and he waved them back into their seats like they didn't have to stand for him. But he liked it. In fact, he would have issued orders to Victor to teach a lesson of respect to any man that did not rise upon his entrance. And there were few men who would willingly go head to head with Victor.

"Good evening, gentlemen. I believe all of you know each other already, yes?" Tony asked as he met with each pair of eyes at the table. All men glanced around the table to see if there were any more surprise guests or empty seats, saw none of either, and said yes.

"Good. Then let's talk. Tom, Gus, it's good to see you. I hope all is well with your families?"

The conversation was always kept light and personal before dinner, and songs from the Old Country serenaded them through the speakers in the ceiling. Business would be discussed after. This was the way it was done, period. Tony allowed nothing to take away from his enjoyment of dinner, especially business. Oh, talk of a sick child or family member passing was okay as this just added a level of sentiment to the ambiance, but that was the limit to anything sad or unsettling. The food was presented as elegantly as it was delicious and plentiful. The house wine was had by all except Tony and son. They were served a select vintage handpicked by the chef. All had their fill without eating or drinking too much. They knew to stop eating each course just after Tony stopped and never to show poor table manners. It was quite a sight to behold, really. All these accomplished men wearing bibs of white over their suits while they ate. But since Tony donned one for each meal, so did everyone present. With

LEFT NO CHOICE

the dessert plates clear and the wineglasses full again, ashtrays and cigars were brought out for all. Most didn't smoke, but those who did couldn't wait to light one of Tony's imported Cubans.

Wednesday's dinners were not just meals; they were events. The food and drink segment alone usually lasted until around eight thirty, and sometimes, if the conversation interested Tony enough, could go until well after nine. Tonight was different though. Tony's mind was filled with the occurrences of the last few days and the unresolved problems regarding them. Making things even more pressured was the fact that over a million and a half of his hard-earned dollars may be lost. Needless to say, Tony's appetite was not good. The table was cleared and cigars were passed a little after eight.

"Gentlemen," Tony said through teeth clenched around his cigar as he stoked it up, "We have some problems."

The dawn would break before the meeting did.

7

As he strolled down the beach of Montego Bay for the last time on this vacation, Michael felt completely rejuvenated and alive. He had never experienced a week quite like it. The sand was warm but not hot and so was the sun. The water was crystal clear, and the sea life wonderful to behold. He'd taken a glass-bottom boat ride his third day and, by the fourth, felt up to snorkeling. The incredible reef, just off the coast, was itself worth every penny he'd paid for the trip. But it was almost over, and his mind turned back to the good ole US of A.

He'd be home in time for the All-Star game and had even caught an Indians game while he was there. He wasn't aware until he turned on his TV the first night that Jamaica received American broadcasting. He didn't watch much TV as most nights he was down at the beach or sitting in the open-air bar. His back was feeling like new, and his step was as lively as ever. He didn't want to leave but promised himself he'd definitely be back. He'd made some great acquaintances and had even accepted the phone number of a woman from Phoenix, in case he was ever in the neighborhood. She'd offered for him to call anytime. Collect. His mind drifted back to the job and almost immediately, to the last night he had spent on it. He wondered if the woman and child had come back yet whose home had been destroyed by that awful fire and hoped they'd survive the tragic news about the man who perished in it.

Then another woman and child came to mind. The one he'd stopped just before he went to the fire. He hoped they too had been able to put that seemingly terrible night behind them. He would never forget the look on both of their faces. Those faces screamed so much fear and confusion. It saddened him even now to recall it, and he couldn't seem to get the picture out of his mind. A final evening swim! That should do the trick! And without another thought, he was wading into the water.

Catherine and Lance were both admittedly too excited and nervous to sleep. Tomorrow was the day. As the last nine days had passed, they both had been on a roller-coaster ride of feelings regarding Jon. At times sure he was alive and at others, shaking with fear that the message would never appear. They had done exceptionally well at consoling and distracting each other considering the circumstances. She had taken no pictures, though. She and Jon had discussed the possibility of their photos eventually making it into the news. That meant no new ones. Too risky to have their faces in the hands of some photo developer in case the National Wire Service was going to spread the word to be on the lookout. Oh well, at least they had the memories. The afternoon they spent at Cannon Beach was one of the best memories. Haystack Rock, a lone-standing obelisk that seemed hundreds of feet high that sat half in the surf and half on the beach was quite a sight to behold. More amazing was how it was reflected in its entirety by the wet sand from the waves that crashed onto the beach, then receded back into the ocean. It was magical, mysterious and awe inspiring all at the same time. They watched people climbing around its base for hours and just couldn't get enough. But even in Cannon Beach the sun does drop below the horizon, so at dusk, they headed back to the car.

She had a surprisingly easy time adapting to her new name. She had been worried that people would be calling her from right beside her and she would ignore them without realizing they were trying to speak with her, but each time she heard the name Catherine or Ms. Lake, her attention was given quickly. It was easy for Lance, too, for obvious reasons. He called her "mom" anyway, and his first name had not been changed. His parents had decided it might be too hard for him, so they risked it a little by only changing his last name, and even then, they only dropped the first letter. If they were still in hiding for one reason or another within two weeks of the coming school year, Catherine would have him start to practice signing his new name, to get into the habit. It could be devastating for all of them if, even once, he were to sign Lance Blake, because that would raise all kinds of questions from the teacher who saw it. The questions would start out innocently enough, but eventually someone would want a real answer as to why he was signing another name to his papers.

On that final night of not knowing, they watched movies and ate popcorn, both hoping to fall asleep in front of the TV. Neither was paying much attention to the movies as their thoughts kept drifting back to next morning's trip down to the store to get the paper. Catherine hadn't told Lance yet, but he would not be going with her to get the paper. She planned to rise quite early and go get one while he slept. Should there be no message, she knew she'd need some time alone to regroup and prepare herself to face Lance. She prayed again that night before she slipped onto the bed. It was a simple yet moving request for divine intervention on their behalf, should that be God's will. She only slept until six. Tension, fear, and anxiety were all doing their combined best to overcome her. She did not shower as she did not want to risk waking Lance, who was still asleep on the couch. She dressed quickly and quietly, then tiptoed to the door.

If she could get down to the store and get the paper without him even waking up, the Lord had already granted one of her simple requests. She jogged down the steps to the car and was driving out to the main street when the realization that Jon might not have made it finally took its toll. It had been wearing her down every day, and now was attacking her with brute force. She wheeled into a parking space down near the entrance and stopped the car. No one would hear her cries, and within a couple of minutes, she battled those emotions back into submission. She called again for help from heaven and drove on to the store.

It was going to be quite a day, Ralph thought as he pulled into the station. He would go home at the end of his shift for the weekend and pick Michael up at the airport Saturday afternoon. He planned on having Michael stay for dinner on Sunday, and Florence had offered to make Michael's favorite meal for the occasion. Porterhouse Steaks, Corn on the Cob, Twice Baked Potatoes, Cornbread, and Peach Cobbler. Ralph had Michael over a lot as Michael was single and not really a night-life lover. They usually barbecued when Michael stayed for dinner, but Ralph would be awaiting his plane, so Flo had volunteered to do it. She liked Michael. Although he was the youngest partner Ralph had been teamed with in years, he was definitely the one she liked the most. He'd help with the dishes and chide Ralph about being lazy until he, too, would make an appearance to help clean up. Then they'd all sit out on the back patio and talk for hours over a few beers or glasses of wine, depending on the mood. It didn't matter to him at all that they were white, and it didn't matter to them or their children that he wasn't. As far as the Davises were concerned, Michael was family.

Flo even fixed Michael up with a date once but that didn't go well. Michael had not been aware when he'd gone over for dinner that night that he would be expected to entertain a lady and was not prepared to. It's not that he felt awkward around women, quite the contrary is true. It's just that being at Ralph and Flo's made him feel like he was at home, and he enjoyed their company so much there wasn't room for anyone else. Both men picked on Flo from time to time about that night too. Whenever the mood was playfully spiteful, if Flo would get a good one off at either of them, they would look at each other, go wide-eyed, and say, "Michael, I'd like you to meet Tonya," and immediately, she would get up and start lightly smacking the closest one of them. She would tell them to stop bringing that up, all the while embarrassed. They both laughed so hard at how she reacted to their impersonation of her that it never got old.

Ralph walked into the station and went to the locker room. Lieutenant Cantonelli was just leaving it as Ralph entered, and Ralph scowled and grunted in his direction.

"What's your problem, Davis? I've got enough going on right now, and I don't need any attitude from you! Understand?"

"Did I say anything to you? I didn't hear me say anything. What's the matter? Too many unsolved cases out there for you? I've got a suggestion. Just come up with some theories and type them in on the reports. Then all those cases will go away!" And with that, Ralph turned to his locker to change clothes while a pair of eyes burned into the back of his head.

"What in the world is that supposed to mean, huh?" Cantonelli yelled. "Are you saying I don't know how to do my job, Sergeant? Is that what you're saying? 'Cause if it is, let me tell you something. You don't have *a clue* how to do my job, so if I were you, I'd shut up and leave the police work that requires thought to the people qualified to think! And since I don't see a detective's badge on you, I guess you're not one of 'em, so back off!"

Cantonelli stormed down the hall fuming and talking unintelligibly to himself. Ralph felt good about getting under Cantonelli's skin. He figured that was only fair since Cantonelli had been getting under his for almost a week.

Gus Cantonelli wanted so badly to beat the living daylights out of Ralph Davis he almost swung at him right there in the doorway. He couldn't though, because Mr. Tracerio was relying on him to help sweep the mess they were all in under the rug, and it would be very hard for him to do if he were suspended for striking a fellow officer. So he held himself in check and would get even with the piddly-ass beat cop when this situation was over. Time was running out for Gus to keep the case off the National Wire. If Mrs. Blake and son did not show up within one more week, he may be forced to put out an APB, or it wouldn't be just a piddly-ass beat cop questioning his actions. It would be at the very least a board of inquiry and possibly the FBI. Sharpe and Greenhill had to find them and soon.

He and the chief still had the other problem to take care of too. The Jeffries issue would be gaining momentum on the priority list as he had not shown up yet either. During the all night meeting with Tracerio, Tony gave instructions that if they had not found Blake and family within ten more days, to start pushing the Jeffries-Blake conspiracy theory and more. Cantonelli was also to put out an APB for the wife and son but statewide only. As long as no one could prove the Blakes had left the state, the FBI would stay out of the case. Danbury was instructed to make the credit card transactions disappear. Without those, there was no proof any of them had left the state. That should buy Tracerio's army at least a month, which had to be enough time to find them.

Right now, all they could do was wait for Blake to come out into the open or use another card again and hope that Sharpe and Greenhill were close enough when he did to strike. But waiting turned Tony Sr. into a maniac, because it meant he was not in control. He'd already upped the bounty to $250,000.00 and had every contractor within their network out looking for the Blakes. Tony was getting nervous. Whenever Tony got nervous, people started to die—on both sides of the law.

Ralph was almost to the squad car when he was called back in by the captain. "Davis, explain to me why you are angering and insulting our best detective. Not to mention that he's our highest ranking one. What is going on with you? Do you know something I don't about his cases? If so, let's hear it right here, right now."

Captain Steve Wilson was also working for both sides but had the luxury of not being called into play very often. His role in the organization was to keep straight cops off the backs of those working for Tony. This was normally a very easy job since very little happened in Albuquerque that required involvement from Tony's friends on the force. That was one of the reasons he'd set up shop there. That and he knew the chief from way back.

"Don't just sit there looking at me, Davis. Say something!"

"Cap'n Wilson, I think there are more leads out there regarding the fire at the Blakes and the missing wife and kid than Gus is following up on. It's been a week and no one's seen hide or hair of them. Don't you think something's wrong with that? Has he even tried to find them? No. He said he's just gonna wait 'til they get back from wherever they went to talk to her. Damn, Cap'n! The least he could do would be to check her credit cards and the airlines. That's only a few phone calls, ya know?"

"For your information, Sergeant, that's already been done. No use of cards, and they didn't fly out of here; they drove. None of the airlines have any record of her or the kid even buying a ticket, let alone using one," Wilson said in a commanding voice. Then he softened and said, "Look, Ralph, Gus is doing everything he can to find them. Just because he's not telling you everything he does doesn't mean he's doing nothing at all. Understand?"

"Yes, Cap'n. But all he had to do was tell me that and none of this cra—"

"He doesn't answer to you, Ralph! He doesn't have to tell you anything! I'm his boss. I'm the one he's got to keep in the loop, understand? So get off the guy's case, Sergeant. I mean it. Look, Ralph, you're a great cop. I truly wish everybody cared as much as you do. But you're not helping matters by winding Gus up. He's a good cop too. Give the guy a break and let him do his job, okay?"

"Ok, Cap'n. I'm sorry. I didn't know he'd done all that stuff already. I guess I misread Gus."

"Yeah you did, Ralph. Now don't you think he should be hearing that apology instead of me? Handle this then get out there and keep the streets safe, would ya?"

"Yes, sir, Cap'n."

Ralph rose, left the office, and went to find Lieutenant Cantonelli.

"Now what do you want, Sergeant?"

"Hey, Gus, calm down. I came to apologize. I shouldn't have been in your face like that. I didn't know all the stuff you'd already done to find the wife and kid, and I promised Michael I'd keep him up to speed. You didn't deserve the attitude I gave you, and I'm sorry. Okay?"

Cantonelli took a deep breath, rose, and extended his hand. "Okay, Ralph. It's all right. It's just that this one's getting to me."

"I can see why, based on what the cap'n said. Hey, Gus, if there's anything Michael and I can do to help, let me know. He'll be back here on Monday. Just ask if you need us, okay?"

"Thanks, Ralph. I appreciate that. I know Michael was hurt over there and this case has meaning for him. I'll try to let you guys know when I find anything."

"Okay, Gus. I'm really sorry man. Good luck."

As Ralph walked away, Cantonelli stood there amazed and relieved. He had no idea what Captain Wilson had said to Davis, but whatever it was, it worked. That was only the third time he had needed Captain Wilson to run interference for him, and the captain had handled it beautifully. Now that he had a little breathing room, he could get back to work for both of his employers.

She took the paper out to the car and flipped through the sections quickly trying to find the Classifieds. She tossed the rest of the paper aside and opened the classifieds to the first full page and saw the heading "Personals" halfway across the top of the page. She folded the paper in half so she could hold it with her left hand against the steering wheel and use her right index finger to guide her eyes. She glanced at each of them, then went through them again, more slowly. Fear began to rise in her as she doing it again for a third time and still saw nothing from Jon. This was the day, wasn't it? Yes. He did say the Personals, right? Yes. She looked at them again. Still not there. Countless thoughts and pictures flashed across her mind in the next fifteen seconds, but all were a distant second to the one out front. *Was Jon really dead? Maybe it was the paper's screw up. Maybe they hadn't put it in yet. Maybe it would be there tomorrow. Maybe th—*

What would she tell Lance? How would he react? What would they do now if Jon really were dead? She lost it, then and there. The sobs were coming from the deepest part of her being, and they were uncontrollable. She fell forward against the newspaper and cried. Her tears made the paper stick to her nose, but she didn't move. For three and a half minutes, she didn't move. Simultaneously, she heard a knock on her window and a muffled woman's voice say, "Miss? Are you okay? Miss? Are you okay?"

Catherine nodded her head yes without raising it from the paper, and with her left hand, waved the woman off. This intrusion was a good one for Catherine, though, as it broke the chain of sobs long enough for her to regroup and get control of herself. She lifted her head off the paper and wiped her face. The paper was wet now, so she threw it over onto the passenger seat. She shook her head a few times quickly as if to clear her vision and awaken her, then she started the car. As she looked behind her to make sure she could safely back out of the parking space, she glanced down at the paper again. It was almost as if she wished it could speak, to tell her why Jon's message wasn't there. The drive back to the apartment was only about a mile, but for Catherine it felt like one hundred. Lance was still asleep when she walked in and she thanked God for that. She set the paper down on her bed and went to shower. The master bedroom in this apartment had its own bath, just like their home in Albuquerque. Normally, she would leave the bathroom door open, so the steam could escape and not fog the mirrors. But this morning, she didn't want to wake Lance, so she closed both the bedroom and the bathroom door almost completely. Lance was not allowed to enter their room without permission, so she figured the paper was safe there on the bed until she came out. She'd wake him and tell him the message had not come after she showered and settled herself down, she thought. The hot water felt good on her skin, almost like a hug, and at that moment, she could use one. The hot water had run out before she realized she had been in there for a full forty-five minutes.

She shut off the water, wrapped the towel around her, stepped out, and opened the bathroom door. As she stepped into the bedroom, she was startled and stopped in her tracks. She grabbed onto the doorframe for support. Lance was sitting on the far end of the bed, classifieds in hand. She stood there horrified at what was about to take place there in the bedroom. She waited for Lance's reaction, and then she would comfort him the best she could. Lance had not heard the bathroom door open or the gasp of breath his mother had taken when she saw him there on the bed holding the newspaper. He was too engrossed in the paper. She could not see his face as he was sitting with his back to the bathroom door.

Suddenly he stood, turned, saw her, and said aloud, "Mom! Mom! Dad's okay! It's here! It's here!"

She was taken aback and speechless. What was wrong with Lance? It was not there and she knew it. Had all this pressure finally pushed her son over the edge? She walked quickly to him, bent down to his eye level, and spoke.

"Honey, I looked already. It's not there, but maybe it wil—"

"Yes, it is, Mom. Look!"

Lance was pointing to the first AD in the Personals section, *on the bottom half of the page.* She hadn't thought to see if the personals had started in the middle of the page somewhere in the previous column, and now could not believe what she saw.

> Lonely, financially stable, middle-aged Caucasian man seeks woman with one preteen child for long-term relationship. Reply to box 2788, photos and telephone number required for response.

Except for the box number, which he had told her would be a variable, the message was Jon's, word for word. Excitement, relief, and hope filled the two of them as if they were one. They hugged, separated, and fell back on the bed laughing and talking. Maybe everything would be okay after all.

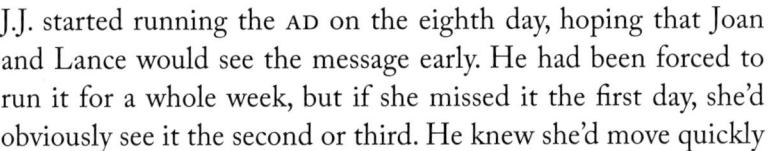

J.J. started running the AD on the eighth day, hoping that Joan and Lance would see the message early. He had been forced to run it for a whole week, but if she missed it the first day, she'd obviously see it the second or third. He knew she'd move quickly to contact the FBI or disappear should the deadline pass as they had discussed it. Ten days was enough. By the eleventh, she needed to be gone. He had arranged with the Oregonian to have any responses mailed to a P.O. Box in El Paso and would drive down there once a week to check the box. He figured Joan's reply would be the only one without pictures but knew how to tell her reply from all the others that came in from the Portland area by one simple phrase.

> You'll get the pictures and phone number if you send me yours first. I am financially independent and don't want to play games with my son's future. If you're still interested, mail them to the following box number and I'll get back to you.

The address provided would allow him to contact her directly, and even though he would send a phone number, he only expected it to ring if the situation turned disastrous. Since the cabin didn't have a phone, he had bought a cellular but knew they were as unsafe as CB radios where conversational privacy was concerned. She'd give him her number in the second letter so he could call her whenever he could. He didn't want her to risk it in the first one, in case it got lost and was opened by someone other than him. That's also the reason she had rented a box at a little place across the river in Vancouver, Washington, after they arrived in Portland. No actual addresses. He was just not going to let chance play a bigger part in their situation if he could help it. He had a lot to do and knew that when the bad guys realized he was back, their search for him would reach a whole new intensity. Should they somehow be lucky enough to find him, he didn't want them to find her before she could escape. If he ever called just to let her know all was well, he'd call collect and always use the wrong name. She would then refuse acceptance of the call, and the operator would disconnect them. That was the little system they'd worked out to let her know all was well. However, should he ever call collect and use his real name, she knew to accept, because he needed to talk with her. He would never place an outgoing call to her on the cellular, so he would use pay phones and that little system. The cellular was only for Joan to call him with, and only in the event of an extreme emergency.

He had finished scouting the area around the cabin a few days before and had already begun constructing the storage facility for the weapons he was buying. He'd purchased a little battery-operated tape deck and a dozen country/western tapes too. While he was up there getting in shape, he figured he'd best master a different accent. What better way than to sing along with country/western artists? J.J. also bought an old four-wheel drive Dodge Ramcharger from a private party down in Santa Fe for seven grand. It was a little pricey for the miles it had on it, but it ran great and everything still worked. He took it to a little shop in Los Alamos after he bought it and had them go through it just to make sure. They replaced a few seals, rebuilt the carburetor, and adjusted the valves, but said other than that, the vehicle was in exceptional condition. He put a Harley Davidson sticker in the back window after having them all tinted as deep as was legal and had big tires put on it for better off-road traction. Behind the backseat, he installed a lockable metal box that would carry rations, weapons, changes of clothes, and anything else he might need if he had to live out of it for an extended period of time.

There was a great deal of open space under the hood of the Ramcharger too, so he had a small air compressor and an upper-radiator-hose steam valve installed at the shop that did the mechanical work. This kind of equipment was not completely unusual for survivalists or lone hunters to have installed, and since J.J. had not been shaving, he looked just like them. Once he got it back, he installed another harness under the hood. This one would carry a semiautomatic pistol and three clips for it. Even if he did get pulled over by the cops, they'd never check under the hood for a concealed weapon. Also, if he was ever being followed, he'd lead them to an out of the way place and then flip a switch on the dash that would activate the steam valve to make it look like his vehicle was overheating. Then he'd get out, open the hood, and have the pistol right there where it was needed if his followers decided to stop.

His diet had not changed much as he had always been health conscious, but his new level of exercise had elevated his appetite, so he was eating more. He'd started with just simple muscle stretches, and even those caused him pain well before he expected them to. It had taken four of the five days he'd been up there so far of stretching exercises alone before he felt limber enough to add strengthening ones to the workouts. The routine was simple. He'd stretch for an hour, then do something else for three or four. Then he'd stretch again, and so on. On the days he'd go into town, he'd stretch before he went and again as soon as he returned. Soon he'd add tumbling and endurance exercises, then later add weapons use while on the move. He figured it would take about a month before he was really ready to go back into Albuquerque. And the first trips there would only be for reconnaissance and supplies. It would be about six weeks before he would feel ready for them, but in six weeks, they would definitely know he was back.

8

Michael's plane from Jamaica landed at four o'clock on Saturday. It had been nearly two weeks since the fire, and Michael seemed to be his old self again. On the drive to Ralph's from the airport, Michael couldn't stop talking about Jamaica. Ralph was happy to see his partner so exuberant and was actually getting excited himself just listening. The drive took about forty-five minutes, and Jamaica was the topic for all of them but the last two.

"Ralph, I'm sorry, man. I must be talkin' a mile a minute."

"Don't worry about it, partner. I'm glad you had such a good time. It'll liven up our conversations while we pull the night shift," Ralph said.

"Yeah, you're right. I'll have the pictures developed by then. I'd rather talk about the trip than anything else with you, anyway, Ralph," Michael said coyly.

"Yeah? Why is that?" Ralph asked with a stunned look on his face.

"Okay, man, I wasn't gonna tell you this, but…," Michael hesitated, knowing he was pulling Ralph deeper into the spin cycle, then went on. "Well, Ralph, it's just that."

"C'mon, Michael. Spill. What's up?" Ralph asked, now completely bewildered and noticeably worried.

"You're breath stinks and you're boring, man. I didn't want to say anything, but since you asked, there it is," Michael said, trying to sound convincingly blunt and compassionate at the same time.

"Oh. Okay. I get it. Man, would you quit doing that to me? I thought you had something serious to tell me," Ralph said, visibly relieved.

Michael laughed as he pushed Ralph toward the driver's door.

"Man, Ralph. You are an easy mark. You should have seen the look on your face," Michael said, smiling broadly. "But you do have bad breath, man. *Real bad.*"

Ralph looked over at Michael and said, "Are you serious?"

He cupped his hand in front of his mouth, blew, then inhaled quickly through his nose. Michael watched, trying not to lose it, but could hold it in no longer as Ralph "tested" his breath a second time. He burst into laughter.

Ralph looked over and said, "I don't smell anything. What the heck are you talking about?"

Ralph pulled the car into the garage as Michael's laughter subsided. Ralph was a good sport. That's the main reason he and Michael got along so well. He was thick-skinned and took a joke well. And although Michael could pull a fast one over on Ralph almost at will, Ralph was no stooge. On the job, he was a wise and cunning mentor to Michael. Michael walked into the house and hugged Flo and the kids. Flo started to smile even brighter when she saw the tears of laughter in Michael's eyes, asking what was so funny.

"Michael's just being a jerk, honey," Ralph said as he hugged and kissed his wife.

"You got him again, didn't you, Michael?" Flo asked, shaking her head.

"Yep," Michael said happily, "I sure did."

"Michael, you better watch it or Ralphy won't invite you over for dinner anymore. And I just happened to make your favorite as a welcome home meal," Flo said.

Michael looked quickly at Flo with a grateful smile and said, "You didn't?"

She folded her arms across her chest and cocked her head to one side while she said, "Yes, I did. Porterhouse Steaks, Twice-Baked Potatoes, Corn on the Cob, and Cornbread. So if you two will go clean up, I'll set the table."

Ralph looked at Michael. "Welcome home, partner. Welcome home."

He then patted Flo on the behind and headed to the bathroom to wash up. Ralph hadn't told Michael what they were having for dinner; he'd only said Flo was making them dinner. Michael watched his friend disappear down the hall, looked at Flo, smiled a thank-you, and turned to the kitchen sink to wash up. The dinner conversation would be a repeat of the one earlier in the car about Jamaica. Dinner ended around eight. Michael tried to do the dishes for Flo since she had made his favorite meal, but she wouldn't hear of it. She threw both him and Ralph out of the kitchen while she cleaned, so they went out onto the back patio with a couple of beers.

Both men had eaten their fill and then some. As they lumbered down onto the patio chairs, Ralph said, "Oh, I missed you, partner. It's been a long week without you here."

"Thanks, Ralph. I missed you too."

"I mean it, Michael. This has been one for the books, I'll tell you that. First, the wife and kid of the guy who died in that fire haven't come back yet, then the captain put Cantone—"

"They're still not back?" Michael asked shocked and dismayed.

"Nope. And I checked on that just before I drove down to pick you up. I figured you'd want to know."

"Yes, I did, *do* want to know. Thanks, man. But that makes no sense, Ralph."

"You're right. Oh man, I'm sorry. I shouldn't have said anything. We can save the work stuff 'til tomorrow," Ralph said sincerely.

"No, no, no, man. It's okay. I'd like to hear what's going on, please. I haven't thought much about work in a week. It's time I got back in the groove," Michael said pleadingly.

"Are you sure? I mean, it'll wait until tomorrow. It's not like we can do anything about it anyway, least of all tonight."

"Yeah, man. I'm sure. Fill me in."

"Okay. You are not going to believe some of this, my friend."

Ralph brought Michael up to speed on everything, from the investigation to his meeting with the captain. Michael became confused as some of the decisions did not seem to be good ones. Ralph agreed. The rest of the evening would be spent talking about it. Flo had come out, heard some of it, and was a little shocked too. Ralph took Michael home about eleven, and they talked about it for another half-hour in Michael's front doorway. Then Ralph left. Michael was unpacked, undressed, under the covers, and asleep by midnight.

Michael woke at seven Sunday morning and went down to the station even though he was not due back to work until Monday. He wanted to take a look at the file on the case while Cantonelli was off, just to see if looking at it could help it make sense to him. It was right in the middle of his desk. Michael looked around, saw that the room was empty, and opened the file. The first thing he saw was something taken off the bankers' desk and Michael froze. It was a family photograph.

Sharpe and Greenhill had been over every inch of New Orleans twice and had turned up nothing. The first time they had been very discreet, trying not to attract too much attention to themselves. This would make it easier for them to be forgotten later should the Blake family's pictures be plastered all over creation by the feds once they started investigating. That angle had proven to be a waste of time, so they stepped out of the shadows wearing disguises and carrying badges. FBI badges. They went to every hotel, motel, travel agent, boat dock, bus station, and even had the airport being watched by a man and woman loaned to Tracerio by a friend there. Still nothing. The third time they called in, Tony Sr. spoke to them personally.

"Marcus, you do whatever it takes to get a bead on them. If that means going back up to Little Rock and asking around again, then do it. I want them found. Do you understand me? *I want them found!*"

"Yes, sir. We'll lea—"

Tony had already slammed down the phone.

"Boy, he must *really* be fuming, huh, Marcus?" Sharpe asked, already knowing the answer.

"Yep. He's hot. Let's get lookouts here at the airport and put a few more at the bus stations and docks, and then we'll head back to Little Rock. I don't want that man to start taking it out on us."

"I hear ya, man. I hear ya. Let's head back to the motel. I'll get our stuff packed up and load it in the car while you make the calls. If we hustle, we should make Little Rock by dark."

"Okay, man. Sounds like a plan. This Blake guy is really starting to get to me too. When we catch up with him, I'm gonna rip his nose off and make him eat it before I kill him"

Greenhill was gesturing as though he had a finger in each nostril and was pulling upward while he spoke. Sharpe got a chill just watching him act it out.

"Man, you are a sick mutha. You know that? Jeez. Make him eat his own nose! Whew," Sharpe said as he winced, then shook his head.

"Well, this guy's got under my skin, man. I want him. I want him *real bad*, now. Let's get outta dodge."

He just stared at it and stared at it. He couldn't believe what he was seeing. The woman and kid in the photograph were the same ones that were in the car that night. Something was wrong here. What was going on? Had that lady set fire to her own house to kill her husband and taken off with the kid? Why? It didn't make any sense! What the heck was going on!

He started reading all the notes in the file and became even more confused. Why had the case been pulled from one detective and given to another? And why just after Blake's fellow employees had been interviewed? Why had an APB not been put out on the wife and kid? Why had Cantonelli not put the description of her car on the wire? They had not been seen or heard from in over a week, so why had Cantonelli not called the FBI? How could the fire marshal rule so quickly on the cause, with almost no investigation? Why had no autopsy been ordered, even if just to solidify cause of death? Why was the captain not digging deeper? *What the heck was going on?*

He left the file as he'd found it and drove over to Ralph's. After ringing the bell twice, he looked at his watch and realized that Ralph was still in church and wouldn't be back for another hour or so. Michael walked around the house and sat on the back patio steps. All kinds of things ran through his mind, and none of them made him happy. A man was dead, his wife and son had disappeared, and officials of both the police department and fire department were doing everything they could to bury it. Who wanted it buried so badly? Who had enough power to get Cantonelli and the fire marshal to bury it? Was the captain involved? Who else could be and why? He had heard stories of bad cops in his young career but had never knowingly encountered one. The reality of the situation hit him harder than anything ever had before. In one hour's time, the highly respected institution he had felt honored to be a part of had crumbled into one infested by treachery and deceit right before his very eyes. The more he thought about it, the more upset he became. Tears began to well up in his eyes. One finally broke free, running down his face. He wiped it away, then rose and walked out to the lone Cottonwood tree in Ralph's yard. He stood there staring out into space for some time, not realizing that Ralph and Flo had returned, or that Ralph was watching him from the back door.

"Man, you never cease to amaze me, Michael," Ralph said from behind the screen door.

Startled, Michael's head snapped in the direction of the voice, then said, "Ooh, Ralph. You scared me, man. I didn't hear you come home."

"That's because I wanted to scare you, man. We saw your car in the driveway when we pulled up, so I tiptoed back here to see what was up."

Ralph paused as Michael nodded with a blank stare, then asked, "What are you doing, Michael? Making a date with my tree?" Ralph smiled and came through the door as he spoke.

"I'm sorry, man. You obviously have a thing already going on with it, so I'll back off," Michael said, trying to sound jovial, but failing miserably. "Actually, I came over to talk to you about that case."

"Okay, sure. What about it?" Ralph's voice rang of inquisitive concern.

"Well, you know that nigh—"

"Would you like to go in the house and sit down while we talk, man? You don't look so good," Ralph interjected.

"No, no. Nah. I-I'm okay. Really. Thanks anyway. I'd rather not talk about it here, though. You mind takin' a ride with me over to the kid's ballpark or somethin'?" Michael asked.

Ralph was beginning to think that what his partner wanted to say would only justify Ralph's own suspicions and this made his stomach begin to turn.

"Sure, man, sure. Let's go. I'll tell Flo we're goin' to the store or somethin,' and I'll meet you around front, okay?"

"Okay."

Michael was leaning on the hood of his car when Ralph came out the front door. Ralph could see that Michael's mind was bearing a very heavy load. He had never seen Michael this shaken about anything.

"I'm ready, man. Let's go," Ralph said.

Michael stopped him in his tracks with a raised palm, then motioned to Ralph to move closer.

"Ralph, I don't want to talk about it in the car, okay? Let's talk about Jamaica, your kids, Flo's cooking, or anything else. Let's wait until we get to the park to talk about the case, okay?"

Ralph squinted slightly as he took in what Michael was asking of him, then said, "All right, man. If that's what you want. Sure."

And as they walked to their respective doors, Ralph asked again, "Are you *sure* you're okay, Partner?"

"I don't know, Ralph. I just don't know."

Ralph tried to start up a conversation in the car but found it quite difficult considering Michael's somber state of mind. It almost seemed to Ralph like there had been a death in Michael's family, and maybe to Michael, there was. Michael's belief in the Code of Honor of all who don the uniform to protect and serve was shattered. It was all he could do not to scream with rage. They sat in the third row of bleachers on the visitor's side of the field. Ralph waited patiently for Michael to choose his words, and eventually, they began rolling off his tongue. He told Ralph about the woman and child he had stopped the night of the fire but that didn't faze Ralph until Michael told him that they were the wife and son. He explained about the photo he'd seen, going through Cantonelli's case file, and about his concerns regarding the investigation and the fire marshal's report. When he finished, he hit Ralph with the same barrage of questions he had asked himself earlier, and like him, Ralph could come up with no justifiable answers. They both now knew that there were bad cops on the force, and even worse; they knew who.

"Man, if we're right about this, it might not be just the captain, Cantonelli, and the fire marshal. If we are right, this thing could go a lot higher," Ralph said.

"That's what bothers me most, Ralph. I don't know who on the force we can talk to. For all we know, internal affairs or even the chief and mayor themselves are involved. Which means we're back to ground zero. We're nowhere."

"If you stopped the woman for speeding, how come they don't know that? You called in the plate number, right?" Ralph asked.

"No, I didn't. When I saw that it was a lady, the first thing I did was get out to talk to her. I don't know why I didn't run the plate, but now I'm glad I didn't. Nobody knows anyone saw them after the fire, and I think we should keep it that way. At least for now. You with me on that, Ralph?"

"Yep, I sure am. God knows what they'd try to pull if they knew what we were talking about. Now I know why you wanted to come way out here. Wow. Man, this is deep!" Ralph said, shaking his head.

They sat there silent for the next few minutes, both pondering solutions. Michael was the first to speak.

"Ralph, I'm going to do a little investigating of my own. I don't want to work with guys playing on both sides of the law. I mean, what if one day I end up stumbling onto something they have to kill me for? Or you? Or what if they go after our families? The way I see it, we've gotta take them down, Ralph. All of them. Before they get to us. The question is how?"

LEFT NO CHOICE

"Very carefully, that's how," Ralph said, and went on, "we have to do this slow, man. We can't let anyone else in on this until we're ready to nail them all, and even then, I think we need to take it to the Bureau. But right now, let's keep our ear to the ground and our eyes on them. Here's the tricky part; watching them without letting on that we are and digging for information on them we'd never need under normal circumstances. That's gonna be mighty tough to do."

"I know it'll be tough, Ralph. I know that. But we need to figure out how to do it. There's got to be a way. There's just got to. I will tell you one thing, partner. I will see them pay the piper, or I'll die trying to get them there."

"I'm with you, Michael. So first, let's go over what we know and who we already pretty much know is involved, then go from there, okay?"

"Okay. And Ralph…thanks."

"All right, all right. You can thank me if we both get through this intact. Right now, let's figure out how we're gonna pull this investigation off right under their noses."

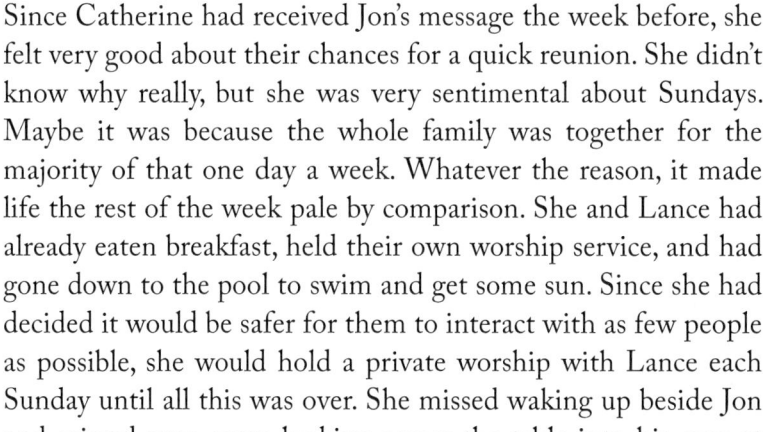

Since Catherine had received Jon's message the week before, she felt very good about their chances for a quick reunion. She didn't know why really, but she was very sentimental about Sundays. Maybe it was because the whole family was together for the majority of that one day a week. Whatever the reason, it made life the rest of the week pale by comparison. She and Lance had already eaten breakfast, held their own worship service, and had gone down to the pool to swim and get some sun. Since she had decided it would be safer for them to interact with as few people as possible, she would hold a private worship with Lance each Sunday until all this was over. She missed waking up beside Jon and missed even more looking across the table into his eyes at dinner. She wondered what he would say about her new hair and eye color, not to mention her attire. It lightened her heart for a fleeting moment as she smiled while picturing his gawkingly confused reaction.

Lance had made a few acquaintances down at the pool that first week, yet Catherine had not. Lance simply told them that they had come here from Las Vegas like he was supposed to and no one dug deeper than that. She had sent Jon the address and telephone number, along with a lengthy and poetic love letter. If there were such a thing as soul mates, Jon and Joan were the definition. Their love had carried them across many obstacles big and small and would outlast this. She knew it. As long as they both lived through it, they would be together again when it was over. She had considered the remote possibility that someone may find them there in Clackamas and enrolled herself and Lance in a self-defense class. If they did come, she wanted Lance to have every advantage she could give him to get away from them. It would also make three nights a week go by quicker while they waited for Jon to come for them, which was in itself reason enough for her to enroll. Lance had taken to the classes immediately and was practicing all the time in the apartment and on the grass outside. Jumping, spinning, kicking, tumbling, falling, and saying "*hyah!*" had become part of his daily activities. He wanted to be able to help his dad if the bad men ever came after them again. Knowing karate would ensure that he could, so he practiced with vigor and enthusiasm.

The pool and Jacuzzi were blessings from heaven for Catherine, especially when she got back from the self-defense lessons. It was easier for her to relax her tightening muscles in the water, and a hot bath was just not as much fun. She and Lance would get home, change clothes, and head for the water. Catherine would slip into the Jacuzzi's warm, soothing motion first, then join Lance in the pool about twenty minutes later. There, they would stay for another hour or so before going back up to the apartment for the night. The time between Lance going to bed and her drifting off to sleep herself was the most difficult time for Catherine. She hadn't slept well since it all began and did not think she would for some time even after it was all over. Jon had suggested she take it one hour at a time, and so would he. They had both agreed that taking things one day at a time was too long and made a joke out of counting minutes. She smiled as she thought back on that conversation. Even with all that was happening that could end their lives, Jon was still able to make her laugh.

"Mom, why don't you come on into the water? It's really warm today!" Lance said.

"I might just take you up on that in a few minutes, Sir Lancelot. I just might."

"Aww, Mom! I asked you to stop calling me that."

She had started calling him Sir Lancelot right after they arrived in Portland because of the courage he had shown through all that had happened. He would never admit it, but he liked it when she called him that. She had told him of the legend of King Arthur and Sir Lancelot, including how brave and strong he was. Lance liked knowing that his mom compared him to someone like that, and Catherine could tell. That was why she hadn't stopped even after he asked her to. She saw many of his father's traits in him, and as the days passed, more of Jon's influences were apparent in Lance. She prayed that he would continue along this path as she knew he would be truly happy if he did. Just as she and Jon were.

"Wherever you are, I'm thinking of you, my love," was the last thing she would allow herself to dwell on before jumping into the pool with Lance.

J.J. had been very busy the first week, actually accomplishing more than he'd planned. That was a good thing, he thought. It would get him back to Joan and Lance faster. The storage facility was almost finished and his body was snapping back into shape faster than he'd expected. He had a few bruises but not many. His body's resilience was remarkable for a man of forty-four. Not because forty-four was old, but because he worked at a bank and did not do much of the physical exercise he was once quite accustomed to. All things considered, he was very pleased, and his confidence with most of his weapons was growing. The only one that was still giving him fits was the compound bow. Somehow, he had lost the knack of judging trajectory, so he'd been spending a great deal of time with it. It drove him crazy because that knack was there the first time he ever loosed an arrow. It was instinctive. Now it was nonexistent. He knew he'd get it; it would just take more work. Everything else was ahead of schedule, so he'd spend his spare time on it until he got it.

He had been singing in the cabin for an hour each night too, trying to adopt a southern accent. On one trip down into Chimayo, he picked up a couple comedy tapes made by a southern guy. Not only was the guy funny, he had a very distinct accent. J.J. practiced and practiced that accent and was finally starting to catch on. The trick wasn't to just have one; the trick was having one that sounded *natural*. With his rate of progress though, he was pretty confident he'd be ready to converse in another month. This was the least of his worries at the moment though as he had bigger fish to fry, literally. When he took the time to rest between grueling workouts and accent mastering, he would go over details for his reentry into the world. A world where people he didn't know or care to know wanted to kill him, his wife, and son over money. Money! How could human beings be so rapped up in that crap that they'd be willing to kill for it?

This thought process he just could not understand but tried to as he needed to know who his adversaries were and how they thought. Once he knew how they rationalized their actions, it would be easier to find a weakness he could exploit. The hardest thing for J.J. to resolve was how to move through them without

LEFT NO CHOICE

their discovering who he really was, all the while taking them down one by one as he went. He had known from the beginning that someone outside the bank had to be in control, he just didn't know whom. Since he'd transferred the bank documents from the motorcycle trailer to the locked box in the Ramcharger, he was able to pull them out and go over them while sitting in the cabin. He knew that somewhere in all that paper was a clue; he just had to find it. With millions of dollars outstanding in loans that were past due to a few select corporations, he was sure Ted Danbury had to be involved. There was just no way Danbury would continue allowing loans to corporations with no consistent repayment history unless he was a player in the money laundering scam.

Before he had been discovered, he had tried to visit a few of the major investors in the bank's high-risk yield portfolio. Many were offshore investors and were impossible to pin down. However, the three local ones he was able to track down were nothing but dummy corporations using P.O. boxes for addresses. On paper, the bank had written off millions over the years in invested capital to those corporations, yet none of Jon Blake's bosses had ever mentioned it in meetings with the Commercial Loan Division. The IRS was most likely being defrauded because the bank could take tax write-offs on the losses they incurred from these bad investments. That meant there were some seriously deep pockets behind this, and J.J. needed to find out who they were. He was sure they were the ones really in charge, so once he took them down, it would be over. He had considered sending everything to the IRS in Washington, but felt they would be like a bull in a china shop coming in. That could give the ringleader time to escape, and he and his family would still be in danger. The risk was too great, so that idea was out. If he'd had just a few more weeks at the bank, he may have been able to get enough evidence together and make all the evidence point to one of their own turning on them.

That was not possible now, so anything that went down they would know was because of him. That left J.J. with only one option. Take them all down himself. If he could get to the leader, the entire group may crumble, so the head of it all was his primary target. How to get to that man was the multimillion-dollar question. He knew the three dead men Ashland had e-mailed Edwards about were somehow involved, and he had collected a little information about them through the bank's records before he was discovered. Somehow, he had to get a closer look at those men's businesses. He knew that the only way to do that was from the inside, so in a few more weeks, inside he would go.

9

Dinner had only been over for five minutes, and most in attendance didn't even have their cigars lit yet, when Tony stood up, began pacing, and started in on them.

"This guy could not just disappear into thin air! He's got to be out there somewhere, and I want him found!" Tony barked at the top of his lungs.

Everybody present except Tony Jr. and Victor was visibly afraid of this kind of emotional outburst from Tony. Normally, Sharpe and Greenhill would not be, but their three-week search had come up empty and they, too, had been called back. Danbury and Edwards sat with their eyes locked on Tony, but otherwise motionless and silent. The chief and Cantonelli exchanged glances quickly, and then the chief spoke.

"Every one of my men that work for you are spending time on this one, Tony, but it's hard to do that from my position without risking the search becoming public knowledge. I even risked pulling the guy's phone records for the last three months without getting a warrant. If one of the regular guys or some flunky we question gets wind of what we're trying to do and leaks it to the press, all kinds of heat will be on the department. And then there's the feds. I can't keep them out of it if it goes public, Tony. And once they step in, the dep—"

"*I know all that, chief! I want answers to the things I don't know!*" Tony said as he slammed his fist down onto the table.

"We got the results in this afternoon on the background check on Blake, Tony. This guy used to be a Green Beret! During his six years, he got commendations out the kazoo. One of them was for Valor. This guy single-handedly saved his entire platoon from a hostile force almost three times their number! He was also exposed to counterintelligence tactics." Cantonelli explained, surprised at his own "courage" in talking that way to Tony. But these words did interest Tony visibly, so Gus stepped out on a limb. "Personally, I don't think a guy with that kind of knowledge and confidence in himself would trust the Bureau to protect his family. I think the guy believes they are safer with him. I also think that's why the man has disappeared. He doesn't have enough to go to the Bureau with, and figures we'll never find him no matter how hard we try, so he's long gone."

Every man at the table was now aligning with that assessment because of this new information, including Tony Sr. His gaze had been fixed on Cantonelli through the first half of his dissertation, but as the wheels in his mind began to turn, he stood and paced while Gus finished. There were eight long seconds of silence, then Tony glanced at each man sitting at the table while pointing repeatedly in Cantonelli's direction, and spoke.

"Okay. Let's say for a moment that some of what Gus says is correct about this Blake character. Let's say that Blake did disappear because he can't or won't go to the feds with what he's got, and does believe we'll never find him. That would mean he's going to do one of only two things now. One: start a new life somewhere and hope that if he can stay out of sight long enough we'll stop looking for him. Why? Because if enough time passes and the feds haven't come around, we'd know he wasn't going to talk. He'd want to keep everything he's already got just in case this plan went bad somehow, so he could still try to use it as a bargaining chip later if he needed to. Or two: that he's a very upset ex-army hero slash protective family man with too much moral fiber. Which means he'd never stop until he puts us all away. The first possibility needs no action on our part as we have nothing to worry about, so that's easy to prepare for. The second possibility, however, leaves us right back where we started. This guy is dangerous, and we need him taken out! So I say it again. *I want him found!*" He slammed his fists on the table again and then called for his car.

Officer Rhodes stood in the alley across from the restaurant as the cars were pulling out. He had tailed Gus to the restaurant from quite a distance but found it fairly easy as Cantonelli's car was unmistakable. This was only the third time he'd had the opportunity to follow Cantonelli since his conversation with Ralph in the park, but this one had produced a few answers. He wrote down plate numbers as the cars left and would run them all the next evening. All but three, that is. Cantonelli's, the chief's, and Tony Tracerio's, his limo was well known around Albuquerque. "Oh, man," Michael said over and over under his breath as they pulled out one by one. Now he wished he had brought the camera. This was big. Although no one had ever said it in an official capacity, the word on the street was that Tony Tracerio owned Albuquerque, but not in the geographical sense. Drugs, prostitution, gambling, extortion, gunrunning, racketeering, and every other major felony you could think of had been attached to his name at one time or another.

Michael wasn't sure how many of the rumors were true as he knew most self-respecting family men would consider drugs and prostitution beneath them. Nevertheless, it had all been said about Tony. Michael now knew the chief and Cantonelli were involved somehow too. Who the other men were he planned to find out the following night. He wanted very much to drive over to Ralph's and bring him up to speed but knew it was safer to wait until the next time they got together off duty. They had not discussed anything while in uniform. It was too big a risk that their radios, car, or even their uniforms themselves may be bugged. Their next get together was scheduled for a Friday night dinner at Ralph's as they both had the weekend off. That was only two days away, so he'd wait until then. It had already been difficult to be around Cantonelli inside the station, and now, it would be even more so. He never ran into the chief during his normal routine, so that helped. At least he wouldn't have to fake it around him too.

The hard part for Michael Rhodes was that he had been hanging around Cantonelli on and off since arriving in Albuquerque trying to learn more about being a detective before he took the exam to be one himself. He couldn't very well distance himself from Gus now without arousing suspicion, especially after his own partner had been in Cantonelli's face about the Blake case. Ralph and Michael had already assumed that Captain Wilson, the fire marshal, and Gus were involved because of the Blake case. However, neither of them would have dreamed that the chief was too. He thanked God again and again that they had not gone to the Chief with their suspicions as he walked the five blocks back to where he'd parked his Grand Cherokee.

Tony Tracerio and the chief. Holy cow! How deep could this thing go? He didn't have a clue. But one thing he did know, he wouldn't stop until he shut them all down, including Tracerio.

LEFT NO CHOICE

He was only twenty feet away from the deer now and still had not spooked it. J.J.'s stalking ability was coming back strong. Moving silently through the brush was slow and tedious but necessary for him to hone his stealth skills. This was the closest he had been able to get so far. Pushing through the foliage without making a sound was not difficult. What was hard was keeping the noise level of the branches swooshing back into place once he'd cleared them to an unintelligible one. That was hard. As was choosing where to place his feet. One branch cracking under his weight and the animal would be gone.

Nineteen feet. He had to get within ten to be satisfied that he could sneak up on a man without being noticed. With the deer's heightened senses of smell and hearing, if he could get within ten feet of it, he could get within inches of a man.

Eighteen feet. The moon was full and reflecting enough sunlight down into the forest that J.J. could now see the breathing motions of the deer. It would be a lot tougher to get closer from here as the bush that lay between them was at least five feet in diameter. He would be just coming through it on the other side if he were to achieve his goal. He pulled the branches apart slowly that were pointing toward him so he could slip between them. Then a shot rang out and echoed through the trees like a pinball. The deer bolted away in two swift bounds and was gone. Bah! No one was supposed to be hunting after dark! And if the guy was just firing his weapon for the heck of it, he was nothing but a fool.

Another shot. What was this guy doing? Didn't he know firing a weapon after dark was the fastest way to get the Fish and Game Wardens in there? Wait a minute—why not see if he could sneak up on that guy? J.J. thought. If he was noticed, he could tell the guy he was going there to tell him he didn't want Fish and Game climbing all over the place. Why was he being so quiet? Because he didn't want to be shot while approaching. It was perfect. So off he went in the direction of the shot. A third shot. He stopped and closed his eyes. He had learned that trick while in the service. Your ears alone could decipher direction of sound better that ears and eyes. His initial path was about ten degrees too far to the right. Either the guy with the rifle was moving, or his initial choice of direction was off. The last one was within a couple hundred yards, judging by the density of the forest, the volume of the shot, and the quickness of the echo.

He moved fairly quickly, all things considered. Trying to stay silent while moving through underbrush was not an easy task. A voice—he stopped and closed his eyes again. Yes, definitely a man and he's moving. J.J. adjusted his path now to one of a pursuit angle. This would allow him to close the distance much quicker, but it would also make it possible for the target to see his movements through peripheral vision. It was a risk J.J. was willing to take as he knew the guy would most likely not be looking to the side while he traveled.

A cough. Seventy-five yards off at two o'clock. J.J. was pleased. He had chosen the right pursuit angle. By the time each man traveled his respective distance, J.J. would be a few feet off his left shoulder. He adjusted his angle once more to about thirty yards out in front of his target. He wanted to have sufficient time to get into an unseen position only a few feet from the target as it went by. He got down on one knee within two feet of the trail on the forward side of a bush and waited. If this guy walked past without seeing him, J.J. would consider this test a success. He walked right by. Without moving from his position, J.J. said in his new accent, "What da heck do you think yer doin'?"

The man stopped in his tracks and spun around. J.J. was hoping he still would not be seen even though he had announced his presence. The drunken man darted his gaze all over the place behind him and said, "Who's out there? Come on out where I can see you."

J.J. slipped back a few feet away from the path, moved quietly to a position in front of the man, then spoke again, "The Game Warden's on the way."

LEFT NO CHOICE

The man spun around again; this time, audibly nervous, "*Who are you? Show yourself!*"

Once more J.J. was moving. His destination this time was going to be a lot tougher to get to quickly and still without being noticed. Ten feet to the rear, on the other side of the path. Crossing the path was the tricky part.

"You better git home whilst ya still can, mister. You hear me, boy?"

The target spun around again, now completely frazzled. The liquid courage he'd started with because of the booze had turned on him and was now darkening his pants and creating a puddle around his feet.

"All right. I'm goin'! Just don't do nothin'. I don't want no trouble, mister. okay? I'll just be on my way, and you won't see me again."

J.J. had already moved away from the last spot as the man walked quickly by but was still close enough to see the wetness on the front of the man's pants. He smiled, shook his head, then rose and headed back to the cabin. His first test of field stealth and camouflage had been a success. By the time he arrived at the cabin, he was feeling even better. Not only had the field test gone smoothly, but also, he may have stopped this vacationing idiot from forcing the Fish and Game Wardens to come in. That was the last thing he needed. Wardens snooping around, looking at IDs, asking personal questions, and making reports. Nope. Couldn't have that. He lit the kerosene lantern and pulled out the first letter Joan had written. They had corresponded by mail twice each at this point, but the first one he received would be his favorite forever.

Dearest J.J.,

Both sun and son have gone to bed for the night, yet there is a smile standing alone in the night sky amidst sparkling stars. Most people would say it's a sliver of the moon, but

I want you to look up and know that it's the smile I have felt in my heart every day since I met you.

Love was only a word in the dictionary before you entered my life. And although there was a definition for the word in that book, there was no way to understand its joyous power just by reading it. I have been given the chance to know companionship in its truest and most complete form…and that form is you.

Each time the breeze blows across my face, I feel your breath grazing my cheek. Each time I hear a phone ring, I know it is you calling out to me from wherever you are as if to say we'll be together again soon. Each night when I lie down and wrap myself tightly inside a blanket, I do so because I long to feel your arms around me once more, and know that you wish them there.

I know these things to be true not because they have ever been spoken with words but because they have been spoken without them.

We have been blessed with the greatest gift God could bestow upon us, my love. The gift of living as one. I have been a part of you since I first heard your voice, and know by the sounds that come from that voice, you are a part of me.

We are as one in many ways, but most of all we are *one life*…for I cannot bear the thought of trying to go through this one without you.

Come to me as soon as you can, for I will be awaiting that moment with unequalled longing. Do not, however, let my request for your speedy return cause you to forgo what you have been called upon to do. I want all of my husband back at my side, including the code of honor that makes you the man I love.

Signed,

Your Lady in Waiting

His eyes began to glisten as he read it again. He missed her. "I'll be there as soon as I can, sweetheart. Just as soon as I can," he said aloud as he folded the letter and held it against his chest.

Catherine was wiping away a tear from reading his response to the same letter. Both times he had written, there was a letter enclosed addressed to Lance and one for just her. She had not read the ones addressed to Lance but had read the ones addressed to her several times. And like him, the first she received was the most moving.

> My Love,
>
> Never before have words on a page moved me with such intensity. I sit here in awe of you, milady.
> In awe of the feelings you shared that filled the air around me so quickly with their meaning that I, too, felt you beside me once again.
> Oh, to have you beside me. That moment is what pushes me on to do what must be done. I have already lived our reunion so many times in my mind it has almost become a tangible memory.
> On that night, when both sun and son have gone to sleep once more, I will come to you wearing the smile of contentment that you have put upon my face since the day my eyes first beheld you.
> And we shall be one. One flesh, one love, one life.
> Look out at the smile in the sky again tonight, for this night it is mine being sent out to you.
> Wrap yourself even tighter into the blanket tonight, milady, for it will be me holding you this night and every night.
>
> With eternal devotion,
>
> J.J.

Love stories have been written about two people less close to each other than this, she thought as she sat curled up on the corner of the sofa crying. She said a prayer for Jon, asking for God's divine intervention in protecting him, and that He allow Jon to come home to her safely, and soon.

10

Laborious though it was, each night before retiring, he stealthily circled the perimeter of the cabin, went back in, gathered all the weapons he had practiced with that day that he didn't want found there, and took them out to the camouflaged underground storage room.

He had dug it out at night by whatever light the moon could cast through the trees. Light emanating from a flashlight could draw unwanted attention as well as blind his night vision, so each night, he went without one. He couldn't dig with a normal shovel in the beginning as this required him to stand out there in the night and that was unacceptable. On hands and knees, he used a small hatchet to loosen the dirt, then would pile it onto the tarp he had purchased. He knew that hunters seeing fresh dirt in the middle of nowhere as they were passing through would make them curious, so J.J. made several trips to a nearby stream each night, following the path the animals had made. He also didn't want to walk into the cabin covered in fresh dirt, so he chose one set of dark clothes to be digging fatigues. By the time he stopped digging on the first night, the hole was more than big enough to hold those clothes and a few of the weapons, all wrapped in plastic trash bags. The nightly routine was tedious to be sure, but necessary. He would get there, disrobe, and wrap his regular clothes and a towel in a clean trash bag. He would then get his digging fatigues out of the hole, put them on, boots and all, and begin. When he was finished for the night, he would put his fatigues back into the hole, then place the cover he'd fashioned over it to hide his work. He'd carry the bag with his clean clothes, towel, and the tarp full of dirt off to the stream one more time.

Once there, he would set the bag aside and dump the dirt into the stream. Although the water was only a foot and a half deep, the current moved reasonably fast. He only had to help the stream a little in its effort to carry the dirt down the mountain. He did wish, however, for the water to be warmer as it was near freezing. He'd wash off the tarp, throw it onto the bank, sit down in the water, and bathe while he pushed what he had just dumped into the stream off the bottom with his feet so the current could catch it and disperse it downstream. The current did its job well. By the time he was clean enough to step out onto the tarp, dry off, and dress, the majority of the dirt was gone. This went on each night until he was finished with his storage room. When completed, the room would be four feet high, five feet wide, and eight feet long. He used a couple of small trees he had chopped down as supports for walls and ceiling. It could be walked by, walked on, jumped on, and perhaps even driven over without being noticed or collapsing.

He had built the entrance in a narrow passage between quite a few trees and a good-sized rock. He fashioned the cover out of three to four inch diameter tree trunks and a great many vines, making sure all the trees were heartily alive when he cut them so if they were walked on they would not crack or break. He then put the brush that he had carefully removed from the spot back atop the cover he had fashioned, and from two feet

LEFT NO CHOICE

away, his handiwork could not be seen. Once the room was deep enough, he was able to bring in his shovel and move much faster although this required more trips to the stream. He didn't want to drag the tarp to the stream for a multitude of reasons, not the least of which was how wide and obvious a path that would create between the storage room and the stream. He also knew that dragging the tarp would be quite loud, and this was equally unacceptable. After three weeks of monotonous work, the room was finished. He was quite glad of this as he was getting really nervous leaving some of his weapons and ammo making equipment under the floorboards of the cabin. He would have waited to purchase the majority of his arsenal until after the room was complete but knew he couldn't dig during the day, which left him free to refamiliarize himself with all those weapons while the sun was out. He didn't want to waste any of his time while preparing himself for whatever lay ahead, no matter how insignificant a loss of time it may have seemed. For this reason, he risked someone walking into the cabin while he was away and walking off with the gear that would not yet fit in the hole.

He had hedged his bet a little, though. He purposely left an extra bow with arrows, a shotgun, and a hunting rifle in plain sight in the cabin whenever he was away. He figured if anybody did walk in with the intent to steal, they'd grab those and run, without even thinking to look around. Nothing ever came up missing, which he was quite happy about. He had the money to replace everything but that wasn't the problem. He was uncomfortable with the idea of having to go back into all the stores he had purchased the original equipment in and do it again. The retraining was going smoothly now and he had even been able to figure out and fix the problems he'd been having with the arrows' trajectories. He was used to lower poundage of pull and heavier arrows. He laughed at himself when he realized that's why his arrows had been missing their marks high. He'd decided the best way to infiltrate and do recon work was as an employee of Johnson Farms, previously owned by one of the men killed in Ashland's memo to Jack Edwards. In the paper he'd picked up, there was a Help Wanted AD running, and he hoped they'd still need people in another week. J.J. had considered the risk in taking a job there but figured they'd never look for him right under their nose.

It also seemed to be a business that had a great deal of employee turnover, so he wouldn't have to worry about a deep background check. These people were used to hiring a labor force and would probably only care if he could do the work. With a change in name, appearance, hair color, and accent, coupled with a letter of reference from a now defunct coal mining company that he'd been employed by for the last eight years, he was confident his real identity was well hidden. He'd gotten the idea for the reference letter from a defunct company on a loan application he'd seen at the bank early in his career. One of the applicants had pulled that one trying to show a stable job history. If you couldn't call anybody because the company no longer existed, how could you prove the letter of reference was a fraud? If it worked for that guy, why couldn't it work for J.J.? It also helped cover his trail immensely because the company he'd worked for was in Kentucky. It was a great deal safer for him to have just arrived from Kentucky than to have been in Albuquerque all these years.

He was only a week away, two on the outside, from going back down the mountain and into their world.

Michael and Ralph drove off after dinner to a little park on the east bank of the Rio Grande and walked to a picnic table some distance from any other. They had talked about all kinds of things in the car but all that changed when they sat down and cracked open their first beer. Michael explained to his partner what he'd seen Wednesday night, and Ralph listened with mouth agape.

When Michael had finished, the questions were more numerous than the answers.

"Okay. Tracerio is obviously using the chief, the fire marshal, and Cantonelli to co—"

"Mmm! And the captain'" Michael interjected while trying to swallow a mouthful of brew.

"And the captain," Ralph agreed, "to cover something up, but what? The fire marshal's office concluded the fire was accidental without investigating, so we can assume the fire was not accidental at all. Which means they were there to kill Blake and set the fire to cover the murder. So how was Blake involved in all this?"

"I don't know, Ralph. He worked at Security Pacific just like the two guys who were at the meeting with Tracerio the other night. Maybe they caught him playing them and wanted him whacked," Michael suggested while shrugging his shoulders.

"Maybe. But this was a sloppy hit, Michael. Tracerio doesn't make mistakes like that. If he did, we'd have put his carcass in the slammer a long time ago."

"Why do you say that? The fire covers the murder, the guy dies…ooh, the wife and kid!"

"Exactly. The wife and kid. How were they able to escape? The only thing I can figure is that this was a botched hit. Either Tracerio felt he had no time to plan it better or things went sour at Blake's because he was ready for them."

"He couldn't have been that ready for them, Ralph. The guy's worm food."

"Yeah, but maybe he stayed to give the wife and kid time to escape. Then they got him before he could get out."

"Okay. I can see that. So where do you think the wife and kid are?"

"Who knows. They could already be dead too and wearing cement shoes right there in the Rio Grande."

"I don't think so, Ralph. I really don't and here's why," Michael said as a new light went on somewhere in his brain.

"Okay, I'm listening. Why?"

"You're Tracerio. You hit a guy and his family, then blow him to kingdom come and burn him to a crisp. You catch the wife and kid after they get away and whack them too. Why would you care if the cops started looking for them then? If you'd already gotten rid of 'em, why not have Cantonelli start looking for her and the kid like she was a suspect in a homicide? She's dead, right? You order her and the kid drowned in the car in the Rio, then if the car is ever found, the story is easy. She must have done him, then taken her life and the kid's because she couldn't live with it. Case closed. Nice and neat."

"All right, I'm with ya. But the fire inspector would come under the gun for misreading the cause if she became a suspect in a murder arson case. How would Tracerio get around that?"

"Hey, everybody makes mistakes, including the fire marshal. Besides, the house was blown into a million pieces. Who could blame the guy for not finding anything under those circumstances? Nobody could. Man, I'm telling you. There's another reason they haven't taken this one public yet. I know it," Michael said with tense conviction.

"Okay. Let's look at it from that angle then. What possible reasons could Tracerio have for not letting Cantonelli officially name her and the kid as missing persons wanted for questioning in a potential murder investigation?"

"Maybe because he doesn't want her listed as missing yet."

"Why not? You said yourself that it would be the cleanest way to get the Department out from under the gun?"

"Hear me out on this, Ralph, okay? What if Tracerio doesn't want this to be taken public because that would mean the Bureau would get involved? Once there's a report of a missing person, they are much closer to being involved. Maybe Tracerio's not comfortable with that."

"Aw, come on, Michael. You know the Bureau doesn't have enough time to follow up on all the missing persons reports they get. Why would Tracerio care if they wer—the fire! Yeah!" When Ralph's train of thought shifted, a whole new set of scenarios rose up to replace the old ones and he became a little excited as he continued.

"Tracerio must know the Bureau would investigate this one because of the dead husband and the fire and doesn't want that. They'd start digging into all kinds of things once they saw how shabbily Cantonelli had handled the case. They'd have the body exhumed, call for an autopsy to determine cause of death, put out APB's on the wife and kid and the car, then start digging into Blake's past, including his job."

"Right. And since we know that the president and a vice president of that bank are playing footsie with Tracerio, that could only mean that Tracerio's using the bank for something that he doesn't want the Bureau to find out about. That also means the wife and kid are probably still alive."

"Why do you say that, Michael? It's been a month now and she hasn't surfaced."

"Because Tracerio could keep this completely within the chief's jurisdiction if he had the wife and kid. He has them dumped in the Rio and some obscure 'witness' comes forward and says he saw a car get driven into the river. Our guys come out and find the car with the wife and kid in it, and the Bureau has no need to come in. Case closed," Michael said as he slapped his right fist down on the table like a judge's gavel.

"All right. All right. So Tracerio has to keep the Bureau out of here because he hasn't found her and the kid yet and doesn't want the Bureau's people to find them first. But why not? Why wouldn't he want the Bureau to find her for him?" Ralph asked, almost to himself.

At this point, Michael took over in the development of their theory, "She must have something that can bury Tracerio! If Blake was on his payroll, maybe he'd taken some hard evidence that could bury Tracerio and gave it to her when things went sour. If that's true, then not only does she have evidence that could put Tracerio away, he knows she's got it."

"Right!" Ralph said, pointing at his partner, then went on, "wait a minute. Wait a minute. If she's got evidence on Tracerio, why not just go to the Bureau with it and have them put her in witness protection? Dagnab it, Michael. We're missing something here. Something just doesn't add up and I think we're overlooking it. I can feel it. Can't you?" Ralph asked, frustrated now.

"Yep. Dessert. We're missing dessert," Michael replied as he looked at his watch, then over Ralph's shoulder.

As Ralph rose and turned to go to the car, he realized why Michael had changed the subject so quickly. A man and woman were walking in their direction. He also noticed that his beer was still half-full when he tossed it into the trash receptacle near the car.

"Half-full or half-empty, which kind of guy are you?' He asked himself under his breath as he opened the car door. "Half-crazy. That's it," and with that he got in.

They were missing something. A key piece to this puzzle that would make the rest of it begin to make sense.

Even though it was just the two of them now, it was still Friday night, so out together they went. Ashland and Covington had said nothing to anyone but each other about the situation since the day Tony had held the meeting in the conference room. But speak about it they had and often. They just couldn't help themselves. They both had an uneasy feeling about Tracerio since that meeting. They had been admittedly scared to death that he would have them killed until they were told of their impending transfers that came with substantial promotions. They had discussed trying to disappear, turning on Tony, and a multitude of other "what ifs" before they were told, but since then, were feeling fairly good about everything. They were to be split up, and that was okay with them although they'd miss their little Friday night jaunts. Covington was headed to Southern California and Ashland to Las Vegas. If they had known the real reason, they would have opted to turn state's evidence in a second.

There was a rumor floating that a bigger bank was considering buying Security Pacific, which could mean even more money and power in a few years. Their speculations on that issue were kept to a minimum as they didn't want word to get out too heavily about the potential merger. If it got around, the cost of the stock would climb and it wouldn't be as big a profit for them. Even though Tony had made it very clear that all conversations about it were to end a month ago, fear of him finding out about their talks was nonexistent. How could he find out? It was just the two of them, after all, and they always spoke in shaded sentences. No one else could possibly decipher what the subject matter was, so why worry?

"I think they went to Canada. He could find solitude and seclusion there, without worrying about being bothered by his past acquaintances. Yep. I'd put money on it. Canada," Covington said confidently.

"Nope. It's too close. I think they moved to Europe. The cost of living is less and it's a lot further from his old acquaintances than Canada. That's where I'd go if I were trying to get away from it all. The south of France. Or Greece, maybe. But definitely *not* Canada," Ashland said without a hint of indecision.

"What about Alaska? Most of his old buddies wouldn't dream of going there, even for a free vacation. And it might as well be Europe, as far away as it is."

"Who would want to move from the deserts of the southwestern US to the cold tundra's of Alaska? No man in his right mind would choose Alas…ooh! Hey. You might just have something there. He doesn't want visitors, so why not go where you'd be pretty sure no one would ever look? Hmm. Very interesting thought, Tim. Very interesting. That definitely has possibilities," George said.

"Yes, I know. Then in seven or eight years, when you're sure your friends have moved on to other things, you just move back down. Simple."

"Why risk coming back? Why not just stay?"

"There'd be no risk to speak of after all that time, really. I mean, think about it. If he had dirt on you, and it hadn't come to light after seven years, would you think he'd ever air it?" Covington asked.

"No, I guess not."

"See. Alaska. Then back in seven or eight years."

"Since I don't think I'll even know you in seven or eight years, I'll concede here and now, and buy the next round as payment."

"The next round nothing. The next three!"

"*Four* and that's my final offer," Ashland said with a smile and a raised hand.

"Done!" Covington said as he laughed.

They arrived home from the self-defense lesson, changed clothes, and went down to the pool. They were both getting pretty good at some of the techniques they were learning. So much so that they had actually been practicing them on each other in mock attacks. They'd made a game out of sneaking up on each other and half-heartily trying to subdue their prey before the victim could respond. Since they both knew positively that the man in both their lives was safe and healthy, it didn't bother them in the least to act out such scenarios. Besides, someday they may actually need them, and in any event, it was fun.

Catherine had noticed Lance was getting stronger, and she was firming up in a few areas herself. She couldn't wait to show Jon. She couldn't send a photo for obvious reasons and had decided not to tell him in her letters either. She would surprise him on their first night back together again. Lance had become a pretty graceful swimmer over the past weeks and had tossed the nose plug in the trash a few days ago. Her little knight in shining armor. He was such a wonderful boy. They had been talking a great deal since the last letters from J.J. about the probability that he would have to start school there in a few weeks. J.J. had made it very clear that he was still a long way from achieving his goal. The phony birth certificate she carried for Lance was going to come in handy, then. J.J. hadn't just changed his last name on it either. He'd made the birth date December 25 and the place of birth Las Vegas. This would be pretty easy for Sir Lancelot to remember, she thought.

On occasion, though, she would grill him as though she were the school principal, trying to trip him up. She never could, which also made Lance feel a little more confident that he could pull it off with a real principal. He would need school supplies and clothes no matter where they were, so the next day was shopping day. She was going to buy herself a journal while getting his supplies too. She would record everything that had gone on since the first night Jon had told her of Ashland's e-mail to Jack Edwards. She felt that if something happened to her and Lance, it would be the only chance that she would ever have to help bring these criminals to justice. She would keep it in the freezer in a TV dinner box. Lance hated TV dinners and she'd only bought the one so she could throw it out and hide the journal in it. No one would ever think to look in there, including Lance. To keep it from getting damaged by the cold and dryness, she would seal it in a freezer bag before slipping it into the box.

The shopping day was tiring, but fun for both. Lance now had enough clothes to get him through the fall. If they were still in Portland come winter, she'd simply get him those clothes then. Winter. It was still almost four months off. Surely, they'd all be back together by then.

11

He was finally ready in every aspect. Physically, mentally, equipment and accent-wise as well as the rehoned skills of his military life. He dressed, grabbed the Sunday paper, and took one final look in the mirror before going out and firing up the Harley. He couldn't believe it. He didn't even recognize himself! The dark colored contact lenses had added the finishing touch.

The beard, the longer hair that was now dark, the contacts, the new style of dress, and new accent had completely transformed him into J.J. Tracker. Even Joan would do a double take before believing it was he. Posing as a motorcycle jockey also allowed him the added advantage of wearing elevator boots with a two-inch heel and a one-inch lift. Wearing them, he stood six feet five. On his new IDs he'd posted his height at six three and adjusted the required descriptive colors of hair and eyes. He wasn't about to try and commute from the cabin on a daily basis, so his first stop was to get a studio apartment in Albuquerque before he applied for the job. That way he'd have an address to put on the employment application and the place to nap between surveillance shifts. Then he'd ride out to the farm.

The Johnson Farms' help wanted AD was still running. From a pay phone in Santa Fe the day before, he'd called to verify that they were still hiring. The starting wage was eight bucks an hour but could go to eight fifty in ninety days if you worked hard. J.J. chuckled over that when he hung up the phone. His salary at the bank worked out to almost thirty dollars an hour, but he would have worked at Johnson Farms for free. He knew Fred Johnson's hot tub electrocution accident all those weeks ago was actually an assassination. Not to mention it happening on the same day as the strange deaths of two other businessmen. Then add into the recipe all three were ambiguously mentioned in Ashland's memo to Edwards, and you have a lead. He knew some of his questions would be answered at Johnson Farms. He just hoped those answers would present themselves quickly.

He'd considered just "dropping in" on Ashland, Covington, or even Edwards and trying to squeeze them for the information he wanted. It was too big a risk, though. If they wouldn't talk or didn't know enough, he'd have no choice but to kill them right then. If he didn't, all involved parties would know he was back as soon as the one he had visited could get to a phone. Even if he did kill them, which he really didn't want to do if he could help it, their death in itself might raise the security around the people in charge, making his work even harder. He needed at least two of them to remain alive to become the state's evidentiary witnesses against the rest in case he could not get to those in charge. That's how he'd get even with Ashland and Covington for trying to kill his wife and son. There could be no bigger punishment for men with big egos and no courage than to hide in fear every day for the rest of their life. That's what he wanted for those two.

If they chose not to cooperate with the FBI, they'd go to prison with everybody else and become toys for some guy named Buford the Butcher. That would be good too. He would have liked to get all this done without bloodshed but knew there wasn't a snowball's chance of that happening. Nope. People were going to die, that he was sure of. Anybody that was carrying weapons had probably killed for their boss before, anyway, he thought. So they'd just be getting what was coming to them.

He rented an efficiency apartment at a motel complex, then rode off to get a job. His plan went smoother that expected, and he was hired on the spot. The reference letter was the kicker. Since the interviewer couldn't call anyone to verify previous employment, all he had to go on was that letter, and of course, J.J.'s responses to his questions. Drawing upon his experience in dealing with men of power from his years at the bank, he was able to make the correct impression of willingness and humility. He'd told the guy he'd be willing to start at the bottom, that he just needed a job. And he was given one. On the clean-up crew.

"Okay. Now all I need to know is when can you start?"

"Today, if that's okay, sir. I'm going crazy not working," was J.J.'s response. It put the finishing touch on a masterful performance.

"Great! Let's get you over to your new supervisor and get you started. I'll have all the necessary employment paperwork put together in an about an hour, so I'll want you to come back here to my office around four. Easy enough?"

"Yes, sir. Easy enough. And thank you, sir. I'll work very hard," he said as he extended his hand in gratitude.

The personnel supervisor walked him through the massive building to his new boss, gave Mrs. Kofax a brief rundown on J.J., then departed.

"Welcome aboard, Mr. Tracker. I only have two simple rules that I expect you to live by. One: get everything done that I tell you to do every day and make sure it's done properly. Two: if you get it all done, come see me and I'll have you help someone else in his or her section. That's it. Nice and simple. Think you can handle that?"

"Yes, Ma'am. I think I can," J.J. said with a nod and a smile.

LEFT NO CHOICE

"Oh, and you can call me Rosie. *Ma'am* is for old ladies, and I ain't that old. Yet," she said with a wave of her hand and a smile.

"I like the way you talk, J.J. You look scary as the dickens, but it sounds like your mama raised you right. I think we'll get along just fine. Now come with me and I'll show you what you'll be doing."

She was the spitting image of the woman on the Aunt Jemima Syrup bottles, and although she tried to exude a tough personality, J.J. could already tell that she was really a sweetheart. He'd like working for her. He also liked hearing that if he got all the things done that were asked of him, he'd be assigned to help others. That should allow him to be put into different areas a lot and also give him opportunity to ask a few innocent questions about the duties of each person he was assigned to. It pleasantly surprised her to see him pull out a little notebook and a pen and take notes of the things she told him. He'd explained that he didn't want to get in any trouble because he'd forgotten to do something and this solidified his "humble blue collar worker" appearance for her. She'd not have to keep an eye on him to make sure he did what he was told, and that's the way he wanted it. The better he did his job, the farther from him she'd stay. That would give him a little room to watch everybody else while he worked.

There were just too many people employed there for all of them to be involved in something that was illegal enough to kill over, he thought. He would look for obscure things that most would never think twice about, such as people coming and going through doors that were restricted areas and faces that wore the look of hidden knowledge. Cold faces that couldn't care less about what was going on in the day-to-day grind. That, too, he had learned in counterintelligence. Those friendlies who were really helping the enemy wore such looks when he'd enter their cities, towns, villages, or encampments. It was unmistakable. Once he saw it, he'd try to watch where they went, because where ever they went is where he needed to go. He'd been offered a choice of a set shift or rotating shifts with a four-day break between midnights and days. He volunteered for the rotating one immediately. What better way to do recon than to be there during all shifts? It would also give him a chance to talk to people who worked on set shifts that he'd normally never have met. Additionally, he could tail Ashland, Covington, and Edwards at different times of the day because of it, and this was icing on the cake. Heck yes, he'd like the rotating shift.

He knew their Friday night drink fest routine very well but wasn't sure if they were still doing it now that Jeffries was gone. Friday was still two days off, so he'd go to their watering hole that night and see if his new style could blend in or not. If it could, he'd be there on Friday. If not, he'd have dinner in the diner across the street and watch for them. The day went smoothly, from job assignments to employment packet, and he was back in the room at the motel by six. He cleaned up, waited a while, then jumped back on the bike and rode over to The Hideaway. There were a few bikes in the parking lot when he arrived at eight, but only a few, and none of them Harleys. He entered and began to worry that he'd not be able to watch them from inside. He was the only one dressed like a real biker in the place. He had pretty much surmised that would be the case since he wouldn't expect bankers to frequent a bar also full of partying bikers. He ordered a beer and moved over to the pool tables. He hadn't played in quite some time but was once pretty good, thanks again to the US Army. He racked 'em up and tested his memory of the fine points of the game. After his first rack, he dropped another fifty cents and played again. He hadn't lost all of his touch and was still good enough to play for a beer here and there.

In order to keep up the beer guzzling biker image, he downed the first one within a few minutes of breaking the first rack and had just been handed his third when he finished clearing the table a second time. From this point, though, he'd carry his beers to the bathroom with him and pour most of each into the toilet while he went, so he could stay quite sober while giving the impression he didn't want to be. By nine thirty the place was starting to fill and not just with white-collar types. There were a handful of bikers and wannabes too. He would *definitely* be able to be inside The Hideaway on Friday. He hung out for a little longer but left the pool tables. The last thing he wanted was to have to make friends that could distract him from listening in on Friday. He sat down at a table near the bar and had another beer.

One guy asked him if he wanted to play a game, and he said nothing. He just shook his head and gave a hint of a glare as if to say "leave me alone," and it worked. From that point on, the only person that spoke to him was the cocktail server. He hadn't seen any of the looks he was after on his first day, but it was just the first day. His crew switched to the afternoon shift on Monday, so he still had a few days of dayshift recon to look forward to. He was pretty sure that if there was something going on there worth killing over, he'd probably get his best look around during the midnight shift and that was two weeks away. In the meantime, he'd learn what he could by just watching what was going on at the farm and listening to Ashland and Covington. If they were still frequenting the place on Friday nights. He'd joined them twice during his first year working on the fifth floor and knew, at least back then, that they had a favorite table. He was sitting at the one next to it and would be again on Friday.

Michael had waited all night to see the cars pull out again, but this time, there was only Tracerio's limo, his son's Jag, some flunky named Greenhill, and another guy named Sharpe. They were all there last week too. But this week the others weren't. Michael had guessed correctly that Tracerio did this each Wednesday and would start watching the place on every one of them, camera in hand, if his shift permitted. As a single man, he had no one to go home to anyway, so watching them was no big sacrifice. He'd found files on Sharpe and Greenhill at the Department, but everything was nickel and dime stuff, and there had been no convictions. There was no paper trail on any of the other guests at last week's dinner, so he figured they were the ones who were far enough removed not to get their hands dirty. He wouldn't risk pulling them up on the system as an inquiry on their files might be noticed and asked about. It just wasn't safe enough. All cops had access to the perp files in the cabinets, though, and since he'd pulled them while on the evening shift, anybody who'd have cared that he was in there had already left.

He and Ralph were still unsure as to the reason for all the events surrounding the Blake case and had still not entertained the possibility that Blake was still alive and that the body found in the fire was that of someone else. Michael and Ralph talked about how the chief had done an excellent job at keeping this one under wraps for so long, especially with a missing wife and kid. How many other times had the chief been able to bury a murder or a disappearance? It was impossible for them to go through normal channels to find out, so Michael did his research in the library. They had fairly recent issues of newspapers there and older ones on microfiche. He would read everything about local events in every paper from the headlines to the obituaries. In the last five days, he'd visited the library four times and had reviewed three weeks' worth of papers.

Blake's house burnt down over a month ago, so he'd considered starting from there and working backward. He ruled that out, though, because it could cause him to miss something that took place in its aftermath. He'd also decided to start tailing the bankers that were at the meeting the week prior once in awhile. Maybe that would lead somewhere. All in all, he was already spending almost all his free time on this one and would until something gave. Ralph wanted to help with the legwork and surveillance, but they'd decided that it would be hard for him to do. For years, his normal routine was to go home after work every night, and they both knew they had to keep up the appearance that all was normal. Michael would have to go it alone. He was very much a loner anyway, so he wouldn't be breaking patterns of behavior with regard to other people in his life like Ralph would. He already visited the library quite a bit, seeing as how he'd worked in one growing up, so that would seem normal too. He'd just be reading different materials than his usual ones, and who could ever find that out?

In all his time in Albuquerque, the only people he'd known from work that he'd ever run into there were attorneys. No cops had ever been in there, so he could do his research without worry. He'd still check books out, now he just wouldn't read them. He wouldn't have the time to, with all the people he was trying to keep up with. Sooner or later, a pattern would show itself surrounding the events of the Blake case, he was positive of it. All he had to do was keep looking through those papers until he found it.

Today had been the first lesson in which they actually did mock attacks with intent to subdue one another, and Lance was very excited. Catherine was nervous and told him so on the way over. He told her she'd do real good and that she could kick some butt if she wanted to. Hearing this from her young son made her laugh and some of the tension dissipated, after she corrected his grammar, of course. What's the worst thing that could happen? That she'd find out she still needed a lot of practice? So what? That wasn't a bad thing. Lance was right. All she had to do was relax and she'd "do good." She chuckled to herself. Besides, what if she really did kick some butt as Lance had put it? She had been practicing with him at home a lot. He was lighter than her mock attacker would be tonight but that wasn't that big a deal. They had been taught to use their attackers' weight against them anyway.

Okay, she decided and then said to Lance, "You're right, son. I'm going in there tonight to kick some butt."

"Yeah, Mom! Woohoo! Now you're talkin'!"

And she did. In fact, she did so well that the instructor himself took a half-hearted shot at her and she put him on his back too. Her confidence began to climb, and her manner began to show it. Lance also did incredibly well for a boy his age and size. He was having a blast doing it too. Catherine watched in amazement as her son did some of the moves they had been taught and could have sworn he'd been practicing more than she knew about. He'd taken to it like a duck to water and was fast becoming a star pupil. On the way home, they agreed to spend even more time practicing and working out. Lance joked that maybe they could even take his dad in a contest soon. Boy, would that surprise him! After he said it, both of them went silent. Both wondered if he was still okay and when they'd see him again. Then Catherine broke the silence by suggesting an ice cream reward for their performance, and Lance perked back up. She changed the subject over to Lance starting school, which was now less than two weeks away. She knew for sure he would be going to school there; she just wished that she also knew for how long.

"Captain, we've got a problem," Cantonelli said as he burst through the door.

"Really? I'd say there better be, Gus. You know better than to just come barging into my office. What's the problem?" Captain Wilson asked.

Cantonelli sat down across the desk from the captain, then said, "Guess who jus—"

The captain had put up his hand as if to say stop, then flicked his head and eyes toward the door. Cantonelli turned and saw it still open. He rose, closed it, resumed his seat, and continued.

"I just took a call from Dennis Jeffries's mother. She said she hadn't heard from him in over a month, so she called his house several times and only got his voice mail. Then, she finally called the bank today and they told her Jeffries had quit over a month ago and that no one had seen him since. Now she wants to file a missing person's on him."

Captain Wilson could see why his lieutenant was worried but he was calm and cool.

"Well, we knew it was only a matter of time before somebody started asking about him. Is she still on the phone?" he asked as he leaned back in his chair, put his elbows on the arms and his hands in his lap.

"No. I told her I'd check into a few things and call her back within an hour."

"Good. I'll call the chief and tell him what's going on. I'm sure he'll want to make a call too. As soon as I've heard back from him, I'll let you know what to tell her, okay?"

"Sure Cap'n. Sure. No problem," Gus said through nervous lips, then rose, opened the door, and started to leave.

"And Gus?" the Captain called out.

He turned and saw the captain again nod toward the door. He stepped back inside the office, closed the door, looking at Wilson. "Yes, Cap'n?"

"Relax. I'm sure this was expected and will be dealt with. There's no need for us to lose our cool, understand?"

"Yes, sir, I do. I'm okay. It just spooked me a little, that's all," Cantonelli replied with a shaky voice.

"That's understandable. But don't let it get to you. I'm sure it will be addressed. I'll get back with you as soon as I hear back from the chief. Go get some lunch and take a breather. By the time you get back, I should have heard from the chief. Now do me a favor and close the door on your way out, okay?"

"Okay, Cap'n. Thanks." And Cantonelli left, closing the door behind him.

"Captain Wilson calling for the chief, please. Thank you. Oh. When do you expect him back? Okay. Just ask him to call me as soon as he gets in. It's important. Thanks."

After Wilson hung up the phone, he also began to unravel a little. How was Tracerio gonna handle this turn of events? What would he want done now? They were all already hanging way out there because of the Blake case, and now this.

"Mr. Tracerio, it's the Chief. He says it's urgent," the butler said while holding his hand over the bottom half of the phone.

"Urgent? Okay, Frederick, thank you," he said as he reached out for the phone. Frederick handed it to him, then turned and left, closing the double doors to Tracerio's study behind him.

Tracerio waited until he was gone, then said, "What's so urgent, Chief?"

"I'd like a moment of your time, Mr. Tracerio. I could be there in twenty minutes."

The only time the Chief ever needed to talk in person was if something was really wrong. Tony did not discuss business over the phone, so if the Chief wanted a face-to-face, there must be a big problem.

"All right, Chief. I'll see you here in twenty," Tracerio said, then ended the call.

The chief was ushered right into the study when he arrived.

"It seems we have a problem, Mr. Tracerio. Jeffries's mother phoned us wanting to report her son missing. What do you want me to do about that?"

"Jeffries was an only child right?" Tony asked as he walked out onto the patio and lit a cigar.

"Yes, sir, he…he was," the chief replied, a little perplexed.

"And isn't his mother his only living relative?" Tony asked, hoping the chief would catch on to where he was going.

"Yes, Tony. She is," the chief responded with some hesitation.

"And if I remember correctly, doesn't she live like a recluse, alone in a big old farmhouse on the outskirts of Omaha?"

"That's what Ashland told us, yes."

"Have somebody call her from a pay phone to let her know you'll start on it right away, then don't file the report. You hear me, Chief? Do not file it. I'll have Greenhill and Sharpe pay her a visit tomorrow night."

"But Tony, if I may ask, what if the Omaha police investigate her death and find out her son is missing too? On top of that, they'll surely check her phone records and find that she made a call to my department the day before she died. And I don't think you want that to happen. Why not just let it get filed? He's been gone long enough that a trail would be almost impossible to find, so I doubt the Bureau would even try."

"You don't get it, do you, Chief. I do not want the feds anywhere near this thing. Period! This little old lady is going to die of natural causes in that old house and that's that. There won't be an investigation. There won't be a phone records search. Then in a week, we'll have our Mr. Jeffries call them because he hadn't heard from her. They'll go out, find the body, call him back, and tell him she passed away. Then our Mr. Jeffries will have the body shipped down here for burial. Case closed."

"Okay, Tony. If that's the way you want it," Chief Richter said as he rose from the chair, hat in hand.

"Yes, Tom. That's the way I want it. You handle the phone call to let her know you'll start on it right away. That will stall her for a day while I get Greenhill and Sharpe moving. I'll take care of bringing Jeffries back to life to make the phone call to the cops up there and the arrangements to have the body brought here. Now get it done."

Tom Richter knew Tony was done talking, so he turned and left. Tracerio watched him leave, then placed the call to Sharpe, who in a week's time would also double on the phone as a resurrected

Dennis Jeffries. Tony was glad he'd decided that the bank should not close Jeffries's accounts and that he'd had his resident artist sign checks for all of Jeffries' bills so the phone would not be disconnected. If this plan went smoothly, that would change in a little over a week. Jeffries could disappear never to be brought up again.

Doris Jeffries lived near Whispering Grove, Nebraska, which had a population of less than eight hundred. She and her now-deceased husband, Frank, didn't like people, which is why they'd bought that little farm soon after Dennis went off to college. Frank had worked hard all his life, and Doris had done an admirable job pinching the pennies so they could afford to help Dennis with his tuition costs and still buy the small farm. The couple was truly beginning to enjoy their lives on their little farm when a drunken teenager changed everything one rainy afternoon. Frank had been coming home from the supply store in town when the youngster hit him head on and both were killed instantly. Dennis was a senior at Bowling Green when it happened but took a semester off to stay with Doris while she mourned. He went back to school a few months later, which left Doris alone and angry. Angry at the entire world.

She and Frank had struggled hard to make a haven for themselves and a young punk from town had taken him from her. The insurance settlement was enough to keep her from having to work the farm anymore, so she didn't. The few fields they did have were let go and so was her interest in caring for herself. The house slowly deteriorated as did what was left of her will to go on. The only reason she still had to live was Dennis. He still called her once a month and had even visited a few times over the years even though he'd told her he was making barely enough money to make ends meet, let alone pay for a flight to Omaha.

LEFT NO CHOICE

She bought that line of crap too. She had never known or even cared to know what most people were making and believed whole-heartedly that the cost of living in the city, any city, had to be outrageous. The truth be told, Dennis had been blowing more money a month on toys, booze, and women than his mom lived on in six.

He'd let her believe that he was living in a one-room apartment, and there wasn't enough room in it for her to stay even a few days. He'd told her that all the time they could spend together would have to be when he could "afford" to fly up to her. He was a true scumbag. His 2,700-square foot home overlooked the eighteenth fairway on one of the nicest private golf courses in town. But all she knew was that her son was a good man who was struggling like she and Frank had, so the calls once a month were enough to satisfy her. He was the only person she ever spoke to other than the few words she'd say at the grocery store on her semi-monthly runs into town. Since Frank had died on those roads, she drove as little as possible on them. Not out of fear, because she couldn't care less if she left this nasty world, but out of remembrance. Every time she got behind the wheel, she relived the accident that took Frank from her and hated it. People had done nothing but cause her problems her whole life, and she wanted nothing to do with them. She'd even loathed having to speak to the detective in Albuquerque about Dennis, but he was all she had. The call she received later was nice, though, she had to admit. Not only were they going to start looking for her son; they were also sending two nice gentlemen all the way up to Whispering Grove tomorrow to talk to her about it. Maybe the world was finally changing for the better.

12

"Just outside Omaha my butt! On this map, that hole in the world she lives in is a good 100 miles from there as the crow flies and probably 150 by car!" Sharpe said as he and Greenhill made their way to the airport.

They would land in Omaha at ten in the morning local time, one hour later than it was in Albuquerque.

"Are you kidding me? 150 miles?"

"No, I'm not kidding you, Marcus. I had a heckuva time just finding that burg on the map. Which reminds me, you did remember to bring the directions she gave Cantonelli on how to get to her place, right?"

"Man, do I look stupid to you? Yes, I brought them. Did you remember to bring your badge?" Marcus asked sarcastically.

"Yep. Got it right here," David said proudly, pulling his jacket open to show Marcus he'd mounted it on his shirt pocket.

"Man, put that thing away. Are you crazy? You can't be wearing that thing when we go through the airport metal detector. Put it in your bag," Greenhill said as he looked at Sharpe's new badge, then the road, then into Sharpe's smiling face.

"I will, man. Relax. I just wanted to get the feel of wearing one for a few minutes. Just think of it, Marcus. You and me as cops. Cool, huh? Real badges too. The chief must have a whole drawer full of these. I wonder if he'd let us keep them?" David said, hopefully.

"I don't think so, David. Too risky. Besides, I don't wanna be a cop, even just for today. I hate cops. They've been a thorn in our sides since we were kids. Why the heck would you want to be one?" Greenhill asked, shocked.

"Because, man. Cops can do anything they want and get away with it. One cop can get away with more stuff than you and I do put together. And if they put a bullet in somebody's chest, it's legal!" Sharpe said, trying to convince his friend to see it his way.

"Man, David, sometimes I worry about you. You ever heard of internal affairs? Sooner or later, they catch up with dirty cops, man. Unless you've got a guy like Tony there to cover you. And they don't make any money. Screw that, man. Now put that thing back in your bag."

Sharpe pulled the badge off slowly, looked at it for a moment, then agreed with Greenhill.

"Yeah, you're right, man. We make a lot more scratch than they do and don't have to worry about internal affairs investigations. But it is going to be cool to pose as one just long enough to get into that old lady's house."

"We'll be playing cop longer than that, David. We've got to have her dig out every letter and photo Jeffries ever sent her so we can go through them before we dust her. Tracerio doesn't want anything left there that could even remotely point to Jeffries working for him."

"That's cool. I get to play cop for a little longer. I'm in," Sharpe said through a wide smile.

"Yep, you sure do. Once we take anything that could cause Tony a problem, we have her put the rest of the stuff back where she got it, then we do her, and we're outta there."

"You did bring everything, right?" Sharpe asked, seriously.

"Yep. It's all in my bag."

"What time's our flight outta Omaha back to here, Marcus?"

"Somewhere around eight, maybe eight thirty. We'll be home by eleven."

"Cool. We'll still have time to down a few tonight then."

"That sounds like a plan. I might even drink one to the old lady. As long as it don't have in it what she's gonna be drinkin' in a couple of hours. Know what I mean?" He laughed at that as did Sharpe.

They arrived at the house a little before two and left just after four. Her cause of death would most likely be ruled heart failure as the liquid Marcus had poured into her coffee caused just that. It would be virtually untraceable, even if the body was found long before the week went by that Tracerio wanted to pass before Sharpe posing as Jeffries made a concerned call to the Whispering Grove police. There had been nothing in the few letters and cards Jeffries had sent her over the years that could be construed as strange. All the photos were quite old, so they were no threat either. They laughed as they watched her grab at her chest and fall to the kitchen floor. Sharpe got down on all fours beside her, with his face only a foot from hers, and told her about her son being dead as she lay there writhing in pain. Then he had the audacity to tell her to say hi to God for him as she took her last breath. They left her lying there as they cleaned all the cups, put two of them back in the cupboard, and filled the third halfway with coffee still in the pot. Then Greenhill put her body back in the chair, and David "dropped" the half-full cup on the floor from table height as if she'd done it. Greenhill then pushed her off the chair, and her limp body fell with a loud thud down onto the spilled coffee and broken cup. They wiped down everything they'd touched, careful not to step in the coffee, then left.

Sharpe looked at his watch as they pulled away and commented happily that they would indeed make it back to Albuquerque in time for a few drinks and maybe even a game of pool or two.

Then he started laughing again and said, "Marcus, Marcus. Did you see the look on the old bag's face when I told her about her son? Now that was a Kodak moment." Then he started mimicking her. Gasping for breath and wearing a mock look of terror and confusion, he fell across the seat into Marcus's lap and pretended to die, tongue hanging out. Greenhill looked down at him and started laughing too. The rest of the drive back to Omaha they kept describing the whole afternoon with her to each other, finding humor in all of it. They loved watching people die. It was their favorite part of the job. But it makes one wonder what look they'd have on their face when death should come knocking on their door. They knew they wouldn't live forever but had no plans to check out until they were finished having the time of their lives. As far as they were concerned, they were invincible.

J.J. had worked very hard for the last three days and had been assigned to help others on each of them. He only heard from those people the things he already knew from the newspaper and TV about Johnson's death, though. Rosie was quite impressed with his work ethic, and as J.J. had hoped, had stopped checking in on him already too. After all, in the last three days, he'd done everything that was asked of him and done it well. On top of that, he wasted no time in seeking her out to be assigned more when he'd finished, so Rosie didn't have to watch him.

Tonight was the night he hoped he would once again be within arm's length of Ashland and Covington. That is, if they showed. He wanted to get there early enough to guarantee his table would be empty. He showered and changed clothes quickly when he got back to his little room, then fired up the Harley, and went straight to The Hideaway. His chosen vantage point was already taken when he arrived by what looked to be two businessmen who were capitalizing on the happy hour specials. He sat at the bar, close to the table, in hopes they'd vacate it soon so he could move in. It was the perfect place to listen in from for a couple of reasons. First, because he could keep his back to Ashland and Covington, leaving no chance of being recognized, and second, that by nonchalantly slouching back in the chair, he'd be within a foot of one of their heads, making it that much easier to hear. The men at his table had just ordered another round when Covington came through the door, followed closely by Ashland. It was only six thirty, but he knew these two would most likely be there until last call. He just hoped the guys sitting at the table he wanted weren't going to stay much longer. He glanced quickly at Ashland and Covington, sizing them up as he'd not seen them in over a month. Both looked a little ragged, like something was eating away at them. He knew what it was too—*him*. They took their seats, and the server removed the reserved sign from the table.

J.J. hadn't even noticed that when he'd walked in, he was so focused on the two guys sitting at the table he wanted. He chastised himself silently for missing that little detail as he knew he could afford to miss nothing if he were to get out of this unscathed. He was on his second beer when the two at the table he wanted paid their check and rose to leave. He was poised and ready to slide over as soon as they vacated. He took a quick glance around the room to make sure no one else was eyeing the table as the place was already filling up. He saw a guy at the far end of the bar by the door point it out to his two friends and locked eyes with him for a second. They started to get up, but it was too late for them, and they had been just too far away. J.J. was already sitting and sipping by the time the three of them showed up and stood before him, drinks and napkins in hand. They were also

LEFT NO CHOICE

white-collar types and the leader seemed to take his style of hair and dress right out of GQ magazine, but not his manners.

"Excuse me, guy. My friends and I were on our way over to this table from the far end of the bar as those guys got up and you know it. Why don't you do the right thing and clear out, huh?"

J.J. was not about to give up the seat but also couldn't afford a scene. Handling Mr. Brave and his buddies without causing one might not be possible, but he risked it anyway. He just hoped using his new accent and a deeper tone would keep his quarry at the next table from recognizing his voice.

"Look, *guy*. Not that it's any of y'all's bizness, but I've got three buddies due in here in 'bout twenty minutes. I got here early so's I could git us a table. I'm sorry if that's gonna screw up yer night, but I'm already sittin' here and I've bin told that possession is nine-tenths of the law. Why don't y'all let me buy you a round er two and if y'all er still here when we leave, I'll come git ya, and y'all can have it. How'd that be?"

The smallest and seemingly weakest of the three spoke next, trying unsuccessfully to mock a southern accent in a humorous way.

"Well, that there depends on whether your friends are as big as you are, gringo."

J.J. looked down at the funny guy and said, "Two of 'em's bigger. The other one's just meaner. He'd already be waitin' for the cops to come git him if yer pal there'd talked to him the way he did me. Heck, the last time somethin' like this happened to Buford, two fellers got cut up real bad. Buford got off cause'n it was self-defense, though."

"Then that's settled! A drink on you it'll be!" he said as the three of them laughed nervously, trying to save a little face during their inevitable retreat.

"All right then. 'Scuze me, ma'am. Could you get these fine gents here a round of whatever they're drinkin' on me? I'd surely be obliged."

She did so, and they went back to the other end of the bar. J.J. wondered if they'd be back in a half-hour or so asking where his friends were. But if they did, he'd handle that then. Right now, he had a clear earshot of the conversation that was going on behind him and didn't want to miss a word. J.J. didn't know it, but that little scene actually sparked Ashland and Covington to talk about the Howard Bell murder. After all, he'd been cut up real bad too.

"Man, do you remember how much blood came out of that guy when Dennis smashed his skull with that bat?" Covington whispered to Ashland. It was barely audible through the din of the bar, but J.J. could make out just enough of the words from where he sat to follow along.

"Do I? Huh! Don't you remember? I had to get rid of that suit. The impact sprayed blood all over it, and I was already ten feet away. It was like a big balloon full of blood exploded midair. It was a gruesome sight and one I'll never forget, Tim," George whispered as he raised his glass to his lips.

"You know what bothers me?"

"What's that?"

"Since he made such quick work of Bell, why couldn't he take Blake out. That's what bothers me. If he had, we wouldn't have been in the doghouse at all with Tracerio. In fact, he'd be patting us on the back big time."

Tracerio! Of Course! Who else in Albuquerque but Tracerio could be running that much money through the bank? Nobody. Okay. Now he knew who was behind it, but what was he doing that produced all those millions? Almost as if they were having one conversation, his answer came in Ashland's next comment.

"The doghouse is right. I still don't know that it's past us yet either, my friend. I mean, look at Bell. We took him out because he was skimming a few measly dollars worth of the powder Johnson was making every week off Tony. *A few measly dollars!* And we let a guy slip through our fingers that could actually bring the law down on him? I'm still sleeping with a gun under my pillow in the guest room," Ashland confided.

"You're sleeping in your guest room?"

"Yes. And I'm leaving a mannequin head in our bed to make it look like I'm still in there. I sent Trudy and the kids to her folks for the rest of the summer right after I got home that night. I'm not takin' any chances," George said.

"Those are good ideas, man. I'm gonna do that too. Angela was wondering why Tracy hadn't called. Where'd you get the mannequin head?"

"The novelty shop in the mall downtown. They carry a bunch of stuff like that."

"Great. I'm going to get one tomorrow for me and have Angela take Christine to her folks until I have to fly to Los Angeles because of the transfer."

"Have you already got a realtor out there trying to find you something, Tim?" Ashland asked.

"Not to buy. We talked about it, and she'd rather lease a place for six months while we sell the house here and that will give her time to look around for a nice home in a nice area."

"That's smart. I think I'll call the realtor in Vegas on Monday and do the same thing. Thanks."

"No problem, George. George, check it out. Over your left shoulder. Is that a beautiful woman or what?"

"Oh yeah. She sure is. I wonder if she'd like to join us."

"I'd better do it, George. I have better luck getting them to come to the table than you do, and I sure was better at it than Dennis."

Ashland laughed at this, saying, "That's no lie. He couldn't pick up a woman with a forklift."

J.J. had heard enough. In fifteen minutes, they had brought him almost all the answers he was after. He rose, leaving half a beer on the table, and went to the far end of the bar.

"Gents? Tommy Joe called my cell phone and said Buford got in a fight with a cop on the way over here, so I'm gonna meet him down at the jail and try to bail him out again. The table's all yers," he said and left.

He straddled the Harley and fired it up. While he sat waiting for it to warm itself, a few key parts to the conversation took first position in his thoughts. Ashland and Covington were being transferred soon. That could mean Tony was expanding his enterprise, which J.J. planned to bring down anyway, so that was no big issue. However, it could also mean he was done with them and wanted them as far from him as possible. But why would Tracerio let them live if he was done with them? They had to be huge liabilities. There's no reason for a guy like Tracerio to do that. There had to be something more to their transfers; there just had to be. Then it all clicked. He was putting them in different cities too. That would make it much easier to kill them both without attracting too much attention. He'd most likely wait until they'd been in their new cities for a few months, then do to them what he'd had done to Johnson, Foster, and Bell. Probably on the same night again too. It would be too risky not to. If one heard that the other had been killed somehow, the living one would most definitely run to the FBI for cover, leaving Tracerio's operation wide open and in danger. Yep. He was going to kill them both, and it was going to be on the same night, but J.J. figured he still had at least a few months before he'd have to worry about that. In the meantime, he had to find a way to get information on the daily routine of Tony Tracerio. Tony was a well-known businessman in town and may have been in the public spotlight at one time or another, he thought. The newspapers! Yes! He'd look for stories about Tracerio in all the old newspapers. Maybe they'd shed some light on his routines. So tomorrow after work, he'd just go down to a library close to his motel room.

Michael pushed his plate toward the middle of the patio table and said, "Flo and Ralph, once again, I've gotta say it. You two should open up a restaurant. The food is so good; you'd have people making reservations weeks in advance just to taste it. I love Momma's cooking, but Flo, your casseroles sitting on the same plate with Ralph's barbecued steaks, ribs, and fish? No comparison. But don't tell Momma I said so."

Flo laughed as she took Michael's plate from the table, "Michael, you are so good for my ego! Ralph, take a few lessons from this man. He knows how to charm a lady."

"Hey! That's not fair, Flo. He doesn't have to live with you," Ralph said, smiling.

"See what I mean?" she said as she was walking into the house with a stack of dishes.

Michael and Ralph laughed. Flo was a wonderful wife to Ralph and he was a good match for her. Michael admired their relationship and had said so. He'd actually confessed that they were the reason he'd not found a steady girl yet. None of the ones he'd dated gave him the feeling he knew existed between Flo and Ralph. They walked out to the back wall, each carrying a fresh beer. The air was crisp and cool, and the sunset had been spectacular this late August night, making the ambiance perfectly relaxing and enjoyable. Michael, being a few inches taller than Ralph, peeked over the wall into the next yard to see if Ralph's neighbors were also outside. The yard was empty and the lights in the house few, so Michael assumed they must have gone out for the evening, leaving it safe to talk with Ralph.

"Are they out there?" Ralph asked.

"No. I don't even think they're home."

"Okay, then. Fill me in. I've been going nuts for days. Was the Chief there again? What about Cantonelli?"

"No. Neither one was. Just Tracerio, his son, and a couple of his flunkies."

"What about the library? Anything jump out at you there yet?"

"No, not yet. But I haven't even made it back to the night of the fire. I'll probably get to those editions tomorrow night or Sunday," Michael said after calculating the speed with which he had been able to go through each edition thoroughly.

"Well, I really wish you'd let me help you, man. It would go a lot faster with both of us doing it."

"I'd love to Ralph, but you said yourself you haven't been inside a library in years, and even then, it was to take a report on some punk who'd started a fight in it and ran out. It's better if I just keep chipping away in there. Things will fall into place, soon. I just know it. Besides, you spend enough time away from your family as it is, man."

"I know, I know. One of these days I'll have more time to spend with the kids," Ralph said apologetically.

"You need to make time, Ralph. You know that. Otherwise, by the time you get around to it, they'll be too old for it. A day will come when they'll think having to spend time with you is taking away from time they could be spending with their friends. You told me that happened to you when you were growing up, and it happened to me too. The time is now, man. I've got the other stuff under control. You just take some time out for your kids. You'll thank me for it, I know it."

Ralph was visibly disturbed by what Michael said. Not because he thought Michael was wrong, but because he knew he was right. Ralph had passed up many an opportunity to spend time with his kids over the years for one reason or another and that loss was starting to weigh heavily on his soul.

"You know what, Michael? You're right. Tomorrow I'm gonna go wherever they want, and have fun with them. That'll stun the daylights out of Flo too. She'll probably think I just found out I had cancer and want to make up for lost time," Ralph said, only half kidding.

Michael spewed the mouthful of beer out through his mouth and nose as Ralph said it because Ralph was right. Ralph started imitating Flo's voice the best he could, asking questions aloud as if he were Flo and Michael were Ralph. "Honey, what's wrong? Ralph, is there something you're not telling me about your last physical? Ralph, honey? If something were wrong, you'd tell me, right?"

This made it even harder for Michael to stop coughing long enough to catch his breath.

Flo had stepped out onto the back patio after hearing the coughing and asked, "Ralph? What's wrong?" in the same tone as Ralph's imitation only moments before, causing both men to look at each other, then laugh. Flo waved them off and turned to go inside, but Ralph called to her to come back.

He walked her into the house to tell her of his decision. Michael moved back up onto the patio and sat down, still chuckling. After less than a minute had passed, he heard Flo ask the third question Ralph had impersonated, almost verbatim. Ralph ushered Flo out to the back patio, and Michael told her of the part of the conversation at the back fence that concerned Ralph and the kids. She chuckled, relieved, and Michael said goodnight. The next night, Michael arrived at the library a little after six and began the tedious task of going through the microfiche. That's when a big biker-type guy walked by and sat in the booth next to him. Michael couldn't help but stare a little at this sight. In all the hours he'd ever worked in or spent time in a library, he'd never seen a man dressed like that in one. Michael rose after a minute and walked to an isle behind the man then back by to get a look at what he was doing. As he passed, he saw the same sight that was on his own machine. He wanted to ask the guy what interest he had in old Albuquerque newspapers but thought better of it and resumed his own research. He made it through the papers all the way back to the one with the story of the fire without finding anything. He had been at it for a few hours, and needed a break. He got up to stretch his legs and use the bathroom but didn't turn off the machine.

J.J. had been looking through the Business and Lifestyles sections for any articles relating to Tracerio. He'd not found anything with Tracerio's name even in it yet, let alone an interview with him. He'd wanted to ask around town about the guy but knew that would be risky. This was the only way to get the information he wanted safely, he kept telling himself, so he trudged on. After almost two hours in front of the machine, he'd had no luck. He rose to ask the librarian if there was a way to find articles relating to one thing if he knew the subject but stopped in his tracks after two steps. As he glanced at the machine next to his he saw three words, and they glued his feet in place—*Fire, great,* and *hills.* He looked around yet couldn't see the man who'd been using the machine but knew better than to stand there and read it. He made his way to the librarian's counter, who told him two things. First, there was no way to search Newspaper Microfiche by subject and their computers were not yet capable of it either. Additionally, the library was closing in just a few minutes, so it would be best if he just finished up and came back another day.

He said okay, and wanting no part of a disagreement with the librarian, he apologized as well. The librarian, who obviously was a little nervous having J.J. standing there, relaxed a little at this gesture of submission. She had been scared of him, and it showed. J.J. flashed her a quick smile and told her he'd be out of there in a jiffy. He walked back to his station and collected all the films he'd borrowed. As he was taking them up to her to leave, he passed the man who'd been seated next to him. A big man, he thought. He made eye contact with the man and said howdy as he walked by, then glanced back as he was exiting to get another look, but the man was nowhere in sight. What was he looking for? What did he expect to find? Who was he working for? J.J. decided to follow him from a distance when the man left, hoping wherever he stopped would provide at least a partial answer. He started the bike and pulled out of the parking lot. Normally, he'd have let it warm up for a few minutes before putting it in gear but didn't want to be still sitting there when this guy came out.

To follow him without being noticed, he had to be completely out of sight when the man came out to the parking lot. There were only a few cars left in the parking lot too, which would have made J.J. stand out like a neon light had he not already left. He noticed a short wave radio antenna on one of the sedans as he maneuvered the bike to the exit. The kind of antenna you'd see on a cop's car. He pulled into the gas station on the corner a block from the library and waited. The corner was well lit and this was the only through street giving access to the library, so he pretty much figured everybody would have to come through this intersection on their way home from there. Within a couple of minutes, he saw headlights approaching from the direction of the library. It was him. He started up the bike and eased it into the lane a safe distance behind the car. The car turned left back toward town but J.J. did not follow. It was the car with the shortwave antenna. This guy was a cop. He'd notice a tail too easily for J.J. to risk it, especially one being done by a loud Harley.

J.J. would have to go up and get the Ramcharger to tail this guy with, or buy a cheap, nondescript car. *The little car would work best*, he thought. The Ramcharger sat high off the ground, so it, too, could be easily noticed. Tomorrow was Sunday, his day off at the farm, so he'd visit the used car dealers that were open and buy a decent car for three or four thousand. This would become his surveillance car, he decided, and headed back to his room for the night. On the way, he remembered that the coming week he was scheduled to work four to midnight. He'd obviously have to postpone any surveillance, so he decided to drive back up to the cabin each night and practice one man assault drills each morning. He'd write Joan and Lance again tonight too. Their last letters were bright and cheery, which let J.J. focus on the task in front of him instead of worrying about them. He knew there was a possibility he may never see them again, but he didn't think much about dying. He knew it could actually assist in causing his death. All kinds of guys from all walks of life were in the service with J.J. and it seemed those who kept their fears to themselves are the ones who made it home. Sadly, the ones who kept thinking about and vocalizing the fact that they were afraid to die were usually killed, so those thoughts were kept as far from his focus as possible.

The best of the best did stay focused, so they missed nothing out there. They saw, heard, and thought of everything that the enemy could use to exploit even the tiniest advantage and lived through it because they had stayed attentive. J.J. had constantly kept a healthy portion of paranoia close to the front of his mind when he was in dangerous areas. That was the only way to be sure he missed nothing. It drove many a good man to the verge of insanity out there. He'd seen it. Never taking a single step without your eyes darting all over the area first, never allowing your ears to be lulled by the rain, always straining to hear what was just on the other side of the prevalent sound. Never sleeping the sleep of the content or the relaxed. Yep. Many good men lost their minds out there and ten times that number had almost joined them, including him. But he knew he was going to have to go through it again, because he had been left no choice.

13

"Keith, I'd like you to meet J.J. He started with us last week on my shift and did an outstanding job. I know you'll be pleased with him. He's a good egg, so try not to drive him outta here, okay?" Rosie said as she introduced J.J. to the afternoon shift supervisor, Keith Marsden.

"Hello, J.J. Welcome aboard," he said, hand extended.

"Hello, Mr. Marsden, It's a pleasure to meet you, sir," J.J. said as he shook the outstretched hand.

Marsden hadn't expected this kind of courtesy from a man of this size wearing those kind of clothes. He leaned back a little in surprise and smiled, saying, "Well, now. I haven't been called 'sir' by anybody but my paperboy in years. I'd much prefer it if you'd just call me Keith. okay, J.J.?"

"I told you you'd like him," Rosie said over her shoulder as she departed.

The afternoon shift duties were quite similar to the morning shift. The few changes were only ritualistic ones, so J.J. had no trouble in adapting. Ritualistic because it seemed Keith and Rosie had different ideas about the best way to do certain things and which order they should be done in. As usual, he finished early his assigned tasks and went looking for more when he caught his first glimpse of "the look." A man around six feet tall, dark hair and eyes, wearing that sullen "you people are just pawns in the big game" look, walked by him. Their eyes had only met for a second but that was enough. This guy was no farm worker. J.J. took a few more steps, then turned and watched him walk through a door that led to the outside. The parking lot was on the other side of the compound, so this guy was going somewhere else on the grounds. He thought about following him and started to, when he heard his name.

"J.J.! Lookin' for me?" Marsden said as he stepped toward him from behind.

"Yes, sir," he said as he turned. "I've finished with the things you wanted done and would like to know what you'd like done now, Keith."

Marsden looked at his watch and shook his head in disbelief. "Man! Rosie told me you were fast, but I didn't think she meant that fast. You sure you got it all done, J.J.?"

I think so, Keith. I'd be much obliged if you'd make sure fer me, though."

"Okay. Let's go see," Marsden said with a trace of disbelief.

He'd seen a lot of people come and go because the workloads he gave kept people busy the whole shift. Once in a while, he'd have somebody come up and say they were done with an hour to go before quitting time, but never before with almost three hours left in the shift. He was sure J.J. had missed something altogether or at least had cut corners on some of the tasks. They went back through all the areas, and as he surveyed each, he was becoming more and more a believer in this big hick from Kentucky. No cut corners, no missed assignments, and still three hours to go. This guy was going to make him look really good.

"Okay! Wow! That's the fastest I've ever seen anyone get done in a shift before J.J., and I've been here almost eight years," Keith said in amazement.

Then he walked J.J. over to where he was working and had him help finish what he'd been doing. That took about an hour and with almost two full hours left in the shift, Marsden had run out of things for J.J. to do. He wasn't like Rosie. He didn't allow his shift's personnel to help each other. He felt he knew how much each person could get done in a day, so if they didn't complete their assignments, they were lazy. And if they were lazy, why make others work harder to cover for them? The only reason he'd allowed J.J. to assist him was that this would give him the rest of the shift to watch his other subordinates even closer. Now he'd be able to see which ones were sloughing off and which ones were really working.

"J.J., were you ever in the service?" Marsden asked as he put his arm on J.J.'s shoulder.

"Yes, sir. I was in the navy fer a spell back when I was a yungster."

"Did your supervisor in the navy ever tell you to find something to do that made you look busy just in case an officer walked by?" Marsden asked, leading J.J. to the obvious conclusion as to why.

With a knowing grin, J.J. said, "Yes, sir! If everything was done, he'd have me do that all the time."

"Now why do I believe that?" Marsden said, laughing and shaking his head. "Okay. J.J., you're now on 'find something to do' detail. Once you find something, though, come let me know what it is before you start, okay?"

J.J.'s thoughts went straight to the door that other man had walked through and suggested, "Well, Keith. Now that you mention it, I saw quite a bit of trash around the buildin'. I'd have no problem at all cleanin' that up. Least ways if'n it's okay with you. I'd like to stay busy if I can, Keith. It makes the day go by faster."

"Okay. Grab that rolling trash receptacle over there and come with me."

Marsden led him out the door toward the employee parking lot, which is not what J.J. had been hoping for but brightened when Marsden walked him over to the side of the building.

"Now, once you've finished cleaning up the lot, start down this side and work your way out to the loading docks. Once you've made it there, stop and come find me, okay?"

"Yes, Keith. I surely will," J.J. said, then started picking up papers, cigarette butts, and other pieces of refuse.

Marsden walked back inside, shaking his head and wondering. Wondering if there were any more like him back in Kentucky that worked just as hard. J.J. flew through the parking lot, sweating profusely due to all the bending and the speed with which he did it. It was a great way to work out though, not to mention the fact that when it was done he'd get a closer look at a part of the operation he'd not yet seen. The loading dock. He'd considered not doing such a great job at picking up the parking lot so he'd have more time to survey the loading dock but thought better of it, for a couple of reasons. He didn't want Marsden to find any of his work lacking, for one. The other was because he knew he'd get to do this nightly if he did a good job and that suited him just fine. Soon, he'd cover the whole perimeter of the facility as the trash man, which not only allowed him a closer look at the whole place, it also allowed him to look for security's numbers and locations and if there were any blind spots in their security he could use. He knew they only ran two shifts on Sundays, leaving only the security team there after midnight this Sunday coming up. He'd use his perimeter trash detail to find or make a way in for that night. Then, with a little luck and a lot of care, he'd get a closer look at what was really going on.

It was a beautiful day to have breakfast out on the east patio, Tony thought as he looked out his bedroom window. He walked to the intercom and told the kitchen staff just that, then showered and dressed. His companion had left a little after midnight and he'd slept well. The Jeffries situation was under control now, and in a few more days, Sharpe, posing as Jeffries on the phone, would bring it to an end. Blake and his family had not yet surfaced anywhere, so Tony was quite confident that he'd not gone to the feds. It had been almost two months since he disappeared. Surely, if he were in protective custody Tony would have gotten wind of it by now. *No*, Tony thought, *he'd most likely left the country*, which would be fine with him. He'd never admit it to anyone, though. He wanted to keep the appearance that no matter who crossed him he'd spare no expense in tracking them down and teaching them a lesson.

It was best for his "boys" to believe that anyway. He was spending a great deal of money on this one even though he was pretty sure they'd find nothing. The reason was simple. He knew it would save him a great deal of money in future potential losses if everybody believed they could *never* hide from him for long. Tony Jr. would be joining him for breakfast too. He did so every Tuesday. That should make for a great morning. His son was taking after him in every way, and Tony was starting to notice. They'd discuss openly Tony's thoughts about Blake's disappearance. Tony Jr. would one day inherit control of the empire, so he wanted his son to know all of his thoughts. That included the ones he'd keep secret from the rest of his people.

Breakfast went well, and business was the topic for only a portion of it. He told Tony Jr. to make sure Danbury, Edwards, Cantonelli, Sharpe, Greenhill, and Chief Richter all came to dinner tomorrow night. He wanted to go over with all of them what was to be done by each to help close the book on the Jeffries situation.

Michael had gone back almost three full months and had still not come up with a solid connection between Blake's death and Tracerio. He was now trudging through the paper almost two months to the day before the fire and on one page, found something that made all those hours in the library worthwhile. His memory clicked as he read the stories, angry with himself for not remembering this series of strange coincidences earlier. He didn't see a connection to Blake, but these articles got the wheels in his mind turning toward an answer. Three businessmen all died on the Sunday before this edition came out. One hadn't been found until that Monday afternoon, but all three died on Sunday. All within a couple of hours of each other. One owned a trucking company, one an egg farm that used trucks, and a downtown produce storeowner. Two were ruled accidental and the other a mugging, but all three happened in one night. He read the articles again. He combined that information with the little bit of scuttlebutt he'd heard around the station at that time and started mulling theories over in his head. The most obvious was that Tony had all three snuffed because they had somehow crossed him. Either by refusing to cooperate with him in some way, or by breaching his trust if they worked for him. Michael couldn't tell for sure.

The strangest of the three was the guy who owned the farm. He died of electrocution in a hot tub. And the investigating officer was none other than *Gus Cantonelli*. As Michael read, he could clearly see how much creative license Gus had tossed in about that one. Strong wind? Come on! The guy had been watching TV from that hot tub for years, the article said. He'd have to have been smarter than that. *Jeez*. What's worse is that police involvement ended right there, too. No further inquiry, no autopsy, nothing. Not even after the other two had been found slain on the same night. That fact alone should have caused Chief Richter or the

DA's office to look deeper into the three deaths before closing the book on them. The DA's office. Why didn't they push for an investigation? Does Tracerio have them in his pocket too? Who didn't this guy have on his payroll except him and Ralph Davis? He couldn't wait to talk to Ralph about this one on Friday night. Hopefully, he'd have worked out a few viable theories by then and Ralph could confirm their feasibility or their absurdity then. Once they'd weeded all the potential theories down to a select few, their real undercover investigation would begin.

Michael's heart began to thump hard enough that he could feel it. He knew he was getting closer to shedding light on the hidden world of Tony Tracerio. He'd watch the restaurant again tomorrow night. Maybe some new players would show up there that could help uncover more of Tony's empire.

"Madison County Sheriff's office. How may I help you?"

Sharpe played Jeffries without error on this Friday afternoon. The sheriff was sending someone out to the southwest end of the county to look in on Doris Jeffries even before he hung up. He had given them Jeffries's home phone number to reach him with and was actually sitting in Jeffries's house when he'd made the call. He'd still be sitting there when the call came back from them. He did an okay job at sounding sad and distraught when they told him about his "mom" and gave an even better performance when he asked them the name of a local funeral home that could assist in her wish of cremation. The officer gladly gave the name of the only funeral parlor in Whispering Grove, and passed on his condolences to "Dennis." Sharpe waited an hour then called the funeral home. He gave the man a credit card number and an address to ship the remains down to. He promised to send someone up to collect her personal effects as it was too hard for him to do. The man at the funeral parlor seemed to understand

and agreed. Now all that would be left was the house she owned and Tracerio had plans for getting rid of that. He'd have "Dennis" donate it to the county for whatever use they saw fit, which would close the Doris Jeffries issue once and for all.

Tony had told all in attendance of their roles during Wednesday night's dinner and all handled or would handle their roles without flaw. Now the chief could act like Doris had never called there and everybody was in the clear. Except, of course, if later on the feds did become involved. They'd eventually find out that the missing "Dennis" had resurfaced from hiding long enough to pay his bills and get his mother's remains shipped down to him. They'd surely question that. But there'd be nowhere to go with it. The guys at the bank would say he'd been talking for the longest time about just packing up one day and disappearing. The local cops would have no record of any wants or warrants for him, leaving the feds without a clue or a trail. Case Closed. Tony Sr. needed the chief to remain in place but at times wanted very much to kill him. He saw the chief as a whiner and a bit of a crybaby, and Tony Sr. despised both. If the chief were not so essential, though, pow! In one ear and out the other. Bye. Done. But for the time being, the chief was quite valuable and not expendable, so he put up with it. After the chief retired and moved away, though, when Captain Wilson was the Chief, Tony would get to whack him. And this one he'd do personally.

When Sharpe had finished with his calls, he and Marcus were to stay in the house and look to see if Jeffries had written down the security code for his phone's voice mail. If they found it, they could leave and check for messages from Nebraska the next day. If not, they would have to stay for the night in case another call came in from there. Tony had told them to leave the lights off after dark, so the neighbors wouldn't get nosy. Jeffries had no basement, leaving nowhere in the house to go where they could turn on a light that would not be seen from outside. The afternoon faded into dusk and dusk into night. They'd given up searching hours ago. The moon was full, though, and it shed just enough light in through the glass doors in back of the house facing the golf course for them to see by. They played cards on the coffee table and drank the booze they'd brought with them. If no calls came in by eleven in the morning, Saturday, they could leave. Then Sharpe would call again on Monday to both the sheriff and the funeral parlor.

The call to the sheriff on the premise that he wanted to thank them for their help. The call to the funeral parlor was to make sure all was going according to plan. If the coroner had decided to do an autopsy, the guy at the funeral parlor would let him know that there'd be a slight delay in getting the remains down to him during the call on Monday. The guy at the funeral parlor wouldn't hide the fact of an autopsy from the son of the deceased, so if there was no holdup on Monday, all was well. They both slept in the living room, and the phones had not rung once. They left Jeffries's house at eleven-fifteen Saturday morning.

During his weeklong perimeter trash detail, J.J. had seen a couple of things that deserved further investigation. The security force at the loading dock was armed, for one. If they were just shipping eggs in cartons, what did these guys need the guns for? The second was because of the two types of drivers. One type fit the stereotypical night hauler of perishables to the supermarkets, but the other type looked like highly trained soldiers on a mission. What added to J.J.'s suspicions was that the security guards only showed up while the soldier types' trucks were backed into the loading platform. Then the security force would disappear when another group of normal looking drivers would be waved through to the loading zone. J.J. was pretty sure that could only mean one thing. The powder he'd heard Ashland and Covington talking about was most likely being distributed from here, in the trucks driven by the soldier types. And they were over the road trucks. That meant this stuff was going to places far from Albuquerque. But how were they bringing it in? He'd seen nothing abnormal where incoming supplies were concerned.

He still hadn't been there for the midnight shift yet. He also didn't know what kind of powder those two were talking about. He assumed it must have been cocaine or heroin as those two seemed to be the most profitable powders on the market. But still, it could be methamphetamine. That was another popular powder among the working class. If all went well, he'd know which one soon. He had noticed, too, that there were two men on each of the over the road trucks, and only one in what seemed to be the local ones. Most people would consider this just plain efficiency to have two guys share the driving, but both men in each of the duos were packing heat. He could tell. He thought about following and disabling one of the big rigs on the road, then subduing the drivers so he could get a look in the back. J.J. figured they had special check-in times and codes that he knew nothing about, so should one not report in, the operation might shut down or security might get beefed up, which was almost as bad. Right now, they seemed quite relaxed in their routine, and he wanted them to stay that way. It would be a lot easier for him to get in and look around. He was off this weekend, so he'd drive up to the cabin, load some carefully selected items into the Ramcharger, and drive it back down. Then Saturday night, no, make that real early Sunday morning, like one thirty in the morning, he'd come back and take a shot at getting past security.

"The DA's office too?" Ralph asked, surprised.

"Yep. How else could all this happen and not be followed up on, Ralph? There must be somebody in their office involved too."

"Maybe. But maybe not. They might just take what information they get from the detectives and decide what to do from there. But to be on the safe side, we'd better assume you're right. Jeez, Michael! This thing is getting big. We're gonna need a lot of help to bring this one down. We're gonna need to bring the Bureau in on what we've found soon."

"Soon, yes. But not yet, Ralph. Not just yet," Rhodes said as he watched the river carry a pretty big branch downstream.

"Why not? We've got enough for them to start an investigation. Maybe they can crack one of Tracerio's guys to get the lowdown on the rest of his game. Michael, I'm telling you, man. This is getting way out of our league," Davis said, with a touch of anxiety present in his tone.

"Yeah, Ralph. Maybe they can get one of Tracerio's own to roll over, but maybe not. As far as we can tell, he's never even been suspected of any illegal activity. That in itself says he knows very well how to cover himself. They don't know that we're onto them yet. I think we've still got a little time to fill in some of the blanks before we go to the Bureau with it. If they knew somebody was watching them, there's no way he'd have met with the chief and Cantonelli downtown like that. We've still got time, Ralph. And I want to use it to make as airtight a case against him and his puppets as possible. If he walks, he'll be coming for us."

Michael's last comment hung in the air thick and heavy over them both. Ralph knew he was right and that if Tracerio did walk both of them and their families would become targets. Ralph was a good cop who wanted justice served as soon as possible, but was also a smart man.

"I'm not putting Flo and the kids in Tracerio's sights, man. Okay, I'm in. Keep digging and see what else you can turn up. I just hope we can get enough to the Bureau to put them all away before they get wise to us. Be careful, Partner. Be real careful."

"I am, Ralph, and I will. And Ralph?" Michael asked.

"Yeah?"

"When this is over, I think I'm gonna apply to the Bureau for a job. I get sick to my stomach every time I think of the chief being in bed with Tracerio. I don't know if I can still work for APD after all this. I just don't know," Michael confided sadly.

Ralph sat there and watched his friend for a long moment, then said, "When this is over, I'll go with you."

Both men looked at each other and nodded. Both tried to smile, but neither could. They knew this was a long way from over and their futures as officers of the law were not the only things hanging in the balance of the outcome. Their lives and the lives of everyone they cared about were too.

J.J. watched as the last car pulled out of the main parking lot. He looked at his watch. It was almost one. Security parked in another area of the facility, so once that car was gone, all regular employees were too. He crawled through the hole he'd cut in the fence on Friday night, then pulled his gear through. He was traveling fairly light but was prepared for the worst. One of the two Beretta's had been fitted with a silencer and so had the AR-15 semiautomatic assault rifle. He chose this rifle because it could be easily modified for his uses, and in its original state was a legal weapon. That meant he could purchase it right off the shelf without having to worry about underworld ties. Its predecessor was the M-16, the rifle US troops used in Vietnam, but the AR-15 only held a few of the characteristics of it. The current model of the AR-15 allowed for greater use of accessories and also operated much better under extreme use conditions. The M16 was known for jamming under those conditions in Vietnam and the US had lost a number of soldiers to that flaw. It was a versatile rifle too, which was a necessity to J.J. He could be as deadly with it at eight hundred yards as he could at close range, if his aim was accurate. He carried these three weapons, five throwing daggers, a hunting knife, two flash grenades, and three frag grenades as well as extra clips filled with ammo. To round out his accessories, he had a flashlight, a pair of field glasses, and a bulletproof vest. He was truly ready to step back into the fray.

He traveled the fence line for about one hundred yards, then closed in on the loading dock from its left flank. There were two security guards on the platform itself, and two more on the grounds twenty-five yards to either side. All were carrying rifles. Using his field glasses, he could see another sentry at the corner of the building that faced the entrance, standing deep in the shadows. He'd not have seen that one at all, but the glow of his cigarette was unmistakable. Okay, so the entire building was being watched. He didn't want to engage them on this recon run if he could help it. Even if they didn't find a body for hours, security would be so tight in the future he'd never get in again without a firefight. What's worse is they'd be looking for it then. He had to get in and back out tonight without being seen or leaving a trace, meaning no residual presence. If he was discovered, though, he was prepared to take the whole place down tonight. He made his way around the perimeter to the opposite side of the main building, where there was less light and only one sentry in view. Stealthily, he moved in on the man's position and didn't stop until he was within twenty feet of him. He couldn't get any closer as the underbrush line ended just in front of him.

There was a side door to the main building just a few feet from this sentry's post. J.J. watched him for a few minutes and recognized his routine easily. Twenty paces toward the middle of the building and twenty paces back. The next time the guy turned to walk his twenty paces away from the door, J.J. would slip inside, if it were still unlocked. He'd noticed that the doors were never locked when he checked them while picking up trash along the building and hoped they didn't lock them on Saturday night. He'd also checked for alarms on them and had oiled the hinges on Friday too. His job was cleanup and maintenance, so

Keith had no problem allowing him to lube all the door hinges. The man turned, and J.J. made his move. He got to the door and tried the handle. Bah! They did lock the place down on Saturdays. He moved back into the brush, then away from the building to a vantage point one hundred yards out on a small knoll overlooking the main building.

Tonight's recon mission was now reduced to plotting sentry movements, their shift change times, and devising tactical escape routes for next week. He'd get the key to that door one way or another from the midnight shift supervisor, make an impression, then make a key of his own up at the cabin. Getting the key should be easy enough. All he had to do was tell the midnight shift supervisor that he was lubing the locks and hinges like he'd done for Keith. If he couldn't get them, he'd spring a window on the darkest side of the building and go in that way. The rest of the evenings of the coming week would be spent doing other recon work. He'd tail Ashland on Monday, Covington on Tuesday, and that cop that was at the library reading about the fire on Wednesday. He didn't have to be at work until 11:45 p.m. That left plenty of time to tail the three of them in hopes of getting more answers.

14

Neither Ashland or Covington had gone anywhere that gave J.J. any answers, but he was hoping that the cop would tonight. J.J. waited down the street from the police station in a coffee shop, watching all the cars that came and went from his seat near the window. He'd been there since three and still had not seen the car he saw coming from the library. It was now five fifteen.

He took another sip of his coffee but stopped mid-swallow. The car was now pulling out of the department onto the street. It turned away from J.J., but before the car had straightened out in the lane, J.J. was out the door. He slid behind the wheel of the little Escort he'd bought and headed off down the street. He caught glimpses of the car a few hundred yards in front of him as he weaved through the afternoon traffic. He kept his distance even though he risked being stopped by a light that the cop would make it through. Better to lose him tonight and follow him tomorrow than to be seen, he thought. He followed him out toward the East End of town, then the cop pulled into an apartment complex. J.J. pulled to the side of the street for a full minute before following him in. As he drove through, he caught site of the cop before he saw the car. The man was entering a second floor apartment in a building near the rear of the complex. J.J. drove straight through the complex and out again, turning east on the street. He drove a couple hundred yards then did a U-turn and parked facing the entrance to the complex. All the stores and shops in this neighborhood were to the west, so he figured if the cop did come out again, that's the direction he'd go. He shut off the engine and waited. He was beginning to think the cop was in for the night when he saw a car coming through the gate. Sure enough, it was him.

He fired up the escort and followed from an even further distance now than before. There were fewer cars on the streets, so he'd be easier to notice, which he obviously didn't want to happen. He followed the cop all the way back to the street the library was on, but as the cop made a left, he drove past. He was going back to the library, but why? If he were on Tracerio's payroll, he could get all the information he needed about Blake from Tracerio, thanks to all Tracerio's men inside the bank. If he wasn't on Tracerio's payroll and was looking for clues, he could get all the information he needed at the police station. So what was he looking for at the Library? Then J.J. remembered something that Joan had written in her first letter. She'd told him of being pulled over by a cop on her way out to the freeway. She'd said he was a big black man too. Could this be him? And if so, he must have seen pictures of the family right after the fire, so why weren't Joan and Lance's pictures plastered all over the place as fugitives? Did he ever see the pictures? Could it be that this cop did work for Tracerio and was instructed not to tell anyone he'd stopped her? No, he thought. That didn't make sense. If he worked for Tracerio, he could easily have yanked Joan and Lance out of the car that night and taken them anywhere he wanted. But he let them go, which meant he couldn't be working for Tony Sr. after all. He only saw her as a woman who'd been speeding. But why, then, didn't he blow the lid off it if and when he saw a family picture?

Joan had written that he'd taken not just a good look at her, but at Lance as well. This guy had to recognize them; he just had to. J.J. was now more curious than before. He sat there for almost two hours churning everything over in his mind when he saw the car pull up to the light from the library parking lot. He followed the man downtown. Once there, the cop turned left into an alley. J.J. drove on and glanced down the alley as he went by it. He saw the parked car and the cop on foot going around the back of the building as he was driving by. J.J. drove about a quarter mile, then pulled off into a side street on the right, which was the opposite side of the street the cop had parked on. He exited the car, then began walking on his side of the street back toward the alley the cop had parked in. He glanced down each alley as he got closer to where the cop had parked. He passed in front of *Ciao Bella*, an Italian Restaurant that he and Joan had been meaning to have dinner in for years, but had just never gotten around to doing. He thought of her for a minute as he inhaled the scent of the cuisine. When this was over, he'd make sure they finally ate there once. He glanced at the window to see the hours of operation and noticed it closed early on Wednesdays. He made a mental note of that and kept walking. When he passed the next alley, he saw a figure of a man in it. The man was definitely trying not to be seen too. J.J. had only needed a quick glance to spot him, and assuming the cop wasn't aware he'd been made, J.J. kept walking.

He walked two more blocks, then walked between two buildings on his right. He inched his way forward until he could make out the corner the cop was standing near and sat down. He was in the shadows now too. He sat with his back to the wall and kept his eye focused on the alley the cop was in.

Officer Michael Rhodes hadn't spotted the car until he was already turning into the alley. He'd seen it drive by as he rounded the back corner of the building on foot, then ran up to the street to watch where it went. He saw it turn right, and waited. In almost no time at all, he saw a man walk around that corner toward him. As he drew nearer, Michael recognized him as the same man he'd seen in the library many days before. Michael figured the guy to be a bounty hunter on Tracerio's payroll, so he ran down the alley, past two buildings, and came back up near the street, but hiding in the shadows. He watched the man walk by and was now positive it was the same guy. After the man walked past, Michael ran across the street to the side the man was on and went down an alley. He walked carefully and quietly, weapon drawn, as he moved behind the buildings in the same direction as the man was walking in front of them.

He peeked around the corner of every building back toward the main street before he passed between buildings, and after crossing between three, saw him again. This time, the guy was sitting in the shadows near the front corner of one. He was facing the alley Michael had used to watch Ciao Bella's parking lot. Rhodes stepped back away from the corner and holstered his weapon. He backtracked a few hundred feet to a small side street that led into a residential area behind the shops. He went down it to the next cross street that could take him past the guy's position. He came back up to the main street one block past him, and approached him from behind. He drew his weapon as he neared the corner where the man had been sitting and took a deep, silent breath as he moved to within a step of it. He wheeled around the corner with his weapon pointed in the direction of where he'd seen the man sitting and announced quietly, "Police officer. Don't mo—"

There was no one there. The man was gone. He looked down the street in all directions and saw nothing. He could feel his heart trying to break free from his chest. He inched down the alley, eyes darting everywhere and weapon at the ready, but it was clear too. As he made his way back up to the street, he heard something behind him. He turned and saw what looked like the silhouette of a man kneeling at the corner of the building. He announced himself as an officer again, louder this time. The figure didn't move. He stepped slowly toward it with the business end of his pistol leading the way. As he got closer, he could see that it was not a man at all but a few bags of trash piled together. He lowered his weapon and took a couple of deep breaths. This was the closest he'd ever come to gunplay and it scared the breath out of him. The guy was still out there somewhere. That was for sure. He checked the alleys to both sides, then made his way back to his car.

He took note of everything as he walked, feeling all of his senses peaking at once. He rounded the corner by the car and checked the alleyways behind it. Nothing. He must have spooked the guy, he thought, as he lowered his weapon and holstered it while he walked back to the car. He took one last look in both directions as he opened the car door, and seeing nothing abnormal, got in. He fired up the engine and had put his hand on the shift lever when he felt something against the back of his head.

"Don't move. All I want is information, then I'll be gone," came the voice from the backseat. Rhodes had been so busy looking around the car for this guy he'd never thought to look *in* the car for him.

"What kind of information?" Michael said as his right hand moved slowly to his holstered weapon.

"Before I ask, why don't you put both of your hands up on the wheel where I can see them, so you don't do something that we'll both regret, okay?"

Michael moved his hands away from the holster and up onto the dash. He thought quickly and rationalized that if this guy had been sent by Tracerio, he'd want to get all kinds of information before he offed him, which gave Michael some time. Right now, though, the best thing he could do would be to follow instructions to the letter, so the guy would relax a little. Once he had, Michael would take a shot at getting out of there.

"Okay. No problem. But do you know who you're mugging, pal? I'm Albuquerque PD, and you might want to think about it a little more before you go through with this," Michael said, hoping to throw the guy off the track, to no avail.

"I said I wanted information, not money. If I get it, I'll be on my way and you won't see me again. If I don't, well—"

Michael could feel the thing pressing harder into the back of his head and asked, "What do you want to know?"

"Good. Maybe there can be a happy ending to this for both of us tonight. Turn off the engine. Left hand. Good. First, I want to know your name. Simple enough?"

"Rhodes. Michael Rhodes. I'm an officer for Albuqu—"

"We've already been through what you do and who you do it for, so let's not cover the same ground twice. Next question. Three months ago, a fire took a man's life in Great Hills. Were you on duty that night?"

"Yes, I was," Michael acknowledged inquisitively.

"And did you go to the scene of the fire that night?"

"Yes. Who are you? And why do you care wha—"

"I told you, I'll ask the questions. Then, maybe I'll answer a few of yours. Maybe. Next question. What were you doing just before you went to the fire? Think carefully now, because the wrong answer here could bring our little meeting to a quick end."

Michael remembered quite clearly what he was doing, but why did this guy care? Tracerio couldn't possibly know about him stopping the Blake woman unless Ralph told him, and Ralph Davis would die before he'd tell Tracerio that. Unless Tracerio had Flo and the kids. Michael started to get angry. Real angry.

"What have you done to Ralph and his family, you lowlife scumbag?" Michael barked.

"I don't know who Ralph is, so why don't we make that the next question, huh?"

"My partner. And you can cut the 'I don't know' crap because we're both smarter than that. Now what have you done to him and his family?"

J.J. began to believe that this man was sincerely worried about his partner, so he took a shot in the dark and went for broke.

"Listen to me. Listen to me! Your partner has no idea who I am and I couldn't care less about him. He's probably watching TV behind a can of beer as we speak! Next question! Did you stop a lady and her kid just before you went to that fire?"

"Man, you're full of it! The only person that knows about that other than me is my partner. So you go tell Tracerio he's goin' down. We've already sent everything off to the Bureau, so he's done! Now the only way you're gonna be able to save your own hide is to hand over the weapon and help us bring him down. You don't do that and you're goin' down with him. Now give me the gun!" Michael yelled.

"You're wrong. You and your partner aren't the only two who know about it. She was there, remember? And you also think Tracerio's behind this somehow?"

Michael thought for a moment. Who else could know? And who was this guy if he wasn't one of Tracerio's hoods? "Correction. We know Tracerio is behind it. I already told you, that's why we've already sent everything off to the Bureau."

"Everything? What about stopping the lady and kid? Did you tell them that?"

"No, only my partner knows I saw them. That's what made me start this investigation. Obviously, you already know I saw them that night, so let's cut the bull! I'm not answering any more of your questions until you've answered these two. One, who are you? And two, how do you know about that?"

J.J. was sure now that this cop was not involved with Tracerio and was lying about going to the FBI. If he had already taken whatever he had to them, he wouldn't still be snooping around in the library. J.J. decided then and there to trust this cop with almost everything.

"Okay. Fair enough. I know about it because she told me you stopped her, and she told me because she's my wife," J.J. said, letting it hang in the air until Michael grabbed on.

"Y-y-you can't be. He's dead. He died in the fire. So cut the bullsh—"

"The guy who died in the fire was Dennis Jeffries, not Jonathan Blake. I worked with him at the bank. He and two others were sent to my house that night to kill me and my family, but it went bad. I was ready for them. The other two split, and I took Jeffries out before he could do it to me," J.J. said impatiently. "Now I'm gonna venture a guess here, Officer Rhodes," J.J. continued as he pushed his finger a little harder into the back of Michael's head, "I got the feeling you've known all along that there was something wrong here. But you don't know whom you can trust in your own department. That's why you didn't tell anybody but your partner about stopping my wife. Right or wrong?"

"Okay. So?" Michael said sarcastically.

"Why do you think we didn't come to the department in the first place, huh? Could it be that we didn't know who to trust either? Let me take you back a bit further, Michael. Two months before the fire, three men died. All on the same night. All three were local businessmen. Do you remember that?"

Michael was stunned, and his voice couldn't hide it. "Y-yes. I remember. Why?"

"Because the next day, I saw an e-mail from my boss at the bank to his, about all three of them. It went something like this: 'Jack. Three for three. Confirmed. One not yet found, but his Bronco is sitting at the bottom of a cliff.' Then I read the colorful findings by your pals in the paper. That's when I realized I couldn't bring what I knew to the police, because for all I knew, it was cops that had killed them! So I started checking into a few things on my own and found out the bank was being used to launder millions of dollars. That's when they caught on to me and tried to have me and my family killed too."

J.J. took a breath, calmed down a notch, and continued. Michael listened to every word.

"Here's the deal, Officer Rhodes. You saw me tailing you, so I had no choice but to have a heart to heart with you tonight. If you were working for Tracerio, well," J.J. hesitated, then went on, "let's just say I'm glad you're not." And with that, J.J. pulled his finger from the back of Michael's head and sat back in the seat. He noticed that all the windows were fogging up.

Michael felt the pressure disappear, then looked in his rearview mirror and saw that J.J. had sat back, so he spun around in the seat.

"Okay. Let's say I forget the fact that you held a gun to the back of my head for a minute, and that you threatened to kill an offic—"

He stopped mid sentence as J.J. held his right hand in the shape of a gun, looked at it, then shrugged his shoulders.

"You mean to tell me you don't even have a weapon?" Michael asked, shocked, and somewhat embarrassed.

"Now, Michael. I don't know that I'd say that," J.J. answered, glancing down toward his knees.

Michael rose up a little more so he could see over the seat, and there in J.J.'s left hand, still poised against the back of Michael's seat, was his hunting knife.

"Officer Rhodes, I've already found some things out that could start the ball rolling for the FBI, but I don't want to just get it rolling. I want no chance left for these guys to walk when it's over. I'd be putting my family's lives in more danger than they are in now. So I've got to keep going until either they're all dead or I have so much proof that Tracerio and his thugs won't even be allowed bail. Does that make sense to you?" J.J. asked with all sincerity.

This man still presented an immediate danger to him and did until he sheathed the long blade. Michael began to smile and his smile turned into a forced chuckle as he said in return, "You know, Mr. Blake, you sound like me talking to my partner. I told him the same thing a few nights ago at dinner. Now why don't you come on up to the front seat and we'll go somewhere a little safer to talk, okay?" Michael offered.

J.J. sat there considering how much to trust this man and the fact that he hadn't told anyone about stopping Joan was, again, the clincher. He flipped the knife to his right hand and sheathed it. When he looked up again he was staring down the barrel of Officer Rhodes's service weapon.

"Okay, dirtbag. Blake had blonde hair and blue eyes. The hair you could dye, but your eyes are brown. Now just who are you?" Michael asked with a deadly tone.

"Contact lenses. Brown contact lenses. Watch," J.J. said as he slowly put his hands to his face and popped both out.

When he looked at Michael again, they were the eyes Michael had seen in the photo. Michael lowered the weapon and repeated his offer.

"Okay, Mr. Blake. I believe you now. Come on up front and let's get out of here."

J.J. moved to the front and Michael started the car, saying, "Man, have I got a lot of questions for you. I hope you've got a lot of time."

J.J. looked at his watch and responded, "Some. I don't have to be at work until 11:45."

"Work? Where are you workin'?" Michael asked as they pulled out onto the street.

"You remember the guy that died in his hot tub?" J.J. asked.

"Yeah. Johnson. Fred Johnson. Right?"

"Right. And do you remember what business he owned?"

Michael thought for a few seconds, then it came to him. "A farm. Some kind of poultry farm."

"An egg farm. That's where I'm working. I figure if Tracerio had him killed, they must have been involved together and the best place to start looking was the farm."

"Mr. Blake. Let me ask you someth—"

"Officer Rhodes, it's J.J. now. J.J. Tracker, actually. Not Mr. Blake. Jonathan Blake will remain dead until this is over, okay?"

"Yeah, okay. Sorry, *J.J.* And call me Michael. Anyway, why were you in the library? What were you looking for in there?"

"You know what's funny, Michael? I wanted to ask you the same question."

The volley of questions from each to the other began, which got them nowhere fast. J.J. finally offered to bring Michael up to speed on all that he knew from the beginning, and Michael could do the same, then both could ask any questions they still had. This worked quite well and both were almost fully informed by the time that J.J. had to leave for work. J.J. left out Joan and Lance's escape path, current location, and the part about where he'd be on Saturday night though. They agreed to meet again on Friday evening at the park down by the Rio Grande, and Michael would bring Ralph. J.J was tempted to go back to Ciao Bella's and end it with Tracerio then. But by the time Michael had told him why he had come downtown, Tracerio's meeting had probably broken up. *That's okay*, J.J. thought. He still had next Wednesday.

The three men met on Friday as planned; all with good intentions, but two full-blown eruptions between J.J. and Ralph had to be stopped by Michael. Ralph kept insisting that J.J. turn himself and his family over to the Bureau and J.J. would have none of it. He gave Sgt. Davis the same reasons he'd explained to Michael, but it was falling on deaf ears. Ralph threatened to arrest him on the spot and take him in and that's when the heated argument really escalated in the park by the river.

"Ralph, you try it and I'm afraid we're gonna be enemies," J.J. said, shaking with anger and disgust. "I couldn't care any less about the APD or the FBI than I do now. You can't protect my family from Tracerio, and you know it! I won't put them in harm's way and I am not gonna make them live like prisoners in the witness protection program! Do you understand me?"

"Then you understand me! I will not risk my career or my family's future over this! Michael and I were going to dig until we got enough evidence together for the Bureau to be able to take over and guess what? You're it! With everything you've got, they can take him down. Now I want you to get your—"

"I don't care what you want, you ignorant pr—"

"Ralph. Ralph!" Michael yelled while grabbing his partners shirt with both hands, "*Listen to me!* If you were in his shoes, would you go into witness protection? Would you? Would you subject Flo and the kids to that kind of life? Would you?" Michael asked, almost screaming.

Ralph sat looking at his partner for a long moment while Michael's question sunk in and hit home. Not only no, but absolutely no; he wouldn't put Flo and the kids through that.

He looked over at the man on the other side of the table, took a breath, and said, "Mr. Blake, I'm sorry. I see your point and Michael's. I wouldn't let them do this to my family, so I shouldn't let them do it to yours, or what kind of man does that make me? All of our collective lives are hangin' out on this one guys. Make no mistake about that. And not just ours; our families, too."

J.J. softened his tone and his demeanor and aligned with the man, saying, "Sgt. Davis, if our positions were reversed, my first thought would be the same as yours. Protect my own family first. I'm sure of it. And look. That's what I am doing. But I didn't start this, and I'm not a criminal. I'm an honest family man who's trying to assist the real law enforcers to bring the real criminals to justice. One way or another."

Both Rhodes and Davis knew what that meant, and Ralph was getting angry again.

"That's called vigilante justice and in this country, it's illegal, Mr. Blake. So now you're asking me and my partner to be willing participants in an illegal activity. That ends our careers and my kids' futures. How can you ask us to do that?" Ralph asked through seething teeth.

"I can't and I won't. If you don't want to help me, fine. I understand. Just don't hurt my family anymore than Tracerio already has. In other words, you forget about ever meeting me and you'll not see or hear from me again. Then, when it's over, you do what you have to do. Just don't do it until this is over."

"I don't know. I don't like this one bit, Blake. I want Tracerio, the chief, and the rest of them as bad as you do. But your way means Michael and I could go down because of crimes you commit. What's fair about that?"

"Answer me this, Ralph. Could you live with yourself if you sacrificed my family's lives when you didn't have to? I could see how easy a decision that would be if I was like Tracerio or your own chief of police, but for God's sake, I'm not like them, and you know it! All you have to do is walk away right now, and I swear I'll never speak of this meeting to anyone. Then your problem is solved. If you don't know I exist, how can you be an accessory to anything I do?"

Silence filled the air for a full thirty seconds as all three men's minds were completely entangled in their own opinion.

Michael broke the silence by saying, "There are three of us trying to accomplish the same thing now, Ralph. It's got to get easier from here. That is, if we all stick together. If you feel it's too big a risk, then I'll understand, man. We've been able to count on each other since we met. So if you choose to stay out of it, you can count on me not to say anything to you or about you where this thing is concerned, okay?"

"Michael, do you realize what could happen here? Have you thought about that? After Tracerio, the chief, Cantonelli, and the rest of them all go down? You'll be next. You've told me many times that your whole life you've wanted to be a cop. Nothing else. Have you even considered the fact that when this is over, you'll be thrown off the force and maybe go to prison? You'll never be a cop again. Your life's dream will be gone. Are you really gonna sit there and tell me that you're willing to throw everything you've ever wanted away?"

"Yes, Ralph, I am. This is the reason I became a cop. To help people that are being terrorized or abused and to bring justice to those who do it. I have to do this, man. Don't you see? If I don't, I become like them. A man who lets others suffer so my life is easier. That's all they do, man. Make others suffer so they can live easier. That's not what I'm about, Ralph, and it never will be. If I lose my badge or end up in jail over this, I'll at least know I did it for the right reason. That I can live with. Do you understand?"

Michael had not expected Ralph to act as he had this night, and from what J.J. had heard about Ralph, he hadn't expected it either. Ralph sat in silence, staring at the ground in front of him, thinking. Both Michael and J.J. looked at each other and then at Ralph, waiting for him to answer. Ralph stood, walked down to the river's edge, and stared out into the night. The choice was not an easy one for Ralph. Flo and the kids meant more to him than anything in his life, and Michael was a close second. He just couldn't let Michael throw his career and maybe his life away if he had anything to say about it, but he knew he wouldn't convince Michael of that tonight. If Blake would just turn what he had and himself over to the Bureau, Ralph, Flo, the kids, and Michael would all be safe from harm and prosecution. Blake's family would probably be okay too, for that matter. But Blake wouldn't do that. He'd made that clear enough. And Michael wouldn't stand by and let Ralph arrest him tonight either. Michael had made that clear too. Ralph needed more time to sort this one out. A lot more time.

"Okay," he said as he turned and walked back to the table, "I'm in. But, Blake, if I catch you doing anything, and I mean anything, that is against the law from this day on, I've gotta take you down. And, Michael, I want your word that you'll back me up on that. You give me your word that you'll help me take him down if we catch him breaking the law, and I'll stand with you. For now. Do we have an agreement?"

J.J. knew this meant Ralph would be no asset. He'd probably take him in right then if he could have, J.J. thought. Ralph Davis was not to be trusted after tonight, and this made J.J. quite angry. But J.J. didn't want him to go straight to the FBI from here either, so he had to keep his anger in check.

"I understand, Officer Davis. I don't plan on breaking any laws, if I can help it. So I guess there won't be a need for you to 'take me down.' I'm almost ready to go to the FBI anyway, if that helps ease your mind any," he said even though he was lying. But he figured this statement might keep his *Judas* from going there first.

"It doesn't. Going now would ease my mind. Anything else just won't do it, but we'll see what else you come up with," Ralph said angrily, then looked at Michael.

"Well, Michael? Can you give me your word?"

Michael sat there, looking into the face of his partner, but the eyes were not Ralph's. He'd never seen this much anger in Ralph before. He locked gazes with J.J. for a long moment, then looked back at Ralph and spoke.

"Yes, Ralph. You have my word. If we learn that he's broken the law, I'll put the cuffs on him myself."

When he'd finished, he looked with a stone face back at J.J. to leave the impression of complete seriousness hang in the air along with his words. He only hoped that the look would be convincing to Ralph. This was the first time he'd ever lied to his partner, and he prayed it would also be the last.

"Good. We all understand each other. Mr. Blake, I really hope you make it to the FBI before I put you together with any criminal activity. And for the record, I do believe the one death you've already caused was in self-defense, so I don't consider it one. But make no mistake about how I feel, because I'm not kidding one bit. I'll take you down without a second thought. If anything else happens that should be handled by the police, you bring it to us, and we'll see that justice is dispensed. You got that?" Ralph said, seething again.

"Yeah, I got that. Good night, gentlemen." J.J. said curtly as he turned and walked toward the Escort.

Michael watched him all the way to his car then said, "Ralph, I'll be right back," and ran over to J.J.'s car.

J.J. rolled down the window and Michael looked in and said quietly, "I'm sorry, J.J. I've never seen Ralph like that. He's a good man even though it didn't seem like it tonight. Meet me here next Friday night at this time. He and I will be here about an hour before that, which will give me a chance to talk some sense into him. Then we can share what we know and hopefully close the books on this whole mess soon. Okay?"

J.J. didn't like having to deal with Ralph anymore, but getting inside information from the cops seemed a necessity, so he agreed. With a few conditions.

"Okay. I'll be here. But I need you to do me a favor, Michael."

"If I can, sure. What is it?"

"Since we never got around to telling Ralph about where I'm working or anything else for that matter, I'd rather he didn't know. It will make it harder for him to pin anything that happens in those areas on me. Okay?"

"Okay, J.J. After the way he acted tonight, I wasn't about to tell him anything anyway. You do what you have to do, but be careful. If he doesn't know it was you, we have nothing to worry about, and I won't have to break my word to my friend."

J.J. looked up at the saddened face and eyes of the man leaning on his window and knew this man meant what he said. He would break his word to Ralph in the name of justice.

"Okay. Next Friday then," J.J. said as he put the escort in reverse.

"Hey! How about Wednesday night in the alley down the street from Ciao Bella's? I'll be there at eight thirty. Then you and I can talk alone."

"I can't. I have to work at the farm all week. Next Wednesday works."

"Okay, I'll see you next Wednesday then."

Michael watched as J.J. pulled out and drove away, then walked back down to the table where Ralph was waiting.

"Michael. You're doing this wrong, man. All wrong. This guy is bad news for us. You need to look seriously at what you're doin' here, pal. If you can convince him to go to the Bureau now, everybody wins, including him. They'll take care of him and his family. What happens if Tracerio finds them and there are no federal agents there to protect them, huh? Have you thought about that?"

"Yes, I have. He said his wife and son are in hiding somewhere that Tracerio will never look, and I believe him. Not to mention that they've already stayed out of sight for months and that's no easy task. Especially when Tracerio's got the chief and the guys at the bank in his pocket. He told me she'd stay in hiding until he contacts her and tells her it's safe. He said the only other way she'd surface is if she doesn't hear from him within ten days of their last contact. Ralph, this guy's no dummy, man. Tracerio's not gonna find her. No one is. Not until she steps back out on her own."

"But what about this guy's game? You know what he meant tonight. He's planning to play judge, jury, and executioner where Tracerio is concerned. We can't knowingly let that happen. He's already admitted to killing one guy. What's to keep him from doing it again?"

"He could have killed me Wednesday night and no one would have known it was him, Ralph. Look, we're the only two that know he's still alive except his family and Tracerio's people. You would never have known it was him, if I had been killed. You'd have assumed it was Tracerio's handiwork. Ralph, he just wants to collect enough hard evidence on the guy to make sure he won't walk. He's not about to kill again unless it's in self-defense. I'd bet my badge on it."

"You already are, Michael. You already are. And then some."

They sat there talking for a while longer, but neither man budged in the slightest toward the other's opinion. When they got back to Ralph's, Michael didn't even go inside. He went straight to his car and drove off. Ralph went inside carrying a heavy heart, torn in two by the fight between his feelings of loyalty and his feelings of survival. The survival of his family and his friend. He knew the only way he could save himself, his family, and his partner from certain ruin was to grab Blake the next chance he got and take him to the Bureau himself. That meant his friendship with Michael would take damage, maybe even irreparable damage. But with all the lives involved at stake, it was a loss he was willing to accept. He walked past Flo without a word, grabbed a beer, and went straight out to the back patio. Flo had never seen Ralph look or act this way, so she followed him.

"Honey, what's wrong?" she asked, frightened.

Ralph didn't answer, which elevated her fear, so she asked again, "Ralph? What's wrong? Talk with me."

The only response he gave this time was to lock gazes with her for a few seconds, but then he looked back out into the night and took another sip of brew. Flo was now almost to the point of panic. She knelt beside him, put her hands on his arm, and spoke again. This time her voice was shaky and broken.

"Ralph. You're scaring me. Don't you dare shut me out. I can't take this, honey. I really can't. I've never seen you this way. Did something happen out there tonight? Where's Michael? Is he all right? Ralph? Talk to me!"

Ralph looked slowly over into Flo's eyes then away again, and this time did speak.

"Yeah, Michael's okay, baby. He's okay," he said as he brushed her cheek softly with the back of his fingers. "But some things did happen out there tonight."

Ralph didn't tell her specifics but confided in her enough for her to understand that Michael's career and their friendship were definitely in jeopardy. She pushed him for more information, but in the end, the only other response she would get was, "Flo, I can't tell you any more than that, okay? I just need some time to decide how I should handle it. You and the kids are my life and I will do whatever it takes to keep you safe, even if it means going against Michael's wishes. Just trust me, Flo. Please? Just trust me?"

She looked deep into his eyes searching for answers that would not come. Finally, she put her arms around him and her head against his chest as her tears began to fall and said, "Okay, Ralph. I do. I do. I love you so much. Just tell me everything will be all right and I'll believe you. Can you tell me that, Ralph? Will everything be all right?"

He pulled her head tighter into his chest. She felt his chest rise as he inhaled long and deep, then fall again as he exhaled just as slowly. He started running his fingers gently over her hair and said in as convincing a tone as he could muster, "Yes, honey. Everything will be all right. Everything will work out just fine, don't you worry."

He comforted her there for a few more minutes, then rose and took her hand. He guided her down the hall, closed the bedroom door, and pulled her tight to him on the bed. He held her there until she drifted off to sleep, but sleep would not come to him until the wee hours, and even then it didn't last long. He woke at four and slipped off the bed. He walked to her side and looked down at her, then reached over and gently pulled his half of the blankets over her fully clothed form. He knew what he had to do, but knowing only made it harder to face. He left the room quietly and made his way to the back patio.

Michael's night was no different than Ralph's. He too had watched the sun make its entrance into this Saturday morning, but no promise of renewed hope came with it. Michael regretted introducing Blake to Ralph. He never thought to consider that Ralph's reaction would have been one of total self-preservation. Ralph had always shown himself to be above that. But even knowing this was not enough to lift the weight from his heart or his mind. His friend and partner wanted to take the quick and easy way out, no matter what the cost was to an innocent family. Michael began to feel sick to his stomach again, so he reached for the bottle of Pepto that was on the table beside him. He wasn't sure how much time Ralph was willing to give Blake to bring down Tracerio, but he was beginning to think it wouldn't be enough. He sat on the edge of his bed contemplating everything he could say to Ralph that might turn him around, but the more he thought, the more he realized everything had already been said. The clock was winding down on J.J., and there wasn't a single thing he could do about it where Ralph was concerned. That left only one option. He'd have to spend as much time as he could helping J.J. Even if that meant risking his badge and his life.

15

Word of J.J.'s dedication to a job well done had made it to Pete Christianson, the midnight shift supervisor. J.J. had no problem getting the key to the building from him for his door maintenance routine.

He used the impression of it to file the blank he'd bought and tried it in the door on Wednesday night. It wasn't a perfect fit, but the tumblers did turn after he'd jiggled it around a bit. He made a few minute adjustments to it and tried it again on Thursday. This time, it was perfect. He drove back up to the cabin at one, Saturday morning after his shift ended to get some rest and collect his gear. He woke around three in the afternoon and spent the rest of the day going over his plan. He knew there had to be a somewhat hidden entrance to the powder room behind the one door, and that it was most likely guarded by security cameras and armed personnel. Cameras didn't bother him although he'd seen none as he could disable those with one round each from the silenced Beretta. It was the armed personnel that had to be neutralized that caused him concern. During his earlier recon trip, he'd made note that all the lights in the main building had been shut off after the final person exited. This would make it easier for him to move around once he was inside and could help solve the problem of how to neutralize any threat. Since he'd be in the main building alone, he could use a dental mirror under the door to see what security measures, if any, were in the corridor on the other side.

He'd looked closely each time he'd seen the door opened and had not seen any cameras there either. J.J. concluded that this operation's security measures were limited to armed personnel and that made things much easier for him. He could eliminate them as he went and didn't have to worry that someone deep inside was monitoring and able to sound an alarm. He took with him the same gear as before, with a few additions. He now carried a gas mask and scuba diver's sized bottle of carbon monoxide. In fact, he kind of looked like a scuba diver. The bottle was heavy and somewhat cumbersome, but it was necessary. It was the only way he could think of to make sentries on the other side of closed doors drop without gunfire. He knew they wouldn't hear it being dispensed through the rubber hose J.J. had attached to it. He also knew they couldn't detect any smell in the air. They'd just breathe it in and pass out before they knew what was going on.

J.J. also assumed the place had never been hit before, so there might not even be guards on duty inside. The security force might be limited to just the sentry's outside the building, which would make J.J.'s mission to shut the powder room down an easy one. The guards outside wouldn't realize something was wrong until J.J. was safely out again and by then it would be too late to save the facility. Since he'd heard Ashland say Johnson was making the powder they'd killed Bell over, he'd done a little more research to narrow down what kind. It was easier to deduce than he'd originally thought it would be. Cocaine was out simply because it was from the Coca plant and there was no way that would grow in the US, and heroin was out because Ashland had said

LEFT NO CHOICE

Johnson was making the powder. That only left one other. Crystal meth. His research had indicated that many of the ingredients for making crystal meth were highly volatile, especially phosphorous. The military had used it a great deal in Vietnam to make incendiary weapons. J.J. had used those weapons himself on combat missions, so he knew a little about its potential dangers but was by no means an expert.

He'd read that there were two types commonly used when making methamphetamine—hypophosphorous and red phosphorous. Hypo was only a nickname used by cops and criminals alike for the less expensive kind, and the name had no scientific significance whatsoever that he could see. It was used by those who could not get their hands on the red as well as those who just couldn't afford it. Hypo was quite a bit more dangerous to work with. Most chemists would leave their lab once they'd introduced the phosphorous into the mixture due to the risk of explosion. With hypo, they always left. The only way to know if you'd added just the right amount of hypo was if the building was still standing after the chemical composition had passed its critical stage. Red phosphorous could cause the same result, but the room for error was much greater.

J.J. figured Tony would opt for the red for obvious reasons. Not only could he afford it, but also it would take one huge mistake by the chemist to blow the lab apart. This worked to J.J.'s advantage. All he'd need to do is pour a substantial amount of extra phosphorous into the mix and leave. It would act as its own time bomb. Without a great amount of added cooling for the spiked composition, the additional phosphorous would heat to a super critical state and explode with tremendous force. The force would definitely level the lab, maybe even the whole farm. The hard part was knowing just how much phosphorous to spike it with. Too little and the lab may just need cleaned up, too much brought a series of other problems. J.J. wanted to destroy the lab, but not the farm. There were a lot of honest people employed there that would be out of work if it went up, let alone the fact that Tony would surely see it as a hit instead of a chemist error if the explosion was that powerful. It would take several minutes for the composition to reach super critical too, which gave J.J. plenty of time to make his exit. The force's strength was the only variable he couldn't control with certainty. If anyone died in the explosion, so be it.

They were scumbags in his mind anyway, so he wouldn't lose a moment's sleep over them. Besides, any deaths as a result of the explosion could only weaken Tracerio's forces. J.J.'s thought on that was a simple "works for me" and actually wished he could corral them all in there before he blew it sky high, especially Tracerio and the chief. He wasn't worried about a big police investigation. His only real concern was being able to go back to work after he destroyed the lab. He wanted to work there at least another week, then tell his boss that he'd been offered another mining job back in Kentucky and that he had to leave immediately. Then no one would suspect him. If he just disappeared or quit immediately, one of his supervisors may say something in passing to the wrong person, and J.J.'s cover could be compromised. Tracerio would definitely want a full description of any employee of the farm that left the day after the lab went up. Even if the explosion in the lab could be kept under wraps, the timing of that coinciding with an employee's departure threw up all kinds of red flags.

He had to make sure he was back to work on his scheduled day unless the farm went up with the lab or he'd finished bringing the curtain down on the whole enchilada. He was going into his four days off in a row sweep, so he didn't have to be back to work until Wednesday morning. Still, he doubted seriously that he could bring Tracerio's whole operation down by then. He finished pulling his gear through the fence at 1:16 a.m. He mounted the carbon monoxide canister to his back and worked his way around the perimeter to the side door. The going was a lot slower and

LEFT NO CHOICE

more difficult carrying the heavy bottle, but he arrived at the last line of underbrush nearest the building without incident.

The sentry was not the same man as he'd seen there the week before. This man was much smaller. He took twenty-three paces to reach the same spot as the other man who had made it in twenty. That would give J.J. an extra second or two to get into the building than he had before. He was glad about that. He needed all the breaks he could get, having to lug the bottle with him through the door. He had more than enough time to get in while the sentry walked away from the door. In fact, he'd already taken two steps inside before the man reached his pivot point. He moved through the main building in the dark, being careful not to awaken the sleeping chickens. He got to the secured door and quietly removed his load. He looked under the door and saw that lights were on somewhere on the other side, but there were no feet visible in the corridor. He took out the dental mirror and slipped it under the door. Angling it around, he was able to see the ceiling above the door and there were no cameras present.

He tried the door, and as he fully expected, it was locked. He grabbed the key he'd made and tried it. No luck. J.J. hadn't expected it to work on this particular door as this area was off limits to all but selected personnel. He pulled the lock picking kit from his pack and went to work. One of the things J.J. had done in his spare time was buy a half dozen different lock assemblies from a hardware store. He practiced picking each of them over and over to improve his skill, and now, he'd see if all that had paid off. It took quite a while, but he was finally able to turn the last of the two, the deadbolt. The doorknob's lock had been much easier and went much quicker. Slow and methodically, he made his way down the twenty-foot corridor, peeking with the dental mirror into the windows of the offices on both sides before advancing to the next. There were four offices total, two on each side. The light he'd seen, though, was coming from just one of them. The one farthest from his entry point into the corridor, on the inward side of the building. He heard sounds inside. The sounds of people talking. He strained to listen and realized fairly quickly what he was hearing was a TV. He used the dental mirror again in the corner of the window and saw a solitary man sitting at the desk with his feet up, watching the TV. J.J. used the mirror to look around the room but saw no others. The man was alone. Except, of course, if you counted his metal companions. The man had a shotgun sitting there on the desk and a pistol in his shoulder holster.

J.J. pulled the mirror back down and looked carefully in all directions again. The sign above the door at the end of the corridor said "Exit," and it had a window in the center. He could see that it was dark in that room too. In fact, it was dark in all directions except this one office. He pulled out the mirror again to take one more look at the sentry. The man was facing almost the same direction as J.J., with one subtle difference. To watch the TV, he had his head turned away from the window and door. J.J. crawled under the window to the door and slipped one end of the rubber hose inside the room under the door. The other end was attached to the canister. After donning his mask, he turned the valve that was near his shoulder very slowly. Although J.J. could hear it, the TV was loud enough to cover the sound of the escaping gas from the sentry. J.J. uncoiled another foot or so of the rubber hose, then rose enough to use the mirror again to watch as the man was overtaken by the gas. It didn't take long before his eyes couldn't stay open. Shortly after that, his head fell back and his hands dropped below J.J.'s view. J.J. let the gas run for another minute, then turned off the valve and removed the tank. He put the tank in the office across the hall where it would not be seen should anyone come by. He'd grab it on his way out.

He went to the door at the end of the hall and used the mirror to look in. He couldn't see any light sources in any direction, so he took a deep breath, removed the mask, put his face to the glass, and peered in. It was another corridor. On the other side of it,

LEFT NO CHOICE

he could just make out another door. It, too, was marked "Exit." That must be the door leading to the outside. J.J. put the mask back on, exhaled into it, and entered the office. The man was out for the count, and maybe dead. J.J. didn't care which, because this man was to die tonight anyway in the explosion. J.J. checked his pulse and found none. He turned off the TV, then moved to the door, and turned off the lights as well. He'd learned a trick in the service about how to see an entrance that's disguised or hidden. First, try to extinguish all light from around it, so the only light visible will be from inside it. If that didn't work, you started hunting. He wouldn't need to do any hunting tonight. As his eyes adjusted to the darkness, a glow became increasingly apparent. It was coming from behind the two filing cabinets against the far wall. The TV the man had been watching was perched upon one of them. He turned the lights back on and went to study the area. Upon very close inspection, he saw faint scratches on the floor in an arcing pattern that originated from the far front corner of the filing cabinets. He looked around them closely for traps and found none. He pulled them gently in the direction of the arc, but they did not budge.

After studying the far side of the cabinet farthest from the door, he saw what looked like a bar protruding into the wall from inside that cabinet. It was a little more than halfway down, so J.J. opened the third drawer of the cabinet. It was filled with what seemed like junk. Extension cords, a small toolbox, and a couple of other nonessential items. On the left side, though, was a tubular piece of metal that protruded out from the side just a couple of inches and ran the entire length of the drawer. It was hidden under all the crap that was thrown in the drawer on top of it. J.J. pulled on what seemed like its handle near the front of the drawer. It took a great deal more force to move it that it looked like it should, but it rotated in place and stopped ninety degrees from where J.J. had started. He tugged on the cabinet again and this time both cabinets moved in unison and with ease. He closed the drawer and looked behind the cabinet again, now that it was a few extra inches away from the wall. Now he could see that the bar from the drawer protruded out from the back of the cabinet and actually went through the wall.

J.J. pushed the pair of cabinets in the direction of the arc, noting that they barely cleared the edge of the desk as they moved. Once they had achieved about 70 percent of their allowable movement, the wall behind the cabinets opened at a seam just a few inches in from where the side of the cabinet met the wall. He swung the cabinets the rest of the way over and the piece of wall opened with them. Now he could see their lock. The bar he'd turned inside the drawer had a U-shaped end that swung down behind the beam on the opposite side of the hidden door to keep the cabinets from moving. But when it was turned, the U-shaped end rotated up and off the beam. This allowed the cabinets to be spun away from the wall, and as the end met with a plate on the back of the hinged wall, it pulled it open with the swinging cabinets. Even though it was a simple design, it was quite effective, J.J. thought.

He pulled the Beretta from its holster and used the business end of it to lead himself into the stairwell behind the cabinets. The walls on both sides went all the way down to a landing some fifteen steps below and around it down more steps. Not a person in sight and no voices that he could hear. He holstered the Beretta and grabbed the center of the U. He pulled on the bar, which reversed the motions of the cabinets and the door. Once he'd pulled it tight, he turned the U back into its lock position against the beam and descended the stairs. He stopped two steps above the landing and removed the mask. From his pants pocket, he took out a black, knitted winter cap and pulled it down over his head. Only his eyes and mouth were visible now. He grabbed the Beretta again and peered around the corner of the landing.

This was it. The powder room. Three men were visible, all at different tables performing different functions. He could see on the far wall a well-crafted miniature lift the size of a twenty-five inch TV. It looked like a square basket with chain-link sides. Inside, the basket were a handful of egg containers like you'd find at the supermarket. He could see against the far wall near the lift a large quantity of those containers. One of the men was filling one with what looked like eggs at that moment. J.J. could see that these eggs were actually plastic containers that were being filled with the powder by one of the other men. Once he'd poured in what seemed to J.J. a carefully weighed amount, he'd put the dome shaped lid on the container and, viola! It was an egg. The third man had to be the chemist. He was combining solutions with a deliberate focus. He was also the one closest to J.J. He swept the room with his vision and the barrel of the Beretta. The only blind spots were the entire right corner and the extreme corner of the room. He'd have to move down a few steps past the landing into plain view of the three men to look for others. He caught a break as he contemplated his next move. As the chemist turned away from him and walked to another table, the guy who'd been putting the eggs into the cartons took two to the lift and the third man was going for more fake eggs. All three now had their backs to him.

    J.J. came down the steps quickly and quietly, with his back against the right side. He could see all the way to the left corner, and it was clear. He spun, putting his back against the left wall, and looked to the right. He could see the feet and knees of a man who was sitting on a stool, and the barrel of the shotgun he had on his lap. He glanced quickly at the other men. The one who'd been placing cartons in the lift and the one reaching for fake eggs were both turning back to their stations now and J.J. would be spotted in a second or two. He had to make his move and fast. He had wanted to avoid gunplay if he could so any deaths would seem like they were a result of the explosion. In one swift motion, he holstered the Beretta and flew down the steps at the man in the corner. The man was taken by surprise, so the second it took him to realize the figure approaching him was not a fellow soldier was all J.J. needed.

    J.J.'s open right hand came down with tremendous force and speed on the man's right wrist, pulling it away from the trigger of the weapon. J.J. slammed his left fist into the man's throat, crushing his windpipe. He quickly grabbed a throwing dagger from the harness behind his neck with his right, then pivoted his head and shoulders where he stood while he let the dagger fly with the force of a fastball. Now was the moment of truth for J.J. All the hours he'd spent training came down to this. The man who'd been getting the fake eggs was the target. He'd been thirty feet away and moving when J.J. released the blade. The man caught sight of J.J. as the blade was crossing the air halfway between them. He took a breath to yell out, but in that little span of time, the dagger connected. J.J.'s aim was accurate, but the blade's rotation speed was not. The handle crashed into the man's forehead above his left eye with enough power to stun him where he stood. He fell to the ground as J.J. was reaching for another and moving toward the chemist. The chemist was not the target yet as he still had his back to J.J., but J.J. wanted to close the distance between them while he sent the second blade at the guy walking back from the lift.

    That man had not seen J.J. The corner J.J. occupied was outside the man's peripheral vision even as he walked back to his station. He would never know what hit him. This time, the point of the blade pierced both skin and skull on its way into his brain. He wavered for a few seconds as if he were drunk and fell forward to the floor as J.J. was now within two steps of the pivoting chemist. The chemist locked gazes with J.J. for half a heartbeat as he completed his turn. J.J. grabbed the man's left forearm with his right hand and clamped down as he hooked his left arm around the chemist's neck. He pulled the man's left arm well up into the center of his back as he spoke.

"You make a sound and I'll snap your neck like a piece of uncooked spaghetti, you got me?" J.J. said through clenched teeth.

The chemist was a small man with the courage to match. He nodded quickly in the affirmative as his eyes shot wildly in all directions looking for help. He was shaking severely and J.J. could clearly tell that living meant more to this man than anything else did.

"Okay. First question. Does Tracerio have any labs other than this one." It came out like an angered statement instead of a question, which elevated the man's fear.

The man shook his head from side to side as best he could under the circumstances.

J.J. tightened his hold, and in the same tone, said, "You're sure."

He nodded.

"Are those stairs the only way into this room?"

He shook his head for a few seconds, then flicked it toward the wall while he raised his loose arm slowly and pointed. J.J. looked over and could now see the disguised door.

"Does that lead to the loading dock?"

He nodded again.

"Okay. Now talk softly when you answer these next ones, understand?" J.J. asked as he tightened his grip for a second, then, slacked back a little.

"Yes, I understand," the man whimpered.

"What's your name?"

"C-C-Carl. C-Carl Townsend."

"Okay, Carl. Which type of phosphorous do you use here, Red or Hypo?"

"R-r-r-red-d."

"And where do you keep it?"

The man pointed over his shoulder and said, "I-I-it's on t-the th-third sh-sh-shelf over there."

"Let's go get some. But, Carl, if you do anything stupid, you're gonna be joining your friends. You understand?" J.J. barked as he nudged the man in the back with his right knuckles, then released him after Carl had nodded.

They moved over to the shelf. The man waved his index finger in the air in front of a series of bottles, all clearly labeled "Red Phosphorous" as well as it's Periodic Table of Elements description. J.J. quickly threw a volley of questions at him while pointing the Beretta at his chest, and the man answered each as he stared into the hole at the end of the silencer. His answers seemed to J.J. to be truthful ones. He'd given J.J. all the information he needed about where in the lab the phosphorous was added to the solution and what a normal amount would be.

"Okay, Carl. You have a decision to make. This lab is getting leveled tonight, one way or another. Either you help me destroy it and leave with me alive, or I spike the mix myself and you die here and now. Which is it going to be?" J.J. said as he motioned toward the bottles.

Carl finally realized what J.J. meant to do and now, in a panic, said, "Y-you can't. This whole place will go up. We'll never get out in time! It's suic—"

"Shut up! It's your only chance to live, Carl. *Now what's it gonna be?*"

"B-b-but Tracerio. He'll kill me even if we do get out."

J.J. raised the Beretta until it was pointing into the man's face and said, "Maybe. But maybe he won't get the chance to. I will kill you and right now. What's it gonna be, Carl?"

"Okay, okay, okay. I'll help you. Just please don't kill me," Carl said, raising his hands torso high and palms extended.

Then he turned to grab a bottle of phosphorous. J.J. holstered the Beretta while instinctively watching the man's hand as he reached for the bottle. His hand was palm out and thumb down. He was going to try to use it as a weapon. J.J. stepped in and delivered a crushing blow to the right side of the man's neck, stunning him. Then he placed Carl in a sleeper hold and held it until Carl's body went limp. J.J. grabbed the man around the waist and carried him back over to his station. He laid the upper half of Carl's limp form on the table, letting his feet dangle above the floor. Then J.J. looked at his watch. He'd been inside the powder room for almost six minutes already and still had many things to do. He'd planned on being out in nine. He quickly wrapped an empty glass beaker in a towel and smashed it on the table. He took a long, narrow shard from it and another towel over to the man with the dagger sticking out of his skull.

It took almost all J.J.'s strength to retrieve the dagger, and he'd had to step on the man's head while pulling to finally dislodge it. He stuck the shard of broken glass in the hole and wiped the dagger clean with the towel. After he slipped the dagger back into its place, he carried the body back over to the lift and put his right arm around the lift's support beam so he'd stay upright. He retrieved the dagger he'd thrown at the other man next, then propped his limp form up against the shelves. J.J. hooked his arm around the upright so he'd stay there. J.J. noticed that he was still breathing too, but time was running out. J.J. went back to the corner and set the guard back up on the stool, then placed the shotgun back in his lap. He went back to the shelf of phosphorous and grabbed three bottles. He quickly opened and poured all three into the main bowl of chemicals. The burner was on already, but J.J. turned it up to maximum. He flew back up the steps to the top. He stopped and listened for a moment as he looked at his watch again. Eleven and a half minutes he'd been down there.

He heard nothing from the other side. He took a deep breath and held it while he opened the secret door and peeked around the cabinet. The man was still in the chair with his feet up. J.J. peeked further around and saw that the room was empty otherwise. He quickly put the body headfirst and face down on the steps inside the passage to the lab. He turned the TV back on, opened the third drawer, and then he exited the room. He grabbed the near empty tank of carbon monoxide and strapped it back on, still holding his breath. He locked the door at the end of the corridor as he went through it but knew there was no time to secure the deadbolt, so he'd have to risk that being noticed later. Once he was safely on the other side of that door, he exhaled the spent air and breathed in new. As quickly as he could, he made his way back to the door he'd entered from, breathing deeply all the way. He stopped there and pressed his face to the floor by the door. He could not see the man's feet on the other side. He looked at his watch again. *Thirteen minutes.* The man's feet came into view a few seconds later, and J.J. watched, in what seemed like slow motion, as the man approached this end of his post. His heart was pounding and the adrenaline was flooding his arteries at full power as the man made his turn.

J.J. watched him for three steps, then stood and opened the door. There was no deadbolt on this one and the lock was a push-button one, so he didn't need the key to lock it as he left. He peeked around the door and saw the man's back. He slipped out, closed the door, and ran back to the cover of the underbrush. J.J. lay there counting seconds as he watched the sentry come back toward the door. He knew the lab would blow soon, but he wanted to be safely back at the Ramcharger when it did. The sentry finally finished his path to the door and turned away. J.J. rose and headed out away from the building and the lights around it. He'd only made it halfway to the hole in the fence when muffled thunder roared toward him from the direction of the building. He looked back as fists of fire punched through the outer walls on the lab side of the building and rose toward the sky. He turned and ran as quickly as he could in a crouched position toward his exit point in the fence. Two more times he heard the thunder roll out, followed by brightened earth and sky before he made it back to the Ramcharger. He looked down from the rise as he removed the knit cap and saw a glow on the other side of the building that lit up both the ground and the night sky.

LEFT NO CHOICE

His plan to level the lab alone had failed. That whole end of the building had gone with it.

He started the vehicle and drove away with his lights off. Three miles later, he turned off that back road onto what could only be described as a dirt trail. He cut across the desert to a paved road that would lead him back to the highway. He wouldn't stop the vehicle again until he reached the cabin. He arrived a little before four and took all his equipment back to the storage facility before retiring for the night. He was physically tired, but his brain was operating at full speed. The first blow to Tracerio's operation had been delivered, and if all went well, Tony would never know it to be anything but an accident. J.J. chuckled as he wondered how the police would handle this one. Two months after the main stockholder dies, the place blows up due to a chemist's error in the illegal drug lab hidden below it. How were they going to keep a lid on all this now? He didn't know, and he really didn't care. Just as long as they did it.

He knew they would. Somehow, Tracerio's boys in blue and his people in the fire department would explain it away as a legitimate tragedy. But J.J. also knew this meant the pressure would mount on those men because of it. Their loyalty to Tracerio would start to wither as his operations crumbled. Maybe enough that they'd take him out before J.J. had to. That was okay with J.J. He didn't care how Tracerio and all his allies went down; he just wanted to make sure they went down. He went over the operation again in his head and chastised himself for the mistakes he'd made. He should never have tried to give the chemist a chance to redeem himself. It cost J.J. almost four minutes and could have cost him a lot more than time. Everybody who was playing on Tracerio's team was now expendable, J.J. decided. No more would he risk himself for these scumbags. They'd chosen their path and would have to suffer the consequences of it. Period. He went over the dagger-throwing error in his mind and could come up with no better explanation for it than being out of practice having to act at that speed. He dismissed it from the front of his mind but in the back was telling himself to practice more as soon as he woke. He hadn't slept well the night before and that restlessness coupled with the events of the last three hours was taking its toll.

He went to the sink and got a glass of water, then nestled back down in the chair and put his feet up on the coffee table. He sipped at it for a few minutes, then put it aside when it was almost empty and laid his head back. He thought of Joan and Lance. He pictured them standing before him in his mind and said aloud, "I'll come for you as soon as I can. Just as soon as I can." And with that, slowly drifted off to sleep right there in the chair.

16

The call had come in around seven from the chief. The news of the explosion at the lab angered Tony so much he hung up on the chief after making some pretty nasty threats. The threats weren't directed at the chief, but at the fire marshal if he screwed up the report on the fire. The chief hung up and called the fire marshal back, relaying almost word for word what Tony had yelled into the phone.

Tony then called his son and through more expletives, ordered that all the men on duty the night before and the other two chemists meet him downtown at Ciao Bella's at nine. Then to call the other three stockholders of Johnson Farms and have them there by noon. In all the years he'd been in business, he'd never encountered as many problems in a three-month span as he was running into now. Then Tony placed a few calls. One to Greenhill, one to Danbury, and one to his partner at Ciao Bella's. Every man and woman in the whole organization was up and moving by eight thirty, including the chef. Tony's staff at the mansion was hopping quickly too. Even though they were not part of the outside operations and had no reason to worry, they did anyway.

The meeting with the security team turned up nothing. No one had seen or heard anything or anyone at any time during the night. The head of the night watch offered the probability that one of the men in the lab must have dropped or spilled something that ignited the blaze. There was no other explanation. The perimeter sweep they'd done within five minutes of the initial blast had turned up nothing. No doors were unlocked and no windows were broken on the nondamaged side and there were eight men outside the building on the side that blew. No way could anyone have slipped by. It couldn't have been a hit. It had to be a mistake on the part of the chemist. He gave Tony the death toll of eight men. The five men that were inside the building and three members of the outside team that burned to death in the explosion and fire. The damage report was as expected. The lab was a complete loss, and about one-third of the main building was destroyed or severely damaged.

Tony turned his barrage of questions to the two chemists in attendance. The lead man did all the talking but both of them believed the same thing. It must have been an accident. Carl or one of his crew must have dropped a container near a burner, catching everything on fire. Carl would never have bungled a mixture badly enough to cause that. And the lead man added, even if he had, there would still have been plenty of time for him to dilute it if too much was used. He further explained that even if Carl hadn't thought of that, there would have been plenty of time for all the men in the lab to get out before it went up. There was no reasonable explanation except the broken bottle. That would cause a fire to spread in seconds, and it could easily have engulfed all the men before they could escape it. The explosion would come when the fire reached the shelf full of phosphorous bottles, and that would only have taken a couple of minutes. He finished by telling Tony that whatever had happened was human error, nothing else.

Tony knew nothing about the composition of the powder or how to make it but was well aware that if a chemist made an error, the whole place could go up. He dismissed all the men who worked at the farm with orders to keep their answers about the fire to either "I have no clue what happened" or "Maybe there was a short circuit in the wiring somewhere," and that was it. Before allowing the chemists or the lead security man to leave, he instructed them to visit the homes of Carl and the other two men whose spouses were aware of what they were really doing and give them his personal condolences and assurances that they would be taken care of. Then he sent them on their way too.

The stockholders meeting went as expected. Tony talked, they listened. There would be no mention of the lab by any of them, period. He'd bury it as a faulty electrical circuit fire that ignited the cleaning chemicals, and the explosions were a result of it. Those eight who died were either making their rounds and got caught in the blaze or got trapped while trying to help the others get out. One of the men voiced a concern about being questioned by the police and specifically, what they should say if they're asked why there were fourteen men there when the place was closed. Tony told him not to worry about it, that he would make sure that never became an issue. He reminded them once again to stick to the story he'd laid out or face his wrath, then dismissed them. He hadn't eaten breakfast and was getting very hungry. He looked at his watch. It was one thirty already. He went into the kitchen to get something to eat and try to calm down. He was on edge, and it showed.

Michael heard about the explosion and fire on the morning news even before going to work. He knew immediately that J.J. was involved and wondered if Ralph would think it too. Ralph had no idea he was working there but knew Fred Johnson had owned it and that Fred was one of Tracerio's men. Michael prepared himself for the barrage of questions and opinions from Ralph about it as he drove. He and Ralph went about their morning routine without a word and silence was still filling the air five minutes into their drive away from the station. They normally got together on Saturday nights but hadn't last Saturday. In fact, they hadn't spoken since Michael left Ralph's on Friday night.

Michael finally broke the silence by asking, "Man, you're sure quiet today. What're you thinkin' about?"

Ralph had been waiting and hoping for Michael to ask.

"Friday night. And last night. We need to talk, Michael," Ralph said, looking across the car at his partner.

"Okay. You wanna get together tonight after work and have a beer?" Michael asked in an upbeat tone.

"It can't wait that long. I mean now. We need to talk now."

"That won't be easy to do Ralph, and you kno—"

"Bull! We sure can. Pull into the parking lot over there!" Ralph snapped.

Michael looked over at his friend and saw a hint of the same look he'd seen Friday night. Ralph was hot and it was going to be up to Michael to keep him from blowing his stack and maybe the case too.

"All right, if that's what you want. No problem," Michael said calmly as he pulled in.

He drove around to the back of the supermarket and, seeing no trucks or people, parked the car. He unbuckled his belt while looking at Ralph, then exited the car and closed the door. Ralph followed a few seconds later. Michael walked over to the wall behind the store about twenty feet from the cruiser and stopped. He kept his back to Ralph purposely in hopes this would make Ralph see just a little of his frustration and maybe back off a bit. It had the opposite effect.

"Turn around and look at me, Michael!"

Michael wheeled in place quickly and responded. "What is wrong with you?"

"You know what's wrong with me, so cut the crap. Blake set that fire, didn't he, Michael?"

"I honestly don't know, Ralph. But I really don't think so."

"Aw, come on! Johnson worked for Tracerio, you told me that yourself. Then a couple days after Blake surfaces, it goes up like a roman candle? Don't play games with me Michael. You know he did it. What I need to know from you is, did you know about it before he did it?"

Michael was shocked to the point of speechlessness by this. He couldn't believe that Ralph had become like this in just a few days. He was losing it. Now, he didn't even trust Michael.

"What are you sayin' here, Ralph?"

"I'm sayin' that your buddy killed eight people last night, Partner. Now how much do you know? What haven't you told me yet, Michael?" Ralph asked as he put a finger into Michael's chest and stepped to within inches of his face.

"Ralph. You don't want to do this. Not here. Not now. Not ever. Now get your finger out of my chest and talk with me like you want to be talked to. Then, and only then, will this conversation continue!" Michael snapped back.

Ralph looked deep into his partner's eyes and saw the depth of Michael's resolve in them. Michael wasn't kidding. In fact, he was actually angry now. Ralph finally realized that he'd get nowhere with Michael that way, so he looked down at his hand, lowered it, and stepped back.

"Okay, Michael, okay. I'm sorry. This whole thing's got me way past the edge. We've been friends a long time, man, and covering each other's back even longer. I'm countin' on that to mean something here. I need that to mean something here. So, please, don't lie to me. What do you know about last night?"

Michael was calmer now that Ralph had backed off, so his response was, too.

"Ralph. I don't know any more than you do. I swear. But I really don't think he did it, man. I really don't."

"And why is that?"

"Think about it, man. You said it yourself. Eight men died. How many more were there that didn't?"

"I don't know."

"Me either. But there had to be at least one left to call AFD and keep the press off the property, right?"

"Yeah, so?"

"So that makes at least nine. Nine guys. Minimum! You think he's gonna get past nine guys?"

"Maybe."

"Okay. Let's say he did. Let's say he got past nine guys and blew up the place in such a way that eight of the nine would go with it. That would take a lot of planning, right?"

"Yeah, it would. What's the point?"

"The point is, if he'd planned it that well, why'd he let the other guy live? You heard him on Friday. 'One way or the other,' he'd have whacked that guy too, if he'd have done it, Ralph. And you know it."

"Not if he thought the guy was dead."

"I'll grant you that, Ralph. But I still don't think he did it. I do have a suggestion that can help us both, though," Michael offered.

"Okay. I'm listening. What suggestion?"

"He's gonna meet us again Friday night at the park. Let's ask him. If he admits to it, or if we even think he's lying, we pull the plug on him right then and there, agreed?"

Ralph looked hard and long at Michael after that, weighing his sincerity. He couldn't be sure Michael was telling the truth but tried to reassure himself by saying, "Does our friendship go that deep? Will you stand with me Friday if I decide to take him down?"

"That's not what I said, Ralph. I said if we, meaning you and I, think that he is lying about doing it, I'll help you take him down. I know you wanna take him down no matter what already, so I need to believe it too. But if I believe he did it, yes, I'll help you. In fact, I'll beat you to it and you'll end up helping me."

Ralph looked at him again for a long moment, then spoke.

"All right, partner. We leave it alone until Friday. But on Friday, you remember what you promised me here today, okay?"

"I will. I will. But you remember that if I don't think the guy was involved, I'm not takin' him in. You'll remember that too, come Friday night, right?"

"Yep! I sure will," Ralph said with a pat on the shoulder. Then he turned and walked back to the squad car with Michael not far behind.

It wasn't normal for Flo to feel so much of Ralph's burden. Then again she'd never known Ralph to have one this heavy before. Ever. Seeing him so distraught all weekend was difficult enough. But Ralph's reaction to the story on the morning news about the explosion sent her way past concern and landed her deep in the center of fear. Fear for Ralph, fear for his career, their marriage, their future, everything. What's worse is that he wouldn't tell her anything specific. She had absolutely no idea what was going on, and he wasn't about to tell her. The one thing he should have told her was that what he knew could get them all killed.

Flo taught fifth grade English during the school year but had summers off to do with as she pleased. During the summers, she worked hard around the house because of her love for cooking and gardening. She'd been chipping away all summer at landscaping changes in the backyard and decided to go to the local Wal-Mart after Ralph had left for work for more gardening supplies. She wanted to get the situation with Ralph off her mind and gardening was her escape. She wasn't doing any digging or building out there. She was changing the look of the backyard by making little flower and plant beds around it. The view from the patio both day and night were already incredible to behold, but Flo was not yet finished. There were a few more colors to be added to one area and ground cover to be placed in another.

As she walked through the gardening section, her mind and heart were still full of the things Ralph had said and worried about the things he'd not said. She was as close to walking around in a dazed stupor as a person could get. She was a little angry with Ralph for keeping her in the dark, which added to her despair.

"Flo? Flo Davis? Hey! I thought that was you! How are you?"

Flo turned around and saw the smiling face of Debbie Wilson behind a half-full cart of her own. Flo forced a smile, but even Debbie, who only saw her a few times a year, could tell something was wrong.

Debbie tried to ignore what she saw out of courtesy, saying, "I haven't seen you since the Policeman's Ball. How are you?"

Flo Davis was not normally one to air family troubles, especially to almost complete strangers, but Debbie was also a cop's wife and that made a difference.

"I'm good. I'm good. And you?" Flo asked, making an effort to mask her thoughts and the fact that she couldn't remember the woman's name.

"Just great! How're Ralph and the kids?"

"They're fine. And your family?"

"Oh, you know. Same ole, same ole. Steve's been under a little pressure lately, but other than that we're doing okay."

As soon as she'd mentioned her husband's name, everything clicked, and Flo relaxed a little.

"Debbie, I know what you mean. Ralph's been under some serious pressures too. I've never seen him the way he's been the last few days." Then in a whispered tone, she leaned toward Debbie and asked, "Is there something going on down at the station?"

LEFT NO CHOICE

Debbie looked around and whispered back, "I don't know, but I'd say there is. And it must be really hush-hush. Steve won't tell me anything."

Flo began to feel better just knowing that someone else was in the same boat she was in and whispered, "Hush-hush is right. Ralph and his partner don't even talk about work at the house anymore. Every Friday night for the last few years Michael Rhodes, Ralph's partner, has been coming over for dinner, and after dinner, we'd all sit out back and talk. But for the last four straight Friday's after dinner, those two jump in Ralph's car and go down to River View State Park to talk. Something's going on, Debbie, I just wish I knew what. Then maybe I could help. But, right now, I feel lost."

Flo was hoping Debbie could and would shed a little light on what was happening. After all, she was the captain's wife. If anybody knew, she would.

"Flo, you're not alone, dear. You're definitely not alone," Debbie said as she waved her hand through the air, then continued. "I've been trying to dig it out of Steve all summer and he won't tell me a thing. He just keeps saying, 'Honey, everything's okay. Don't you worry. It's no big deal,' and asks me to leave it alone, so I do. For a few days," she said with a chuckle.

Flo chuckled too, then said, "Well, if you ever get it out of him, Debbie, would you let me know? I'm getting a little worried," Flo admitted.

"I will. They always stick together, so I think all of us wives should too. If I hear anything, I'll call you, and you do the same, okay?"

"Okay. Thanks, Debbie. I really needed somebody to talk with today. You have no idea how much better you've helped me to feel than when I walked in here."

"Likewise, Flo. Definitely. So you're doing some gardening, too, I see?"

"Oh, yes. I love to garden."

And that quickly the subject was changed. The two of them talked for quite a while, giving each other gardening tips and advice, then went their separate ways. Flo did feel better and hoped Debbie could find out from her husband more than Ralph had told her. Debbie even took her home number down so she could call Flo if she was able to get anything out of her husband. Flo decided not to tell Ralph about running into Debbie. In fact, Flo had decided to quit pestering Ralph about it altogether. She'd help him any way she could once she'd heard from Debbie. Until then, she'd do whatever she could to cheer him up without pushing him. After she left Wal-Mart, she went to the grocery store. She picked up all the things she needed to make Ralph's favorite meals for the rest of the week. She knew how to please her man, and she set out to do just that.

J.J. woke around two in the afternoon and, after cleaning up again, went straight down to a local pub in Chimayo to have a few beers and watch the news. He'd been torn between that and practicing with the daggers, but his curiosity and desire for information won out. By now, the reporters would have been able to interview the fire department and the police, so J.J. would be able to get a good idea how Tracerio was going to spin the incident. If he let the truth come out about the meth lab, J.J. would prepare a package with all that he'd collected and add typewritten notes regarding everything he knew about Tracerio's involvement. Then he'd have it delivered as if it came from George Ashland to the Bureau's office in Santa Fe, and anonymously to the TV Stations in Santa Fe.

Once they had the package, he'd write Joan, then just go back up to the cabin and stay while the FBI and the media worked the case. If all went well and Tracerio was brought down in the wave he created, he'd come out of hiding and assist the Bureau in bringing down those in Tracerio's army that had escaped prosecution. If, however, Tracerio did as expected and covered up the truth about the lab, J.J. would keep going after him from behind the scenes. He'd considered bringing the FBI in before Tracerio could get rid of all evidence pertaining to the lab's existence. In fact, he'd been really tempted to. But he knew that meant there would then be undercover agents all over the place. That brought two problems into play that he could not accept. The first was that the influx of undercover agents would definitely hinder his movements, but the second was far worse. Since he wouldn't know who the undercover agents were, he could end up killing one or more by mistake during his mini campaigns against Tracerio. That was absolutely unacceptable, which brought J.J. back around to the beginning again.

The only way he'd go to the Bureau and the press was if they were already involved, and that could only happen if Tracerio let the truth be known about the existence of the lab. Even then, he wasn't sure how long it would take them to sort through all the people and evidence before they could make a case. The worry about that was simple. The more time it took to make a case against him, the more time Tracerio had to cover his tracks or disappear all together. J.J. planned to stay in the shadows no matter what for just that reason. He could do things the law would not allow the FBI to do, from illegal search and seizure, to eliminating conspirators with extreme prejudice. He just had to wait and see how Tracerio would play it.

The news came on at five, and the explosion at the farm was the lead story. The initial findings of the investigation were that an electrical short circuit had started the fire, and the explosion occurred when the fire reached the gas main. The business would be closed until the official report from the fire department came out. All employees were being contacted by phone to let them know not to come to work until further notice. A sidebar about Fred Johnson's death was mentioned, but nothing big in that regard. J.J. hung around the bar for another hour or so after the news to cover his reason for being there, then went back up to the cabin. He'd drive down to the motel to check his messages the next day to make sure he'd been called. If he hadn't, he'd head for the farm at his normal time on Wednesday morning.

When he got back up to the cabin, he immediately changed clothes and made his way out to the storage facility. He grabbed his throwing daggers and his bow and began sharpening up on targets that were thirty feet away. He didn't want another mistake like last night's to be repeated. After working out for three and a half hours, he went back to the cabin and wrote Joan and Lance. Lance would start school the following Tuesday and he wanted the letters to arrive before that. Once he'd written a pretty lengthy letter to each of them, he would go out into the night to work out some more. Things were definitely going to start heating up now, and he wanted to make sure he was ready to handle it.

Michael hadn't told Ralph of the meeting he was to have with J.J. on Wednesday and was very glad of it. This was only Monday and the whole day there'd been tension between the two. Neither would admit it, and both tried to cover it, but it was there.

Michael went to the firing range after work and Ralph went home. He could tell something was up as he pulled into the driveway as Flo and both kids were standing in the yard waiting for him. All had big smiles, and all waved as he pulled in. He couldn't help but smile back as he hadn't seen this sight in a long time. It changed his mood completely. By the time he got out of the car, he was laughing and waving too.

"What's all this?" he asked, visibly pleased.

"We just wanted you to know that we love you, dear, and we decided to declare this night as 'Dad night.' We're going to have a great time too. The kids have pulled a couple of games down from the closet for after dinner, and there's a twelve-pack of Lowenbrau in the fridge," Flo said giddily.

"Lowenbrau? Wow! You sprung for Lowenbrau? This must be 'Dad night,'" he said with a broad smile as he tossed the hair of his two teens then hugged and kissed his wife.

"That's not all. Tonight's menu is Shrimp Cocktails and Crab Cakes for appetizers, then Stuffed Pork Chops, Twice-Baked Potatoes, and Corn on the Cob, and for dessert, we're having Cherry Cobbler. Welcome home, honey," Flo said with a wink and a smile.

The rest of the evening would be a memory he'd cherish for the rest of his life.

"I've told you a hundred times, Deb, that nothing's going on," Steve Wilson said with a chuckle. "Now stop asking me or you'll have me worrying about you, okay?" He said with a kiss and a hug.

"Okay. okay. I'll stop. But I've gotta tell you, honey, it's not just me," Debbie said as she walked back toward the kitchen.

"Not just you? Have you been listening to my mother again?" he asked with a laugh.

"No," Debbie said from the kitchen. "I ran into Flo Davis at the store today. She said her husband Ralph has been acting weird too."

Steve froze in his tracks for a second, then walked toward the kitchen but didn't enter. He stood at the corner, out of Debbie's view, and asked, "Weird how?"

And from the kitchen, she told him everything Flo had told her. He stood there by the door listening as if he were in shock. He was quite glad she couldn't see his face now as his features were reflecting his resentment, anger, and fear all at once. The thing that struck him the hardest was the secretive talks Davis and Rhodes were having in the park. His thoughts became a conversation within his mind.

They rode together all day long, giving them all the time in the world to talk, so why the need for out of the way meetings? And why stop talking about work in front of his wife? Unless they knew something. Something that could put her in danger. They hadn't come to him with whatever it was they were discussing either. Under normal circumstances, they'd bring anything to him in a second if it were big enough to act the way they were. So why weren't they? Because they do know something. But how much? And who have they told? The chief and Tracerio need to know this, and they need to know this right now!

He did his best to cover the wave of anxiety through dinner and then made an excuse that he needed to go to the store afterward so he could get out of the house. He had never told Debbie of his involvement with the Tracerio organization. In fact, she didn't even know about the money he'd been stockpiling from it. He drove to the chief's house, then they took a drive together. Wilson explained what his wife had said and the chief's face filled with the same horror that had overflowed on Wilson's just a few hours before. Davis and Rhodes were on to them. There was no other possible explanation. They knew something. That was a fact. But they also knew not to bring it to either the captain or the chief. That meant they knew too much! Both men were in up to their eyeballs and both knew they'd be ruined if that ever came out. But neither man wanted to kill cops, or know of someone killing cops, for that matter. They knew Tracerio would have both men killed and probably their families too.

That would bring down the heat. Internal affairs would be all over it, and Tracerio would expect the chief to handle it. There was no way the chief could interfere with IAD. They'd spot his involvement in a second, and then, he'd be a target for Tracerio, so that was out. But they couldn't just let Davis and Rhodes keep going either. How could they cover their own backsides with Tracerio without becoming accomplices to the murders of Davis and Rhodes? And if Davis and Rhodes lived on, how could they cover their backsides where the law was concerned?

Wilson called his wife and told her he'd run into the chief in the store and they were going to get a beer together. They drove off to a secluded spot of their own, which was an empty warehouse, and the captain called Gus Cantonelli. He told Gus where to meet them but didn't say why. Between the three of them, they had to figure out what to do. Cantonelli arrived about forty minutes later, and by that time, the chief and the captain had already come up with a risky but feasible plan. A plan that could save all three of them. First, the chief had Captain Wilson bring Cantonelli up to speed with regard to what his wife had heard from Davis's wife. Then the chief laid out all the possible outcomes for them that he and Wilson could think of, but none of them were good. Then Chief Richter told Cantonelli of the plan he and Wilson had devised.

"We wait until Friday afternoon to tell Tracerio about Davis and Rhodes. Tracerio will obviously call Sharpe and Greenhill to have them dispose of both of them down at the park later that night, then go to Ralph's house and take care of Ralph's family. Do we all agree that's what Tony will do?" Richter asked, hoping for unity.

Both men looked at each other and after processing it, did agree that Tony's most likely response would be that. Then Richter continued.

"Okay. So Sharpe and Greenhill are sent to the park to kill them both. They wouldn't know it was coming, so they'd be sitting ducks and would wind up dead for sure, right?" Again, he paused, waiting for both to acknowledge. Both nodded.

"All right. What if we beat Sharpe and Greenhill to the park? I mean all three of us. Then all three of us take them out before they can kill Davis and Rhodes. Once they're dead, they can't tell Tracerio who did it, right? And when we step out of the shadows, Davis and Rhodes will know it was us who just saved their lives and the lives of their families. Then we've got our best shot at saving ourselves from going down with Tracerio."

Wilson had already heard all of this once and, in fact, had actually assisted in coming up with it, so he was obviously in. Cantonelli's response was the unknown. Gus could just as easily agree tonight, then go tell Tracerio about the plan these two had, and be Tracerio's hero. Tracerio would have the chief and the captain whacked then cover Cantonelli's involvement. The captain and the chief had discussed this possible move by Gus before he had arrived, mainly because the captain could see it developing as Chief Richter was explaining the plan to him earlier. Captain Wilson was not a stupid man, especially when it came to the criminal mind. Cantonelli had been contemplating exactly what they'd thought as the chief spoke.

"Okay. I agree. Let's do it," Cantonelli said.

Richter and Wilson exchanged glances and the Chief was next to speak.

"All right. Good. In a minute, we'll drive over to the park and scout it. But before we do that, I've gotta say something to both of you. Now, I know all of us are aware that any of us could go to Tracerio and let him in on our little conversation. Then he kills the other two, and the blame for any police involvement in criminal activity falls upon them. Which leaves the one that's still alive in Tracerio's good graces, and out of harm's way where an investigation is concerned. But let me dispel that myth right now," he said as he looked hard into the shocked eyes of Gus Cantonelli. "Tony Tracerio doesn't give two nickels about anybody but himself and his son. That means that every cop on his payroll will go down when the investigation starts. And I'm not talking about jail. I'm talking about six feet under. That man can get away clean if he kills everybody on the force that knew him, and he knows it. Think about it for a minute. There is no way he'd save our butts with his on the line. No matter what mess we'd saved him from. We're only useful to him while we wear these badges and can cover up his actions. The minute this goes public, and with at least four dead cops it *will* go public, the one left alive is a walking dead man. What's one more cop dead when you've already killed four? Not a thing, that's what. He'll plug all leaks and erase all loose ends. Period. So I suggest we keep this little conversation a secret, and we'll all get out of this alive and well. Comprende?"

The Chief's words struck pay dirt. Cantonelli's delusions of grandeur disappeared as he looked at the situation from the same depth as Richter and Wilson had earlier. But now, he was full of questions.

"Yeah, chief. I understand. But even after we save Davis and Rhodes, Tracerio will just bring in other goons to whack them, and Davis and Rhodes will know it. That means they'll take this thing public on their own, doesn't it? What do we do then?" Cantonelli asked.

This brought a whole new twist to the discussion. From there many questions flew into the air, and even though they'd be there for hours, they would not come up with enough answers for them. They decided to meet again in the same place the following night at seven.

17

"Mr. Tracerio? There's a man here from the fire department to see you."

"Thank you, Frederick. Bring him out here to the patio. I've been expecting him."

"Who is it, Dad?"

"The fire marshal. Bill Wilkes. He's here to tell me what really happened at the farm."

"Do you mind if I stay and listen?" Tony Jr. asked.

"Of course not. Don't be silly. I'd rather you heard what he has to say, too, son."

The news Tony would hear from Wilkes was not much different from what he'd heard the morning before. In fact, it would confirm it. There were just no signs that the lab's explosion was caused by sabotage.

"All the bodies had sustained a level of damage from flying debris and the fire consistent with an accident. All the men in the lab were probably standing, except one, when it went up and he was probably seated on a stool in the corner. As for the man who'd been upstairs, I believe he died of suffocation as he was attempting to make his way down into the lab. Presumably because he was going to try to get everyone out after the fire started. He just never made it. It's hard to tell though, because the wooden stairwell acted as sort of a catalyst to burn his body so severely that an autopsy would be the only way of knowing what really killed him. Other than that, the three men who were outside died in the explosion or the fire that followed."

"Bill. You did not order an autopsy, though, right?"

"No, sir, Mr. Tracerio. I knew you'd not want that done."

"Good. Okay. Thank you for coming, Bill. Give my best to your family."

"Yes, sir, I will. Good day, gentlemen." And with that, he was gone again.

"Dad, do you really think this was an accident? Carl had worked for you for years, and he'd never even come close to having something like this happen," Tony Jr. said.

"Son, when I first heard, I thought it was a hit. But after everything I've been told, I just don't think so anymore. I believe Carl or one of the guys with him in the lab screwed up, and that screwup cost all of them their lives. I wasn't sure until I heard from Bill, but what he just said sums it up for me."

"Now what, Dad?"

"Whaddaya mean, now what? As soon as the farm is operational, we rebuild the lab. I figure we'll be down about two weeks. But in two weeks, we'll be back up to speed."

"Okay, Dad. Is there anything I can do in the meantime?"

"As a matter of fact, there is, son. You get hold of all our people that distribute, and let them know what's up. You make sure they know we'll be up and running again in two weeks and also that I'd be extremely disappointed to hear that they'd jumped ship because of this little setback. You make sure they are really clear on how upset I'd be. Okay, son?"

"It's as good as done, Dad. Well, if that's all, thanks for breakfast. I'll see you tomorrow night at Ciao Bella's."

"Okay, son. Until then."

"Okay, you two. I've been thinking about this since we left here last night. I've got an idea, but I really need you both to hear me out before you ask questions or chime in, okay?" Chief Richter asked.

"Sure, chief," Cantonelli said, while Wilson nodded.

"Gus, last night when you brought up the fact that Rhodes and Davis would go public, it bothered me. Not because of you, but because I believed you were right. All night, I played this one out in every conceivable direction, and the only way I could come up with to save all of us was this." Richter paused, but not for effect. He truly regretted having to speak these words.

"We don't stop the hit on Davis and Rhodes, or Davis's family. We let it happen. Then we do an investigation of our own into their murders—a real investigation. I'm talking about assigning a task force to bring their killers down. I will announce it as APD's priority one case with Steve calling the shots from his office. Gus, you'll be lead man in the field investigation. All you have to do is make sure you collect your clues and evidence legally and without looking like you had inside information. Starting with the explosion at the farm, which will provide evidence of the hidden lab. That decision won't come under scrutiny, either. Since Johns—"

"The hell it won't Chief," Cantonelli interrupted, "everybody from internal affairs to the media would be asking about that one." And then did a mock interview with himself as a reporter. "Detective Cantonelli. What made you decide to go out to Johnson Farms and start looking around again? Hadn't you already investigated it and agreed with Fire Marshal Wilkes that it was electrical failure? So why go back?" He finished in an interrogative tone, hoping to stress his point to both men that his carcass would be hanging suspiciously out in the wind. Then, without stopping, went on saying, "They'll smell the stink on that one and start looking closer at me, chief. That might be okay with you, but it's not even clo—"

"Gus! Listen to me!" Chief Richter interjected loudly. "Your reason for going back sometime next week is simple. Johnson died there a few months ago and eight more men would lose their lives in the same place in the same summer. That's nine deaths in three months out there. That alone made you curious enough to look again. But the clincher to looking really close was this question: 'Why were so many men on duty in a place that was closed? It was a farm, not a gold depository. Something was wrong with that picture.' So you had to go back out there, but this time, you'd turn the place inside out with a microscope. That's when you discovered the presence of the lab, which made you look a lot closer at Johnson's death. Then, when you reopened his case, you stumbled onto the second strange coincidence. Two other men died the same night as Johnson. There's our angle to spark a department wide investigation into a possible connection between all those deaths and to look for others.

"During that phase of the investigation, we look at Blake's death, and you check to see if the Blake woman had ever returned. You discover that both her and the child are still missing, causing your suspicions to grow. You take what you know to your captain, who comes to me with it. I get a judge to order an exhumation and autopsy of Blake's body to determine true cause of death, and that's when we find out it isn't Blake at all. It's one of his coworkers. Then we can investigate the bank and their files, which leads us to evidence of money laundering. That, and the Blake woman's disappearance, forces us to bring in the Bureau. Then the heat will really be on Tracerio and his entire organization. Now in all of that, there have to be at least a handful of his people who will be willing to give him up to stay out of prison. Then the

Bureau's got him cold. Now, somewhere along the line, he may try to implicate us as conspirators, but we can cover that too."

The chief had obviously been up all night, both Wilson and Cantonelli thought. Both sat silently as the chief had spoken and could see the logic clearly. The chain of events made sense up to this point, but there were still concerns and it was Captain Wilson who brought those up.

"All right, Chief. So far it sounds good, but three things worry the hell out of me. Tracerio's gonna be coming after the three of us and our families with everything he's got once Gus discovers the lab. That means none of us are safe and neither are our families. But if we sent our families away or put men out there as our own personal security force before we knew who was behind it and how big his operation was, we'd come under suspicion. The Bureau's men would want to know why we'd done it. We investigate people all the time without taking such extreme personal security measures. Their agents aren't stupid. They're going to at least toy with the idea that we must have known something more than we'd let on. They'll eventually speculate that we knew it was someone powerful and maniacal enough to kill us running the show. And there's no way we could know that unless we had inside information, which means we become the Bureau's target too. That gets compounded if Tracerio names us as coconspirators. The Bureau will definitely follow up on that. Then, there's the initial problem that jumpstarts the other two. Tracerio really *is* going to try to kill us!"

"That's not all we have to worry about either, Captain," Cantonelli said in a strained tone. "They're also going to want to know why we didn't act on the Blake woman's disappearance earlier. How the hell do we justify that?"

The chief had actually begun smiling as he listened to both men, which added to their confusion and fear. However, he was smiling because he had known they would say those things but already had answers. *Viable* answers.

"I've already figured out how we can handle those concerns, you two. First, we can put men on as personal security for us and send our families away because of a threat Gus will receive in his mailbox. It will also give us good evidence to cast disbelief on our involvement should Tracerio choose to point fingers our way. The letter will be untraceable because it will have been made using words clipped from various newspaper articles glued to a piece of common typing paper. It will say something like this: 'Back off now, or you and everybody involved will be joining the other two. There will not be a second warning.' That justifies the moves to protect our families and ourselves and lends credibility to our story that we were not involved with him. After all, if Tracerio had any of us on his payroll, why would he need to drop such a tediously constructed letter that could never be traced to threaten us with? He could get that done by picking up a phone or having someone follow one of us to a grocery store or something. And that would be smarter as well as easier. That way it left no paper trail. But our story will be that he didn't want us to know who'd sent it and that's why he'd gone to such lengths to disguise its origin. Now we take that one step further. He would only disguise a threat to stop the investigation if he were trying to keep us from discovering his involvement. And trying that proves we could not have been involved."

The chief let this sink in, then continued on. "Now, where the Blake woman and kid are concerned, we take a little egg on our faces. The story there is that the ball got dropped because every one of us thought somebody else must have already seen and talked to her since it never came up again. We never assumed she and the kid were still missing because we received no complaints or even so much as a call regarding them. It was an innocent mistake of 'I thought he had, he thought I had.' We'll definitely take a thrashing in the press and look like incompetent fools in the eyes of the Bureau, but it will end there. Besides, looking like fools may be a pretty damn good idea, and here's why. We've been in such a peaceful community for so long we've lost our paranoid thought pattern. That will help explain our initial conclusions about the other deaths. We'll be pressured to resign due to incompetence, so be prepared for that. I plan to announce mine not long after it's asked for, anyway. I won't fight it. I'll simply agree that I screwed up and don't deserve to lead the police in protecting the people anymore. Of course, I'll announce that my last act as chief will be to do everything within my power to bring this crime wave to a halt and the perpetrators to justice. You two should consider the same thing. You'll be out of a job, but that's definitely better than being in prison, or being *dead*, isn't it?"

Both Wilson and Cantonelli sat in silence absorbing Richter's words. They had been filled with hope for a way out of all this, and neither man could see any other way that was as promising. They'd live in constant fear and paranoia while the investigation and the trial ran their respective courses, but then they'd be in the clear. That is, as long as Tracerio never found them. Wilson was very uncomfortable with that.

"Chief, since we're probably going to end up losing our jobs anyway, and then most likely fending for ourselves, why don't we turn State's evidence on Tracerio right now? Our lives will be in danger either way, but at least then we won't have worry about what happens twenty years from now. We'd all have been in witness protection for so long he'd never find us," Wilson said.

The chief smiled again, this time a little on the devious side, then spoke.

"Who said we'd definitely have to worry about Tracerio? I plan to make sure that sadistic beast dies in a shootout somewhere along the line. His evil kid too. We're going to end up storming his place eventually, and during the firefight, they each take a bullet or two. Then there won't be any trial, and we won't have to hide. Plus, if we do this right, we might not have to leave the force at all, even after I announce that I will resign. The entire city may see us as the humble heroes who just made a few mistakes, and then put our lives on the line to rectify them. It's entirely possible they'll ask us not to resign. It might actually accelerate your careers and get me a raise. Is that enough reason not to turn ourselves in right now, gentlemen?" Richter asked with a hint of sarcasm.

Again both Wilson and Cantonelli sat there in silence. They had spent more time in the presence of the chief in the last two days than in all the time they'd worked for him combined. Both could see why he'd made it to chief. He was a deep thinker and a rational one, even in the face of extreme consequences. Richter said no more while he let them absorb everything. He could see by the looks on their faces that they were about to come on board, so there was no need to speak further. Now he just had to wait for them to say it. And say it they did. The rest of the evening was spent working on minute details and potential surprise occurrences. The first detail to be agreed upon was that the chief would definitely tell Tony about Davis and Rhodes this Friday and the second was that they were not to be put under any type of surveillance at all, especially Friday.

The way his family had rallied to lift his spirits had done wonders for Ralph. He carried that enthusiasm into the workday on Tuesday. Michael asked him what had caused him to be in such a delightful mood. Ralph told him everything that had taken place at his house the night before, down to the smallest detail.

Michael hadn't seen his friend feel this good about life in a long time. In fact, Ralph's exuberance actually raised Michael's spirits too. They spent most of the day talking and joking just as they had done every day before this started.

"We still on for dinner at your house this Friday, Ralph, or should I make other plans?" Michael asked as he pulled back into the station.

Ralph flashed a quick glare in Michael's direction, and said, "Of course we're on. And we're still on for 'dessert,' too. I've got a feeling, though, that you may not like it. It may be too bitter for you, partner."

"You may be right, but I'll decide that for myself, if that's still okay with you," Michael threw back.

"Yep. It is. Just remember our agreement. That's all I've got to say about it," Ralph said.

"I won't forget. But remember, we don't throw it away unless we both taste the same thing, Ralph. And that's all I have to say about it."

Michael was confident J.J. would let him know the following night whether he had been responsible for the fire at the farm but would tell J.J. to deny involvement to Ralph no matter what. Michael knew J.J. was doing what he thought was right, and no innocent people, as of yet, had been harmed. And as long as it remained that way, Michael would support J.J. the best he could.

J.J. had spent the last few days working out, except for the time it took to mail off the letters to Joan and Lance. He met with Michael on schedule, and they discussed everything—almost. J.J. would neither admit nor deny being the cause of the deaths and the fire as he didn't want Michael to be putting himself and his career in jeopardy. J.J. did say, however, that if he were going to take out the farm, it would only be done because of the drug lab that was hidden in its bowels. He went on to say that maybe the chemist at the lab had made a fatal mistake while combining ingredients and that may have been what caused the explosion.

Michael informed him that even knowledge of the drug lab's existence could send Ralph over the edge, so it was best not to say anything except that he hadn't done it. J.J. then suggested that he bring up the possibility that Tracerio himself did it. Maybe Fred

LEFT NO CHOICE

Johnson wasn't the only one who'd stiffed him, and Tracerio was making a point. Michael agreed with this idea whole-heartedly. Once they'd finished briefing each other on current developments, the conversation turned to family and friends. Right there in the alley down the street from where Tony and a few of his cronies were having dinner. They covered pretty much every major event in each of their lives through abridged versions. In fact, they were already out of things to talk about when the first car pulled out of the restaurant's parking lot.

Two of the cars were new to the scene and both drivers seemed a little angry when they pulled onto the street. They gunned their engines and screeched their tires as if they couldn't wait to put distance between themselves and Tracerio. Michael jotted down plate numbers as J.J. called them out from behind the lens of the camera. J.J. was no expert with a camera but was fairly confident he'd gotten shots that were in focus and discernable. The meeting had lasted until after ten, which had been the longest Michael had seen thus far. Before both men went their separate ways. Michael reminded J.J. to show up a half an hour later for Friday's meeting than he had last week. J.J. finally said what he'd been thinking since Michael had suggested that the first time. Why? Ralph was going to feel the same way whether he was fifteen minutes, thirty minutes, or only one minute late. There was nothing they were going to do about it. J.J. admitted that he'd rather not attend at all, but Michael nixed that quickly. If J.J. didn't show, Ralph would surely believe he'd been responsible for the fire and go straight to the Bureau. J.J. hadn't thought of that and thanked Michael for looking out for him. Then J.J. made a joke that maybe those two should start their own private detective agency when it was over. They both chuckled then parted company.

Michael ran the plates on the two new cars the next morning before he went on shift and both were rentals but from different companies. He called both agencies anonymously and complained that his car had been struck by the driver of their car and was able to get names and addresses of the drivers. One was from a suburb of Phoenix known as Glendale and the other from San Antonio, Texas. Michael guessed that both were somehow connected to Tracerio through the drug trade and had flown in because of the loss of product. That gave Michael a solid foothold on the belief that Tracerio's lab on the farm must have been huge. To be able to supply at least three cities from that one place? No wonder there were so many security guards there when it went up. He must have been supplying the whole southern center of the country from there. But not anymore, thanks to J.J.

Michael knew that J.J. was responsible, mainly because J.J. hadn't denied it. All J.J. did was offer optional theories as his way of saying nothing. Michael respected him for that, especially because J.J. hadn't flat out lied to him. He also felt pretty confident Ralph would buy J.J.'s theory that Tracerio did it himself as a follow-up to the Johnson murder. Now all they had to do was get through Friday night. If Ralph didn't try to arrest J.J. then, Michael was pretty sure he'd be able to get Ralph to back off completely. Michael had evidence of men from other cities in cahoots with Tracerio now in the form of photos and recorded rental car receipts. He could have the DEA put tails on both men, if they weren't already watching them, and before long, the DEA would nail them for something. Add that to the photos Michael had taken, a real investigation of the fire at the farm, and bingo! you had Tracerio under indictment for drug trafficking.

And that should be enough to clear J.J. of having to testify, even though the evidence of money laundering he had would be quite useful. Add that to the exhumation of the body believed to be him, and the bank topples along with Tracerio. Then it's all over and the good guys win. Michael smiled as he ran that thought through his head. Two beat cops and a banker take down one of the most powerful organizations in the southern half of the country. Michael was still shocked by one thing and couldn't get around it. He'd heard many times that no self-respecting family

LEFT NO CHOICE

man would come near the drug trade. He had no experience where this was concerned, so he didn't know if that was true or not. He hoped it was true, and that a man named Tracerio being the kingpin of the organization was just coincidence. That would mean Tony's operation was not just one appendage of a bigger one although Tony's was big enough. Michael figured Tracerio had to have several hundred men and women on his payrolls in one capacity or another.

Some were legitimate employees performing legitimate tasks and knew nothing about his other life. But how many of his employees were a part of his criminal activities? It was obvious now he was doing business in more that just Albuquerque. The more Michael thought about it, the more the sheer magnitude of the situation stunned him. High level public officials on the take and possibly involved in major felonies. High profile businessmen sheltering a distributorship of drugs that were being marketed in at least three states. One of the country's largest banks laundering the money. *Man!* What else could he find out in the course of investigating Tracerio? Maybe J.J. would have more for him on Friday.

Catherine and Lance received the letters on Thursday and both read theirs in private. The relationship between these three people was as wonderful as it seemed. Both brightened up when they read what he'd said about it being half over as that gave them some sense of time to work with. Both were very glad he'd made it this far and were worrying less and less each day about the danger he was in. Well, that was partly because he didn't tell them much of what he was doing, and partly because the things he did say were toned down quite a bit. Nevertheless, he'd said that with the Lord's help, they should all be together again by Thanksgiving.

18

Friday's workday had been especially hard on Ralph and Michael. Not because of criminal activity, but because it had been quiet all day. The two had nothing to do but count the hours until the shift was over.

Their conversations had been few and even those had been spawned out of necessity. Both men were preoccupied with what would happen later that night. They finished their shift as usual, checked out, and went to their respective homes. Michael would go over to Ralph's about an hour later, then after dinner, they'd drive to the park to meet with J.J. Then would come the moment of truth for their friendship.

As soon as he'd seen their cars pull out from his office window, Captain Wilson got on the phone.

"Chief. They're gone."

"How long ago?"

"Just now. I can still see their cars driving down the street."

"Okay. I'll take it from here."

"Yes, sir."

The chief left his office quickly and drove a dozen blocks to a pay phone. It was far enough from the station that later investigations would not be able to assume the call to Tracerio's house had been made by a cop. He used a glove to dial and hold the phone as usual, then told Tracerio about Rhodes and Davis's secret meetings. Tracerio blew up, as expected. Once Tony had finished his colorful dissertation, Richter suggested he might want to strike that night in the park down by the river. Richter told him they had probably selected the place because it was secluded, which meant there would be very few, if any, other people around. Tracerio took the bait down in one gulp. He thanked the chief, then hung up.

His next call was to Greenhill's cellular phone. He explained the situation and told Greenhill what he wanted done. He further instructed him to get Davis's address from his driver's license once he'd been dispatched, then go to the man's house and take out the family. Tracerio instructed Marcus to make the whole thing look like a double robbery. That way, the chief could explain it away without too much heat. First, the hoodlums had robbed and killed the men in the park, then gone to their houses afterward in their own cars to take everything that wasn't nailed down. They'd even stolen the keys to their houses and used those to gain entry. Marcus understood clearly what he was to do. After hanging up with Tony, he called Sharpe. He explained the situation to him and told him to be ready in fifteen minutes. Sharpe asked why so early, and Greenhill impatiently told him that he wanted to get a good look at the park before dark, and before the two men showed up.

David Sharpe was no dummy and knew before Marcus had said it why he wanted to go so soon. But David had company, and she charged by the half-hour. She hadn't been in the house five minutes when the phone had rung. He had an argument with her about payment not being due because no services had been rendered. She argued back that his having to leave was not her problem. She was absolutely willing to stay and carry out her part, so the money was due. He got really irked then and dragged her kicking and screaming by the hair toward the door. As she fought harder and started calling him names, Sharpe pulled a blade from his pocket and flashed it in her face. He told her that if she didn't shut up and get out without another word, she'd look so bad the next day she'd have to pay somebody to be with her.

She left and Sharpe finished getting ready. Greenhill arrived a few minutes later, and they drove down to the park. They had never done a cop before, let alone two. These two sick fools had killed old ladies, kids, entire families, and even babies, but never cops. Most would think they would rather not add two cops to their exploits, simply because of the intense heat that came down when cops got whacked. But these two were actually looking forward to it. They talked about the challenge of killing somebody who might actually shoot back. Both joked about it, but their plan after the walk-through proved it had all been just that—talk. They were going to be in separate areas of the park under the cover of trees with rifles. Both rifles would have silencers and scopes. The descriptions given were cause for another little foray into battle over who got to kill whom.

Greenhill said that no black man deserved to be shot by some white trash hoodlum, so he said he'd take Rhodes. Sharpe argued that affirmative action was for chumps and pansies and he was neither. He wanted Rhodes. Then Greenhill used his own budding prejudices against him. He asked Sharpe to state which of them had better vision, and since Sharpe wore contacts, there was no contest, but he wanted to know what that had to do with the price of tea in China. Greenhill calmly explained that a black man was harder to see in the dark, so he should take him. As Sharpe laughed and asked what kind of bull Marcus was pulling,

Marcus told him the truth. They'd probably only get one clean shot off at each of them, two if they were lucky. That meant every shot had to count. Period. Sharpe had lost the argument on that logic, so he changed the subject as they finished the drive back to Marcus's house to get changed and get the rifles. Their attire would be all black, with the facial mask to match. They wrapped the now loaded weapons into midnight blue blankets and went back to the park. They parked the car just off Mantano Road and walked a mile down the riverbank to the park. Their masks and black pullover shirts were wrapped in the blankets with the rifles.

The shirts they wore as they walked were light colored cotton, so they'd blend in with any hikers. They'd even grabbed two fishing poles and had the ends sticking out of the blankets for effect. They didn't know it, but by the time they'd done all this and walked halfway to the park, someone else had already set up shop. And as fate would have it, in the very same spot Greenhill and Sharpe were heading for.

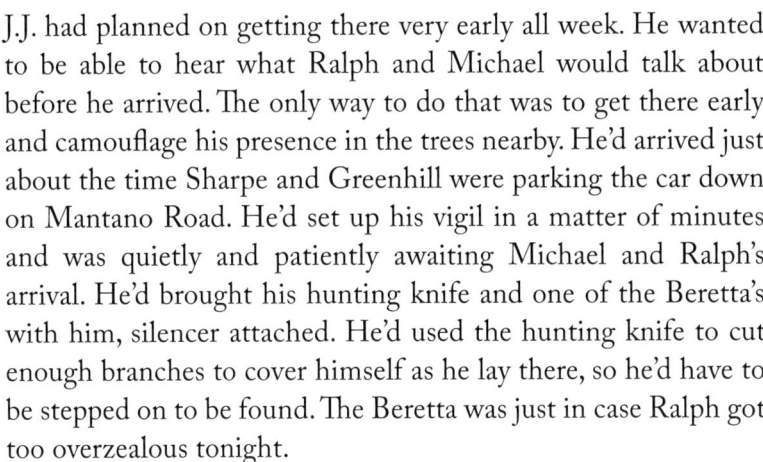

J.J. had planned on getting there very early all week. He wanted to be able to hear what Ralph and Michael would talk about before he arrived. The only way to do that was to get there early and camouflage his presence in the trees nearby. He'd arrived just about the time Sharpe and Greenhill were parking the car down on Mantano Road. He'd set up his vigil in a matter of minutes and was quietly and patiently awaiting Michael and Ralph's arrival. He'd brought his hunting knife and one of the Beretta's with him, silencer attached. He'd used the hunting knife to cut enough branches to cover himself as he lay there, so he'd have to be stepped on to be found. The Beretta was just in case Ralph got too overzealous tonight.

J.J. had no plans to use it although it was loaded and a round had already been chambered. But if Ralph decided to pull a gun on him to increase the advantage in trying to arrest him, J.J. would use it to disarm him if Michael did nothing. J.J. had been practicing on swinging targets the size of fists all week up at the cabin and was confident he could shoot the gun out of Ralph's hand without injuries to any other part of his body. J.J. was also wearing the bulletproof vest under his oversized shirt, in case Ralph actually did get a round off. He wanted to avoid all the gunplay, though, which is why he decided to get there ahead of them. If what he heard was bad news for him, he'd tell them from the bushes that their relationship was over and that he only ask that they not go to the FBI for seven more days. He was sure Ralph would say something really idiotic and macho, and maybe even draw a weapon and point it in J.J.'s general direction. That's when J.J. would shoot it out of his hand and state that they'd both already be dead if J.J. had wanted it that way.

Then he would ask again for seven more days. On the following Friday night, he'd either turn himself over to them there in the park, or a federal agent would come down and tell them personally that he already had turned himself over to them. The other option, that Ralph would come on board and help was still the one he wished for. He didn't blame Ralph for acting the way he was. Ralph was taking care of himself, and he wasn't breaking any laws in doing so. J.J. did feel that Ralph was somewhat of a hypocrite, though, because he was only serving and protecting his own family. Still, all in all, he'd like to have Ralph patrolling the area around his house. Ralph was a good and honest cop and deserved J.J.'s utmost patience and consideration.

He'd just finished camouflaging his position when he heard something. He closed his eyes and focused his hearing. It was footsteps in the brush. Somebody was coming his way and from behind. Not just one, but two people. By the sounds of it, they were about ten yards to the rear and to his right and closing. He lay there still while a bug of some kind climbed over his hand. The footsteps were farther apart now, and the sound was much closer. That meant they were slowing down as they neared the clearing just as J.J. had. He was fairly sure they didn't know he was there, because they would have been much quieter coming in if they had known.

Finally, he heard a voice whisper, "Okay. I'll set up here. You're gonna circle twenty-five yards or so to my left away from the water and set up. You take the one on our left, and I'll take the one on our right. If they don't come to this end of the park, we'll pull back and circle around for a clean shot. You got that?"

"Yeah. I got it. What's the signal to fire?"

"I was getting to that, David, relax. Take an end of this string with you. Pull on it three times to let me know you're in position, then once after they arrive to let me know you've got a clear line of fire. Twice, if you don't have a clear line and have to move. Then once again when you're repositioned and ready. When you feel me tug on it three times in a row, wait ten full seconds and then fire. If I only tug once, we abort and fall back into the woods. If I tug twice, it means I'm coming to you. And the last thing. If more than just the two of them show up, I'll take the two closest to the river, and you take whoever is farthest from it. Once they're down, we move in. You got all that?"

"Yeah, yeah. And if I see something that doesn't look right I'll pull hard and hold it for three seconds before I release it, okay?"

"Okay. Good Idea. Now get moving, man. We're running out of time. They'll be here soon."

"I'm gone."

J.J. listened as the second man departed. These two were here to kill Michael and Ralph! How did these two know where they'd be? The only people that knew were the three of them and Ralph's w—. Oh, man! She told somebody. Not good! His thoughts flew in all sorts of directions. He would have to move and move fast to neutralize the guy behind him. That meant it would be noisy, giving the other jerk time to make a play of his own. J.J.'s fear wasn't that the second sniper would come toward him. In fact, J.J. wanted him to. His real fear was that the man would disappear before J.J. could get to him. He thanked God that he'd chambered a round in the Beretta before they had arrived as that would save him at least a second and maybe two. He'd have to roll over somehow to get a decent shot off. And even though he knew the general direction and distance the voice had come from, he wasn't sure enough to just roll and fire. He tried to turn his head to the side slowly to get a look over his right shoulder, but nothing entered his vision. The leader was more behind than beside him.

Just then, he heard something else. Leaves and branches moving. Once. Twice. Thrice. The other player must be in position. J.J. then realized what his best time to attack would be. The sniper behind him was going to pull on it three times as the signal. J.J. now knew he'd hear it being pulled, so that would give him ten seconds to neutralize this assassin and get at least a distraction shot off at the second one before he could fire his weapon at Michael or Ralph. He thought about just pulling the string once after neutralizing the first one but that was risky. If the second man heard the Beretta's "burp" or the commotion of the first one hitting the ground, he may still fire. Nope. J.J. would have to take them both.

After the assassin behind him pulled on the string, the man would have to direct all his attention down the barrel of his rifle. That was the best time for J.J. to roll into action. He'd have to wait two seconds for the man to get the rifle into position, and then he'd make his move. J.J.'s best guess placed the man five or six feet behind his right foot and out to the right another three or four feet. It was gonna be tight. It was still light enough for J.J. to see movement, so he turned his head slowly in the direction of the second assassin to see if he could get a fix on his position. No way. There was nothing in his line of sight but a lot of bushes and quite a few trees. Using the hunting knife was out. J.J. would never have enough time to take this man out with it and still put the other man down. It was the Beretta for both. There was no other way. He heard a car door, then a second one. The park was empty now. It would be a lot harder for these two to step into the open to make sure they'd killed both men if other people were there. On second thought, it was better that it was empty. Innocent people might become targets to cover the hit as a random killing spree. There they were. Michael was carrying a six-pack and Ralph was a step behind him on the right.

"Hello, round heads. You're about to be run over by the Greenhill express." J.J. heard whispered from behind him.

He couldn't yell out to Michael and Ralph. The second man may already have them in the crosshairs of his scope, and he'd have time to get a couple of rounds off at them while the one just behind J.J. put a quick burst into J.J.'s general area. Michael and Ralph were about sixty yards out now and getting closer with each step. J.J. decided not to wait for the signal. The farther away from the kill zone Michael and Ralph were when he spun into action, the better their chance of survival. It was now or never. The one behind him was obviously watching them approach, so he'd be startled by J.J.'s movement. J.J.'s heart was beating with the speed of a hummingbird's wings now, and the adrenaline was flooding his senses. J.J.'s arms were already extended out in front of him, so he pulled his left arm in a few inches and put the palm of that hand against the ground. Fifty yards.

He could make out Michael's voice now but couldn't tell what he was saying. He tightened the muscle in his left arm and slowly pushed his upper body away from the ground an inch at a time. Forty yards. He turned his head to the right without sound breaking the silence, and pulled his right arm back toward him until his elbow was below his shoulder. His grip on the Beretta unconsciously tightened to the force of a human vice. Thirty yards.

He took a deep, deliberately slow breath and loosened his grip on the Beretta. With his grip that tight, the Beretta would be hard to wield and the speed he'd need to adjust its line of fire once he moved would be dangerously hampered. Twenty-eight yards.

"That's right, come to Papa. It's almost time to say good night." J.J. heard whispered from behind. J.J. was almost positive of the man's position now. Twenty-five yards.

It was time. He was as ready as he'd ever be at that moment. With the speed of a gymnast, J.J. shifted his weight to his left arm and pushed off the ground with his right knee and elbow. He spun up onto his left hip and brought the business end of the Beretta around and up. The noise was as if someone was jumping into a large pile of leaves, but it was too late to change that now. His adrenal gland sent everything it had into his bloodstream and the surge into his brain was almost dizzying. He was committed now; there was no turning back. As his right arm came up and around, it threw the branches he'd used to cover himself up to the right, momentarily blocking the vision of the man behind him. He could see the target's upper body now and brought the barrel of the Beretta to a stop with the bullet's trajectory on a collision course with the man's throat. The man was so stunned by the surprise movement so close to him that he froze. His eyes and mouth were open wide with confusion and disbelief as J.J. squeezed off the first and second rounds one after the other.

The first blew through his chin like a baseball through a plate-glass window. The second left the barrel during the recoil of the first and crashed through his skull just above his nose. J.J. had no time to waste now. He didn't know how the second sniper had reacted to the noise, so he had no choice but to charge him. He caught a glimpse of the white twine they had spread between them as he sprung to his feet, but his gut told him pulling on it would be a waste of time. A deadly waste of time. He leapt through the brush like a deer, his eyes darting back and forth from the string to the line of sight above and in front of it. He had traveled only about ten yards when he saw something in the brush. It was a man's eyes, and they were fixed on him. He was only fifteen yards away, and J.J. had a clear line of sight. He brought the Beretta up with the swiftness of a champion boxer throwing an uppercut. He had just zeroed in his aim when he heard the man whisper, "Marcus? What are you doin'?"

J.J. didn't answer with words. He popped three quick rounds out of the Beretta, and although the first missed its mark, the second and third did not. The force of the second bullet's impact into the man's left shoulder sent him sprawling backward and the third ripped across the side of his head as he fell. The man let out a loud groan as the second bullet invaded his body, tearing flesh and shattering bone. J.J.'s bullet had destroyed the man's clavicle. As he fell from the third, he screamed in agony. J.J. moved in on his position with the Beretta leading the way, watching carefully for signs of retaliatory movement.

"Michael! Ralph! Snipers in the trees! Hit the ground, *now*!" He yelled as he closed in on the second man. He had moved to within five yards of the assassin before he could see him clearly. The man was reaching for his rifle as J.J. heard Ralph call out.

"Blake! Is that you?"

"Yes! Just stay down!" J.J. yelled back.

"Where are they, Blake? Give us their position!" Ralph yelled.

J.J. was now within ten feet of the second sniper. The man was bringing the rifle's barrel up toward J.J. as he yelled, "Die, you worthless piece o—!" The man was wearing a full facemask similar to J.J.'s, but his eyes showed that he was overflowing with crazed hate and in enormous pain. J.J. had been led all the way in by the Beretta, so it was already in position to defend without question and terminate, if necessary. He side stepped to the left away from the rising barrel and sent another round across the man's chest into the barrel end of the rifle's stock. The rifle twisted out of the sniper's hand and fell to the ground.

"You worm! Where is Marcus? *Marcus!*"

The man's right hand was up and pointing at J.J. again. J.J. could tell that his left was out of action. J.J. decided to do the same with his right. He swung the Beretta over and sent a bullet in the direction of his right hand. The bullet went through his hand like a locomotive through a plywood fence. Pieces of bone and flesh flew in all directions as the slug exited as did what was left of the man's self-control. He screamed the scream of those defeated and in agony, then fell back blubbering like a coward.

"Blake! What is happening out there!" Ralph yelled with a voice saturated in fear, anger and confusion.

"It's clear! There were two of them. One is in the trees fifteen feet from the table. He's dead. The other is right here in front of me, and as you can hear, he isn't." J.J. announced, then had an uneasy thought.

"Ralph! Michael! Are either of you armed?"

"We both are!" Ralph yelled back.

"Good. There may be more than these two! One of you check the man in the trees by the table, and the other cover us against an attack from the other side of the park. I'll cover this way!" J.J. yelled through deep breaths.

"Got it!" Ralph yelled back.

"Hey! I didn't have time to check the one by the table after I dropped him! Make sure you approach his position with caution!" J.J. ordered.

"Wait. Stop! Which of you is coming into the tree line?"

"I'm coming in while Ralph watches our backs from the table!" Michael yelled back.

"Okay. Change of plans! Michael you come to me and watch this one. I know exactly where the other one is, so if he is alive, I'll have the best shot at protecting myself!"

Michael looked quickly over at Ralph. Ralph kept his eyes and the barrel of his revolver pointed toward the main clearing of the park but didn't hesitate to speak.

"He's right, Michael. Do as he says."

LEFT NO CHOICE

Michael looked like a hunchback as he quickly made his way to the edge of the trees. He stopped there and peered in. He could see nothing human.

"J.J. Call out so I know where you are!"

"I can see you, Michael. Five feet to your left and fifteen feet in," J.J. said in a normal tone.

Michael's heart was making almost as much noise as his footsteps in the brush. He wound his way into the trees, then stopped a few feet in and looked around. He took a few more steps, and saw J.J. He was wearing all black, including a mask. He looked like a movie version of a ninja, Michael thought.

"Okay. I see you. I'm on my way."

Michael had heard the sniper moaning and crying, which helped guide his vision to J.J. The woods were dark, and if he hadn't heard the crying, he still wouldn't have found J.J.

"Man, Ralph and I never realized. We'd be...we'd be dead, J.J. Thank you," Michael said sincerely. But J.J. was not in the mood for conversation. Not until he was sure about the other player.

"No problem, Michael. Just keep your eyes on this guy and keep a watch out into the forest for movement. I'm going back down toward the river. That's where the other one is. I'll announce myself as I come back toward you. If you see something and you don't hear them first. Don't call out and don't hesitate. Drop them. You got it?"

J.J. spoke as though he was back in Iraq teaching a soldier how to stay alive. Michael picked up on it too.

"Yeah, J.J. I got it."

"Good. Be right back. Ralph! What you'll hear behind you is me going toward the river, so don't worry! Just keep covering from that side, okay?"

"Gotcha, J.J.!" Ralph yelled. Both Michael and J.J. caught it; that was the first time Ralph had called him anything but Blake.

J.J. made his way carefully back down toward the river, using the string as sort of a guide. The Beretta was out in front.

Instinctively, he'd counted the rounds as he'd fired them. He'd used six of the fifteen round clip. That left nine. More than enough to go back over there with. He paused as he caught sight of the body. Looking carefully, he could see no movement, but he could see the rifle. It was lying across the man's torso and the barrel was pointing in J.J.'s direction. The man's left hand was on the ground beside him, but his right was not visible. J.J. circled around toward the river above the man's head. As J.J. circled trying to get a look at the right hand, he saw reflective sparkles like stars in the night sky, but they were on the ground and on the man's face. What was left of it, that is. J.J. knelt beside him and appraised the damage. His forehead was still there even though there was now a good-sized hole in it. But his lower jaw was history. The first bullet had shattered his chin and broken his jaw. His eyes were wide open, and still carrying the same look he'd had when J.J. fired the first round. The Greenhill Express had made its last stop.

"This one's dead. Michael, I'm coming back toward you! Ralph? How's the park?" J.J. asked as he worked his way back to Michael.

"It's clear here. For the moment, at least."

"Okay. We'll be out in a couple minutes."

"Gotcha. Don't touch anything of theirs if you can help it, J.J. okay?" Ralph asked from the picnic table. That was the second time he called him J.J.

"I haven't yet. But now I'll make it a point not to. Thanks, Ralph. Michael, I'm coming in."

"Okay. You're clear."

J.J. entered and said, "Which of you two normally does the interrogations, Michael?"

"We both do, but under the circumstances, J.J.," Michael said slyly from behind a wide grin. "I think it would be best if Ralph got a shot at this one."

J.J. smiled back, knowing then that Michael had also caught on to Ralph's change of heart.

LEFT NO CHOICE

"I agree. You go switch places with him and send him in. I'll prepare our witness," J.J. said coyly.

Michael looked at J.J. for a second, then understood and left. It would be best if he didn't see what J.J. meant by prepare him.

"Ralph! I'm coming out. Don't shoot me, you crazy hunk of lard!" Michael said jokingly. All three men chuckled, easing their tension a little.

"Don't tempt me, Michael. Call me crazy again and I just might," Ralph said in a mock threat.

"All right, then. Don't shoot me, you hunk of lard, 'cause I'm comin' out!" Michael threw back.

All three men let out a small laugh. The tension was still there, but it was lessening by the minute. The worst seemed to be over, and they were all still alive.

"That's better! Smart guy." Ralph said through his light laugh.

Once Michael had taken four steps toward the tree line, J.J. knelt beside the now whimpering sniper. The man's eyes were full of fear and sadness. Quite a difference from ten minutes ago, J.J. thought. He took one more careful look out into the trees around him, then holstered the Beretta. Sharpe watched as he did this. J.J.'s right hand disappeared behind his back. When it reappeared, so did J.J.'s hunting knife. A higher level of fear instantly appeared in Sharpe's eyes, and his whimpering increased to crying. J.J. pulled Sharpe's mask up off his face, then put the point of the blade inside Sharpe's left nostril. He tugged it slightly. It cut into Sharpe's flesh like a razor, but J.J. had only tugged on it enough to get his attention. It worked. Sharpe began to speak.

"Please don't kill me. Please? I promi—"

"Shut up, dummy! Now, you better pay real close attention to what I'm about to say, because I'm only going to say it once. There will be no second version. Do you understand?" J.J.'s tone was filled with so much anger and disgust Sharpe knew he wasn't making an idle threat. Sharpe didn't move because of the blade hovering deep in his nose, so he composed himself the best he could, swallowed, and spoke.

"Y-yes. I-I do. No P-p-problem."

"Good. First, how many of you were sent here?"

"J-just two."

That jived with what J.J. had heard from the bushes, so now he was pretty sure there were no others.

"Okay. By now you know your pal is dead. You'll be joining him in hell tonight if you don't tell us everything we want to know. But you won't have the luxury of dying by a bullet. Nope, if I feel even for a second you're stalling or lying to me, I'm gonna saw off your nose and make you eat it. Once the nose is gone, I saw off your ears, then the fingers, then the toes. Then I start feeding you chunks of your own flesh. You'll die one gruesome, slow death tonight if you waste my time, jerkface. Have you got that?"

"Y-y-yes. I-I-I g-got it."

"J.J. It's Ralph. I'm coming in."

"Okay, Ralph. You're clear. Straight ahead ten feet or so."

J.J. let that graphic picture set in for a few more seconds, then said in a maniacal tone, "Man, I really hope you forget. I really do. I haven't gotten the chance to do this since I was in Black Ops. And if I were you, I wouldn't count on either one of these guys to save you since you just tried to kill them. My guess is they both want you dead right now too. So just hesitate once. Or stutter too much. That would be good. That's all the excuse I need right now to butcher you. Seventeen out of nineteen others thought I was messin' with them, and all seventeen found out the hard way that one shot was all they were gonna get. The other two are probably at home with their families right now. So you make the call, you measley leech. Which is it gonna be?" J.J. even surprised himself at how convincing he sounded.

The ploy worked. Sharpe was so frightened by the picture J.J. had laid out for him that he was willing to say anything.

"I'll tell ya everything ya wanna know, mister, I swear it!" Sharpe said, shaking uncontrollably. Then his curiosity bested him. "Mister, could I ask you somethin' without it gettin' me killed?"

"You can ask," J.J. said flatly. He could see that the man was clearly broken.

"Who are you?"

J.J. grinned a devilish grin. This man hadn't heard Ralph call him Blake. And since J.J. was still wearing his own mask, his identity was still a secret.

"Well, what do we have here?" Ralph asked in a mock fatherly tone as he stopped and looked on. He owed his life to J.J., so he said nothing about where J.J. was holding the knife. Besides, if J.J. had wanted to kill him, Ralph thought, he would have already. Ralph put his hands on his hips, and spoke again.

"Son, didn't I tell you that playing with guns could get you hurt? You never listen to me." Ralph said to Sharpe, shaking his head in mock disappointment.

"Ralph Davis, I'd like you to meet." J.J. looked at Sharpe, and as Sharpe remained silent, J.J.'s eyes widened and a grin began to grow on his face. He looked at Sharpe's nose and started to lean in.

"S-sharpe! D-david Sharpe."

"Ooh, that was close, David. I was gettin' excited," J.J. said with enthusiasm.

"Ralph, me and David here have been having quite a heart to heart conversation. He promises he'll answer any question you ask him. Won't ya, David?"

"Y-y-yes. Yes. Everything I know."

Ralph could see now what J.J. was doing. It was illegal, but this man had been sent to kill him, so Ralph didn't care. In fact, he rather liked it. There were many perps he wished he could interrogate this way.

"What's the other shooter's name?" Ralph barked out.

"Greenhill. M-marcus Greenhill," Sharpe spat out quickly.

Sharpe looked at J.J. as he answered but got no response. J.J. was just staring at his nose. Then Ralph fired question after question.

"Who sent you here to kill us?"

"T-Tracerio. Sr. Tony Tracerio Sr."

"How'd you know where we'd be tonight?"

"Tracerio. He told Marcus."

"How did Tracerio know?"

"I don't know. Marcus didn't tell me," Sharpe said as he began to cry, afraid J.J. wouldn't believe him. But J.J. did believe him and interrupted Ralph to say so.

"That's bull! You kno—"

"No, Ralph. I don't think he does."

"Really?" Ralph asked, a little surprised at being interrupted, "And why is that?"

"Because," J.J. explained, "Tracerio is an egotistical, self-centered maniac. He's not the type who would tell his grunts everything he knows. I heard these two when they first arrived. The one over there was the leader. I'm sure of it. This pile of dung here is probably just the hired help. But I'll tell you how we can find out how Tracerio knew," J.J. offered.

"How?" Ralph asked curiously.

"*Michael! Come on in! They were alone!*"

"Michael?" Ralph asked, bewildered.

"*Are you sure?*" Michael called back.

"No, not Michael, Ralph. Just hang on a second."

"*Yes, I'm sure. Come on in!*" J.J. yelled.

"Then if not Michael, who?" Ralph asked impatiently.

"Just hang on a second until Michael gets here, Ralph. Then I'll explain my thinking, okay?" J.J. asked respectfully.

Ralph looked down at the man who'd just saved his life and gave him the benefit of the doubt.

"Okay. No problem."

Once Michael had joined them, J.J. brought him up to speed on what had been said so far. Then he asked the question that sent Ralph reeling.

"Obviously, Tracerio found out about you two meeting out here on Friday nights at this time, so somebody had to tell him that. That means somebody that works for him must have tailed you here at least twice, overheard it from one of you, or someone close to you. Can we agree on that?"

Both Michael and Ralph hesitated for a moment, then agreed.

"All right. That makes it easier. I have told no one of our meetings out here. Have either of you told anyone?"

Michael's response was instantaneous.

"No. I haven't."

"I haven't either," Ralph said, now more confused.

J.J. looked up at Ralph and calmly asked, "Ralph, did you tell your wife?"

It took a few seconds, but Ralph's bewilderment turned to despair. He pulled his cell phone from his pocket and called home without a word. Flo answered on the third ring.

"Hello, Davis's residence."

"Flo, it's me."

"Hi! Boy, this is o—"

"Honey. Honey, listen. Have you told anyone, and I mean anyone about Michael and me coming out here to the park on Fridays? Think hard, please, okay?"

"No, I haven't said anything to any—. Wait. Yes, I did. I ran into Debbie Wilson at Wal-Mart and we talked for a while. I think it was Monday. She said her husband had been uptight a lot lately and I told her you had been too. Then I told her about you and Michael going off to the park every Friday night. Why? What's wrong?"

Ralph couldn't believe his ears. He stood there stunned beyond the ability to move for a few seconds. Flo's little conversation had almost cost him his life tonight.

"Ralph? Talk with me, honey. What's wrong?" Flo pleaded.

"Flo, everything's okay. Relax. But I need you to do something for me, okay?" Ralph asked nervously.

"Okay. What?"

"Grab both kids and go downtown to a hotel for the night. Not a motel, a hotel. You got that?"

"Ralph, why in the world woul—"

"Don't ask questions, Flo. Just grab your cell phone and the kids and go, now! I'll call you in a few hours, okay?"

"What's wrong, Ralph? Are we in danger?"

"*Flo*! Just get the phone and the kids and go! *Now*! I'll call you soon."

"Okay. I'm going. Bye!" she said as she slammed down the phone.

Both Michael and J.J. watched as Ralph deflated into a mass of regret. They waited in silence. He stood there thinking of all the things that could have happened that night. A seemingly innocent comment made by his loving wife to the wife of his boss, who was also his enemy, could have ended all their lives. He finally regrouped and spoke sorrowfully.

"It was Flo. She told Captain Wilson's wife on Monday when they ran into each other in Wal-Mart. Then Wilson's wife must have told him. I'm sorry, you two. I'm real—"

"No time for that now, Ralph," J.J. interjected. "We still have a lot to do here, so don't worry about it. Besides, your wife might have just given us everything we need to take Tracerio down." J.J. waved an open hand palm up over Sharpe, then continued.

"You wanted evidence of Tracerio's involvement. Here it is, in the guise of." J.J. raised his eyebrows as he did his voice, signaling the dazed man on the ground to speak.

"Sharpe. And yes. I'll testify. I'll tell you everything you need to know to put him away. Names, dates, everything," Sharpe was fading from consciousness fast as he spoke. "But I want immunity.

You have to guarantee me immunity. And now you need to get me to the hospita…" He passed out mid-sentence.

J.J. checked his pulse, and although it was slow, it was pretty strong.

"He just passed out. He'll be okay," J.J. told them.

"J.J., if the Captain told Tracerio, then the chief and Cantonelli must know too. And they must have known Tracerio would want us killed," Michael said.

"That's right, Michael. I'd say it's time to pay a visit to the home of our dear Captain," Ralph said emphatically. "J.J. I can never thank you enough for what you did tonight, but I hope you'll accept my apology for being such an ogre."

"Apology accepted, you crazy hunk of lard," J.J. said, mocking Michael. Michael and Ralph both chuckled as did J.J.

"Okay," Ralph said with a pat on J.J.'s shoulder, "You're allowed to call me crazy. You've earned it, but only this once." Then he put an outstretched hand in front of J.J. They shook hands meaningfully, and their feud was instantly replaced by the most powerful bond of all—trust.

J.J. explained to them that Sharpe still didn't know his true identity and that he'd like to keep it that way for a while longer as it added to Sharpe's fear of him. Then he slapped Sharpe in the face a few times and awakened him. Ralph read him his rights, and then Sharpe made a comment about getting to a doctor before saying anything else. J.J. slid the blade back into his nose immediately.

"Listen, David. We haven't forgotten that you came here to kill these two men. That means that they don't like you, and neither do I. So we couldn't care less about you seeing a doctor until we're good and ready to take you. If you die out here like your buddy did before you tell us everything we want to know, none of us will lose a bit of sleep. So I suggest you answer all the questions we ask as quickly as you can. Or I start cutting, and you start chewing. Have you got all that, David?"

Sharpe answered affirmatively and all three men took turns firing away. It would be fifteen minutes before Sharpe slipped into unconsciousness again. J.J. couldn't wake him this time, but the three men had already learned just about everything Sharpe knew about Tracerio's organization. The decision that had to be made now was where to go from here and how to get there. Sharpe was still alive and would live through all this, J.J. told both cops reassuringly. He explained that he'd seen more than his share of wounds like this, and men had survived for many days without medical attention under much more severe conditions. The discussion then turned to the Bureau, and all the ramifications of going to them.

All three men were torn on that decision. Since Sharpe had admitted he and Greenhill had been ordered to go to the men's homes after they left the park, even Ralph became unnerved a little. Going to the Bureau now meant that all three of them and their families would be in jeopardy until the trial was over and might not even be safe then. The trip to the Bureau was voted down unanimously.

They were going to have to try to finish it themselves and finish it tonight.

"Victor, there are three good men out there. They can handle any surprises. Tonight is a night of celebration, not a night of business. For once, would you just sit down with us and relax? Have some dinner and a glass of wine." Tony Sr. said.

"No, thank you, sir. You pay me to make sure you can relax. And that's what I'm going to do," Victor said standing near the door of Tony's private dining room.

Tony looked at his son, then at the ladies they had brought as dates. The look on his face was one of pleasant disbelief. He shook his head, then raised an outstretched hand in Hanes's direction.

LEFT NO CHOICE

"You hear this? Even when I offer a night of enjoyment, he chooses to work. I offer to arrange a lovely companion to spend the evening with and what did he say to me? 'No thank you, Mr. Tracerio. I already have one,' and he places his hand on his holster," Tony said, placing his own hand on his jacket pocket. "Son, of all the boys you met at that school, you definitely picked the one who grew up to be one incredible man. To Victor!" Tony Sr. said, raising a glass in his direction.

"To Victor!" came three voices in unison.

Victor Hanes bowed slightly in their direction, said thanks, then returned to watching the people in the bar through the window in the door.

"Vic, Dad's right. Just this once, why don't you join us? I'm sure Miss Violet has a friend who'd love nothing more than to join us as your escort."

Violet smiled slyly and nodded. Then she gave Victor's handsome frame the once-over, and her smile turned to one that had seductively wicked thoughts written all over it. Both Tonys caught the look and the slight movement in her seat. Tony Sr. looked quickly at his son, not knowing what his response would be. He was not aware that these two had swapped women many times in school and were not bothered in the least when one's date showed interest in the other. In fact, quite often they used it to increase their own level of enjoyment.

"Hey, Vic," he said smiling and laughing, "I think Miss Violet wants to volunteer to be your escort herself." Then he leaned over toward her and said in a lower tone, "You like that, huh? Baby, if all goes well between you and me tonight, and I mean real well, I'll see what I can do about getting you a proper introduction, all right?"

She nodded with excitement, then leaned to him and planted a French "thank-you" kiss on him. Tony Sr. watched from the other side of the table then smiled broadly.

"I think I know now why you and Vic get along so well, Son. You share everything. That's good. Why not? Neither of you are married, so I say, Enjoy!" And with that, he raised his glass while his smile turned to light laughter.

The dining room was now filling with sexual energy, and Jacquelyn, Tony Sr.'s date, decided to make his night more memorable. She began teasing him with gentle touches on the inside of his thigh now and again. Then once, when she'd risen to go refresh herself, had parted her legs more than necessary as he helped her to her feet. Her dress fell away from her thighs, and Tony caught a glimpse of what was yet in store for him.

Tony had called ahead and asked Joseppè to prepare an array of succulent dishes for dinner. Joseppè outdid himself, if that was at all possible. The feast was spectacular as was Furia's choices of vintage wines. The courses were served one by one, in the tradition of the Old Country, and there were five in all. Jacquelyn and Violet ate sparingly from each course, while the two men ate a touch more than their share. Young Tony had commented on their lack of appetite, jokingly, and both ladies in turn seductively said their reasons for not filling up on food. The traditional cigars were lighted after dinner, and as the men smoked, Jacquelyn and Violet told abridged versions of their life histories. Once the cigars were half consumed, all five people migrated out to the lounge. Tony had also requested live music for the night. He'd told Joseppè it was because he wanted to dance. He would dance, to be sure, but not because he really wanted to. Making numerous trips out onto a dance floor would ensure that every man and woman there would see him. What better witnesses to his whereabouts for the night could there be? Thirty people were more than enough witnesses, especially because only a handful of them were connected to Tony in any way.

19

"Flo. Collect all your things honey, but don't check out. Yes, I realize you just checked in. Just do it, okay?. Use the rear exit when you leave. I'll meet you out back in fifteen minutes," Ralph said at the end of the call.

"Okay. That's done. How far from Chimayo is this cabin of yours?" Ralph asked J.J.

"Not that far. About a twenty-minute drive. I can get there from here in just over two hours driving the speed limit."

"And you're sure my family will be safe there?"

"Positive. Where do you think I've been staying since this started?"

"Okay. I trust you, J.J. Let's do it."

J.J. jogged back down the road a half mile and grabbed the Ramcharger. Neither Ralph nor Michael had ever seen him in it, so when they drove by it into the park they wouldn't have known it was his, or that he was already there. J.J. backed it up to the edge of the pavement, pulled the accessories fuse, and opened the tailgate. Then he ran back to where Michael and Ralph were standing over Sharpe. J.J. had brought a couple things with him this trip. A camera and a flashlight.

"J.J. why don't you let me and Michael handle this part. Then once we've got enough pictures of this scene, we'll move over to the other area and you can carefully wrap the rifles and the fishing poles back into the blanket, okay?"

"Thanks, Ralph. I was gonna ask if you would. I have no clue what you guys would want on film for evidence."

"No problem. Just step back and enjoy the view for a few minutes," Ralph said cordially.

"Yeah, J.J. I think you deserve a break anyway," Michael chimed in with a smile.

Once all the photos had been taken, Michael and J.J. carried Sharpe out of the brush and Ralph carried the weapons. They put Sharpe on the tailgate of the Ramcharger and J.J. proceeded to tie him up while Michael and Ralph grabbed Greenhill's body. By the time the two cops had brought Greenhill's body over to the Ramcharger, J.J. had field dressed Sharpe's wounds and was ready to move him into the backseat. He and Michael did so, and then Greenhill's body was placed in the rear area of the Ramcharger, and tied down. Neither Ralph nor Michael was happy about doing things this way. But both men also knew that if an ambulance or a cruiser was called, Tracerio's crew would find out their hit had gone bad and try to cover their butts. Right now, they had at least an eleven-hour advantage and wanted to keep every second of it.

Sharpe had said he and Greenhill were to dump the two bodies in the river so they wouldn't be found until the next day. Tracerio didn't want them found that night, because then the cops may go to their homes before he and Greenhill could ransack them. Greenhill was to call Tracerio at eight the next morning to inform him of their success. That's when the panic would start setting in from Tracerio's side. Greenhill would obviously never make that call. J.J. suggested they take Sharpe up to the cabin and try to rest him enough to make the call if they still needed more time. Both men agreed that was a good idea, and Flo would be there to make sure he did it if she hadn't heard from Ralph by seven thirty. They blindfolded and ear-plugged Sharpe, so he wouldn't know where he was calling from, or be able to give clues on the phone should he awaken during the trip up there. J.J. had told them of his little arsenal and given a rundown of all his weapons. There were enough guns and ammunition there for all of them, so they'd have no reason to stop at their homes for weapons. Both Sharpe and Greenhill had been wearing vests under their shirts, so Michael and Ralph took them because J.J. only had the one he was wearing in his inventory. There was only one other problem. Sharpe had said they were supposed to drive Ralph's car back to his house to do the hit there. That way, if his wife or kids had seen a car pull in, they'd think it was Ralph and not think twice about being suspicious. Ralph usually parked in the garage, so the car wouldn't be seen anyway. But if one of Tracerio's men saw Ralph behind the wheel while they drove through town to the hotel to get Flo, their element of surprise would be gone. So Ralph would drive the Ramcharger and Michael would drive Ralph's car.

J.J. would ride with Michael, hunched down in the seat to look like Sharpe. Should they see a cruiser, they'd turn off before they crossed its path, so it wasn't the police cruisers they were worried about. It was any of Tracerio's people that might be out and about. Ralph had argued that the little game of musical drivers was overkill and unnecessary, but J.J. reminded him of what was at stake, for all of them. That shut Ralph up in a hurry. They met Flo in the rear parking lot of the hotel where Ralph had instructed her to wait. Ralph had the kids sit in their mom's car, while he and Flo walked a dozen spaces down to the Ramcharger, where both Michael and J.J. were waiting. Ralph did a quick introduction, then gave Flo the abridged version of the night's events as Michael and J.J. stepped away to keep watch. She almost lost it when he told her about the captain's involvement, so he mercifully spared her the details of how close they'd all come to dying that night. Instead, he played the hit down somewhat and said that he and Michael had been ready for it. Then he showed her the man in the backseat and told her what she was going to have to do that night. Flo was a strong woman and took that part of the news well. Ralph never told her about the dead man in the back. She didn't need to know.

J.J. and Ralph switched keys, and Ralph had Flo and the kids pile into his car and stay low. There was a freeway onramp a half mile down, so Ralph figured he'd be safe driving his own car that far on the city streets. Michael would ride with J.J., keeping an eye on Sharpe as they drove. Since the situation had come under control and there wasn't much to do on the drive, Michael would have the time to ponder some things.

"J.J., let me ask you something. Why were you there so early? And why were you hiding in the trees with a weapon? I thought you trusted me, man," Michael said, a little put out.

"I do trust you, Michael, and I did then too. It was Ralph I wasn't sure about. I wanted to hear what he had to say when he thought I wasn't around. If I'd heard him say anything to you about taking me in tonight no matter what, I was going to say what I had to say from where I was laying. If he tried to come in after me with his weapon because of it, I was prepared to shoot the weapon out of his hand, then disappear back into the trees. But if Ralph's end of your conversation gave even the slightest indication that he was willing to give me the benefit of the doubt, I'd respond differently. I'd have retreated, circled around, and approached from the parking lot. Neither of you would ever have known I had been there the whole time, but I'd still have found out what I needed to know. You see, if I would have walked up and he tried to arrest me for any reason, there would have been a serious altercation. Somebody could have been seriously hurt, and I was trying to avoid that at any cost."

Michael took everything in that J.J. had said, then responded, "Okay. I see your point. Ralph's probably going to be thinking about it too, now that things have calmed down for the time being. I just hope he doesn't take offense to it and get really angry. None of us need that right now."

"No, we don't. That's for sure. But if he does, he does. I can't and won't feel any regret for the decision I made. I had no clue what his intentions would be, especially after what you told me on Wednesday. I would have put money on the fact that he had every intention of taking me in tonight. That left me no options except the one I chose."

"I see that now, J.J. I suggest you explain it to Ralph on the way back down to Albuquerque. It might even be a good idea to get it out before he figures it out."

"No, I don't think so, Michael. He may never figure it out at all. Did you tell him that I was going to show up late?"

Michael thought for a moment.

"No, I don't believe I did. Why?"

"Then I doubt he will figure it out. He's probably under the impression that I just arrived a little early. Then, while waiting for you two to show, I saw the assassins in the trees and turned the tables on them before they could carry out their plans."

"Okay. But what if he asks you why you were carrying a weapon? And not just any weapon, but a Beretta equipped with a silencer?"

"Hmmm. Good question. Let me think about that one for a minute."

They drove in silence for a while, then Michael asked, "Are they behind us?"

"Yep. Right behind us. I've been watching closely to make sure of it. Besides, I told Ralph if he needed me to stop for any reason to just flash his high beams once. And if he needed me to speed up, that he should switch lanes momentarily. We're still in good shape. I wonder what's going on in that car right now, though. I feel really bad for Ralph and his family, especially the kids. They must be frightened out of their minds."

During the ride, Ralph did his best to describe everything to his two teenagers he thought they could handle. To his and Flo's surprise, they weren't scared in the least. In fact, they were both excited about being involved in their dad's work. Ralph lectured them about being cautious but disguised it as "police cadet training 101." All three listened intently. By the time he turned behind J.J. into the cabin's driveway, all three of his kin knew what their role was to be for at least the next nine or ten hours. J.J. walked back to Ralph's window, said hi to the two smiling teens in the backseat, and suggested that Flo and the kids stay in the car until he and Michael could get Sharpe inside and make a perimeter check. Ralph agreed and stepped out of the car but stood by the driver's door, weapon at the ready.

Once J.J. had done a quick perimeter sweep and lit two kerosene lamps inside the cabin, he and Michael carried the still unconscious man inside. J.J. didn't want the two teens to imbed in their minds the picture of this seriously wounded man wearing blood soaked gauze, but it was just a one-room building. The bathroom was a nearby outhouse. He stood there for a second, then had an idea. The double bed was a cheap, possibly hand crafted wooden one with posts on all corners. The posts only rose a foot or so above the mattress, but that was enough. He and Michael pulled the bed away from the wall and put the mattress on the floor in its place. They flipped the bed frame up on its side and hung a blanket over it, creating a makeshift partition. They laid Sharpe down on the mattress and quickly redressed his wounds using the first aid kit from the kitchen.

Sharpe rose to a state of delirium as the antiseptic was poured into his wounds but never to full awareness. J.J. had been worried about blood loss but relaxed when he saw that the field dressing he'd done at the park was working well. The bleeding had stopped, and Sharpe's breathing as well as his pulse was quite stable. He'd live for now. J.J. cut holes clear through the mattress where Sharpe's biceps, wrists, knees and ankles would rest, then used lengths of rope to lash him down tight. He had become one with the mattress and would not be able to free himself. Ralph had come to the doorway once to find out why it was taking so long and saw what they had done with the bed. J.J. told him why and explained from behind the partition that they were just dressing the wounds and would be done shortly. Ralph was grateful for J.J.'s quick thinking with regard to the partition and said so. He went back outside to wait by the car again after that.

Michael and J.J. both came out when they were done and escorted Ralph's family inside. Ralph and Michael brought in firewood from the stack on the side of the cabin while J.J. showed Flo where everything was in the kitchen. He then walked her and both kids to the outhouse and apologized for not having a real bathroom. They went back into the cabin, and while Ralph got the fire going, J.J. and Michael took Greenhill's body out to the storage room. They wrapped it in the tarp, then virtually emptied the storage room. The two men loaded everything into the Ramcharger except weapons for Flo and the two teens to protect themselves with, should anything unforeseen occur. Ralph's reaction to this surprised J.J. He was actually grateful J.J. had thought of it. Each man took a student and gave them crash courses on the use of the weapons they'd possess. Ralph's family was no stranger to firearm use and safety, so the lessons went quickly.

J.J. then told all present that the call sign for anyone who approached the building once they'd left would be "Robin hood and his merry men." Flo, Ralph, and both kids snickered at this. Ralph reminded J.J. of Flo's cell phone and said they could use that to identify themselves as they came back. But J.J. hit him with two possible scenarios that made that idea a bad one.

"Flo, if things go bad and Tracerio's thugs discover what's really going on, they may call your cell phone to find out where you are. They'll say they're with one law enforcement agency or another and that something's happened to Ralph and Michael. Then, they'll say they want you to stay where you are and that they'll send men to protect you. Then they'll ask for your location. I'm telling you right now that will happen. Then while they've got you on the phone, they'll try to trace the call. I have no idea if they have the equipment to do that or not. But I suggest we assume they do have it and will use it, just to be safe."

J.J. paused for a moment to gauge the group's responses. All were silent and paying attention, so he continued.

"The other problem is, there's no way to charge the battery up here. So if you left it on all night, it may be dead by morning. Then we wouldn't be able to reach you on it anyway. Here's what I suggest, turn it off now and leave it off until seven twenty in the morning. If all goes well, we'll be contacting you around seven thirty. If you haven't heard from us by eight, immediately call information, and get the number for the FBI office in Albuquerque. Not the one in Santa Fe, Flo, the one in Albuquerque. Call them and tell them who you are and that you have proof of a drug ring involving Tracerio, the chief, and other high ranking officials, and that they're after you to kill you, but do not tell them where you are. Tell them you're in Socorro, and that—"

"Socorro?" Ralph asked, lost.

"Yes, Socorro. If the agent who picks up the call is also on Tracerio's payroll, and she gives her true location, all three of them will be in grave danger. Hear me out, people. There is a method to my madness."

No one else had thought of the possibility of the wrong agent picking up the phone but were extremely glad J.J. had.

"Okay, we're listening, J.J. Go ahead," Flo said, paying complete attention.

"Tell them that you'll meet them at the Old San Miguel Mission there at ten. Can you remember that?"

"Yes. We've been there before. I can remember that."

"Good. Don't forget that. The Old San Miguel Mission, at ten o'clock. Make sure you get all this said within ninety seconds, no matter what. Don't let them interrupt you, and don't let them stall you; ninety seconds and off. That way they can't trace the call's origin. Then as soon as you hang up, drop everything, and the three of you drive straight down to the Bureau's office in Santa Fe and turn yourselves over to them. That way, once—"

"I get it," Michael said, enlightened, and took over. "If the wrong agent picks up the phone, he'll head for Socorro himself, or call and have someone else go. But either way, they'll be looking for you in the wrong half of the state, Flo. They'd never expect you to just drive into their office in Santa Fe on your own after that."

"Right," J.J. said. "As long as you get it all said and are off the phone in ninety seconds, you'll have a safe drive down into Santa Fe. Remember, Flo, call the office in Albuquerque but go to the one in Santa Fe. Then the three of us will contact you there as soon as we're able. Do you understand all that, Flo?"

"I do. But I still don't get the need for a password."

"Fair enough. Since we will have no way to contact you by phone, we may have to come back here for one reason or another. I'm sure you'd assume everything is okay if you see our car, but that's how these two were going to get into your house without being noticed tonight. They were goi—"

"My house? What do you mean, my house?"

J.J. looked at Ralph. Ralph had not told her that part of Tracerio's plan, but after hearing what J.J. had said, realized how important it was for her to be suspicious of everything until this night was over.

"Honey, they were supposed to drive my car to the house after they killed us and just walk in using my keys," Ralph said.

"But why? Why would they come to our hou—*oh my!* They were going to kill us, too, weren't they? Ralph? Weren't they?" Flo said, jolted by fear.

"Yes, they were," J.J. answered, "We are dealing with ruthless murderers here, folks. We should not be trying to hide that fact. They will use any means necessary to kill every person that gets in their way, so we have to be prepared for any unknown surprises. It is the only way we'll all get out of this alive. Now, Flo, the reason for the call sign is if for any reason things go bad here," J.J. said seriously, then softened his tone.

"Flo, if anyone, and I mean anyone comes here to the cabin and does not call out 'Robin hood and his merry men!' start shooting at everything that moves. Even if it's any or all of us that show up, require the correct password to be said before allowing anyone to enter. If we show up and give a false one, something's seriously wrong and you should call the FBI immediately and then prepare to defend yourselves. Now, is everybody clear on all this?"

Five voices answered yes.

Then J.J. finished by saying, "Flo, one more thing. If someone other than us shows up and gives the correct one, use your best judgment. I'd suggest you not give yourselves up until the media has arrived and at least six or seven marked cars are in sight. Real police won't storm the place without trying to talk you out first. That should buy you enough time to use your cell phone to call a couple of TV stations and get them up here before you and the kids walk out. If the police show up and try to storm the place without giving you a chance to walk out safely, they are not to be trusted, and I'd defend the cabin if I were you."

Ralph looked at her and the kids, and said, "He's right, honey. You think you three can handle all this tension for a few hours?"

All three said yes and hugged him, then watched as the three men left the cabin. It was just past 11:30 p.m. now. J.J. was a little perturbed with Ralph for not explaining everything to his family. It had cost them a half-hour's time already and could have ended up costing a lot more. Michael stepped quickest and climbed into the backseat of the vehicle so Ralph and J.J. could talk easier. Michael had noticed J.J.'s frustration but hoped he could keep it in check until all was over. As they pulled away from the cabin, Michael shifted the subject.

"So, J.J. where do we go first? You've got more intel on Tracerio's people than we do."

J.J. looked at his watch and stepped a little deeper into the gas pedal. "To a bar called The Hideaway."

"A toast! To us, and our careers! May we do as well apart as we have done together," Covington announced with his glass held high.

"Here, here!" Ashland said, raising his own to meet it.

"Well, Tim. Take a good look. This is probably the last time we'll ever have a drink together in this place," George said as he surveyed the room.

"Yep! I do believe you're right, there, George. As of Monday, you'll be trying to find a new place to sip suds and fondle females in Las Vegas, and I'll be doing the same in LA. I'm gonna miss this, man. I wonder how long it will take once we find our new Friday night haunts to get privileges like we've had here? I mean they hold our table every week, we run tabs, and we get really fast service even when the place is packed."

"I don't know. But my guess is it may take a while and a lot of bucks spent."

"That's okay. With the raises we get starting on Monday, we can afford it. By the way, when do you fly out?"

"Sunday morning. And I'm really looking forward to it. Living in a hotel gets old quick. The movers were actually a day early coming to pack us, so I've been in the thing over a week. I'll be in my own bed Sunday night but with the way Tracy's been talking on the phone, I may not get much sleep," George said with a grin.

"Ooh. Sounds to me like Tracy's preparing a private party for the two of you, huh?"

"Well, yes, Tim. We haven't seen each other since I sent her to her mother's."

"That's right. I had forgotten that she had left almost two weeks before I sent Angela and Christine to my mom's. Wow, you must be suffering from 'lackanookie,'" Covington said with a laugh.

Ashland was overtaken by this and spit the mouthful of beer he was drinking back out through his mouth and nose as he burst into laughter. This sight was enough for Covington to join him. Both men laughed with great intensity, causing a curious cocktail server to come over.

"What's got you two all fired up? I figured you'd be in mourning. Don't you both start new jobs on Monday?"

"Yep!" Covington replied, "But we're not in mourning, we're having a wake! So bring us another round, my dear, if you will! Then tell me you'll come back to my hotel with me, even if you won't."

"Oh, you just wait by the door holding your breath, Tim. You and I have been down that road, remember? You, booze, and romance don't mix worth a darn. But I'll tell you what, how about I buy you both a round as a going away present?"

"That would be wonderful!" George said, raising his glass.

"I called Tracy before we left the office. She said she's already got the whole house set up, and man, is that a relief," George said.

"Angela left the picture hanging and the garage to me. She said everything else is done, though"

"When does Christine start school?"

"Wednesday. She's nervous too. You know how it is, George, new city, new people. She hasn't met anybody there, yet."

"She's a sweet girl, Tim. She'll make friends in no time."

"I know. But try telling her that. You may as well talk to a baked potato. She'll be okay after a few days, though."

"Did you talk to Angela today?"

"Yep, around two. I told her I'd call her before I flew out tomorrow night."

"You're flying out tomorrow?"

"Yep, at eight. Then I can spend the whole day Sunday relaxing with Angela and Christine before starting the new grind on Monday."

"That's good. Taking the whole day to relax. I plan on doing that in my hotel all day tomorrow. I'm not leaving that room for anything tomorrow. I'm ordering room service, watching TV, and tuning out the whole bloomin' world."

"Well, you go right ahead, there, dear friend. I'm hoping to be ordering a little room service too. But I don't plan to be eating it alone tomorrow if I can help it," Covington proudly announced.

"Good for you, Tim. More power to ya. My date tonight is going to be with Miss Michelob, here. I know she won't let me down."

"You're right about that. In fact, when you two spent last Friday night here together, didn't she make sure nothing stayed down?" Covington said, and the two were laughing again.

"This being our last night here together, I say we get more ripped than we've ever been, George. Whaddaya say?"

"Now you're talkin', Tim! Now you're talkin'! Waitress!"

The two would close out their memories in The Hideaway with unequaled flair and exuberance. They tried their hand at a few pool games, then darts, then went back to pool. They were buying drinks for just about everybody they came in contact with. They would even have a few drinks with a big biker dressed all in black just before closing.

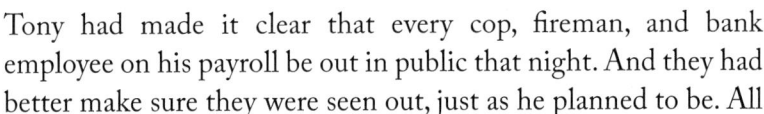

Tony had made it clear that every cop, fireman, and bank employee on his payroll be out in public that night. And they had better make sure they were seen out, just as he planned to be. All of them not on duty were to be in a public place no later than seven and had to stay in plain sight until after midnight. That would give them all ironclad alibis should a police or internal affairs investigation start digging deep because of the death of two cops. He and Tony Jr. would do the same. They would stay in the lounge at Ciao Bella's until closing. He wanted nothing left to chance with regard to the night's hit. He also ordered that no one go near that park, or the homes of Davis and Rhodes, for any reason. All his people were to stay as far from potential incrimination as possible. If they went to a nightclub, they were to introduce themselves to quite a few people and be big tippers. That way the servers and bartenders would remember them. If it was dinner, they better go to a place that had a lounge to hang out in after eating. If they went to a late movie after dinner, they were to tell their server at the restaurant which movie they were going to see. Asking if and where they'd seen it, then announcing that's where they were going would seem inconspicuous enough. Once they arrived there, they were to buy something at the concession counter before going in and were to buy something else at the midway mark of the flick. They had to have fairly long conversations with the person behind the counter both times, too. They also had to remember names. Upon their departure from wherever they were last, they were to thank some employee for being so nice and exchange names. There was no way he could take any heat for the deaths then. The investigators would have nowhere to go except where he wanted them to go. It was a mugging that turned deadly, and a couple of robberies afterward that had too.

"Why are we going to a bar? What's there, J.J.?" Michael asked.

"Yeah, I'm curious too. What's the thinking there, J.J.?" Ralph asked.

J.J. reminded them of the three men who came to his house and told them of their normal Friday night routine. He also informed them of Tracerio's plans to have them transferred to different cities, and his conclusions regarding those transfers.

"You two have your badges with you, right?"

"Always. We are required to carry them at all times, why?" Ralph asked.

"Because if plan A doesn't work for getting them out of the bar without incident, you'll have to pop them for drunk in public as plan B. First, I'm going to go in and sit down near these two jerks and keep an eye on them from inside. They didn't recognize me the last time, thanks to the beard, the contacts, and the fake accent, so I doubt they'll catch on if they're three sheets to the wind."

"Fake accent?" Ralph asked. Michael had heard it the first time he'd ever met J.J. But after J.J. knew Michael was no threat he stopped using it around him. To illustrate his point to Ralph, J.J. adopted the accent again at that moment.

"Yep, that's right, mister, a fake accent. Them fellers was only a hogs width away from me when three other slicked up fancy lookin' dudes tried to make me leave mah table. I was a mite ticked 'bout it. So I told them three city slickers I was meetin' a couple a buddies there, and Buford, he's the mean one, wouldn't take kindly to knowin' what they'd done to get it. Whadda you think there, mister policeman?"

Both Michael and Ralph sat there during the entire dissertation thoroughly enjoying themselves.

"That accent, Ralph," J.J. chided.

"Okay. So let's say we have to grab them, what do we do? Pile them into the Ramcharger?" Michael asked. Ralph took it from there.

"Sure, they'd fit. And if anybody asked, we could tell them it was an undercover unit. They wouldn't know if it was or not. And I doubt they'd give us any grief since they'd be coming out of the bar at closing time. They'd just be glad it wasn't them getting arrested. But my question is, once we've got them, where do we take them?" Ralph asked.

"Your place, Ralph. You grabbed the garage door opener from your car like I asked you to, right?"

"Yep. I got it right here," Ralph said, holding it up for J.J. to see.

"Okay, then. We use it to open the garage door, and we drive right in. Then no one sees us unload the drunks, and we hog tie their butts together in a bathroom."

"Wait, J.J. That's kidnapping and false imprisonment. I can't do th—"

"No, Ralph, it isn't. It will be perfectly legal, and here's why. I, Jonathan Blake, brought two peace officers to an establishment where two of three men who'd tried to kill me were drinking. The two officers chose not to make a scene, so they waited out front for the two to exit. Then once you had them in custody, you could not take them back to the station because of evidence you have that corruption is rampant inside your own ranks, from the chief on down. So the safest place to incarcerate these two criminals who were involved in the same conspiracy as those members of the police force was in your home while you continued the night's investigation. We can say the same thing about why we didn't take Sharpe in, or report immediately the other guy's death. You two have complete autonomy right now. The only one who doesn't is me. And I'm willing to risk it now. We're too close to closing him down to quit now. I am right about the autonomy thing, aren't I?"

"Actually, explained that way, yes, you are. It will also justify why Michael and I couldn't call for backup. With what we learned from you, the shooter, and these two bankers, we had no choice but to act alone. Plus, we have enough probable cause based on the statement of the shooter to snare Tracerio's hide without worry that he'll walk. Okay, J.J. I'm in. Let's go get them."

"After a quick stop. We need handcuffs, gents."

"J.J., it will take too long to go to both our houses to get ours. We've got the rope. We can use it," Michael suggested.

"Nah. Rope takes too long. Besides, witnesses would question us as to why we were using rope instead of real cuffs. Then they might call the station, and the cat would be out of the bag too soon."

"So what do we use then, J.J.?" Michael asked before he'd thought about it, then in unison he and Ralph both said, "Zip ties!"

"Yep. Zip ties. There's a Wal-Mart right down the block from The Hideaway that's open twenty-four hours. We can get the size we need in there. If they're still too small, we'll link them together. You two can do that while I'm in the bar."

"Gotcha," Ralph said, then made an observation.

"You know, for a guy who works at a bank, you know a lot about our line of work, J.J."

"I'm a former US Army Green Beret, Ralph. Six years of wars, enemy action, and counterintel. That's where I learned it all."

"That explains everything. No wonder you had the balls to go after Tracerio alone. You have counter-terrorist training, too, right?"

"Yes. That's why I was so specific with your family back there, Ralph. I hope now you can understand why."

"I can, and I do. But as good as you are now, you must have been almost unstoppable then. Why'd you get out and become a banker, of all things? Why not a cop, or a fed?"

"I never liked the killing. I was in great shape and wanted to stay alive. So I figured the best way to stay alive was to be surrounded by the best-trained soldiers the army had to offer. That's why I volunteered for the Green Beret. But when it was over, I wanted to put as much distance as I could between myself and bloodshed. That's when I went back to college and majored in finance. Who'd have thought I'd be right back in a war zone because I became a banker?"

"No kidding. I wouldn't have," Michael said.

"Nor did I," said J.J. "Nor did I."

20

They usually only danced at weddings and only out of respect for the families of the betrothed, but tonight, they actually were enjoying it. Both men had been asked to the floor by a number of women, and neither man refused even one. During one slow, romantic song that both Tonys were already dancing to with women who were not their dates, a man asked Jacquelyn to dance. She accepted, but it ended quickly when Tony looked at Victor.

Victor slowly and gently made his way out to them and asked to cut in. The man tried to brush Victor off, saying that he would just have to wait for the next song. Apparently, he had no idea who Tony Tracerio was, Victor thought. Victor made no scene although he could have ripped the man apart right there. Instead, he glared with displeasure at Jacquelyn as their eyes met while she rotated. He then flashed a quick look in Tony Sr.'s direction, and she understood. She was Tony's date tonight. Just Tony's. It did not matter how many women he danced with; she must reserve all of hers for him. She stepped away from the young suitor without incident by stating that she needed to use the ladies room. As the young man left the floor, Victor stopped him and quickly explained whose date that was. The moment the man heard the name, Victor could tell he had definitely heard of Tony even though he had obviously never seen him before. The young man apologized again and again and beseeched Victor to pass that on to Tony. Victor patted him on the shoulder and smiled. Then he walked the young man over to the bar.

"Doug! Doug!" he called out, trying to get the bartender's attention.

The man next to him was completely intimidated and stood as though nails were piercing his feet. The bartender finally heard Victor beckoning him and approached.

"Doug, this is my new friend." Victor hesitated with a smile, waiting for the man on his right to state his name.

The man caught on and filled in the blank, looking first at Victor, then at Doug.

"R-R-Richard. Richard Payne."

"Richard, this is Doug. Doug, Mr. Tracerio has requested that Richard and everyone in his party be his honored guests this evening. Mr. Tracerio will take care of their bill," he said, then looked at the confused man beside him. "Richard, how many are there in your party?"

"F-Four. Including me."

"Splendid! For the rest of the night, you and your friends have whatever you wish with Mr. Tracerio's compliments. And I suggest you accept graciously. Mr. Tracerio's feelings may get hurt if you don't drink up and have a great time. His only request is that you don't ask either of the ladies at his table to dance again. okay?"

Relieved, the man smiled, and looked at Victor with admiration. He accepted excitedly, then quickly went back to his table after placing a drink order with Doug. Victor watched as he sat down. The three young men with him leaned in toward him as he explained what had happened. They high-fived each other, then smiled and held their glasses high toward Victor. He bowed slightly and smiled. His behavioral sciences degree had been quite useful. Again. Victor had learned how to control the outcome of many situations without needing to resort to violence, but violence was still his passion. He was truly a dangerous man. His skills in all aspects of human relations were exceptional. He was capable of showing very convincing speech and body language patterns toward a passive, relaxed demeanor, while deep within desired to kill without hesitation. One might say he had the makings of the textbook serial killer. He did a quick walk-through of the place sizing up all the patrons again. The few moments he'd been distracted by Richard were more than enough for one of Tony's enemies to move in close, too close. He talked with each of the three men Tony had on watch as he made his circle, and all said things were normal; then he went back to his vigil by the dance floor.

The live music had lured many couples who'd come just for dinner to stay, and the place was still packed at eleven. Victor made a mental note to mention this to Tony in the morning. Ciao Bella was capable of making Tony a lot more money than it already was. But Tony wouldn't need to be told. He had noticed it too. In fact, he and his son had been discussing that very thing during one of the band's breaks. They were having an especially great time, and even discussed making this a Friday night stop. Their wineglasses were never empty, Doug had seen to that. When they'd first come into the lounge they were sipping the wine, but once enough had been taken in to numb their senses, they stopped sipping and began to drink. They were slowly getting drunk—father and son. Victor didn't mind it. In fact, just the opposite was true. He was in charge of their security this night, so he was quite confident they were safe. He had rarely witnessed this sight and was pleased at how much fun they seemed to be having. Their lives were filled with tension and worry, so being able to do something like this was a good thing, he thought.

They were the life of the party, and by midnight, the party was bigger. Normally on Fridays, Ciao Bella closed at midnight, but not this Friday. Everyone who had stayed was so completely taken in by the atmosphere they had called friends to come down. It was wall-to-wall people in Ciao Bella, and the bar was raking it in. There had been no talk and little thought of Sharpe and Greenhill since they'd left the mansion. These two had never failed Tony before, so he was quite sure they'd have no trouble carrying out their assignment. Tony Sr.'s joy was not just increased by this belief; it had actually spawned it. Two unwitting, know-nothing beat cops had stuck their noses into a place they didn't belong, and that was that. They and their families would pay with their lives for that stupidity while father and son danced the night away. At one fifteen, Doug had come over to Tony and told him that by law the bar had to close at two, so at one thirty, Tony took the stage and the microphone. Once the din had quieted enough, he announced that every Friday until further notice, Ciao Bella would bring in live music for all to enjoy. A thunderous roar of applause and cheers followed, and he stood there for a moment with his arms raised high leading them on.

Young Tony and Victor exchanged knowing smiles. Tony Sr. had found his happiness again. He had not been seen in this good a mood since long before Maria's passing, and both Victor and Tony Jr. knew it. They had the same thought as they smiled at one another. What he'd found here tonight would help him finally get over her loss, and they believed it would allow him to enjoy the rest of his life.

They pulled into the parking lot at the bar a little before one thirty. J.J. didn't feel there was time to stop for zip ties first, so he dropped the fastest runner in the group, Michael, off there, then he and Ralph drove straight to The Hideaway. J.J. had already entered when Michael got back to the vehicle.

"Michael, I want to thank you. You are a good man and a better friend. You've saved me from making a few of the biggest mistakes of my life the last few weeks. There's no way I'll ever be able to make that up to you. But I promise you this. If we make it through this, I won't ever argue with your gut instincts again. You are a great cop, Michael Rhodes, a great cop." Ralph's emotions climbed to the surface as he spoke and it touched Michael just as deeply.

"Thanks, Ralph. Hearing that from you means a lot to me. You are the reason I've come this far, man. I've learned a lot from you. You're the best partner I've ever had, Ralph," Michael said.

"Wow. Thanks, partner. Wow. Do you really mean that?"

"Yeah, man. I do. Very much."

Michael had meant it. Every word of it. But the mood was too heavy for him, so he quickly lightened it.

"I mean, since I've never had a partner before, you're definitely the best one."

After a few seconds of silence and a quick look at each other, both men laughed lightly. Ralph shook his head then looked back at Michael.

"Okay, okay. Michael, you can be a real jerk sometimes too, do you know that?" Ralph said, looking at Michael's sheepish grin. Then both men sat quietly while they waited for J.J. to come around the corner.

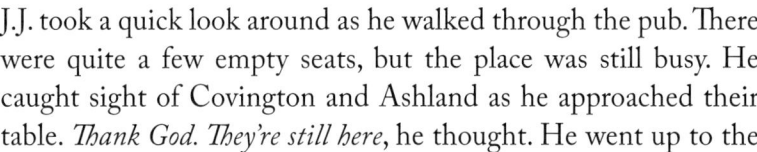

J.J. took a quick look around as he walked through the pub. There were quite a few empty seats, but the place was still busy. He caught sight of Covington and Ashland as he approached their table. *Thank God. They're still here*, he thought. He went up to the bar directly behind Covington, noting that the adjoining table was empty.

"You made it just in time, friend. We're announcing last call in five minutes," the bartender said, "So what can I get ya?"

J.J. turned for a second to see what the two men were drinking but could only see Ashland's bottle of Michelob.

"Y'all got Michelob on tap back there?"

"Nope. Just Michelob Light."

"Well, that'll just have to do then, won't it, Barkeep? I'll take a large pitcher. It's been a long day on the road, and I'm as dry as a bone."

"You sure? It's almost closing time. I don't think you'll have enough time to finish it. How about a mug instead?"

"No thanks. I'll take the pitcher, if'n it's all right. If I don't finish it, it wouldn't be the first time. But I 'preciate the offer. It's right nice of you to think of savin' me money like that, though. Thank ya kindly."

"No problem, buddy. One pitcher, comin' right up."

J.J. took the pitcher and sat down at the table next to Ashland and Covington's. He only had a few minutes to work with, and he had no clue how to get them to invite him over to their table, if they would at all. He poured himself a glass and took a healthy swallow. For effect, he'd rather have just downed the first glass, but he'd need to stay sharp to stay alive this night. He looked around and met Ashland's glance. Ashland was smiling, obviously feeling no pain. J.J. immediately raised his glass and nodded with a hearty smile. He could now see that both men were clearly inebriated.

"Hey! How's Buford and the boys?" Ashland slurred out happily.

Covington looked at Ashland, then in the direction Ashland was looking. He too, seemed to be enjoying himself immensely.

"Yeah! You're the guy! The country boy from a few weeks ago! We really liked how you handled those three wannabes. We were sitting right here and heard the whole thing. We would have bought you a beer if you hadn't left."

"Why, that is a mighty kind thought. I 'preciate that. But can you fine gents keep a little secret?" J.J. said as he leaned in toward them.

Both men said yes in their own way as they leaned toward him.

"There is no Buford. I made him up. I jus' didn't want them fellers to start a fight. I hate fightin'," J.J. confided in a half whisper.

Both Ashland and Covington broke into laughter and Ashland actually slapped the table.

"Tim, we got ourselves a right smart dude right there," Ashland said in a horrible attempt at matching J.J.'s accent.

"Why, thank ya, mister. That's a mighty fine compliment. Your accent needs a little work, though, if'n you don't mind my sayin' so too awful much."

Covington laughed and pushed Ashland.

"Yeah, George. It needs a lot of work."

"I'm J.J.," he said, extending a hand to Covington, "J.J. Tracker."

"I'm Tim, and this right smart dude here is George," Covington said as he took J.J.'s hand. Ashland rose and reached across the table, also shaking J.J.'s hand. Neither man was even close to realizing that J.J. was really Jonathan Blake.

"Pleased to meet ya, Tim. Pleased to meet ya, George."

"Last call for alcohol! Last call!" the voice yelled behind them.

"Okay, Tim. It's your turn to buy our last drinks here at The Hideaway. So get me two!" George said.

"All right, George. You got it," Covington said, rising from his seat.

"Hey, Tim, wait just a second, okay?" J.J. asked. "I've got this here whole pitcher of beer, and I can't finish it by myself. Would you two gents like to help me polish it off?"

"Yes!" Ashland said. "No sense in letting perfectly good beer go to waste. Just grab two glasses, Tim, and we'll have a drink here with our new friend J.J. Come on over here and sit with us, J.J."

"Why, thank you, George. I'd like that," J.J. said as he slid over to their table. He was careful not to stand as he wasn't wearing his elevator boots tonight. Those just wouldn't be practical for the firefight he was expecting shortly.

Covington returned with the glasses. Once he and George had toasted their new friend with full glasses, the conversation turned to jobs, families, and the like. J.J. was surprised that these men, who were so paranoid a few weeks before, were letting a complete stranger sit with them. *The booze must have temporarily overrun their sense of fear*, J.J. thought. Besides, they had seen him here before and nothing happened to them, so why would they think anything? He let them ramble for a few minutes about leaving for good and where they were going, then started a story of his own. He needed them to stop talking and start drinking. J.J. spun a yarn about his life story that had both men engaged while they gulped down the beer. He told them of his kin and their antics as well. There was barely a swallow of beer left in the pitcher when closing time came, but J.J. was still nursing his first glass. George and Tim needed a pit stop to the bathroom before leaving, they'd said, and J.J. agreed and followed. Both men were staggering noticeably, and J.J. smiled as he watched.

George's shoulder slammed into the doorjamb as he entered the restroom and Tim used it to hold himself steady as he entered. They were obliterated. There were only two urinals in the place and both were closest to the door. Ashland and Covington were in no shape to walk far, so they stepped up and put a hand each on the wall to steady them as they purged their bladders. J.J. headed into the stall. He was glad, too. He really didn't want to stand beside these men at the urinal on the off chance they might realize he seemed shorter than before. He also didn't want them to get too long a look at his profile; they may recognize him from that viewpoint. He stood in there motionless, then flushed as they did and stepped out. They talked as they walked to the front, and J.J. mentioned that neither one seemed in any condition to drive. It was a shot in the dark, but since everything had gone so well so far, he thought he had to take it. And it worked. Both men dismissed the comment at first, but then J.J. reminded them that it would be pretty hard to board a plane from a jail cell. They stopped, looked at each other, and agreed.

J.J. then offered to drive them, so they wouldn't have to pay for a cab. He'd brought his big unit tonight, and there was plenty of room. He told them that he just wouldn't feel right knowing they could wind up in jail if they tried to drive. Besides, they'd been so nice to him, he'd be honored to return the favor. They agreed again and thanked him. They even offered to pay what a cab would have cost. J.J. told them to wait by the door and he'd go get the car. He walked quickly around the side of the building to the Ramcharger. Michael and Ralph were sitting in the front seats. He went to the driver side and told them to get in the back; all the way in the back and down out of sight, explaining why as they moved. He closed them in and fired up the Ramcharger.

He drove around to the front while Michael and Ralph moved weapons out of the way so they could hide. Ashland and Covington were leaning on the railing as he approached. He left the motor running and got out. He told them to wait there a second longer, then opened the passenger door and flipped the front seat forward. He wanted both men in the back. He suggested that Covington climb in first so he could help pull George up into it while J.J. steadied him from behind. Tim did so and, because he was distracted by the task of having to help George, never looked behind the seat. They got George up and in, then J.J. flipped the passenger seat back down into place and closed the door. He suggested to both men that they lean forward and hold on to the back of the seats to assist them in remaining steady. They did so in unison like a man and his shadow. He had their trust now and soon would have a lot more.

He circled around behind the Ramcharger and swung quickly into the driver seat, asking, "Okay. Where to first?"

"Let's take George to his hotel first. He's in a lot worse shape than me!" Covington said humorously.

George wasn't about to argue. "Yep! I sure am! I spent a lot of your money tonight, Tim."

"You sure did, George. I just wish they'd have let us run a tab tonight and mailed me the bill."

"Hey. You're the one who told them last week we were moving. If you hadn't said anything, maybe we could have. But no, you had to say something, and they put us on cash. Idiot," Ashland said, his face against the back of the front seat.

"I know, I know. George, would you quit bringing it up already? Jeez. I mean it's not like we were going to stiff them for the bill. We would have paid anyway. This way we just paid sooner," Covington threw back in a justifying tone.

"Which hotel are you staying in, George?" J.J. asked, now driving out to the main street.

"Guess!" George said with a laugh.

J.J. faked the best laugh he could as he said, "George I need to know. I need to know which way to turn out here."

"The Marriott on Louisiana North East."

"George, there's only one Marriott in town, so it's the one on Louisiana. Don't mind him, J.J. He's drunk," Covington said, slurring his own words.

"Okay. Just rest there, you two. I'll get you there in a jiffy. I'm gonna drive on the side streets though, so's I can avoid the cops. You fellers just enjoy the ride."

He looked in his rearview mirror and could see neither man. He adjusted it down so Covington's reflection would be visible and glanced occasionally at Ashland. He pulled the directions to Ralph's house from his pocket and read them again. The two drunken men were silent and unmoving there in the backseat. They had fallen asleep, or possibly passed out. J.J. didn't care which. He pulled into Ralph's driveway while pushing the button for the garage door. It rose, and he drove in, positioning the vehicle dead in the center of the garage. The antenna dragged against the door making some noise as he entered, but neither man seemed to notice. Once inside he closed the garage door. He opened the Ramcharger's door and got out but did not close it. He reached under the seat and grabbed the Beretta. Then he walked around to the rear of the vehicle to let Ralph and Michael out, but the tailgate was too close to the door to open. He waved to get Michael and Ralph's attention, but it was unnecessary. Both men were already looking at him through the glass. He could barely make them out through the deep tint, but because the door was open, the dome light was on. He gestured as though his hand were a gun, and then pointed toward the men in the backseat. Then he raised a finger to his lips, meaning to do it quietly. Both Ralph and Michael nodded and rose slowly. Both men had revolvers in hand, and both weapons were locked and loaded. J.J. moved over to the passenger side of the Ramcharger and opened the door. It was time to wake the scumbags up. J.J. looked at them for a moment before waking them. These two evil jerks had tried to kill him, his wife, and his son. They were about to know that terror.

"Okay, boys! Time to get up! Let's go!" J.J. said. But this time, he spoke in his normal voice.

Both men stirred, but not much. J.J. slapped his hand repeatedly on the side of the Ramcharger and said again, "Okay, boys! Time to get up! Let's go! Let's go!"

This time both men did begin to move although they still hadn't caught on to the voice. Covington was the first to raise his head completely and noticed immediately that they were not in the parking lot of the Marriott.

"J.J.? Where the hell are we?" Covington asked, completely bewildered.

"We're at the home of Ralph Davis. A sergeant with Albuquerque PD, and he's right behind you," J.J. said, pointing.

"What?" Covington asked as he turned.

Ralph's weapon was in his right hand, and his badge was being displayed in the air by his left.

"Hello," Ralph said with a serious glare. "I suggest you do as the man says."

"What's going on here, J.J.?" Covington said as he turned back around. Ashland was rising now.

"The name's not J.J. It's Jonathan. Jonath—"

"*Blake! No!*" Ashland shouted, his voice trembling in fear and disbelief.

"Yes, George. It's me. And you'll join Dennis Jeffries right here, right now if you jack me around!" Jon said angrily as he raised the Beretta into plain view. "Now get out and lie face down on the floor. Now! Move it!"

"Okay, okay. Just don't shoot," Ashland said, raising his hands as he stepped toward the door.

Jon Blake grabbed his arm and pushed him to the floor as soon as he was out. Then Jon motioned to Covington, who'd now seen both Michael and Ralph, to do the same. Covington stumbled out of the vehicle and Jon pushed him face down onto the floor beside Ashland. Both men were firing questions and excuses nonstop as they got out and were still doing so after Ralph and Michael had climbed over the seat and out. Jon told them to shut up but that didn't stop them. Then he grabbed both by the hair, pulling their heads off the floor and said it again. This time both men listened. Ralph zip-tied Covington's hands and Michael did Ashland's while Jon covered both. Jon Blake was not enraged, but the level of disgust he held for these men made it seem that way.

"All right. Now we're gonna get up and walk inside. If one of you falls, I'm gonna shoot you in the first leg that hits the ground. If one of you speaks, I'm gonna shut you up with a bullet. Make no mistake about tonight, gentlemen. Life as you have known it is over. The decisions you make now can either allow you a chance to live, or cause your death, tonight. And, personally, I don't care which you choose. I owe you a bullet each anyway."

Michael and Ralph pulled both men to their feet. Before they went into the house, Jon told them to stop and turn around. Right there in the garage, he explained the harsh reality of their future, if they had a future.

"Here's the deal, weasels one and two. Either you turn state's evidence against Tracerio, or you *become* evidence. Of two homicides. I will not play around with you on this. It will be just as easy to dump your carcasses in the river as it was…what was that sniper's name?"

"Greenhill," Michael said.

"Marcus Greenhill," Ralph corrected sarcastically.

"Greenhill, yeah. Thanks. You'll be floating with him. He thought I was bluffing. Well, I'll tell you right now that this is no game. You two tried to kill my wife and son and I want you dead. Oh man, do I want you dead. So just give me a reason. Be as stupid as…"

"Greenhill," Ralph said in assistance.

"Marcus Greenhill," Michael said, mirroring Ralph's earlier sarcasm.

"His buddy Sharpe was smarter. After he saw what happened to Greenhill, he decided not to test our resolve. He's alive because he chose to come clean. With everything. I suggest you follow his example. Especially since he named you two and Jeffries in the Bell murder."

Jon had told both Ralph and Michael of the conversation he'd overheard these two having weeks before, so even though they knew Sharpe had said no such thing, they showed no surprise. Jon was using a top-notch police interrogation tactic and was doing it expertly.

"So, I'll sum it all up for you before we begin. Murder, attempted murder, numerous counts of felony conspiracy, felony bank fraud, money laundering, income reporting violations, and tax evasion are just the crimes we can prove you committed. You two are going away for life, and you know it."

Jon stopped for a few seconds to let the two men, who were sobering up quickly, absorb everything. Then he pounded the last nail of fear into their proverbial coffin. He glared angrily at both.

"Tracerio won't be able to protect you two, either. He's going down tonight too. No more money, no more power, no more pull. He'll be just another lowlife scumbag in the next cell that wants you dead. Unless you choose to cooperate. That's your only possible option to survive. And maybe, just maybe, if you come through with enough information to take Tracerio's whole operation down, including his out of state drug ring, the FBI or the DEA may put you into witness protection. But I'll tell you right now, what you know had better be huge in their eyes. So your choices are simple. You can die right here and now, you can become some guy's toy and die in prison, or you can spill every detail you have and hope it's enough to impress the feds. That's it. The choice is yours. So I'll start with you, Tim. Do you choose the death penalty?" Jon said, raising the Beretta to Covington's forehead.

Covington swallowed, shook his head no, and agreed to tell everything. He even tried to sell the three men on how good the information was. In turn, Ashland did the same thing. Jon asked what they knew of the order to hit Ralph and Michael and both seemed genuinely surprised to hear about it at all. Jon recognized that Tracerio hadn't told them and planted another seed. He told them Sharpe had confessed that he and Greenhill were to dispose of both Ashland and Covington once they'd moved and that it was to be done by Christmas. That's the reason Tracerio hadn't told them about the hit. Tracerio had already cut them loose. He just hadn't told them yet. Both men stood in silence after that, but each man's eyes were fixed to a point out in front of him, realizing that Blake was telling the truth. Jon then asked about the Tracerio estate's layout, security, armament, and personnel. Both men hesitated out of fear before responding that they'd never been there and didn't know. They even started to cry as Jon raised the Beretta again, pleading for him to believe them. Jon did believe them. Michael grabbed two fifty-foot extension cords from the wall, and Ralph led the way into the house. There was a bathroom on the first floor big enough for both men to lie down in. Jon tied Ashland and Covington back to back on the floor of the bathroom. They weren't going anywhere. He then waved both Ralph and Michael out into the garage for a small conference.

"Okay. I'd love to tape their mouths shut, but Ashland has a tendency to throw up. He'd choke to death on his own vomit and that we couldn't explain away. So here's what I'm thinking."

J.J. proceeded to tell the men of his plan and both agreed it made sense. Then all three went back inside. Jon spoke while Ralph went to his bedroom.

"Okay. Here it is. Sergeant Davis is going to hook up his video camera and place it in the hall on a tripod. You two will proceed, one at a time, to tell everything you know since day one of your involvement. Including what crimes were committed, by whom and to whom, as well as approximate dates and times. It's a four-hour tape, so you'll have plenty of time to get it all out. When we return, we'll watch the tape. If we like what we hear and it jives with what we already know, we'll take you and the tape to the FBI If we don't like it, or if you say anything on it about being coerced, threatened, or wanting to talk to an attorney, you die. If, when we watch the tape, either of you looks like your trying to free yourself at any time, which will be impossible anyway, you both die. Oh, the house you are in was left to Ralph's wife by her parents. It's a ten-acre ranch. So no one could hear you scream if you try it. But that also means you'll be screaming on tape. And if you scream on tape, you die; point-blank, period. I'm not kidding. If you have to go to the bathroom, do it where you lay.

But I'd suggest you hold it. Ralph might just go berserk when we get back if you've messed up his floor. Have we got all that so far?"

Both men said yes almost immediately.

"Good. Last thing. Michael here's gonna read you your rights once we turn on the tape. The correct response is, 'Yes, I understand,' and 'No, I don't want an attorney.' Anything other than that and you both get a bullet. Any questions?"

"Y-y-es," George said, blubbering and crying like a coward. "Once we say all this on tape, the FBI won't need us anymore. They'll just send us away with Tracerio. And we'll be dead anyway. So why shouldn't we just let you kill us now?"

"Well, George. I'm glad you asked. Because the FBI will still need you. They'll need your live testimony to back up the validity of the tape. Juries are funny, and defense attorneys are slick. Some slime-ball lawyer will say the tape was coerced, and since you're dead, reasonable doubt hangs in the air for Tracerio. The Bureau won't want to risk that over your two asses. So if I were you, I'd make sure this tape is as juicy as it is convincing. Now, any more questions?"

Both men shook their heads and voiced their answer at once.

"No? Well then, let the truth set you free. Ralph? Are you ready back there?"

"Yep, all I need to do is hit record."

"Great. Michael?" Jon asked.

"Ready when you are, Ralph."

"All right. Three, two, one and…," Ralph said and pointed to Michael. Then Michael began.

"Tim Covington and George Ashland; you are under arrest for the murder of Howard Bell and the attempted murders of Jonathan Blake and his family. You have the right to remain silent. Anything you say can and will be used against you in a court of law. You have the right to—"

Michael finished, and the moment of truth arrived for Covington and Ashland. Did they test Jon Blake's resolve or not?

Was Blake serious about Greenhill? Had he been stupid enough to underestimate Blake's anger and resolve? In the end, neither of them would be that stupid. Both men started talking as soon as they had declined having an attorney present. Covington stopped, and Ashland began his confession.

Tony and his entourage left at quarter to two soused and happy. The ladies were clinging to them but not out of desire to be close. It was to hold them up. They had indeed surpassed their normal intake of wine. Victor chuckled quietly as Tony Sr. flopped into the seat of the limo. In all the years he'd been around Tony, he had never seen him this intoxicated. Tony Jr. wasn't in much better shape, but he was able to get into the car without making a spectacle of himself. The ladies climbed in, and with one final look around the area, Victor closed the door and went to the front. Once inside, he put the window down that separated the two inner areas of the car and asked young Tony if he were going home or to the mansion. With a glassy-eyed smile, he looked at his father. His faculties were not completely saturated as he considered what it would be like seeing his dad the morning after. He wanted no part of that hangover and told Victor to take him to his own home.

Victor acknowledged the request then closed the window as the driver pulled out. He called the lead man for Tony Jr.'s night security team and informed him of the decision. There were three men on duty at his house—two outside and one inside. Tony Jr. had argued many times with Victor that he could take care of himself or Victor would have had five men there on a shift instead of three. It had been incredibly difficult getting young Tony to accept the three. He then checked in with the security team at the mansion, and the response there was that all was quiet. Victor instructed the man on the other end of the phone to have a fairly large basin and a towel put in Tony's room on the nightstand near the bed but did not say why. Then he looked at his watch. It was 1:55. Sharpe and Greenhill should have completed their tasks about an hour ago, he thought. They were probably out somewhere getting drunk themselves by now. He wondered what the look was on the two cops' faces as they felt the bullets penetrate their bodies and wished he could have been the one to pull the trigger. But his duty was to protect Tony, not to eliminate outside threats. Still, he thought as they drove toward the mansion, he would really like to trade places with Sharpe and Greenhill for a few clean-up calls. They were having all the fun. Maybe one day, somewhere down the road, he would request to handle a future problem or two. He longed for battle, but moreover, he longed to kill.

"What was all that about a ten-acre ranch? Ralph's house is barely on a half-acre," Michael asked as they pulled out of the garage.

"I know that, Michael, and you know that, but they don't. They were asleep the whole way here. For all they know, they really are on a ten-acre ranch."

"Smart thinking, Jon," Ralph said from the backseat.

"Thanks, Ralph."

"Where to now, Jon?" Michael asked.

Jon Blake looked at his watch, and was about to speak when Ralph spoke out. "Captain Wilson's. It's time we invited his ass to join the party." Ralph said with contempt.

His loathing for that man and what he'd done was getting the better of him. A battle raged inside him. The battle between duty and revenge. Revenge was winning.

"I want to see the look in his eyes when he realizes we aren't dead. I want to see the expression on his face while we cuff that dirty loser right in front of his wife. Then I want to read him his rights. I just pray he resists arrest," Ralph said, holding his sidearm up as if he were inspecting it.

Jon and Michael looked at each other quickly, and then Jon looked back at the road. Michael, however, turned around in his seat.

"Ralph, I know the feeling, man. I want the jerk too. But if we go over there and he gets the word out before we can get to him, Tracerio's place will be locked down so tight we'd never get in. But think about this, Ralph. A few hours from now, he hears a knock on his door. He opens it, and on the other side are men from the Bureau. They flash badges and take him into custody on the spot. All night he's been thinking his problems are over. That you and I are gone and so are his worries. And in one swing of his front door, his whole world crashes down around him. They put him in their unit, and he looks at his house. Just then it hits him. This is for real. He can't run, and he can't hide. He has nowhere else to go. He'll know fear, Ralph, and hopelessness. And when the cell door shuts, he'll think he's reached bottom. That he can fall no further. That's when we walk up to the bars, smiling, and he realizes we're alive and well. It will be enough to send him over the edge. Him, Chief Richter, and Cantonelli. Think about that."

Ralph sat quietly looking off into space while Michael spoke, and the picture he'd painted was vivid enough to appease Ralph. Ralph began to grin.

"Yeah. I like that idea, Michael. I really do. That is worth the wait. Those dirty conniving worms won't be able to believe their own eyes."

"Agreed," Jon said. "So, now that that's settled, I suggest you prepare yourselves. Because our next stop is the Tracerio Estate. It may have been easy to take out his two hired guns and two unsuspecting bankers, but I've got a feeling taking his house will be a completely different story. We can't afford any mistakes, gentlemen. We won't get a second shot at him this way."

Then the three men discussed infiltration strategies and individual assignments, from entry to exit. Jon did most of the talking, while the other two men paid close attention. They knew he was the best choice to lead the assault. Ralph had spent some time in the service, but he'd never engaged in actual combat. Michael's entire experience was limited to his academy training. He'd not had to fight for his life on the job either. Because of these things, their egos were pushed to the back burner. And with good reason, their desire for survival was taking up the front one.

Flo had been keeping a close eye on the man strapped to the mattress. Even though he had moaned and squirmed occasionally, he had yet to achieve full consciousness. She'd replaced all three bandages at midnight, noticing as she did that the bleeding had almost completely stopped. Both children were fighting to stay awake but were losing the battle quickly. It was a little after two and there were only five and a half hours to go before she'd hear from Ralph. She prayed silently on and off throughout the time she had already spent there in the cabin. This was the first time she had ever so much as glimpsed the amount of danger Ralph faced every day, and now she was being drenched in it. Anxiety was taking its toll on her emotions, but the kids could barely tell. She had done a miraculous job of hiding it around them. "Just a few more hours," she kept repeating to herself. She stoked the fire again and added two more logs. It was crisp up there during the day and got downright cold at night. She wondered for a moment what it must have been like to live in the times when this cabin and outhouse were deemed luxuries.

She brushed it off and took another walk around the cabin. She wasn't tired. Fear and anxiety had taken care of that. But she was nervous and walking seemed to help, so walk she did. She told the two children it was to make sure the area around the outside of the cabin was safe—and they had believed it. Truth be told, it was so she could get out of their sight for time to collect herself and refortify her confidence. She was scared to death of all the things that could go wrong before the night was over. Just a few more hours, she told herself as she circled the cabin again; just a few more hours.

Ashland was truly feeling sick and lay there in his own vomit but kept on talking. Everything he could remember was coming out of his mouth. He'd even backtracked to interject instances that he hadn't remembered the first time through the series of events. Covington said nothing. In fact, he was asleep. He'd begun a slight snore a little while ago, but George did not wake him. He just talked louder. He would wake him when it was his turn to speak. George Ashland wanted there to be no question in anyone's mind that watched this tape of his willingness to assist in bringing Tracerio to justice. He truly believed it to be his only hope for survival. So much so that he apologized to Jon Blake and family on that tape for attempting to kill them. He said this way out of the sequence of events, but he wanted Jon Blake to hear it early in his confessions.

George did not want to die and he did not want to go to jail. He'd rather spend the rest of his life in hiding under another name than die or face life in prison. He planned to be the best witness the authorities would ever have. He gave specific details of the money laundering process, where it was coming from, how long he'd been a part of it, everything. No way was Blake going to be able to come back and feel it necessary to kill him, no way. He just hoped Tim would do the same thing when it became his turn.

21

Tony Jr. and Violet got out of the limo then were helped inside by one of the men on guard there. Tony Sr. was still awake. Victor had heard him and his son exchanging pleasantries and thanks for the night out together before young Tony turned and headed up the walk to his door. Victor watched them all the way into the house before instructing the driver to head for home.

As soon as the chauffeur closed the door and began walking around to his seat behind the wheel, Victor felt the car sway slightly. Tony Sr. and Jacquelyn were undoubtedly going to get a head start on the night's horizontal mambo, he thought to himself. He wondered if Tony Sr. would even be able to perform. He knew young Tony well enough to know that a few bottles of wine would not deter him, but he was not sure about the old man. Tony Sr. was in great physical condition for a man of fifty-seven, but he had consumed a serious amount of vino. Victor began to picture what Tony Sr. must be attempting to do in the seat behind the glass and shook his head hard to try to erase it. Picturing his boss having sex was not his idea of constructive thought. He instructed the driver to drive especially slow and carefully but did not explain why. It wasn't necessary. The driver could feel the car's movements too.

Harry, the driver, smiled at Victor and said, "No problem, sir. I was thinking the very same thing."

Victor did not smile in return, so Harry quickly lost his. Victor did not want Harry to think it would be all right to go back and tell the rest of the staff what was going on in the limo. Hanes knew the best way to do that without words was to show displeasure at Harry's enjoyment of it all. The limo came to a stop out front of the mansion at 2:45 a.m. One of the men stationed out front went to open the door of the limo but was stopped one step short by Victor's upraised hand. Victor motioned with his head for the man to return to his post, and then walked around to the driver and told him to take a walk. Harry told Victor he needed to put the car away. Victor was unmoved. He told Harry quite abruptly that he could return in fifteen minutes to get it. Harry reached for the ignition to turn off the engine, but Victor's hand rose again.

"Leave it running and put the A/C on its highest setting, Harry. Thank you. If you don't see me standing here when you come back, it will be safe to assume Mr. Tracerio has gone inside," Victor said as he opened Harry's door. Then as Harry walked toward the house, Victor said, "Harry, you did a great job driving home. The ride was smooth and even. Thank you for that. Also, let me thank you in advance for your discretion regarding Mr. Tracerio's choice of entertainment and location this evening. Have a great night"

Harry showed a touch of impatience as he turned around but replaced it with a smile and a respectful nod as he resumed his walk to the house. Victor walked back out to the front of the hood after closing Harry's door slowly and leaned gently against the car. He could feel movement. He stood there patiently, waiting for the movement inside the car to stop. Once it had, he waited an additional three minutes, then heard a knock on the glass. He walked around to the passenger side and opened the door.

"Welcome home, sir," he said.

As Tony got out of the car, he locked glances with Victor for a few seconds and then put his hand on Victor's shoulder.

"You are a good man, Victor. Tell Harry he can come and put the car away now, and that I, too, thank him in advance for his discretion."

Tony smiled and winked at Victor as he squeezed his shoulder then assisted Jacquelyn as she got out of the car. Victor had spoken quite softly to Harry and was surprised Tony had heard him.

"I'll do both right away, Mr. Tracerio. Good night, sir."

"Good night, Victor," Tony said, and then turned to Jacquelyn. "Shall we retire?"

Jacquelyn leaned to Tony and whispered, "If that means go to bed, yes. But don't expect to get much sleep, Tony."

"Really?" Tony asked as they walked toward the house. "And what makes you think I would want any sleep tonight?" Then he stopped and spoke again to Victor, who was still standing by the car. "Victor, tell Frederick I'd like breakfast for two on the east patio but not before ten."

"I'll take care of it, sir."

"Thank you. Good night, Victor."

"Good night, sir."

He watched Tony and Jacquelyn walk into the house before he moved again. He was more than a little surprised at the man's stamina and recuperative ability. It wasn't an hour ago Victor had almost poured him into the car, and now, he was walking and talking as though he drank nothing but water. Victor dispensed the orders to Harry, then left a note under Frederick's door regarding Tony's wishes for breakfast. His task was done for the night, and he was very glad of it. It was now ten past three, and he was tired. So tired, in fact, that he didn't even walk out to the security building to check up on things before turning in.

"There are two men on the grounds out front, and I count five cameras. But those are just the ones I can see. There are probably more. I didn't see motion sensors but that doesn't mean they don't have them. I wish Sharpe had stayed awake long enough to give us a rundown on Tracerio's security," Jon said to Michael and Ralph.

He was looking over the top of the side wall near the front corner of the property. The wall was eight feet high, so Michael and Ralph were holding his feet as if they were a team of acrobats. He swept the grounds with the field glasses again but could see nothing new. He lowered them and asked the two men to let him down.

"All right, guys. Listen up. I have to do a quick recon probe of the grounds. It is our only chance to hold onto the element of surprise. You two drive away quietly and come back here in thirty minutes. The less time the Ramcharger is parked here, the better. I'll be back here by then. Michael, grab the rope in the back, and while Ralph's driving, put knots in the rope about every foot or so. Big ones. When you return, pull the unit as close as you can up beside the wall and drop the tailgate. Then one of you can stand on it and watch over the wall for my return. Don't throw my end of the rope over until I get back here, okay? Oh, and be careful not to gun the engine or spin the tires crossing the curb. The noise may alert them that something's up. I've already pulled the bulb so the dome light won't come on. You got all that?"

"Got it," Michael said.

"Piece of cake. But J.J., are you sure this is just a recon probe? You aren't going in there to take the whole place on alone, are you?" Ralph asked suspiciously.

"Ralph, for three of us to get all the way in unnoticed and safely, a recon probe is absolutely vital. I'm not filled with bravado, and I'm not stupid. I want to live to see my family again. By the time you get back, I'll know where the holes are in their security and the number of men guarding the grounds. Then the three of us will have a better shot at being successful."

Ralph still seemed unconvinced, so J.J. repeated himself.

"Look, the chances of me going in there alone and coming out alive are slim, Ralph. Real slim. My family is important to me, and I absolutely want to see them again. okay?"

"Okay," Ralph said in a hesitant tone, but not one of belief. "Thirty minutes. No more. If you aren't back here by then, we're coming in."

"Understood, Ralph. Loud and clear. okay. I've got 3:23. I'll meet you back here at 3:53."

Then they boosted J.J. over the wall, and he disappeared before Ralph could say any more. Ralph and Michael got back in the Ramcharger and drove slowly and quietly away.

"What I didn't mention, Ralph," J.J. said as he donned the night vision goggles, "was that the chances of three of us coming in and surviving are worse."

Then he crouched down and started to circle the grounds. He was careful not to venture too far from the wall as he circled around toward the back. He noted camera positions as he moved and found many blind spots near the wall, but very few near the main house. He counted four buildings all together. The main house, the garage, the pool house, and what looked like a guesthouse. The guesthouse was very well lit inside for this time of night, so he took a closer look at it and the grounds around it through the field glasses. Rising up out of the ground and into the wall near the corner closest to him was a very large PVC pipe. That meant groupings of cables and wires. *Too many to be just TV and phone*, he thought. He crawled quickly and silently toward the building another ten yards, then looked through the glasses again. The light inside the building flickered slightly but enough to notice. He saw it again and again, but not in a sequential pattern. There was a TV on in there. There had to be. There was no chimney, so it couldn't be a fireplace. He inspected the roof and saw no exhaust pipes protruding through it for a stove either. Then it dawned on him. This was no guesthouse. It was the estate's security house.

It wasn't big enough to have lodging capabilities, and there were no signs of it having a kitchen. It had to be Tracerio's surveillance building. It was partially visible to the two goons on the back porch too. He quietly climbed the tree beside him high enough that he could see into the surveillance building. A man's head was visible. He was leaning back in a chair. J.J. could see the TV too. The guy was watching some after hours smut flick. J.J. watched him for a full thirty seconds, but the man never once took his eyes off the TV to look at the monitors on his right. He looked over to the back patio again, but only one goon was visible. The branches of the tree were blocking his line of sight to the other one. He used his field glasses again and took another look at the roof of the surveillance building now that he was in a position to see the whole thing. There was a large electric cable connecting it to the house. He followed the cable to the main house and down the wall. Bingo! There, on the wall, were the electric meter and the main breaker panel. He swung the field glasses back to the window of the surveillance room. The sicko was still glued to the TV. He could see no telltale signs of electronic security around the glass but had the feeling it was there just the same. He lowered the glasses.

He moved through the tree until he could see both goons on the back patio and the one in the building. Then he propped the goggles up onto his forehead and pulled the silenced AR-15 down from his shoulder. He scoped the goon farthest from him on the patio and adjusted the focus. He was talking to the other guard, but neither man had their weapons in the ready position. J.J. centered the crosshairs on the man's mouth and waited for the man to open it again. Two seconds later, he squeezed the trigger. There was no time to make sure the shot was on target. The second goon needed to be taken out before he could sound an alarm. J.J. moved the rifle barrel a few inches to the right. The back of this man's head was in the crosshairs. J.J. fired again. The bullet found its mark as the man was turning around to see where the first shot had come from. J.J. quickly panned their area with the scope and saw no movement from either of them. He looked into the window again. His hopes were that the man in there was too engrossed in his movie that he had not seen the other two fall. He hadn't moved. Yet. J.J. jumped down from the tree and ran across the grounds toward the front of the house. He was taking a huge risk as he was out in the open running between the two buildings, but there was no time to waste now. If the man kept watching his show, J.J. could get into a position to take out the two in the front without being noticed.

He stopped his run abruptly at the corner. He brought the rifle up as he looked around the corner and scoped in the farthest goon. This man was smoking a cigarette and had just exhaled heavily when J.J. released another whisper of death from the rifle. The round punched through his temple like a hammer through drywall. J.J. quickly brought the crosshairs over to the falling stiff's comrade. He had not yet seen the hit but must have heard it. He spun around toward his fallen friend while J.J. was sighting him in. The man's move put the back of his head smack in the middle of the scope. J.J. fired again. In the light of the front steps, J.J. could see the results of this bullet's exit. A spray of blood, flesh, and bone filled the air on the other side of this one and drifted to the ground as he fell. J.J. was hurrying now. There was no telling when the guy near the monitors would notice the bodies and break the silence.

J.J. spun in place and raised the rifle again. This time at the lock on the main electrical panel a few feet from the corner. He blew the small lock from the side and opened the box. It was slightly noisy, but speed was more important now than stealth. He was running out of time, and he knew it. He left the box open and the main breaker lever exposed. He would shut off the power to the whole place soon but not just yet. He knew that as soon as he did, the goons inside the building would go to full alert. The longer he could keep that from happening, the better. Below the electric breaker was another box. J.J. recognized it immediately. It was the main phone system connection. A small cable protruded from the bottom of the box and disappeared into the ground. He'd have to apologize to Ma Bell soon, he thought. He shouldered the AR-15 and pulled the Beretta into play as he ran back to the surveillance building. He tried the door handle. It was unlocked. He swung it open and stepped in while raising the Beretta. The man in the chair spun to see who had entered but would never utter a word. The bullet entered his left cheek and buried itself into the console after blowing away his lower right jaw.

J.J. did a quick vision sweep of the building but saw no one else. It was only a one-room facility. Even the sink and toilet were in the open. Probably so the man on duty could watch the monitors no matter what he was doing. *A smart move on the part of the designer*, J.J. thought. He looked for a long second at each monitor but none gave him a look at the inside of the house. He turned off the light switch and closed the door as he left. He ran back to the box and donned the night vision goggles. He severed the wire for the telephone system with a quick flick of the knife, then put it away as quickly as he'd grabbed it. He pulled down on the lever, and in an instant, the whole place went dark. The front door was the closest entry point from there, so he sprinted toward it. He stopped abruptly as he passed by one of the windows. He had seen movement. He backed up a step and crouched, raising the Beretta. A man with a pistol in hand was feeling his way out of the room he was in, presumably heading for the front door. J.J. didn't want him to make it, but there was a problem. A big problem.

The whisper of the AR-15 and the Beretta were quiet enough not to be heard inside, but the sound of shattering and falling glass could wake everyone. He took a quick breath and a huge gamble. He ran to the front of the house and did a baseball player's slide in the grass about twenty-five feet from the front door. He brought the AR-15 up and aimed it at the door's opening point. He saw the man's silhouette through the windows on the side of the door, but the man was obviously crouching. J.J. could also hear him calling to the men out front. There would be no response, meaning there was no way this goon was going to open the door without looking through the window first. J.J. changed the barrel's trajectory and waited. The man's face came up to the far window about three feet off the floor. J.J. had been aiming at the near window. He quickly adjusted his line and squeezed off two rounds. The sound of shattering glass was there, but it was muffled greatly because of the window's small size. J.J. could not see the man's head after the shots but wasn't sure he'd connected.

He rose and held the AR-15 in the attack position. He began to charge the door when he saw movement again. He had missed. The man was pointing his sidearm in J.J.'s general direction from a low position in the near window. Most of his frame was behind the door. J.J. acted quickly. He stopped, knelt, and then raised the barrel of the rifle. He put the area of the door that was serving as cover for the man's body in the crosshairs and fired five rounds, one after the other. The noise of the bullets hitting the steel centered door was thunderous. He heard the glass break and the sound of a weapon discharging as the night vision glasses gave him an extremely exaggerated look at the muzzle flash from inside the door. He rolled to his left and rose again on one knee. This time, he had a solid angle on the goon. He wasted no time. Three quick rounds shattered the glass, and most likely, the man's skull. J.J. watched the silhouette fall backward, then lowered the rifle barrel a few inches. He peered into the dark house through the window by the door but saw no movement. He took off toward a large window without another moment's hesitation. He leaped up into the glass like an oblong cannonball and had the same effect it would have had. Glass flew in all directions and cut him in a few noncritical places but at least he was in. Using the AR-15 as a wedge had worked well.

He shouldered the AR-15 and pulled both Berettas from their holsters. His best guess was that the front door was two rooms to his right, so to the right he would go. Not to get to the front door but to get to the staircase. He was going up. A shot rang out behind him as he entered the main foyer. He felt the searing heat and spiking pain as the bullet plowed non-stop through the flesh of his left arm. He instinctively dove into the foyer to the right, away from the apparent aim of his attacker. He looked up the darkened staircase, which in his goggles glowed an eerie shade of green. No movement there. He rolled back into the doorway, facing the direction the shot had come from. Not a moment too soon either. This goon was only two steps away from the foyer himself, and coming on fast.

J.J. didn't have time to raise the pistol high enough for a head shot, so he parked the aim of the silenced Beretta into a direct line with the goon's genitals and fired three quick rounds. He rolled to his left immediately after squeezing the trigger the third time. As he rolled, a chilling scream of panic and disbelief filled the air. He came to a stop after two full revolutions and raised the Beretta again. The man was now lying on the floor of the foyer, face down. His head was turned, and he was looking at J.J. as if he still could not believe he was the one who had lost their battle. J.J. didn't give him time to contemplate it or time to plead for his life. J.J. could not risk being merciful or forgiving tonight. If he was to get out alive, there could be no one left in his wake that could take him down from behind. Besides, J.J. thought as he lined up the Beretta's muzzle with the man's right eye, he should have thought of all that before he chose this type of life. Then J.J. popped off a single round, but it was enough. This goon would bother him no more. He rose as quickly as he could, feeling fully the pain of his arm's missing flesh and the rush of air as it poured into the wound. He counted the dead in his head as he moved.

They totaled seven. But he was sure that there were more. So sure, in fact, that he ejected the round in the chamber into his hand and switched clips in the Beretta while he leaned against the inside wall of the room to the left of the foyer. He had only fired it seven times that he could remember. But this was not the time to be gambling with the count.

He heard movement upstairs after he chambered the first round. He took a deep breath to calm himself, then swiveled around the corner with the Beretta leading the way. He heard heavy footsteps above and to the left. He closed his eyes and listened for another second. The sound was descending. There was another staircase! Tracerio was coming down the other way! He went quickly back through the rooms to the left, listening for the sounds again. He heard a doorknob being twisted vigorously, then the sound of a windowed door slamming open against a wall. The garage! They were headed for the garage! J.J. raced back to the front door and spun the deadbolt. He opened the door with a slam of his own and ran through it. He jumped off the front patio into the grass between the driveway and the house. At a dead run, he made his way toward the garage. He could hear a car being started, and the engine gunned. The garage doors were not open, but J.J. knew that was because he had cut the power. He dropped the silenced Beretta and grabbed a grenade. He pulled the pin and lobbed it in the direction of one of the six garage doors.

He chose the farthest one from the house as his target, gambling that Tracerio's only bulletproof vehicle was the limo and that would be parked at the far end of the garage. He couldn't see Tony Tracerio wasting any of his precious time if he didn't have to, including something as trivial as walking by the limo to get to the car he would drive himself. The chauffeur could walk to the far end to get it, because Tony probably always got picked up out front. The grenade blew as the sound of spinning rubber against pavement filled the night. J.J.'s hunch about the limo had been sound, but he had missed one small detail. Tony had two limousines. A second after the last garage door exploded under the force of the grenade, the fifth one was splintered to pieces as a car smashed through it. J.J. didn't trust his grenade aim at a moving target, so he pulled the AR-15 down from his shoulder and dropped to one knee. He threw off the goggles and sighted in on the speeding car's left front tire. Two rounds met the air, then the tire. The car didn't stop, though, so J.J. targeted the rear tire on the same side. It took three shots to hit that one. The car still did not stop.

Sparks flew in all directions as the rims hit the pavement and J.J. lined his sights again. This time, at the right rear tire. The car was moving away from him at a forty-five-degree angle, so the tire was not completely visible. He steadied his aim, closed his left eye, cross-haired up, and let two more bullets fly. The car was almost to the gate when the bullet struck. This time, the car slipped out of control. It slid gradually to the left and then fishtailed back to the right as the driver tried to correct its line. The rear end smacked into a tree near the driveway thirty yards or so from the gate, and came to a halt.

"Get out of the car in five seconds, or get blown up with it!" J.J. said as he pulled another grenade from his belt.

The driver's door opened and the man who'd been behind the wheel got out with his hands high in the air.

"Don't shoot! Don't shoot! I'm unarmed, and I won't give you any trouble!"

"Tracerio! Step out, or you die in a coffin made by Cadillac."

"Tracerio? Mr. Tracerio's not in here," Harry said. "I'm the only one in the car. I heard all the gunshots, got dressed, and got out of that house. I'm not a gunman. I'm just a driver."

J.J. stood and put the grenade away, then raised the AR-15. He jogged quickly over to the car, keeping the driver in his sights. He told the driver to open all the doors and the trunk or be shot where he stood. Harry quickly obliged. J.J. started moving laterally as soon as the trunk lid popped and that movement saved his life. The bullet took off a small piece of his left ear as it passed, and the burning made him wince heavily. He dove to the ground. He spun around in the grass until he was facing the house. One of the upstairs windows was not reflecting the little bit of moonlight the same as the others. It was broken. The gunman had fired from there and was probably still there. J.J. saw the muzzle flash from another window and instinctively covered his head. The bullet whizzed by with the sound of a screech owl and buried itself with a thud into the lawn a good seven or eight feet behind him. Then another muzzle flash from the first window again. There was no way one man could move that fast, J.J. thought as he covered his head again. There were still at least two men in there firing at him.

J.J. risked heavily that neither man could see him lying on the grass. The last two bullets were just too wide. He propped the AR-15 up on his elbow and sighted in the second window. If the muzzle flash happened again, he'd use the sniper's trick he'd learned in Iraq. He'd send a bullet into the window just below the glow of the flash. A head shot was too risky but directly beneath that glow were two arms and a chest. A much bigger target. There it was again. Same window. He squeezed off four rounds in succession, then rolled toward the first window. He heard a woman scream, and then heard her cry out in agonizing pain and terror.

A woman? Tracerio had a woman on his security team? Just then the confusion cleared as she screamed again.

"Victor! Help! Tony's been shot! Victor! Can you hear me?"

J.J. lay there in silence, watching carefully for another muzzle flash. He glanced quickly at his goggles on the ground fifty feet away. They may as well be a mile at this point, he thought. Then the woman screamed again.

"Victor! Do something! Why won't you answer me?"

Victor wasn't about to answer her. He was not going to move from his position. He knew the assault team was down there on the grounds somewhere. He just needed to know where. He stuck the barrel of the rifle out the window and stepped aside. He fired a quick three round burst, then stooped by the corner of the window and waited. He knew of the sniper's trick too. He didn't have to wait long. The return muzzle flashes pinpointed a man's position for Victor, so he quickly brought the rifle up and sprayed half a dozen shells in the immediate vicinity. He waited for a full fifteen seconds, then called out.

"Harry! Did I get one of them? Where is he?"

No response came, so he yelled it again.

"Harry! Answer me! Did I get him?"

The only sounds he heard in return were the cries of the woman a few rooms down. He looked out the window slowly, trying to catch a glimpse of the car and Harry. The car was there, and the doors were all open, but Harry was nowhere to be found. He listened carefully for telltale noises from below, but none came.

"Victor! Get in here! Right now! Do you hear me?"

It was Tony. He was still alive. Victor felt relieved and answered back, "On my way, Tony!"

He moved quickly through the upper floor's hall to the room Tony was occupying.

"Are you okay, Tony?" Victor asked as he entered.

"I will be. As soon as we get those motherless pigs. Where is everybody?" Tony asked, bleeding from the right side of his upper chest.

"Dead, I believe. I don't know how many there are, but whoever they are, they're pros."

"I can see that. How many do you think there are?"

"Hard to say, Tony. But my guess is at least two, maybe more. I'm going to see if I can draw them away from the house. That way you can get out of here."

"Not a chance! No one is gonna make me run from my own home. These suckers are going to pay for this. Help me up. There's only a few of them, and we know this house better than they do. We have just become the hunters."

After Tony reached his feet, Victor handed him the weapon he had dropped. Tony ordered Jacquelyn to stay put, and he and Victor went on the hunt.

J.J. had heard the second voice call for Victor and could only assume by the tone that it had been Tracerio himself. J.J. seized the opportunity to get his goggles and the silenced Beretta back. Once he had them, he went back into the house. He worked his way through the first floor carefully, listening for any and every imaginable sound. There was a very gentle breeze riding the air in Albuquerque, and it seemed to wish to be a participant in the night's events. It added an unsettling whisper to the house as it entered the broken windows. The chill it carried was not enough to warrant a sweater but, on occasion, would deliver a shiver to the spine. J.J. finally stopped in the main dining room, which was on the back side of the house. It opened into the main hallway very near the foyer, directly across from the large living room in the front of the house. He squatted against the side wall beside the hutch, hidden from view by the twelve-seat table. He took the AR-15 from his shoulder, replaced the clip, and chambered the first round. He put the weapon back on his shoulder and then pulled his shirtsleeve up and looked at his watch—3:39. Ralph and Michael would be back soon. It was time to finish it.

They had been driving for about ten minutes, discussing strategies and potential variables, when Ralph asked Michael a question that made both men go silent.

"You don't think Blake's going to try to take that place on his own, do you, Michael?"

After a long pause, Michael looked over at his partner, and said, "Ralph, I just don't know. The man is obviously experienced enough to think he can, but he's definitely not stupid. I just don't know."

"Think about it. Asking us to drive away for fear of being seen made sense at the time, but this whole area is all large estates and mini ranches. We haven't seen a single car since we left. What if he was trying to get us out of the way so he could go after Tracerio himself?"

"I still don't think he would do that, Ralph, but I wouldn't put it past him either. One thing is certain—he's an expert. And having been in the army's elite strike force, I'd have to assume he's stormed places with superior manpower before."

"Exactly. And he obviously survived every one of them."

The men looked at each other for a long second, then said in unison, "Let's get back there."

Ralph slowed and wheeled the Ramcharger around, then put his foot to the floor. Michael climbed into the back and readied the weapons they would carry onto the grounds. Both men's instincts screamed out that J.J. had lied to them and was attempting to take the whole place down alone. Ralph was the first to voice it.

"Why would he pull such a crazy stunt? It's an absolute suicide mission to go in there alone. I don't give a rat's ass how good he was in the Green Berets. That was twenty years ago, Michael. This guy is unbelievable!"

"Stay cool, Ralph. Stay cool. He might be there waiting for us just like he said he would be. We don't know what he's done yet."

"Are you kidding me? Are you really expecting me to believe that crap? No way, partner. No way. I'll bet that Blake's either already dead, or close to it. *Stupid egomaniac!*"

Michael wanted to argue but couldn't. He believed the same thing Ralph did. Jonathan Blake was going to end the threat Tracerio had placed on his family's lives tonight, or die trying.

"Can you make this heap go any faster, Ralph?"

"I've got it to the floor, partner. She's still climbing even though she isn't climbing as fast as our cruisers do," Ralph said as the speedometer needle passed the seventy-five mark on the gauge.

"Hey, Ralph?" Michael asked as he climbed back to the front.

"Yeah?"

"If we're right about him going after Tracerio alone, we'll know it the minute we pull up. And if that is what's happening, I say we crash the gate with this thing. Screw going in silent and slow."

Ralph looked at Michael with an appreciative glance.

"Do you think this old monster can take that thick, reinforced wrought-iron gate?"

"If he's already swapping lead with them, she's gonna have to."

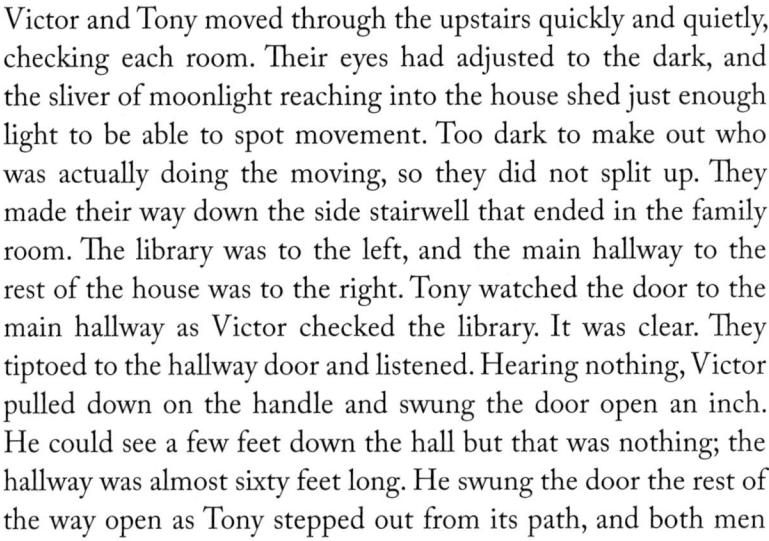

Victor and Tony moved through the upstairs quickly and quietly, checking each room. Their eyes had adjusted to the dark, and the sliver of moonlight reaching into the house shed just enough light to be able to spot movement. Too dark to make out who was actually doing the moving, so they did not split up. They made their way down the side stairwell that ended in the family room. The library was to the left, and the main hallway to the rest of the house was to the right. Tony watched the door to the main hallway as Victor checked the library. It was clear. They tiptoed to the hallway door and listened. Hearing nothing, Victor pulled down on the handle and swung the door open an inch. He could see a few feet down the hall but that was nothing; the hallway was almost sixty feet long. He swung the door the rest of the way open as Tony stepped out from its path, and both men stepped quietly into the corridor. Then they stopped. A sound, then another, the sound of metal sliding against metal. The sound of a clip being replaced, coming from somewhere down near the main foyer.

They stepped quickly toward the foyer, guns out front and ready to fire. They had traveled a half dozen paces when another sound stopped them in their tracks. The sound was faint, but nevertheless unmistakable. Someone had just chambered the first round of a fresh clip. The sound was coming from in front of them and to their left. It was coming from the dining room. Tony tapped Victor gently, then slid his hand up behind Victor's neck and pulled him down to Tony's height.

"Dining room. You cover the kitchen door, and I'll take the hall. He's got to come out of one of them. Go," Tony whispered softly, yet sternly. Then he pushed Victor's neck away and started moving toward the door fifteen feet farther down the hall. He was bleeding more quickly now, and dizziness was creeping in, invited or not. He stopped and knelt near the opposite wall, with his Glock 19 pointing head high at the doorway.

Victor had taken a position near the only other way out of the dining room, the kitchen. It and the dining room shared a wall and a door. The man would have to come through the kitchen to exit this way, so Victor decided to try and outflank him. It was risky, but if he could get past the small table and the pantry to the island in the center of the kitchen, he'd have a clean shot as the man walked past. Additionally, the man would most likely not see Victor until it was already too late to do anything about. Victor took a deep breath and rounded the corner into the kitchen area. He felt his way with his free hand, making sure he would not run into a chair or something. He made it past the table and turned left toward the island. He'd walked four steps, again with his hand out front feeling for the island, when fate stepped in.

"Ralph, the mansion looks completely dark, man. I don't see a single light on in the whole place," Michael said as he sat back down in the passenger seat.

He'd been sitting on the door, his upper body out the window, looking over the wall at the main house as they drove toward the front gate.

"None? As in not one?" Ralph asked, surprised.

"Not one. And you know what that means."

"That crazy fool! He did go in there alone! Idiot!"

"Yep. That's the way I see it," Michael said. "He got inside and killed the power so they'd be blind and he wouldn't. He's crazy, man. There are a lot of guns against him in there, and they might have night vision goggles too. What is he thinking?"

"He isn't thinking. That's the whole problem. All right. we're gonna have to crash the gate. Belt up and hold on, Michael."

They were only a few hundred yards from the street the main gate was on. Ralph buckled up, then wheeled the corner with tires screeching. Silence was no longer an option. The gate was two hundred yards away.

J.J. heard it. It was faint, and only lasted for an instant, but it was there. A sound in the room behind him. A sound like something being bumped. He rose slowly and moved silently toward the door between the two rooms. The goggles gave him a great advantage in the dark, but they couldn't help him see through walls. The doorway into the next room was in the corner. There would be nowhere safe for him to hide to get a look into the room before entering. To make things worse, the person who'd made the sound had already had time to prepare for an entry. His aim was probably already fixed on the doorway. J.J. decided to take no chances.

He peeked inch by inch around the corner and saw that there was a wall on his left and a counter on his right, extending ten feet or so into the room. It would provide adequate cover but that was not the problem. It was only made of wood and probably very thin wood. It would provide no protection from bullets being sent through it at him. There were also cabinets hanging from the ceiling above the counter, but between them it was wide-open air. He could not see a man or even signs of a man in there. Which meant that the man was hidden and waiting. J.J. crouched there for a few seconds thinking. He knew that to enter the room without at least a general idea of the man's location was definitely dangerous and possibly deadly. So he reached for a grenade.

Tony had heard the noise too and was now inching his way down the outside wall of the dining room toward the hall door. His night shirt was now soaked with blood, and he was leaving a light trail of it on the floor wherever he went. He fought off the dizziness with all his will. He was in a game of fight to the death, and there were no rules. Should he lose consciousness, he would lose his life. He stood at the corner, pooling all the strength and focus he had left in him to make his move when he heard another sound in the kitchen.

Victor heard the item hit the floor between him and the table but did not move. He was not about to give away his position by firing at an obvious decoy. He decided he would wait until the man entered the room, thinking that it was clear, and then take him out. He smiled as he sat there on the floor, proud of himself for thinking of all this in less than three seconds. Victor was downright lethal in a face-to-face fight but had never heard the sound of a grenade hitting a floor before. The second to last thing he would ever hear was J.J.'s AR-15.

J.J. knew that once he tossed the grenade, he'd have to get out of there and fast. If the appliances were gas instead of electric, the whole kitchen would become an incinerator. But there was a second problem. He'd have to run through a doorway that he had not checked, and he knew there were at least two men carrying weapons. The other was probably right on the other side of his exit door, waiting to ambush him. It made the most sense to have one man watching each exit from the room. He holstered the Beretta and pulled the AR-15 back down from his shoulder with incredible speed and silence. He tossed the grenade into the kitchen over the counter with his left hand and then immediately grabbed the rifle's stock with it as he spun to the left.

He took two quick steps toward the door, then, without stopping, pulled the trigger of the AR-15 and held it in. He showered the wall with a waist-high inch or so apart curtain of lead as he now ran toward the door. He dove out into the hallway as the grenade went off.

"Punch it, Ralph!" Michael yelled as they approached the gate.

It was truly a formidable obstruction and neither man knew what would happen. They both knew that what happened in the movies did not necessarily reflect the truth. All it would take was one iron rod to pierce the sheet metal or the glass of the passenger compartment or a blowout while the vehicle's weight was too far to one side, to cause them both serious injury or death.

Both Michael and Ralph ducked toward the center of the vehicle a second before impact, but the explosion they heard as the Ramcharger's grille smashed into the foreboding gate was not the sound they expected.

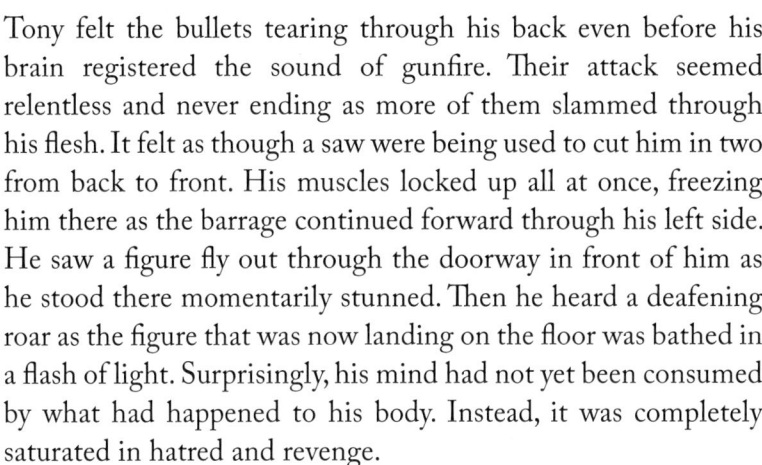

Tony felt the bullets tearing through his back even before his brain registered the sound of gunfire. Their attack seemed relentless and never ending as more of them slammed through his flesh. It felt as though a saw were being used to cut him in two from back to front. His muscles locked up all at once, freezing him there as the barrage continued forward through his left side. He saw a figure fly out through the doorway in front of him as he stood there momentarily stunned. Then he heard a deafening roar as the figure that was now landing on the floor was bathed in a flash of light. Surprisingly, his mind had not yet been consumed by what had happened to his body. Instead, it was completely saturated in hatred and revenge.

His legs weakened and began to buckle as he lowered the Glock toward the man hitting the floor. The man's feet were nearest Tony, but Tony only cared that he could finally see his prey. His eyes filled with the wildness of the criminally insane as he screamed, *"Your turn to die, you motherless fool!"*

He had at least ten rounds left in the Glock, and he was going to use them all. He pulled back on the trigger and held it there as he fought to stay on his feet. The glow from the kitchen allowed him to see the power of the Glock at work. Bullet after bullet blew through the man's pants, then his clothes, shredding the flesh beneath. Tony screamed every foul name he could think of at the man on the floor as the powerful thunder from the Glock cracked the air again and again. Tony raised the weapon as his legs finally gave way, trying with his last conscious breath to send a message from the Glock straight into the man's brain. He would never raise the gun high enough to send that message. The great

Tony Tracerio fell to the ground while one bullet remained in the Glock, but he wouldn't have time to fire it. His time was up.

J.J. felt the bullets ripping into his legs, and the impact as they smashed into his vest. The first bullet had blown through his calf even before he hit the ground, stunning him, and leaving him no chance to react. He could feel himself slipping from consciousness into the land of nightmares as the onslaught continued. The fear of impending death washed over him like a tidal wave, drenching his mind in the unknown and unwanted. The pictures in his mind swirled around and around as if he were caught in a whirlpool and being sucked down. He could not hear Michael or Ralph calling to him. He could not feel their hands upon his face. And even though his eyes were open, he could not see. Then, as if someone flicked a switch, even the lights in his mind went off, turning everything black and silent.

22

Michael took J.J. to Mercy Hospital while Ralph searched the rest of the estate. Once he had extinguished the relatively small fire in the kitchen, he went outside and flipped on the main breaker. Then he made his way slowly through the house. He discovered the butler and maid hiding in her closet. She was obviously terrified and being comforted by the butler. He took them outside quickly, zip-tied their hands and feet, then went back in. He found another woman curled up on the floor crying in an upstairs bedroom. Everyone else was dead. Ralph ushered her outside, then zip-tied her hands and feet as well. He then went back in and completed a sweep of every room.

The grounds were now easy to cover with the lights on. Almost every inch was illuminated. He went through the other three buildings and found only one other survivor. The man was hiding in one of the cars in the garage. He identified himself as Harry Gilliam, the chauffeur. While Ralph was taking his new captive back to where he'd left the other three suspects, his cell phone rang. It was Michael.

"Hey, Ralph. We're here at the hospital, and he's going into emergency now. I showed them my badge and ID and told them not to call the press due to the impending investigation. I told them that I'd found him lying on the ground in an alley. Then I said th—"

"Michael. Make sure they don't call this in, man. You know they are required to report all Goss," Ralph said urgently.

"Already handled. They only have to notify the police of a victim with gunshot wounds. Since the police brought him in, they have no reason to call. I told them all information regarding his condition was to be brought to me and me only. The doc asked why and I told him that there were extenuating circumstances surrounding this shooting that led us to believe that this was an assassination attempt, not a random act of violence. So announcing his presence to anyone would be reckless endangerment. The doc instructed his staff to keep quiet, then went off to the operating room. He's in bad shape, Ralph. Real bad. I don't know if he'll make it, man," Michael said sadly.

"He's a strong man with a strong will, partner. If anyone can pull out of this, he can," Ralph said with equal sorrow.

"You're right about that, Ralph. He's definitely a fighter. So what now?"

"You stay there, where you can stay in contact with the doctor. But stay out of sight. The last thing we need right now is for one of our own to bring someone in and see you there. I'm going over to the house to check on our two bankers. I'll call you from there."

"Okay. Be careful, man. This isn't over yet."

"Agreed. I'll call you soon," Ralph said.

Ralph piled all the suspects into the limo that was still in the garage, got the keys from the chauffeur, and drove over to the house. They were all bound, so there was no threat of attack or escape. He walked through his door at 4:40. He went straight to the bathroom, finding both men right where he'd left them. They were sound asleep. He quietly removed the VHS tape from the camera and took it to his bedroom.

He skipped through the tape quickly, listening to a few things here and there. All he wanted to do was make sure there was enough said on the tape to justify calling the Bureau. Ralph didn't care that the tape showed both men tied up during their confessions. Its future admissibility as evidence was a problem for the attorneys to fight over. There was more than enough said to suit Ralph's immediate needs, so he picked up the phone.

"Michael? It's Ralph. The bankers did their duty. This tape seems to have everything we need. I think it's time to call in the cavalry. Whaddaya think?"

"Well, there's no possible way we can run all these perps down on our own before word gets out. I'd say our best bet is to hit them all at the same time, and for that, we'll need the help of at least..." Michael paused to total the number of houses they'd have to storm, but Ralph had already done it.

"Ten agents. Two per house. That covers the chief, the captain, Cantonelli, Tracerio's kid, and the fire marshal. Did I miss anyone?"

"Just the guards who survived the Johnson Farms blast and the off duty ones at the mansion."

"I forgot about them. Okay. Most of them we can pick up later, I think. But the Bureau should bring at least two more in to watch the mansion. That makes twelve. Man, this is huge. How's J.J. doing?"

"No word yet. They're still working on him. What are you going to do about Flo and the kids being up there with the other shooter?"

"I'll call her as soon as she turns on her phone and tell her the coast is clear to come home. As far as the shooter goes, I'll give the Bureau his location and have them pick him up."

"I don't think that's a good idea, man."

"Why not?"

"'Cause if the wrong agent goes to the cabin, the shooter may either be snuffed on the spot or pulled out of there and hidden. He's too important to our case, man. I don't think we can risk that, Ralph."

Ralph paused to digest Michael's words. Michael's point was a solid one.

"Okay. You're right. I'll play that one by ear until I talk with her in a few hours. So for the time being, let's not mention the cabin to them. This tape is more than enough to get them down here anyway. I'll call them right now. I'm not going to call the Albuquerque office. I'm calling DC and having them wake up the head honcho here. Then I'll go on conference mode with them all, so there will be a record of it in Washington just in case the head honcho here was also on Tracerio's payroll. I figure that's the best way to make sure the sting actually goes down."

"Good idea, Ralph. If the head agent is dirty, he'll do everything by the book to cover himself with Washington once he learns that Tracerio is dead."

"Right. And if he's not dirty, he'll do it by the numbers anyway. So either way, we win."

"I'm in. I'll stay here and guard J.J. Call me if you need me."

"I will."

Ralph's phone call to Washington was tedious and ridiculously slow at first. He had to let his call be traced and then for the Bureau in Washington to pull him up on their computer to verify he was who he had claimed to be so they could take what he had to say seriously. Once they had, the Bureau's machine was on the move. The conference call was an ingenious idea. The men in Washington and the local field office supervisor had heard everything Ralph had to say in one shot. The call lasted almost an hour, but about halfway through, the lead agent grabbed his cell phone and called his office right there in Albuquerque, while Ralph and the boys in Washington listened in. He told the night shift operator to wake all available agents and have them get down to the office and ready to go by 6:15. Once he hung up, he apologized and asked Ralph to continue. When Ralph had finished, the lead agent, Ken Crane, asked him to bring the two bankers and the tape to his office downtown as soon as possible. Crane told Ralph that he would be there within thirty minutes himself. Ralph agreed and all parties hung up.

Ralph called Michael again and let him know what was going on. Michael informed him that J.J. was still in surgery, then commented that this was probably a good sign.

"Yes, it is," Ralph said. "If they're still operating, they must still feel he has a chance."

Ralph woke the two bankers, let them use the bathroom one at a time, and then drove down to the Bureau's office on Silver Avenue in the limo with all six suspects. By the time he arrived, Ken Crane was waiting on the front steps with two other men. The two men escorted all six of Ralph's charges inside, and Ralph went off with Crane to his office to view portions of the tape. It was now 6:05.

At 6:15, the receptionist buzzed and said that all but three available agents were waiting for him in the conference room. Crane thanked her and told her to let them know he'd be in there at 6:20. He asked Ralph to give the briefing. Ralph's heart skipped a beat. He did a good job at hiding it, but he was very excited to be giving a briefing to an FBI sting team. He filled them in on the who, what, when, where, why, and how, then Crane took over. He assigned two agents to bring in each of the five men Ralph had named, then sent four more to Tracerio's Estate and still two others to the hospital to relieve Michael. He instructed them not to use police band frequencies for any reason as those conversations may be intercepted and some of the suspects may flee. Crane looked at his watch. It was now 7:05. He instructed all teams to be in position and ready by 7:40. Then, if they had not heard from him by 7:45, to start waking people up.

Ralph told Crane of his concern for Blake's life and that under no circumstances was he going to tell Michael to leave Blake in the hands of Crane's men. Crane understood and empathized with Ralph. So he caught the two men who were to go to the hospital and told them to support Michael but not to take over for him. Then Ralph called Michael and told him to expect them. Ralph went with him to the observation booth connected to the interrogation room where Ashland and Covington were being held. Both men stayed true to their word and were repeating what both Ralph and Crane had heard on the tape. Ralph went with Crane back to his office, where Crane poured him a cup of coffee and started asking a few questions of his own. The questions were personal ones as Ralph had given quite a detailed explanation of the events leading up to that morning.

Ralph kept a close eye on his watch. Flo would be turning her cell phone on at twenty after seven, which was now only a few minutes away. She was expecting to hear from them by seven thirty. He would need to get away from Crane to make that call, so at twenty-two minutes after, Ralph would suddenly need to go to the bathroom.

The kids were asleep, and had been for hours. The man tied to the mattress had not woken up once, and Flo had not slept at all. With all of the tension, she had not been forced to battle it either. Worrisome thoughts had flown through her mind over and over again all night long like nightmarish Indy cars circling the track. They filled her with anxiety, almost to the point of mental torture. She held on, staying very focused under the circumstances. Finally, it was time. She looked at her cell phone for a long moment, then at her sleeping children, then back at the phone. She closed her eyes and prayed, holding the phone to her chest like one would hold a cherished gift. She opened her eyes and pushed the on button, bringing the phone to life.

She considered checking for messages but discarded the idea quickly. J.J. had been specific about the contact time. She looked at her watch, looked at her phone, and waited. It was twenty-three after.

Ralph excused himself by asking where the restroom was, then actually did use it. Afterward, he slipped outside to the Ramcharger to call Flo. It was 7:25. The relief in Flo's voice was unmistakable, and although Ralph dearly wanted to just talk with her, he could not bring himself to. There was too much to be done and he would soon be missed inside.

He asked about Sharpe, and she told him he had not moved. Ralph asked if she thought she could tie him up, then she and the kids could load him up and bring him back down to the house without risking their safety, and Flo immediately said yes. She explained that each time she had checked on him, he had been nonresponsive but breathing. She told Ralph that since he was actually a very small man, he would be no problem to handle. Ralph cautioned her about the possibility that he may be faking, then told her a policeman's trick to finding that out. If she was to brush his eyelash quickly with her finger and his eyelid twitched, he was awake. If it did not move, he was truly out cold. He told her there was no way to control that response, so this test was failsafe.

They arranged to meet at the house at ten. But if a problem of any kind arose, she should call him immediately. He asked her not to call him unless it was truly an emergency, because of who he was currently working with. Then they hung up. Ralph did not want her bringing him to either FBI office because he didn't know if there were any agents on Tracerio's payroll. He would get Sharpe from her and bring him to the hospital himself at ten.

Ralph had already decided to keep his prisoner a secret at first. All he had to say was that he still didn't trust anyone until he saw all the men he had named being brought in. After all, Ralph's own leaders were involved, so how could he trust anyone else? Ralph knew this explanation would be enough.

Ralph went back to Crane's office but found it empty. He asked someone in the hall where Crane was and they pointed to a door down the hall. Ralph looked in the window and saw Crane leaning on a desk. He seemed to be talking into some kind of microphone. Ralph knocked on the glass and Crane nodded and waved him in. Ralph stood there listening as the sting was setting up. All teams were checking in and then, at precisely 7:45, made their respective moves. Within five minutes, three teams had reported in with confirmations of their apprehensions, but the other two had as yet been unable to locate their quarry.

23

The blackness faded almost unnoticeably to gray. Voices. He heard voices. The gray seemed to be softening. Where was he? Then the gray turned to white. An almost painful, blinding white. He kept fighting the pain to open his eyes wider so he could survey his surroundings. It seemed an eternity had passed before colors started to make their way into his vision. Shapes formed around the colors as the fog slowly lifted from his brain.

His concentration was so focused on seeing that he didn't even hear a voice say, "Don't leave him alone for a second, is that clear?"

Then it went black. When he next awoke, he was able to make out the spot that was above and in front of him—a TV. As his head cleared his eyes regained complete focus. The sterile aroma that filled his nostrils finally registered, and everything came together. He was in a hospital! How on earth had he wound up in a hospital? Just as he reached into his memory to recall why, a voice called out.

"Dr. Grand! Dr. Grand! Mr. Blake is regaining consciousness!"

He saw a tower of a man enter his vision from the right. Why couldn't he move his head? He tried his arms. No good. His legs wouldn't move either. He tried harder, to no avail.

Dr. Grand's hand swept expertly across Blake's face, settling on his brow. Blake could feel his right eyelid being opened gently and saw a few flashes of light as the doc checked his pupil response. Grand moved to his left eye and repeated the procedure, speaking to him as he did so.

"Sir, you are in Mercy Hospital, and I'm Dr. Grand. You were brought here almost a week ago, and frankly, I'm amazed that you ever woke up. We pulled four bullets out of you, and had to close up wounds from three others that passed clear through. What in samhill happened?"

"Dr. Grand, we'll take care of the investigation, you just do what you can to keep this man alive, okay?"

Blake knew the voice, but was too groggy to place it.

Who are you? he thought. He tried to speak, but the effort was fruitless. *Come closer so I can see who you are*, he thought.

God, he wished he could speak. He tried again. A throbbing pain rose to jackhammer proportions in his head and it seemed like every blood vessel in his skull would explode at once. He closed his eyes to lessen his gray matter's workload. What had happened? Why couldn't he remember? He felt the touch of gentle fingers on his forearm. Then a peaceful, tingling sensation climbed up the inside of his arm and spilled into his body and mind. He breathed deeply, and then drifted mercifully back to sleep.

"J.J.? Can you hear me? J.J.?" a voice asked softly from his bedside as he stirred.

J.J. kept blinking as he opened his eyes wider, but he was unaccustomed to the light, making it difficult to see. He finally won the battle and turned his head to the right. It was Michael. His gaze was still glassy, but his mind was clearing quickly. He noticed another man standing in the room behind Michael, a man he did not recognize.

The man had a serious look on his face, but Jon Blake could not tell if it was a look of impatient indifference or one of contempt. He was big and had his arms folded across his chest.

"Hi, Michael," Blake said in a very raspy voice. How many days has it been since the firefight at Tracerio's?," he asked as quickly as he could.

"Um, let's see. Eight."

"Are you sure?" Blake's urgency was unmistakable.

"Yeah Jon, why?"

"Nothing, it's okay. Sorry. Who's the bouncer?"

Michael stopped smiling for a second and looked quickly behind him.

"He's with the Bureau. He's here to protect you while you recuperate, J.J. Don't worry. He's on our side. His name is Dawson. Special Agent William Dawson. And his partner, Agent Jim Streeter, is outside in the hall. You're in good hands, J.J., and you are safe. So just relax and heal. You took a monstrous pounding from Tracerio's Glock. You almost died, man. The doctor didn't give you much of a chance to pull through," Michael said in a solemn voice, then smiled. "I am so glad to see you. I knew you'd make it, man. I have to admit, that both Ralph and I were scared when we found you lying on Tracerio's floor. You were a mess, J.J. But once they started pouring blood back into you here, I knew you'd survive, so did Ralph. He's a little tweaked at you, though."

"Really? Well, he'll get over it. Where's Tracerio? Did you guys get him? And what abou—"

"Whoa, J.J. Slow down, man. Tracerio's dead. He was lying on the floor a couple feet behind you. He was unconscious but still alive. He died on the way here. And a lucky thing for you that he passed out when he did. If he could have stayed conscious for another few seconds, you'd probably be dead too. There was still one round left in his Glock when we found you two. And from the looks of things, you were down before he was. It was one gigantic mess there."

Jonathan Blake heard everything Michael had said, but his mind was already moving on before Michael was finished.

"What about Tracerio's kid? And the chief? And the captain? Did you get them?"

"Hey, man. Relax, okay? Everything's gonna be fine."

"I need to know, Michael. Did you get them?"

Michael Rhodes looked deep into the eyes of the man lying in the bed. He saw the anxiety building within him and caught clearly the urgency in Blake's wilting voice.

"Lucky for us, none of Tracerio's neighbors called 911 when the gunfire began. I guess they all had a pretty good idea who Tracerio was and were too afraid that if they called, he'd come after them for it. So the Bureau's men were able to nab Cantonelli and Wilson, but by the time they got to the chief's house, he was gone. Somebody must have warned him we were coming. But with the help of the video your pals from the bank made, the Bureau put out a nationwide APB on him and on Tracerio's son."

"Tracerio's kid got away, too? How is that possible? I thought I got everybody at Tracerio's, Michael. How did I miss him?"

"Apparently, he wasn't there when you went in. The Bureau's boys found a cell phone upstairs in one of the bedrooms and did a last number redial. Then they had the phone company run down the number and the time of the call. The number dialed was Tony Jr.'s house, and the call was made about ten minutes before we found you. The phone was registered to a guy named Hanes, Victor Hanes. When we questioned the maid, the butler and the chauffeur, we found out that Hanes was Tracerio's head of security. He's the guy you took out with the grenade in the kitchen, so he must have made the call before he came downstairs."

Blake lay there stunned, feeling the uneasiness that had started in his gut now overtake his entire body and mind. Two of the biggest and most dangerous men had escaped. After all he had gone through to make it possible for his family to come out of hiding, it was still not safe. Not until the chief and Tracerio's son were found and brought down. He had used their system to contact Joan the day of the battle at the mansion. That meant he had until 3:00 p.m., two days hence to reach her or she may surface on her own, thinking him dead. He'd have to find a way to escape his guards. He would contact her by phone once he was free of them and bring her up to speed on most of it. He longed to hear her voice and the voice of his son. The thought of talking to them lifted his spirits somewhat.

"Michael, what about the people from the bank? Did Ashland and Covington give all their names?"

"Yes, they named four others; two mules and two big shots. We had them all in custody within a few hours of the Bureau's initial sting."

Blake knew that a mule was merely a courier.

"Big shots? Which ones?"

"A guy named Edwards and the CEO himself, named Dan—"

"Danbury. Ted Danbury," Blake interjected.

"Yep. That's the guy. Edwards was the vice president you told me about, right?"

"Yes. He's the one. How many of them are out on bail?"

"Only the two big shots from the bank. The two mules turned state's evidence just like Ashland and Covington, so they are in protective custody. The judge wouldn't grant bail to Wilson or Cantonelli. Sharpe is in the room next door with two of the Bureau's men on him too. The federal prosecutor assigned to the case made him a deal, and he spilled his guts about everything. Between what he told them and what was on the video from the other two, the Bureau was able to make all the arrests. In fact, they have requested that Ralph and I be temporarily assigned to their detachment here until this is all over. That's why I'm here now, instead of in jail, or suspended pending the outcome of the investigation. Ralph is down at the station working with the team assigned to track down the chief and Tony Jr. He'll be glad to know you're up and around, but he'll probably never tell you that," Michael said with a smile.

"I bet. So what happens to me now?" Blake asked solemnly.

"Well, I won't lie to you, Jon. If the federal prosecutor decides to, he could prosecute you for a few dozen offenses, including multiple counts of premeditated murder. But I don't think he will as long as you assist in bringing the whole Tracerio operation down. I mean, he made deals with some real scumbags, so I doubt he wants the press to have a shot at him for treating you with less fairness than he showed them. But you shouldn't be worrying about all that now, man. You just heal and give us time to track these other perps down."

Blake knew that Dawson could hear everything he said and was most likely hanging on every word. He decided to use that to his advantage.

"Michael, you're going to have to find them. I couldn't help you even if I wanted to. My legs won't move, man. And now that the Bureau's men are on it, I think it's all going to be okay. As long as the men assigned by the Bureau weren't on Tracerio's payroll, that is," Jon said, looking at Agent Dawson, then back to Michael.

Dawson fielded this one before Michael could say a word.

"Mr. Blake, based on Tracerio's obvious connection to law enforcement officials, no agent who has ever had contact of any kind with Albuquerque PD has been assigned to this task force. Many agents have been brought in from other offices. The director doesn't want to take any chances on this one. If Tracerio does have someone inside our ranks, they could alert Tracerio's son and the chief of our movements, making it impossible to apprehend them. The official findings given to the public have been kept to a minimum, and your true identity has been suppressed. We don't know how deep this thing goes yet, Mr. Blake, and until we do, we're not giving the press anything they don't already have. We couldn't keep a lid on the arrests we made, or that Chief Richter and Tracerio escaped. The press was all over the arrests within a few hours, and we had to use them to assist in finding the two fugitives. Pictures of both men have been plastered all over the newspapers and the TV. Right now, the media only knows that an FBI sting operation has commenced that involves respected members of the community and some public servants. If you feel up to it, our investigators and the federal prosecutor need to ask you some questions about what you know."

Jon looked at Michael, then back at Dawson.

"I'll be more than happy to help them anyway I can, Agent Dawson. How soon can I see them?"

"How about a half-hour?" Dawson said as he pulled out a cell phone.

"Okay. A half-hour it is."

"Jon, are you sure you're up to it?" Michael asked, with a hint of reservation and caution.

Blake watched Michael's eyes flash from the direction of the agent behind him back to his own, then heard him whisper almost unintelligibly three words.

"Cover your ass."

Blake grinned at his friend.

The meeting of the minds was becoming tedious, and the discussions regarding the whereabouts of the two fugitives were becoming heated. The only thing the investigators had in the way of a lead was the flight Tony Jr. had chartered a few hours after the assault on the mansion. The pilot had flown him, Richter, Richter's wife, and two other men to an obscure airfield near the city of Hermosillo, Mexico. From there, the trail went cold. They had interviewed Harry, and he told them of young Tony's companion that night. Violet was no help. She only knew of the call Tony Jr. had received and that it made him angry and obnoxious. Immediately after he hung up from that call, he had thrown her out of the house half-naked, without even calling her a taxi or offering her a ride. She told them she had heard yelling in the house as she walked toward the street. She had used her own cell phone to call a cab, and while she waited for it, Tracerio's car came powering out of his drive and sped down the street. Her story checked out as her phone records and the cab company's log both verified it.

They had questioned all the spouses of the men they had been able to identify that were on duty at the Tracerio Estate but learned nothing. They had also found four of the six Johnson Farm's security guards that were on duty the night of the explosion and fire. Those interrogations were fruitless. The other two guards had not yet been found. They had disappeared the day after the shootout at the mansion without a trace. So many disappearances without viable trails to follow caused the tension in the task force to elevate to a crescendo. Peter Jackson, the task force commander, and Donald Goldstein, the federal prosecutor, were both showing it.

"We have you and nine other people working on this, Pete! It seems to me that you could come up with more in a week than this!" Goldstein said as he tossed the file across the desk at Jackson.

"Look, Donald! We are not incompetent, and you know it! I have two agents in Hermosillo talking to every pilot, every cab driver, and just about anyone else who might have helped them leave there. They have already hit all the hotels and motels too. If they left that city, we'll find out how and when. But it is gonna take time. The job my men are doing is not the problem here, so get off it!" Jackson yelled back, throwing the file on the floor. Then he stood, slapped both palms abruptly on the desk and fired away at Goldstein again.

"We are on the same team here, Donald. Everything that can be done is being done! The DEA is running down Tracerio's distribution centers, your boys are going through the bank's records, and my men are either babysitting witnesses or pounding on doors in two countries. Now if I've missed something, I'd like to know just what you think it is!"

Goldstein, known for being a crafty litigator, had no comeback for that outburst. He looked for a long second into Jackson's unwavering, contemptuous glare, and leaned back in his chair. Goldstein realized then and there that intimidating this man was impossible; he was not the type to cower in the face of a verbal attack directed at him or his team.

"Okay, Pete. Your point is well taken. You aren't the only one under the gun here, though. I'm feeling pressure from above on this one. Even my boss in Washington is starting to take heat, so he's dumping it on me. I'm sorry. I know you're doing everything you can to get them. I was taking my frustrations out on you, that's all. My fault. What else do you think we can do?"

Jackson sat back down as the phone rang.

"Goldstein," Donald said as he picked it up.

Jackson listened to Goldstein's side of the conversation. Although Goldstein only said a few words, Pete Jackson knew what it was about.

"Blake's ready to talk?" Jackson asked.

"Yep. Let's get over there. Maybe he can fill in the missing pieces to the puzzle," Goldstein said as he rose and put on his suit coat. Then he pushed a button on the phone.

"Mary? Agent Jackson and I are going over to the hospital. Forward all our calls to our cell phones, okay?"

"Yes, sir."

"Thank you."

They drove over without talking. Both men were silently running through their minds all the questions they were going to ask this man. Neither Goldstein nor Jackson were prepared for what they were about to hear. They introduced themselves, then Jackson recited Jon his rights, explaining that he had to as a formality. Then they gave brief rundowns on their own duties. Goldstein asked Blake to start from the beginning and walk them through everything.

"Mr. Goldstein, I would be happy to," Jon said.

"Great. I'll record this conversation, if you don't mind," Goldstein said as he pulled out the miniature recorder.

"No, I don't mind at all."

Michael was standing near the wall, behind the two men who had just arrived, wearing a look of shock and concerned disbelief while he looked at Jon Blake. He wanted to stop Jon from talking but didn't know how without being ejected from the room, and most likely, the case.

"All right, Mr. Blake. The tape is rolling. Just begin whenever you're ready," Goldstein said confidently as he sat down.

"Thank you. I'll begin with this. I want deals of complete immunity from prosecution for any offenses even remotely connected to this case for my wife, Ralph Davis, his wife, Michael Rhodes, and myself before I tell you a thing, and I have a lot to tell. I want them in writing, signed by the attorney general, and I want them notarized. Once I have them, you get everything I know, and I promise you, I know a great deal more than you do."

Jackson and Goldstein looked at each other. Both men were visibly confused, surprised, and dismayed. Ever the litigator, Goldstein threw it back at Blake.

"Mr. Blake. You have willingly committed numerous felonies, including murder. Although I do understand that you feel justified in your actions, our laws do not allow vigilantism in any degree, let alone the level you have taken it to. So this I will tell you. If the information you have is good enough, I will take it into consideration when I decide whether or not to prosecute you. Should you decide not to cooperate, I will make sure you feel the full force of my office and the power it wields. Do I make myself clear?"

"Perfectly," Jon said calmly.

"Then let us begin again," Goldstein said, with a glance at Jackson.

"We will begin when I have those deals *in writing, signed, notarized, and in my hands.* Complete immunity from prosecution for *anything* relating to this case, or you take your chances in court. Good luck finding a network, a newspaper, or a jury that won't side with me. The cops were dirty, the fire marshal was dirty, my bosses were dirty, and I'm pretty sure that the investigator I hire will find that at least one agent in the Bureau's office here in Albuquerque is dirty too. Then I'll have him dredge up the deals you've already made with the guys who were actually involved with Tracerio. You want to play games? Play. I've faced a lot worse than you in the last few months, and I'm still here. Now, if you do as I ask, I will help you get them all. If you don't, read me my rights again and hand me the phone. *Now, do I make myself clear?*"

Michael tried diligently to hide his smile. He had already seen this man under fire but was astounded again. Jon's intensity and constitution were plainly visible. His chances of winning were pretty good too, and Goldstein knew it. Especially since Goldstein had already offered deals to those who had turned state's evidence. If Blake brought the media in on this, there was no way in the world Goldstein could come out of this case unscathed. Even if he did prevail where Blake was concerned, the scars would short-circuit his career. But there was a problem.

"Mr. Blake. I do not have the authority to make such a deal. I need to talk with my boss in Washington. But I assure you, he will not make such a deal without first knowing what you have. So why don't you tel—"

"There's the phone. Call him. We're wasting time. You tell him that I'll either be very outspoken in backing you and your efforts to bring these men to justice, or I'll become the nightmare that puts the depth of the corruption here on every newscast and front page in America. You have until tomorrow at noon. And since you are recording this, I know there will be no possible way you can screw up what I said. I want everyone I've named to be granted full immunity for *every single deed* even remotely connected to the Tracerio organization or their activities, period. There are to be no timeframes mentioned, either for the commitment of the acts, or the prosecution of them. Immunity on all events, for all time. You bring me that, and I help you bring down one of the biggest conspiracies in recent history. You don't and at 12:01, I call my lawyer. Now if you'll excuse me, all this has worn me down and I'm tired. Until tomorrow, gentlemen."

And with that, Jon looked at Michael and asked, "Could you get the nurse? I'm getting dizzy again and my legs are throbbing."

"Sure thing, Jon," and Michael hurriedly left the room.

Michael wasn't the only one who had enjoyed Jon's dissertation. Both Jackson and Dawson ate it up. They knew Blake wasn't a criminal and, in fact, had saved them a great deal of work. If anyone deserved immunity, it was him.

"Okay, Jon," Jackson said calmly, "you rest, and we'll be back tomorrow. Although I cannot speak for the Mr. Goldstein's division of the justice department, I can honestly say I will do my best to make sure your requests are granted. I'll call the director as soon as I get back to the office."

Goldstein looked sharply at Jackson, who was staring at him with serious eyes. They left the room without another word, but once in the hall, Goldstein started in. Jackson would have none of it, and finally ended their quarrel with three powerful sentences.

"Goldstein, just because your ego has been beaten to a pulp, there is no reason to treat that man in there with anything except respect and gratitude. If it weren't for him, Tracerio would still be operating and getting stronger by the day. So I suggest you remember what he's already had to endure just to protect his family and stay alive and get him those deals."

Jackson did not give Goldstein a chance to respond to what he had said. As soon as he finished speaking, he turned and walked toward the elevator. Goldstein stood there in the hall burning holes in Jackson's back with his stare. Not because he thought Jackson had spoken out of turn, but because Jackson had been right on the money about what he was feeling, no matter how much effort he had expended trying to conceal it. Blake looked at Dawson after the others had left, and Dawson was smiling. Dawson nodded four times while his eyes were locked with Jon's, saying everything without words that he wanted Jon Blake to know. Blake smiled back then spoke.

"I don't know you Agent Dawson, but I mu—"

"The name's Bill, not Agent Dawson, Mr. Blake."

Blake smiled at him then responded.

"Thank you, Bill. Please call me Jon. I apologize that you had to hear all that, but I hope you can understand my position."

"I do, Jon. I do. And off the record? If I would have thought of it, I'd have done the same thing."

Jon looked into the face of the man before him and saw that he was speaking the truth. He was about to speak again when Michael entered with the nurse. She tended to Jon's needs and requests, then departed, leaving only Michael, Bill, and Jon in the room. The three men talked fairly openly while the sedatives Jon had received took effect and Jon drifted off. Michael had heard the way Bill and Jon were talking, so he thought it would be okay to tell Bill a little more about the man sleeping a few feet away. He told Bill of Jon's military background and a few other things that were not public knowledge. Michael was careful not to say anything that could put Jon in harm's way. He didn't know Bill Dawson well enough to tell him just how good Jon Blake was under fire.

Jackson called the director as soon as he got back to the office, and the director made a few calls immediately thereafter. Jon Blake would have his deal, and just about anything else he wanted was the word from the top. Goldstein would not even have calmed down enough to call his boss in Washington before his boss had called him. The papers were drawn up for all of them and taken back to Jon Blake at ten the next morning. He looked specifically for the wording he'd requested and smiled when he saw it word for word. The men who'd drawn it up had not caught one very important fact about the sentence structure of the agreement. Probably because what Jon planned to do after his body healed had never crossed their minds. This document did much more than give Jon, Joan, Michael, Ralph, and Flo immunity from everything they'd already done.

Jon Blake now had one of the items he needed, but there were many more yet to be attained or learned. And he had to get them during the interview with Goldstein, because the day after that would be too late.

Ralph had learned a great deal about the Bureau's tactics and procedures with regard to fugitives and was secretly amazed at the technological resources at their disposal. His was mainly a consultative role as he and Michael knew the most about Tracerio, other that Blake himself. But Ralph and Michael had been assigned before anyone knew Jon Blake would pull through so, at the time, they were the resident experts on Tracerio's organization. Ralph and Michael had told them what they knew, using the logic to justify their actions that Jon Blake had suggested. The information was indeed helpful. As was the information from some of Tracerio's other people, except two.

Captain Wilson and Lieutenant Cantonelli had opted to hold out for complete immunity, so they were no help. They were gambling their futures on Tracerio's ability to disappear. Should he avoid capture long enough, the prosecutor may just grant them immunity in exchange for Tracerio and Richter's whereabouts. Cantonelli didn't have a clue where they had gone. He was just doing what Wilson had told him to do during the few moments they had spent together before their initial interrogations. Wilson did know. At least, he knew of the place they had set up before all this went down. He assumed Tony Jr. would still go there even though Tony would only stay long enough to get confirmed reports of who was still running, who was in jail, and who was dead. Once he knew all those things, he would disappear. Probably for good, seeing as how his father was dead.

Wilson and Cantonelli would just have to wait it out. If Tracerio and Richter were found before the two dirty cops negotiated their own deal, there would be no chance of one. Tracerio had to avoid capture, he just had to. It was the only chance these two men had of avoiding certain death, one way or another. If they were put into the general population of any prison, their lives wouldn't be worth a wooden nickel. Cops did not survive in prison very well, or for very long, especially higher ranking ones. Then there was the worry of retaliation from Tony. In prison or not, they were still within his grasp. Their only hope was to help lead the Bureau to Tony under a deal of immunity and pray that they kill him. It was a long shot, but it was all they felt they had. They held up well considering the fact that they had not been able to speak with each other but once. And that was just for a few moments while they were locked up in adjoining cells in the holding area. Neither had rolled on the other although both were told the other had.

Cantonelli almost cracked once. The barrage had been relentless until his attorney showed up. Relentless enough that he almost crumbled on the captain. But his attorney put a stop to it before the two agents could get him to spill anything incriminating. Wilson was hanging tough. They would not break him, no matter what. He only had to rely on Cantonelli. Since Cantonelli's greatest fear was going to prison, he was pretty sure Gus would keep his mouth shut. After all, rolling over on the captain would not get him immunity, just a reduced series of charges. He'd still be sent to the big house. Wilson had made it very clear to Gus that his only hope of avoiding prison was to hold out until the search for Tracerio and Richter was abandoned. Once the search was called off, he and Gus would step in, dangling the biggest fish if they were set free. Gus believed him. Gus asked where they were, but Wilson just laughed. He then used that information to instill fear in Cantonelli. He told Gus that if Gus rolled over on him, not only would he take Gus down, he would use Tracerio's rendezvous point as a bargaining chip to save just himself. That would leave Gus high and dry and on his way to prison.

Wilson did have a problem that even revealing Tracerio's whereabouts may not cover him from, though, his wife Debbie and Florence Davis. Debbie had no idea that her husband was involved in organized crime. In fact, finding out that it was really true had left her angry, vengeful, and scorned. She had been living a lie her entire married life. He had stolen many years from her, and she wanted him to pay. She and Flo told the FBI investigators everything about their conversation in Wal-Mart. Then Debbie told them about hers with her husband. Coupled with the statement from David Sharpe about the hit that had been ordered on officers Davis and Rhodes; Wilson was in deep trouble. These two dirty cops were going to do everything they could to walk, but in the end, it probably would not be enough. At least, that's what the investigators had told them, and they weren't the only ones. Unfortunately for Wilson and Cantonelli, their own attorneys had said the same thing. Which is why Wilson had convinced Cantonelli to hold out until the time was right to play their own game with the federal task force.

Jon Blake gave detail after detail of his ordeal with incredible acuity. He told them everything; except where his wife and son were. They tried to pry from Blake his wife's whereabouts, but he refused time and time again. He finally told them with great contempt that their deal would be off if they kept pushing. She was safe and that is all they needed to know for the moment. Once Tracerio and Richter were safely in custody or dead, he would contact her, and she would surface. Goldstein's comeback was for them to go into witness protection, but Jon was ready for that.

"Listen to me, Donald. I know without a shred of uncertainty that my wife and son are safe right where they are. There is no reason on God's earth that I should or will jeopardize Joan or Lance just so you can get your hands on them. They are not costing the government one dime or wasting the services of even one agent. When the time is right and the coast is clear, I will contact them. But until I decide that time has come, Joan and Lance stay right where they are."

Goldstein's ego was rising to the surface again as Jon spoke. He was not accustomed to being told no by anyone this often.

"Mr. Blake, your wife is a key witness in a criminal investigation. We need her testimony, and if necessary, I will put a team of agents on her trail. So I strongly sugges—"

"That's a lie, and you know it, Goldstein! With the confessions you already have from Ashland and Covington, you don't need her at all. You just want her because you don't have her. You know that, I know that, and so does every other person in this room. So hear this, Mr. Goldstein, compromising the location of my wife and son just to soothe your bruised ego is not going to happen!" Jon yelled emphatically.

"Mr. Blake! I don't think you realize whom you are talking to! I'm not some two-bit flunky that will shy away just because you speak with conviction. I am a federal prosecutor for the United States Government. And if you do not divulge their location this instant, I will charge you with obstruction and throw you in jail until you rot. Now this is your last chance. Mr. Blake, where are your wife and son?"

Jon watched as Goldstein became so enraged the tips of his ears turned red. Goldstein was seething now and had thrown his most powerful card face up on the table. He was grasping the handrail on the side of Blake's bed with both hands and leaning over Jon's face. Jon raised up until he had breached Goldstein's space, then spoke.

"Donald, does the obstruction charge have anything at all to do with the Tracerio operation?"

"Don't toy with me, Blake. You know very well that it does. Now answer the question!"

Goldstein was determined to make a stand and break Jon Blake. He was so saturated by his loathing for Jon's words that he had not even caught Jon's point. Each man's gaze flashed back and forth between the eyes of the other. Goldstein's eyes showed hatred, but Jon's were reflecting total serenity. Jon smiled, then moved his face laterally to whisper in Goldstein's ear.

"Donald, I hate to have to be the one to point this out to you, especially when you are already in such a foul mood. But, Donald, you can't charge me with obstruction or anything else for that matter. The document I have clearly states that all the parties named are immune from prosecution regarding any issues related to the Tracerio case, and it was signed by your boss. I do have a suggestion, though, if you are willing to sit down and hear me out."

With that said, Jon moved his face back over to match gazes with Goldstein, then lowered himself back onto the bed. Goldstein realized he was not dealing with a fool and his expression reflected that. Blake was right. Goldstein couldn't charge him at all. Realizing the full impact of his defeat, Goldstein composed himself and sat down.

"What is your suggestion, Mr. Blake?" he asked as calmly as he could. But the attempt he made at disguising his tone failed miserably. His words carried his defeat mercilessly to all the ears in the room.

"I said earlier that one of my reasons for not coming forward in the beginning was to avoid having to live in hiding and in fear for my family. I still feel that way now and always will. But I promise you this. Should it come to pass as the trials progress that testimony from my wife or myself become absolutely necessary, I will deliver us both to your office within seventy-two hours of your call. But you are going to have to be able to prove that you need us, Donald. I'll want to know specifics and make that determination myself before I bring Joan and Lance out into the open. I know you are a great attorney, Donald. Probably one of the best in the justice department. Which is without a doubt why you have fought with me so much. You hate to lose a fight, no matter how trivial it is. I would rather have a man with your level of intelligence, tenacity, and fortitude in the prosecutor's chair against these scumbags than any other man in the country. You don't cower, and you don't give up. But I'm not your adversary here, man. I'm asking you to take everything and everyone I've already placed in your hands and see that justice is done. Remember, Mr. Goldstein, we *need* them to be put away for what they've done too. Which is why Joan and I will testify if it becomes necessary. It just isn't necessary now. Haven't Joan, Lance, and I already sacrificed enough, Mr. Goldstein? Please do what you can to ensure we don't have to sacrifice any more, okay?"

Jon's words blanketed Goldstein with such wisdom that all his feelings of animosity and contempt were smothered. The only emotions left in Goldstein were compassion, respect, and righteousness. Every man in the room felt the power of what Jon had said and were showing it. Donald Goldstein looked at Jon, then to the floor as he clasped his hands together and put his elbows on his knees. He sat there for almost a full minute, while all others remained motionless and silent. All the eyes in the room were now on Donald Goldstein, and all minds were hoping for the same thing to come from his mouth.

"Okay, Jon. You and your family have already been through enough. I won't call on you to testify unless I have no choice. Now I have a request too."

"What's that, Don?"

"Don't tell anybody you outsmarted me. I have a reputation to uphold," Goldstein said as he stretched his hand toward Jon.

Everyone in the room smiled or laughed as the two shook hands, including Jon and Donald. Jackson patted Goldstein on the back and squeezed his shoulder as he smiled and nodded at Jon. As Mr. Goldstein headed for the door, each man there shook his hand and offered their gratitude for what he had just done. Goldstein stopped at the door and turned. He looked admiringly toward Jon, then spoke.

"You rest and heal, Jon Blake. I'd love to stay and chat, but I have several trials to prepare for and a few of confessions to shore up. You tell your wife and son I said hello and not to worry. I should have no problem making my cases from these three men's statements alone. And, Jon? Thank you, for everything."

Then he turned around and left. The atmosphere in the room was now celebratory. All three agents were congratulating Jon for standing up to Goldstein and moreover, for swaying his mindset. Jon joined in with Jackson and his boys for a few minutes. The jovial atmosphere subsided eventually, and Jackson announced that he was leaving to go help Goldstein. Jon stopped him before he left. Jon's legs weren't working yet but he had no more time. He knew there was no chance he could elude these agents, but he still had to contact Joan and right away.

"Agent Jackson? Could you get hold of Michael Rhodes and Ralph Davis for me? I would like to thank them. In person, if that's possible."

"No problem, Jon. I'll arrange for both to come by shortly."

"Thank you. I'd rather see them one at a time, if that's okay."

"Sure. I understand." Then he turned to the agents and said, "set up outside this room. Mr. Blake is no longer in custody, but I want him to have twenty-four-hour protection until he leaves this hospital. All right, gentlemen?"

Both men voiced their acknowledgement, then Jackson left. Michael arrived first, about thirty minutes later.

"Michael," Jon whispered as soon as they were alone, "I need a huge favor."

"Sure, Jon. Anything, just name it."

"Hand me a piece of paper and a pen," Jon whispered.

Michael looked on as Jon wrote on the paper and saw Jon wincing a bit each time he had to move his left arm more than an inch or so to hold down the piece of paper. When he finished writing, he handed it to Michael.

> I need you to get me a clean cellular phone, and I need it by tomorrow morning. Then I'll need you to get me out of this room to somewhere safe so I can call Joan. I have to call her no later than tomorrow at three or she's gone. Then I need you to make the phone disappear where it will never be found. You are the only man I trust with this, Michael. Can you do it?

Jon watched Michael's face as he read. When Michael finished, his expression showed the loyalty Jon Blake already knew was there. Then Michael nodded and tore the paper into small pieces.

"You hungry, Jon?" Michael asked as he ripped.

"No. I ate a little while ago. Why?"

"I am. I'm famished," Michael said as he tossed all the small pieces into his mouth and began to chew.

"Thank you," Jon said. His emotions of relief and gratitude had finally made their way to the forefront of his mind.

Michael's lips curled up as he chewed, then he winked at Jon and pointed to Jon's water glass with raised eyebrows.

"Sure, Michael. Have as much as you want," Jon said through a light laugh.

Michael drank, swallowed, belched, then spoke.

"Don't thank me. You took out two assassins that were seconds away from killing me, and I'll always be in your debt for that."

They talked openly now about many things. Their conversation was the most enjoyable Jon had partaken of since the Sunday before he saw the e-mail on Ashland's computer. Three months had passed since then. And there was still more that needed done after his body healed, yet before he could again be with Joan and Lance.

When Joan first heard it ring, she froze where she stood. For days she had been watching the mail closely for word from Jon, but none had come. The fear that something had gone seriously wrong had been slapping her around without remorse for days, showing no signs of letting up. But the phone was ringing now. Could it be Jon? Or one of Lance's friends? Why would Jon call instead of write? Had something happened? Was it finally over? These and many other questions raced through her mind as she reached for the phone.

"H-hello?"

"Hi, honey. How are you?"

Joan's excitement elevator blasted through the top floor and shot straight up into the Heavens. Their reunion may have only been by phone but that did not stop either husband or wife from breaking through and letting go. They talked for fifteen minutes about her and Lance and how they had spent their summer. Then Jon asked if Lance was there.

"No, darling. I'm sorry. He's at school. But I can have hi-"

"No, Joan. It's all right. I was hoping to catch you alone," Jon said sadly.

Joan's heart sank as the fists of fear slammed into her belly, turning her stomach, and causing her to feel dizzy. Something was wrong!

"Honey, there are still two men out there who can hurt us. They both evaded capture and disappeared into Mexico. At least one or maybe both men have the money and the means to come after us, Joan. So until they're brought down, you and Lance can't come home," Jon said, his voice and his heart both breaking at once.

Joan could see his face and feel his pain even though they were thousands of miles apart. She could sense what Jon was about to say and knew that nothing she could do or say in return could convince him to let it go. So she decided not to make it harder for him.

"Then what the heck are you waiting for, honey?" Joan asked in as cheerful a voice as she could muster.

"Joan, I don't think you understand. That means I can't com—"

"I know what it means, Jon," Joan said, full of hope. "It means that you have to find them before we can be together again. Lance and I are fine and will be as long as you are, honey. I'm not sad about this, Jon. I'm just so glad that there are only two left. You take all the time you need to finish this, Jon, okay? Lance and I both want you with us, the whole you. If that means we need to wait longer for that, then so be it."

The tone she was speaking in renewed Jon's strength and his confidence. Miraculously, her voice had also lifted the weight from his heavy heart. He was trying to fight back tears as he smiled.

"I love you so much, Joan. And God willing, I am going to finish it soon. Would you tell Lance I love him and give him a really long hug for me? One that lasts so long, he'll try to squirm away. Then remind him to picture that it is my arms around him. Would you do that, Joan?"

"Well, as long as he doesn't throw me for trying, I will. He's getting pretty good at karate, Jon. You'll be so happy for him."

"I already am, my love. I already am. Of both of you. Thanks for understanding, Joan. I don't think I coul—"

"Jon, would you just stop already? It's been less than four months, and I'd wait a hundred times that long just to know that when you came home, you came home at peace. So I'll ask you again. What the heck are you waiting for? You just go out there and kick some major bad guy butt. Then someday, we'll tell this story to Lance's children. We'll call it... *The Legend of Grandpa Blake*. Yeah, that's it. What do you think?"

"I think you're crazy. That's what I think. Grandpa? You just wait until I see you again, honey. I'll show you I'm no grandpa." Jon said, laughing.

Joan's voice changed to one filled with seduction.

"I'll tell you what. For every day we have to be apart from now until it is over, I want a passionate night with you as..." she hesitated for a second, then went on, "you figure it out. And I promise you, I'll make you tired enough to feel like a grandpa."

"That's a deal, honey. That's a deal and a date! I'll contact you soon."

After Jon put the phone down he sat there for a long moment in silence. Then he looked over to where Michael was standing.

"Michael! I'm ready!"

Michael walked over and asked, "Is everything okay?"

He handed Michael the phone and smiled. He told Michael pretty much everything Joan had said, and Michael laughed with Jon when he mentioned Joan's comment about telling Lance's children the legend of Grandpa Blake. Michael started guiding his wheelchair back through the courtyard toward the door as he laughed heartily and chided Jon about growing old. Halfway to the door, Jon looked toward his right shoulder and spoke.

"Hey Michael?"

"Yeah Jon?"

"How would you feel about being an even bigger part of the legend of Grandpa Blake?"

LEFT NO CHOICE

Next...

Take the plunge with Jon as he goes after Tracerio and Richter. The search will cover a lot more ground than Hermosillo, Mexico, and Jon will have no choice but to make a deal with someone from his past to continue the hunt. A deal that will change the Blake family's lives forever. The Legend Of Grandpa Blake has just begun.

ABOUT THE AUTHOR

Having grown up in the small town of Windham, Ohio, I've loved writing and creating characters since I was able to read. Although she didn't know this until recently, my seventh-grade English teacher had the biggest impact on my dream of putting stories on paper. And what's really funny is that I'm very sure she didn't like me very much. I was shy, awkward, overweight, easily run over, and an outcast. Definitely not a candidate for junior high heartthrob.

But one mid-year homework assignment and the subsequent events stemming from it changed the way I looked at life. We'd been asked to write a short story that would be read in front of the class. I spent quite a few nights working on mine too. I never would have believed what happened next and still become lost in God's glorious and mysterious plan even now.

After all of us had stood and read our stories, which took two days of class time, she read our grades aloud. It was the first and last time I can ever remember one of my teachers doing this. I was quite nervous, thinking I was about to get the worst grade in the class. She went down the list, calling out names and grades, and although as of yet no one had received a failing grade, she had granted no "100 percenters" either…until she read my name and grade. I was the only one she gave that grade to, and it made a world of difference to me in confidence and self-worth.

From that day on I started coming out of my shell, and by the time I had graduated high school, I had even acted in the school play as one of the lead characters. I learned how to believe in myself and to become the driver of the vehicle carrying my own destiny. From then on, I was considered a lucky man, harvesting great career successes in the auto industry.

But what is luck? I've heard it described as fate, the will of God and just as many other things as you can imagine. But the definition I'll share with you is the one I believe to be the most fitting.

> Luck is the exact moment where honorable preparation can successfully handle the opportunity God sets before us on the time line of our life.

May God allow each of us to be lucky in all our honorable endeavors.